Cardan was aware, first, of a lapse of time. Then he sensed that he was on his feet, held upright by something that gripped him under each arm, and at the waist, knees, and ankles. What felt like a set of padded clamps pressed against the sides of his head. There was a faint prickling sensation across his forehead and along the top, both sides, and the back of his head. It felt to Cardan as if a great many sharp points were evenly pressed against his scalp.

Directly behind him, there was a conversation going on that he couldn't quite get into focus. After each comment, words formed in Cardan's consciousness, as if an interpreter were translating the discussion for his benefit. The lag between gabble and translation decreased, and it suddenly occurred to Cardan that he seemed to be getting the meaning a little ahead of the translated words. He listened carefully, and heard:

"Very well. Now, your recommendations as to this planet?"

"Wipe out the dominant life form, then settle the planet."

"You consider the dominant life form might be more dangerous than useful?"

"I do. At present they have a passable civilization, and use atomic fission in weapons and embryonic power applications. They are plainly split in competing geographical fragments. Progress is going on. Who knows when their science may develop beyond science? We should wipe them out now, while it's easy."

"You're certain they're not dangerous as yet?"

"Positive. I checked that carefully."

"Then I agree. 'Fix them while they're little, or when they're big they may fix you.'"

"Yes, sir," said Skaa. "Exactly."

"Well, now that that's settled, let's hear this creature talk. A life form as weird as this one shouldn't die without a few words on record."

Books
by Christopher Anvil

The
POWER of
ILLUSION

Christopher Anvil

Edited by
Eric Flint

THE POWER OF ILLUSION

This is a work of fiction. All the characters and events portrayed in this book are fictional, and any resemblance to real people or incidents is purely coincidental.

Copyright © 2009 by Christopher Anvil. Afterword copyright © 2010 by Eric Flint.

A Baen Books Original

Baen Publishing Enterprises
P.O. Box 1403
Riverdale, NY 10471
www.baen.com

ISBN: 978-1-4516-3760-1

Cover art by Bob Eggleton

First Baen mass market printing, November 2011

Distributed by Simon & Schuster
1230 Avenue of the Americas
New York, NY 10020

Library of Congress Cataloging-in-Publication Data:
2010029993

Printed in the United States of America

10 9 8 7 6 5 4 3 2 1

Table of Contents

Acknowledgments

"A Taste of Poison" © 1960 by Christopher Anvil. Originally published in the August 1960 issue of *Astounding*.

"The Gold of Galileo" © 1980 by Christopher Anvil. Originally published in the October 1980 issue of *Analog*.

The Day the Machines Stopped © 1964 by Christopher Anvil. Originally published by Monarch.

"The Missile Smasher" © 1966 by Christopher Anvil. Originally published in the July 1966 issue of *Analog*.

"The Problem Solver and the Killer" © 1966 by Christopher Anvil. Originally published in the August 1966 issue of *Ellery Queen's Mystery Magazine*.

"The Hand From the Past" © 1972 by Christopher Anvil. Originally published in the May 1972 issue of *Alfred Hitchcock's Mystery Magazine*.

"The Problem Solver and the Hostage" © 1966 by Christopher Anvil. Originally published in the February 1966 issue of *Ellery Queen's Mystery Magazine*.

"The Problem Solver and the Defector" © 1966 by Christopher Anvil. Originally published in the December 1996 issue of *Ellery Queen's Mystery Magazine*.

"Key to the Crime" © 1966 by Christopher Anvil. Originally published in the September 1966 issue of *Shell Scott's Mystery Magazine*.

"The Problem Solver and the Burned Letter" © 1967 by Christopher Anvil. Originally published in the April 1967 issue of *Ellery Queen's Mystery Magazine*.

"Warped Clue" © 1966 by Christopher Anvil. Originally published in the April 1966 issue of *Mike Shayne's Mystery Magazine*.

"The Coward" © 1966 by Christopher Anvil. Originally published in March 1966 by *Adam*.

"A Sense of Disaster" © 1979 by Christopher Anvil. Originally published in January 1979 by *Fantastic*.

"Destination Unknown" © 1958 by Christopher Anvil. Originally published in the March 1958 issue of *SF Adventures*.

"High Road to the East" © 1968 by Christopher Anvil. Originally published in the May 1968 issue of *Fantastic*.

"A Tourist Named Death" © 1960 by Christopher Anvil. Originally published in the May 1960 issue of *IF*.

"The Knife and the Sheath" © 1974 by Christopher Anvil. Originally published in 1974 in *Future Kin*.

"The Anomaly" © 2010 by Christopher Anvil.

"In the Light of Further Data" © 1965 by Christopher Anvil. Originally published in the July 1965 issue of *Analog*.

"Apron Chains" © 1970 by Christopher Anvil. Originally published in the December 1970 issue of *Analog*.

"The Power of Illusion" © 2008 by Christopher Anvil. Originally published in the October 2008 issue of *Jim Baen's Universe*.

PART I

RESEARCH EAST

A Taste of Poison

James Cardan strained to move his left arm, which lay dead still across his chest. But like everything else he'd tried to move since he came to, the arm lay where it was.

Cardan knew that he was on his back, lying as if he'd been thrown down bodily. It was perfectly dark where he was, cool, and very quiet. He could sense the position of his limbs, and with his outstretched right hand could feel a little of the smooth surface he was lying on.

But he couldn't move.

Cardan forced himself to think back, to see if he could find out what had happened.

***

He had, he remembered, been driving back from the meeting he'd called at the branch office in Milford. As the car's headlights reached far ahead in the moonless night, his mind circled back again and again to the problem the meeting hadn't solved. The violent arguments as to if, how, and when the company should install an electronic computer were still echoing through Cardan's consciousness as he spotted his shortcut up ahead.

Cardan glanced in the rearview mirror, and let up on the gas. He tapped the brakes lightly, and swung off onto a back road that cut over the ridge and around hairbreadth curves to join Route 36. He slowed the car for a moment to study the water trickling down the hilly dirt road, then stepped on the gas.

As usual, he got going too fast, and the car went into a shuddering vibration on the corduroy ridges of the road. Cardan grunted, slowed down, and reached over to press in the lighter, meanwhile shifting his dead cigar to the other corner of his mouth.

The trouble, he told himself, guiding the car with automatic skill around the swinging curves, was that no one seemed to know how a computer would actually work out in any specific case. Cardan believed that his own special skill, which had put him at the head of the firm, lay in his ability to draw out the truth in what a man said from the general mass of overstatement, obscurity and prejudice. But in this problem, his special skill was of no more value than a water pump with its intake pipe in a dry well. After he separated out the obscurity, overstatement, and prejudice, there was nothing left.

The lighter popped out, and Cardan waited till he came to a straight stretch, then groped for it, keeping his eyes on the road. He puffed the cigar alight, and felt around to get the lighter back in its socket. He drove steadily for some time, then pressed harder on the gas to gather speed for the last uphill stretch before he reached the top.

For the sixth or seventh time since leaving the meeting, Cardan's mind was sifting over the violent partisan arguments. Cardan, who despised yes-men, and only hired anyone who plainly had the backbone to stand up and state his own opinion, now asked himself how he had come to end up with such a bunch of bull-headed egomaniacs.

The car topped the rise, dipped down around a sharp curve—and Cardan brought the car to a sudden stop.

A medium-sized pine lay across the road directly in front of him.

Cardan shifted the once-more-dead cigar to the other side of his mouth, and jabbed the lighter back in its socket. The road was so narrow that there were few places where he could turn around, and to back down the steep curving slope at night would take a long time.

The lighter popped out, and he puffed the cigar alight, thinking furiously. The tree ahead wasn't too big. "Let's see," he thought, "didn't I get one of those all-steel rubber-handled hatchets with a leather case and put it in the trunk about the same time I got the chains—after the car got stuck on that hunting trip and we had to wrench branches off the trees to get some kind of traction?"

Cardan cramped the wheels of the car toward the side of the road where there was the hill instead of the ravine, made sure the parking brake was set, shut off the ignition and got out. He stretched his cramped limbs, drew in a deep breath, was surprised to smell a faint geranium-like odor, and—

—Found himself lying on his back in a cool dark place, able to sense the position of his body, but unable to move.

Feeling a sense of grim satisfaction that he had at least discovered part of what had happened, Cardan filed away that geranium scent for future reference. Before he had time to do anything else, a vertical gray line appeared on the wall opposite him. The line rapidly widened to a gray block, with the shadow of a low mound at its base. The mound moved, like a loose pile of rope from which a free end rose up of its own accord, to hold horizontally what appeared to be a short length of pipe.

There was a hiss, and a geranium-like scent was strong in the air.

Cardan was aware, first, of a lapse of time. Then he sensed that he was on his feet, held upright by something that gripped him under each arm, and at the waist, knees, and ankles. What felt like a set of padded clamps pressed against the sides of his head. There was a faint prickling sensation across his forehead and along the top, both sides, and the back of his head. It felt to Cardan as if a great many sharp points were evenly pressed against his scalp.

Directly behind him, there was a conversation going on that he couldn't quite get into focus, while somewhere in front of him and off to his left there was a sound of splashing.

Cardan cautiously tried to move his limbs, and got no response. He mentally summarized what he knew of his situation and discovered that all he knew was that he was unable to move and was in a dark cool place where he had seen a shadow that made no sense, and now heard various sounds that added up to nothing familiar. He wished to get out of this place; but paralyzed from head to foot, how was he to do it?

Cardan mentally grumbled to himself, and an habitual impulse went out that would ordinarily shift a dead cigar from one corner of his mouth to the other. Then there was a pause corresponding to the time needed to puff the cigar alight, and then Cardan was deep in thought. His thought wasn't in words or logic, but was a mental groping, with an inner sensation like that of a man in a darkened room searching through the things in his pockets for a match.

In time, Cardan's thoughts seemed to gradually focus, and then come to a point, and there rose up from the depths of his unconscious a mood, a set of attitudes like those of a man who fits the point of a wedge into a crack, then eyes it calculatingly, and reaches for a sledgehammer. At the same instant, he thought, "Somebody wants to know something." With this thought impulses started out along certain nerves that would ordinarily slightly narrow his eyes, and adjust the cigar between his clamped teeth at a certain specific angle that produced, in even his most pugnacious associates, a twinge of foreboding followed by a state of maximum alertness.

Then he became aware of an odd effect that had been going on for some time without his being conscious of it.

From behind him came the conversational gabble he had heard before, an out-of-focus noise like an earnest discussion being carried out on the other side of thick wall. But now, after each comment, words formed in Cardan's consciousness, as if an interpreter were translating the discussion for his benefit. The lag between gabble and translation decreased, and it suddenly occurred to Cardan that he seemed to be getting the meaning a little ahead of the translated words. He listened carefully, and heard:

". . . zz brgt hvd gdn nbbbn how does that show up on your dwell meter now?"

". . . grbbl bbz mddb jj still too big a spread. Am I doing something wrong?"

". . . Bb zbbd zd you're overcorrecting. Here."

"Oh. I see."

Just before the two sounds merged, Cardan was sure that he was getting the meaning a fraction of a second ahead of the translated words. It seemed first the meaning came to him, and then a part of his own mind translated the meaning into words. He puzzled over this, which seemed to be a kind of electronic telepathy.

Behind him, one of the voices said, "Higher. We don't want to unblock that far down."

"Here?"

"A little radially. There."

***

There was a stinging pain, as if a spark had landed between Cardan's shoulders and expanded in a puff of flame through his chest, neck, and head. Cardan suddenly realized that he could now move the muscles of his chest, neck and head, but could not move even this part of his body freely, because of the clamps that gripped him. He tried to open his eyes, and found that they were partly open already. All he could see was a general dull gray shadow.

From off to Cardan's right, a voice spoke sharply. "Is the receiver ready?"

To Cardan's front and left there was a splash. "Taking a bath," came a new voice. "Why? The specimen's not ready yet, is it?"

"I don't know about the specimen. But I just got the warning signal from Control."

There was a low muttering noise, and a loud splash. Cardan, peering into the dimness, tried to look not quite directly at the source of the noise. He saw a vague series of upright wavering forms, which seemed at first like streamers of a dark flame, and which then produced a mental picture of snakes weaving upright in a circle.

Behind him, a voice said sharply, "There. It had a thought."

"Where?"

"Gone now. But it must be coming to."

To Cardan's right, a voice said sharply, "Hurry!"

From the place Cardan was watching came a sound like a sail slatting in the wind, and then a low brisk rubbing sound. He could now only make out a vague mass.

Gradually, Cardan was forming an opinion about whatever it was that had captured him. The thought caused a chilly sensation to travel up and down his spine, and this in turn caused his jaw muscles to set an imaginary cigar at a more pugnacious angle. Simultaneously, the muscles around his eyes tensed. His face, in the shadowy room, took on a look which often created a paralytic hesitancy in people who had succeeded in getting him at a disadvantage.

Meanwhile, in the depths of his mind, an intense sifting process continued, and Cardan was aware, now and then, of a vague mental image.

Behind him, a voice said, "*There*. No, my mistake. Wait. *There*, again."

The excitement, Cardan realized, sprang up each time

he saw a mental picture. Cautiously, he formed a fuzzy mental picture of a wrist watch floating in space.

"It's almost conscious," said the voice.

"Keep an eye on it. I'm going to have a spare contact put on standby."

A voice from the right called, "Specimen ready?"

"Not yet. It's slow coming to."

"Hurry it up. *Receiver!* Control red!"

The low rubbing sound out in front of Cardan stopped abruptly. Behind him, a low voice said, "Try the stribulator."

A vague scatter of sparks crossed Cardan's field of vision.

To his right, someone called sharply, "Control red-yellow!"

"Coming." A clicking thumping noise rapidly approached.

There was another vague scatter of sparks across Cardan's field of vision. An instant later someone called tensely, "Control yellow!"

It was clear to Cardan that something was about to happen. He peered alertly into the gloom, and was rewarded when a very dim light snapped on overhead, revealing a thing like a dentist's chair, with a variety of padded armrests held up by jointed, faintly glimmering polished rods.

"Control blue-yellow!"

Into this chair hurtled a sizable monstrosity, like a tangle of snakes around a central mass. Cardan, trying to get it into focus, had the impression of a kind of squid, which hastily distributed its arms on the multiple rests, gave a final twitch, and sat intensely still.

A humming tone sounded. To Cardan's right, a crisp voice spoke:

"Sector 139, sir. We have a planet, and a specimen of a moderately intelligent race."

The thing in the chair opposite Cardan stirred, then spoke in an incisive voice, entirely different from what Cardan had heard before.

"Spotlight," it said sharply.

***

A sizable lens overhead gave a feeble glow, like a flashlight with nearly dead batteries. The creature in the chair leaned forward, as if peering at Cardan. The central mass of the creature, seen from directly in front, looked like a huge inverted horseshoe. Cardan made out a faint reflected glimmer in the dark space inside the horseshoe-shaped body, and suddenly realized that that dark space might be one huge eye.

After staring at Cardan for some time, the thing drew back with a faint leathery creaking sound.

"Enough," came its voice. "Dim that light."

The feeble glow faded out. Cardan thoughtfully filed away the information that these creatures might have uncommonly sensitive eyes. He also noted that they seemed to have some kind of scientifically-assisted process, by which a distant authority could communicate through the body and senses of a "receiver."

The creature opposite Cardan spoke, using the tone of a busy person who has no time to waste. It said, "This is the dominant species?"

"Yes, your excellency."

"Is it intelligent?"

"Moderately so, sir."

"Has it constructed artificial aids? Can it manipulate tools?"

"Yes, your excellency, to both questions."

"Then where is its eye?"

There was a little pause, then the hesitant answer, "It has microeyes, your excellency. They're a . . . a little hard to find. High up, in the receptor head."

Another little pause followed. "Oh. I see. Yes, of course." Cardan thoughtfully noted the irritation in the voice, "All right," it said, "now, directly below the microeyes is a vertical ridge with two small holes at the bottom."

"Air-duct openings, your excellency."

"And below that?"

"The food-intake and mastication apparatus."

"How does it communicate?"

"Well, sir, we think it can talk. But there are technical difficulties with this specimen, and—"

"None of that. Can you or can't you get it to talk?"

"Well, you see, your excellency—"

"Yes or no?"

There was a silence. A somewhat more authoritative voice spoke up, and Cardan recognized the executive protecting his assistant from an angry superior.

"You see, Chairman Thall," said the new voice, "the specimen's vocal centers have been zzztically stimulated under anesthesia, and calibrated. Naturally, I know nothing of the details. But I have heard the creature make sounds while unconscious. What Mr. Stol meant to say—"

The chairman gave a low, inarticulate sound that

translated an instant later as "Gah." Then it said sharply, "Listen, will it talk to me *now*?"

Yet another voice cut in, "No, sir. The technicians have had hours to run through the standard routines. But they're hung up. Why, I don't know."

"Ah," growled the monster in the chair, and Cardan listened intently to the antagonism in the voice. "So it's you again, Skaa? Another planet, eh?"

"Yes, sir. My ninth."

"And the technicians have had several hours to 'run through the routines'—is that what you said?"

"That's right, sir. They have."

***

There was a pause, then the voice spoke more smoothly. "Well, then, suppose you describe this planet to me yourself."

"Gladly, sir. The planet has suitable gravity and atmosphere. About a fourth is land area. Day on the planet is blinding, but night is just about right. We have carried out a quick examination, and find that most of the plant life is edible. A number of the animal forms, however, are evidently poisonous to us."

"What do you mean, 'evidently'?"

There was a silence, and Cardan sensed a developing tension in the room.

"Well, your excellency," said the voice of Skaa, "as you know, I am a believer in the direct methods of General Meio. Rather than spend the next hundred years carrying out elaborate tests to see what might be poisonous, I offered a bonus to volunteers, who ate samples."

"How many volunteers did you lose this time?"

"Thirty-nine and three still doubtful."

"Forty-two! Just what is your total by now?"

"Eight useable planets discovered, and three partly settled. Has anyone a higher record?"

There was a long silence. Then the creature in the chair spoke in a voice that had an undertone like snapping sparks. "How do you replace these losses?"

"I give the surviving volunteers their bonus, and a steep increase in mating allotments. I up the general mating norm. Between one planet and the next, there's time to raise a new set of basic workers, and train up replacements from the crew for any technical spots vacated."

"So far, you've been lucky. If the odds—"

"The devil with the odds."

Cardan admiringly told himself that this Skaa was no yes-man. On the other hand, Chairman Thall sounded as if his patience was strained to the breaking point. Cardan's imaginary cigar shifted around thoughtfully.

Chairman Thall's voice, rigid with self-restraint, said, "Very well. Now, your recommendations as to this planet?"

"Wipe out the dominant life form, then settle the planet."

"You consider the dominant life form might be more dangerous than useful?"

"I do. At present they have a passable civilization, and use atomic fission in weapons and embryonic power applications. My examination was quick, so it's hard to say if they have fusion or not. It doesn't matter. They are plainly split in competing geographical fragments. Progress is going on. Who knows when their science may develop beyond science? We should wipe them out now, while it's easy."

"You're certain they're not dangerous as yet?"

"Positive. I checked that carefully."

"Then I agree. 'Fix them while they're little, or when they're big they may fix you.'"

"Yes, sir," said Skaa. "Exactly."

"Well, now that that's settled, let's hear this creature talk. A life form as weird as this one shouldn't die without a few words on record."

There was a grating noise from here and there around the room, like bones being ground up. This translated belatedly as a sound of hearty chuckling.

Cardan's face smoothed out as if a switch had been thrown, disconnecting the muscles of his face from what went on in the brain within.

The creature in the chair leaned forward.

"Speak up, specimen."

* * *

Feeling his way cautiously, Cardan said in respectful tones, "Yes, your excellency?"

There were numerous small creakings, clicks, and stirrings in the room. Cardan gathered that he had a sizable audience. From behind him came vague mutterings, and Cardan remembered that to these huge-eyed creatures, thought without mental images was unthinkable. For their benefit, Cardan produced a mental picture of a vague, many-limbed creature.

The monster in the chair said, "You've heard our conversation, then?"

Cardan said humbly, "I heard you talking, your excellency."

The creature spoke to Cardan in the tone of an adult speaking to a child. "I mean, did you *understand* what we were talking about."

Cardan made foggy mental pictures of undistinguishable objects. He said, "I lost track, your excellency. I mean, I figure the boys below can handle it. It's not my job."

A slight pause followed, filled with numerous creaking noises from around the room.

"Boys below?" said Chairman Thall inquiringly.

"Yeah," said Cardan. "I mean, yes, your excellency."

"You mean to say, *the people down on your world?*"

Cardan visualized a vague, slightly lopsided sphere. "Well, no, your excellency. The guys *underneath*. What I mean— It's a . . . a" He pictured a vague mass with odd bumps sticking out here and there, then let it fade out. "I can't think of the word."

The creature seated before Cardan snapped, "Psychotechnicians! What is the intelligence of this creature?"

"As a rough estimate, your excellency, we would say the intelligence factor is around forty."

"Forty! What is the use of talking to an idiot?"

Cardan judged that the time was right for the first rap on the wedge. He said plaintively, "Your excellency, maybe I'm no brain, but you won't find a harder worker anywhere under the sun. Or under the moon, either."

At the word "moon" there was a general creak and clack all over the room. Someone spat out a low curse.

"Moon!" thundered the chairman. "Does this planet have a *moon?*"

"Yes," said the voice of Skaa angrily, "it *does* have a

moon. Planets often do, you know, and this has only *one* moon, anyway."

"How bright is it?"

"I don't know. As it happens, it's in the planet's shadow right now."

"Specimen," snapped the creature, turning in its chair, "how bright is your moon?"

Cardan visualized a huge dazzling disk. "It's better not to look straight at it, your excellency."

"I see. Someone snap on that spotlight. Is it brighter than that?"

The feeble glow lit up behind its lens. If this bothered the big eyes of the aliens, Cardan could imagine what moonlight would do. For the benefit of the psychotechnicians, Cardan visualized a mental comparison showing the glaring moon on one side, and a faint glimmer on the other side. Aloud, he said, "It's a whole lot brighter than that, your excellency."

Skaa's voice cut in. "After all, it's only *one* moon, your excellency. It can be devegrated; it wouldn't cost too much to zzzpostuzztalate the whole thing."

"Might not cost much," snapped the chairman, "but if you know anything, you know it only takes one single mistake, and the whole surface will crystallize over with an albedo like polished chromium."

"There is that *possibility*, but—"

"You should have *told* me there was a moon. Now just keep quiet."

"It doesn't make any—"

"Shut up, I said!" The chairman's voice rose menacingly, and a tight silence gripped the room.

***

Cardan, satisfied he had the point of the wedge driven into the crack, bided his time. Meanwhile, he let an occasional vague mental image drift through his mind, to keep the psychotechnicians occupied.

The monster in front of him grumbled, "Seeing that you won't give me the information you ought to, I'll have to wring it out of this alien idiot here. Who knows what else you haven't told me?"

"Sir," said Skaa stiffly, "if you'd asked me, I'd have told you. But—"

"But you're in a hurry to go out and discover another planet, and run up your record? And let somebody else come here and do all the work?"

"I think," said Skaa coldly, "that my record justifies my actions. If you want to call a Board of Inquiry, I'll be glad—"

Cardan, who wanted to use this antagonism for his own purpose, suddenly realized that the situation might blow up prematurely. In a loud voice, Cardan spoke up:

"Why should I tell them about Underneath? Who *are* those guys, anyway?"

Skaa's voice cut off abruptly. From that direction, Cardan could hear several low earnest voices, as if Skaa's subordinates were trying to argue him out of a head-on clash. The chairman—the monster seated directly opposite Cardan—was also silent; Cardan thought he could understand the situation. Settling planets must be like opening a great many boxes, an unpredictable percentage of which contain booby traps. After the first ruinous explosion, the man in charge will insist on precautions. But new workers, hired after the wreckage from the explosion has been cleared away, will come to doubt the need for precautions. Cardan could imagine that the chairman must ache and yearn for a *small* explosion, to teach the headlong Skaa some caution. And right now, the chairman was probably relieved that the alien idiot had opened its mouth just in time to prevent a showdown.

"Hm-m-m," said the chairman, twisting around with a leathery creak, "so, you don't like moonlight, eh?"

"No, your excellency," said Cardan. He decided it was time to tap his wedge in a little farther, and let a vague mental picture of the moon drift through his mind, followed by a sharply visualized rectangle. Behind, there was a murmuring, as the psychotechnicians conferred about this new phenomenon.

"Now," growled the chairman, "your planet has only *one* moon, hasn't it?"

"That's right, your excellency. There's only one big moon."

"One *big* moon!" the chairman exploded. "Are there any small ones?"

"No, your excellency," said Cardan humbly.

"All right," growled the chairman. "Now then, what was that remark about 'boys below'?"

"Well, just that, your excellency."

" 'Just that'? Just *what*?"

"I mean, they're underneath. You know."

There was a sound as of steam escaping under pressure. "Psychotechnicians!" roared the monster.

"Yes, your excellency?"

Cardan let a vague image drift across the sharply

defined rectangle as the chairman said furiously, "Is this specimen evading my question on purpose?"

"No, your excellency. The creature is stupid. It just doesn't understand."

"Then how am I to get an answer out of it?"

"If you could get it to start talking, your excellency, it might be possible to guide the conversation, and get at the information indirectly."

"I see."

Skaa's voice cut in irritatedly. "How can anyone get information out of an idiot? Can you squeeze blood out of a vacuum?"

"Keep out of this," said the chairman warningly.

Cardan, sensing another premature crisis, drew in his breath and sneezed loudly, then sneezed again, and again.

The chairman swiveled around angrily. "Now, what's wrong with *you?*"

In the background, Cardan could hear low voices arguing with the muttering Skaa. Very humbly, Cardan said, "I'm sorry, your excellency. My nose tickled. I sneezed."

"All right," said the chairman ill-temperedly, "now let's get on with this." He added angrily, "And I *hope* there will be no more interruptions."

***

Cardan stood in humble silence, and made his mental image of the rectangle clearer and sharper, while allowing a fuzzy blob to half-form and drift over it.

Behind Cardan, there was a low confused muttering. Off to his right he heard Skaa spit out an epithet, while another voice pleaded urgently, "No, no, don't do it!"

The chairman was saying angrily ". . . Picture is pretty

confused and I want to fill in the details. At least, do your best and *try* to understand. Now when you speak of this 'underneath,' do you mean—"

Behind Cardan, one of the psychotechnicians muttered, "He isn't going at it the right way."

"Well, don't get mixed up in it. There's nothing *we* can do. But, say, look at this image."

Cardan was very gradually enlarging the rectangle.

One of the psychotechnicians said, "Remarkable image persistence for this creature. Almost like an entirely different—"

To Cardan's right, Skaa's voice was gradually becoming louder, despite the clamor of pleading voices around him.

". . . Do you mean," the monster in the chair facing Cardan was saying, "that they are *physically* underground, or—"

"All I know, your excellency," said Cardan quickly, "is my own job, and what I read in the papers, and—"

"All *right*," snarled the creature, leaning forward, "start there then. What *is* your job?"

Cardan had the momentary balancing sensation of the man who eyes the wedge as he readies the sledgehammer. Then he began to speak, his voice earnest, eager to please.

"I'm a dollar-mender, your excellency. I mend dollars. Some get torn, and others get wrinkled. I put them in the 'In' slot, and throw the switch down. Then when the red light flashes, I take them out the 'Out' slot, and feed them in the drier. Oh, I forgot. I throw the switch up after I take them out of the machine. See, because the cycle's finished.

Then I take some more dollars off the belt, and put them in the 'In' slot, and throw the switch down. When the red light flashes, I take them out the 'Out' slot and—"

There was a universal creak and clack all around Cardan. The faintly visible chairman had what seemed to be a stupefied look. As Cardan rattled on, Skaa's voice cut in sarcastically, "Fill in the details. Very important, you know, to fill in the details. Yes, sir. Here we stand, officers of the Fleet. We could be doing our duty. But instead here we stand, awash in claptrap. 'Throw up the "Up" switch. Reach in the "Out" slot.' Oh, this is a dangerous alien race, I tell you. We must proceed with great caution, as our noble leader here—"

The chairman's voice came out in a crackling roar. "That will do! *Guards!*"

Cardan, satisfied that the situation had come to a head, and that his reputation for stupidity was now unshakably established, suddenly altered his mental picture. Within the rectangle, he visualized numerous radiating lines, drawn from a common center. Slowly, then faster and faster, these lines began to whirl. The rectangle enlarged, and the whirling lines spun faster, till they filled his entire field of mental vision.

Behind him, Cardan could hear the sudden exclamation. Concentrating hard, he made the spinning spokes whirl yet faster, the central hub enlarging till it in turn filled his entire field of vision.

He then immediately visualized everything he could think of. Slide rules, microscopes, cameras, photographs, paint brushes, apples, revolvers, ammunition, graph paper, pencils, pens, atomic models, ring stands, hunting rifles, lions, cats, dogs, bears, maps on old parchment, algebraic formulae, tables of integrals, radar sets, oscilloscopes, vacuum tubes, condensers, transistors, remembered drawings of futuristic devices, lightning bolts, coils of wire hanging in space. As fast as he could think of anything, he pictured it, and thrust it aside to picture something else.

Behind him rose a scream, a wild shriek that wavered over the hubbub to bring a sudden silence, and then a roar from the chair, "*Now* what's happened?"

"Sir . . . your excellency," shouted the psychotechnician. "It's *changed!*"

"*What do you mean?*"

"The alien isn't the same any more. *Its intelligence factor is over three hundred!*"

Judging that this was the moment of maximum confusion, Cardan spoke in a voice as coldly flat and authoritative as he could make it. "You are no longer talking to the dollar-mender. I am an Underman. I now occupy this body."

There was a tense silence, and Cardan, moving fast, said flatly, "My mind is now shielded from your technology." He had visualized a gray blur, like blowing fog. "I will remain here only long enough to deliver this warning:

"The planet below is occupied by many power groups. They are rivals, and have for generations hidden their newest advances from one another. To avoid a childish secrecy which hides things from itself as well as others, they have built complete, self-sufficient installations underground. Only those of the highest ability can go below, and these must mate only among themselves. In these conditions, progress has been swift. *But no new device is permitted on the surface until it is certain that it cannot suggest secret developments to a rival.* The devices visible to you are obsolete surface devices, which give no measure of the present power of this planet." Cardan paused for just an instant, then added:

"You are warned. You now have sufficient information to make your decision. If you attempt to injure anyone below, you will be destroyed. If you wish to depart peacefully, you will so signify by returning this captive unharmed. You will then leave.

"Our wishes for your happiness and advancement go with you.

"Good-by."

Cardan visualized a spinning mass, which withdrew to show whirling spokes, then a rectangle that enclosed the spokes and then that shrank, till the spokes slowed and vanished, and then the rectangle itself was gone.

For a long moment, Cardan waited, like a general whose reserves have been sent into action. The silence stretched out.

Then, suddenly, the creature before Cardan said, "*Wait!*"

"Too late, your excellency," said the psychotechnician, "he's gone. He's broken contact."

There was another silence, then a creaking and a stirring in the room.

To Cardan's right, there was a ponderous clanking, as of a many-limbed creature being led off with all its many limbs in chains.

"Wait, guards," said the chairman, a hint of benevolence

mingled with the triumph in his voice. "What do you say now, Skaa?"

Skaa said slowly, "I can see I must have been wrong somewhere, your excellency."

"You *admit* I was right?"

There was a long pause. The chains rattled. Reluctantly, Skaa said, "Yes."

"Ah-ha." The chairman's tone was almost genial. "And do you apologize for what you started to say back there?"

Another pause followed. Then, in a tone of deep depression, the words, "I apologize."

"Good. Fine! Guards! Unchain him!"

There was a clatter and thud that went on for about thirty seconds.

The chairman's voice said, "Now, Commander Skaa, as soon as possible have this specimen carefully set down on his home planet. Then get out of here. And take my advice. Don't mope over this. You're still young. There are other worlds to conquer. When you bite into something and taste poison, the only thing to do is spit it out. That's common sense."

There was a faint hiss nearby, and Cardan smelled a strong, familiar, geraniumlike odor.

* * *

Cardan was vaguely aware of a lapse of time before he felt a sensation like a puff of flame that burst through his body from the back to the ends of his limbs. He sat up to see the gray light of dawn in the east. He was in his car behind the wheel, with the engine turned off and a medium-sized pine dragged to the side off the road ahead.

Cardan pressed in the car's lighter, and felt in his inside

coat pocket for a cigar. Stripping off the outer wrapper, and biting off a bit of the end, he put the cigar in his mouth. The lighter popped out, and he puffed the cigar alight.

"Hm-m-m," he said, looking out through clouds of smoke. A section of his mind was trying to argue him around to the belief that he had fallen asleep and dreamed the incident.

Cardan snorted. He rolled the window down a little way, and took a light cautious sniff of the outside air. It smelled .fresh, and free of any geraniumlike odor. Carefully, he got out, and bent to look at the wet dirt of the road. It was covered with numerous thick curving marks, as if a multitude of flexible-limbed creatures had hastily bundled the tree off to the side of the road.

"You *see*," growled Cardan, to the skeptical part of his mind. Grumblingly, it subsided. He shifted the cigar around to the other side of his mouth, picked up a small piece of branch on the road to scrape the worst of the mud off the bottom of his shoes, got back in the car, slammed the door and started the engine.

"Hm-m-m," he said again. It had just occurred to him that he had just about decided to get a computer. He fished around to find the reason for this development, and found that a number of ideas had rearranged themselves, under the crystallizing influence of some comment he had heard recently. But what was the comment?

He was well down the winding dirt road near the highway when it came to him. It was a remark he had overheard in that dark room: "You never know when their science may develop beyond science."

Cardan shifted his dead cigar from one corner of his mouth to the other.

An intense curiosity was starting to develop within him.

"... *What was beyond science?*"

The Gold of Galileo

As he neared the curve at one hundred and ten miles per hour, Marius "Doc" Griswell kept his foot hard on the accelerator. His sleek sports coupe whipped up a cloud of moonlit snow as it went off the blacktop, to smash head-on into the stone wall.

The police, hastily called, found no skid marks.

***

James Cardan shielded his eyes from the wintry sun, slammed the car door, took the morning paper from the rack by the variety store entrance, and read the headline:

RUSSIAN REACTOR HIT
IN NEW MYSTERY BLAST.

Cardan paid for the paper, and, as he slid back behind the wheel, he glanced again at the front page. Separate from the main article was a familiar face, under the words: "Nuclear Scientist a Suicide?" Cardan, startled, skimmed the article:

". . . famous atomic scientist, Marius 'Doc' Griswell
. . . Director of Research for giant Hanwell
Industries . . . died in an auto crash last night . . .
considered a maverick for his theory that particle
speed and position can be simultaneously
determined . . . attempted to prove his theory
with a huge 'cold fusion' reactor called the
'asterator' . . . keen analytical mind . . . much in
demand lately to investigate the worldwide rash
of nuclear accidents . . . 'We will miss him,' said
Nobel prize winner, Dr. . . ."

✳ ✳ ✳

Cardan, frowning, drove slowly across the tracks, past
the big familiar sign "Research East," then parked in the
freshly snow-plowed lot, and went inside. He unlocked a
door lettered, "James Cardan, President," went through
the outer office into his inner sanctum, tossed the paper
on his desk, and hung his coat and hat in a small closet. He
sat down, and, still frowning, took out a cigar.

Why should Doc Griswell commit suicide?

Cardan reread the article. The night had been clear,
and Griswell knew the road; but there was no sign he had
braked. Yet he had been in good health, respected, happily
married, and highly paid by Hanwell Industries, whose
president, Eli Kenzie, was Doc's personal friend.

Cardan groped for matches, lit his cigar, and sat back.
Finally, he shook his head, looked at the headline, and
carefully read the lead article. Two sentences stood out:
"This explosion brings to six the unexplained nuclear
blasts since the first at 3:26 p.m., September 29th, in the

English Channel" . . . "as in the U.S. accident of November 9th, an explosion took place after the reactor had been shut down following an earlier alarm." A list of unexplained nuclear accidents followed:

1) 9/29 U.K., 3:26 p.m., submarine
2) 10/24 China, 10:23 p.m., missile
3) 11/9 U.S.A., 7:17 a.m., reactor
4) 11/17 U.S.A., 9:19 a.m., missile
5) 11/26 France, 3:09 p.m., missile
6) 12/9 U.S.S.R., 6:02 p.m., reactor

Cardan at last folded the paper, and reluctantly turned to a problem he had put off in the hope that it might solve itself.

He had, during the start of what had looked like an impressive business expansion, hired people he expected to need later. The expansion had then evaporated, and now the need was to economize. Yet there was no one Cardan wanted to let go. And, as sure as day followed night, once he let them go, business would pick up, and he would have to scratch and scrabble to rehire them. But when would business pick up?

Scowling, Cardan unfolded the paper. Following the sports pages, the business headlines sprang up at him:

MARKET SLIDE CONTINUES!
ECONOMISTS ALARMED
AMEX CRASHES
ANOTHER GREAT DEPRESSION?
ADMINISTRATION URGES CALM

As Cardan knocked the ash off his cigar into the square glass ashtray on his desk, the phone rang. Grateful for the interruption, he picked it up, and a deep male voice said, "Jim?"

Cardan recognized Doc Griswell's boss at Hanwell Industries, and cleared his throat. "Eli."

"Have you heard about Doc?"

"I just read it in the paper."

"I got it last night. I came in early, to think things over."

"Why did he do it?"

"I—" Kenzie stopped, and began again. "You know, Doc thought a lot about that asterator project of his. I'm sorry, now, that . . ." His voice trailed off.

Cardan sat still, frowning.

Kenzie said, "I don't want to tie men up in that project. But I think, out of respect for Doc . . . I'm making a mess of this, Jim . . . Look, would you be willing to take on Doc's asterator? Don't rush it. Look into it, see what you think. After all, Doc was a genius. Maybe a fresh set of minds . . . The device hasn't produced yet, but, you know . . . fusion power . . . And if there's anything in it, we'd be glad to give you a participation. We might even sell the whole thing to you for the right price. What do you say?"

Cardan set his cigar carefully in the ashtray.

"How much," he said warily, "do you have in mind if we work on this for you?"

***

Out in the company lot there were now two cars and a third pulling in. A slender, dark-haired man got out and his sharp features, as he looked at the second car, registered annoyance. He glanced up, and suddenly grinned.

At an upper window, a blond athletically-built man grinned back, with a slightly rueful expression. It might be childish—it *was* childish—but he took pleasure in getting here ahead of Mac. Since Cardan got here early, the whole place tended to, as if somehow it were a question of status to be early.

Behind the blond man, the intercom buzzed. Cardan's voice spoke inquiringly. "Don?"

Donovan said, "Right here."

"Mac in yet?"

"He's on the way up."

"We've got a job to talk over."

"Want me to tell him?"

"I'll let him know."

* * *

Cardan relit his cigar as Donovan and Maclane straightened from the newspaper looking grim.

"Is either of you," Cardan asked, "familiar with what Doc was working on?"

Donovan shook his head. "Only vaguely."

Maclane hesitated. "I've heard Doc's argument. But it involves mathematics I don't understand."

"How did he expect to get 'cold fusion'?"

"Doc argued that nuclei aren't statistical abstractions, but have definite structures. He said that to fuse two nuclei, there ought to be an optimum approach based on their actual structures. He said our nuclear fusion program only considers high-energy approaches. He claimed to have the mathematics to show that in certain cases a low-energy approach should work."

Donovan said, "Did he explain it?"

"Mostly by mathematics. The rough general picture I got was of electrical or magnetic fields, varied by computer according to nuclear location and attitude, rapidly bringing pairs of nuclei together. The advantage, if the method worked, was that there would be no plasma to wrestle with."

Cardan sat back, frowning. "Did you see any apparatus to *do* this?"

"No. Doc quit talking once he had the asterator."

Cardan described Kenzie's phone call. "Since we need the work, I didn't want to turn him down. But there's something Kenzie is very carefully not mentioning."

Maclane nodded. "We could be taking on a lot more than we bargained for. Doc wasn't easy to understand. To give you an idea, he was criticized for suggesting that particle speed and position could be simultaneously determined. You'd think if that *wasn't* what he meant, he'd have said so. But he acted sometimes as if he thought people deliberately misunderstood him, so why explain? It dawned on me finally that possibly that wasn't what he was arguing. He could have meant that the particles would naturally interact with the fields, to come together *somewhere* in the apparatus, with this 'optimum approach.' We wouldn't necessarily *know* their speed and position. But Doc never cleared up the point. There are bound to be other things he never explained about the asterator. It may be a nightmarish job to begin where Doc left off."

Donovan shrugged. "How can we lose? If the method works, we buy a participation. If not, remember, Kenzie's still paying us."

Cardan studied the glowing tip of his cigar. "Any chance of the asterator itself causing trouble?"

Maclane looked puzzled. "Trouble?"

"Trouble. Kenzie isn't *actually* doing this out of sentiment. If so, he'd just have some of his people keep on with the work. He implies it's sentiment, to provide an explanation that isn't subject to logic, or to questions of profit and loss. But in carrying out this sentimental gesture, just incidentally, the asterator moves around. Now *we've* got it."

Maclane blinked. "I hadn't thought of that."

"Any chance that it may be at some crucial point? When *we* run it, could it—say—turn into a little supernova?"

Maclane shook his head. "I don't think, from what Doc said—"

Donovan, scowling, said, "Remember that 'analysis of a sample' we did for hire a few years ago? Nobody told us they had reason to believe the sample contained a hallucinogen."

"I remember. They said their lab people were out with the flu."

Cardan picked up his cigar. "Let's go slow with this. There's some reason Doc slammed his car into that stone wall."

***

As the days passed and the weather worsened, Cardan took cheer from the fact that now he didn't have to let anyone go; but he lost an equivalent amount of peace of mind from the monstrosity rapidly taking form in the building around back known as "the hangar."

Shipped in sections, the asterator left everyone who looked at it speechless. To make things worse, there were the experts who came along from Hanwell Industries.

Sporting mindless grins, they tended to jump at slight noises; they laughed heartily at the sickest jokes; they had to visibly put their minds in gear to answer a simple question. Donovan and Maclane, supervising the work, began to acquire a sleepless look.

Cardan himself, over a period of years, had been occasionally subject to what, for lack of a better name, he called nightmares. One chill night, at two a.m., he found himself sitting among tangled sheets in the quietly ticking blackness. Against the windows, there was a rattle of sleet. Cardan didn't move.

His occasional nightmares, if that was what they were, tended to occur with craftmanlike attention to detail. Grafted onto actual incidents in his life, they frequently seemed linked also to other nightmares, so that Cardan woke to the impression of living several interconnected lives at once. Sometimes, among the confusion of events, he found something of practical value, and he now carefully thought things over. If there was a lesson here, he wanted to find it.

Finally he got up, pulled the sheets straight and went back to bed. He knew that the psychologists would probably suggest he was suffering some unacknowledged strain. But, of course, that wasn't it.

Just before he fell asleep, he remembered something. The asterator should be ready to test tomorrow.

***

The morning found Cardan pulling into the freshly snow-plowed company lot in a not very pleasant frame of mind. He had barely gotten through the drifts on his shortcut over the hills this morning. So many cars were already here that the work might be proceeding without him. .

Cardan went to the rear of the hangar and opened the door. Before him loomed the high, shadowy, faintly echoing interior. Against the gray light from the wide, paned doors on the far side, stood a towering frame like the gimbals of an enormous gyroscope. Within the frame was what looked like the broad side of a giant's discus, resting on its edge. Near the base, a knot of men dispersed, leaving Donovan and Maclane, dwarfed, looking up at the asterator. Then Donovan called out, his voice intense and faintly echoing: "Rotate both rings."

There was a hum, the disk moved. There swung into view against the light, the arching slender girders of an inner frame anchoring cables that stretched to the disk. Swirling out from the bulging central part of the disk were raised spiral arms reaching almost to the rim where each ended in an oblong, faintly outlined.

Donovan's voice was strained. "Stop!"

The hum died. The disk hung motionless.

Cardan looked up at it uneasily. He took time to light a cigar, then walked slowly toward Donovan and Maclane.

As he came closer, Cardan had a sense of the hulking weight of the apparatus which seemed to lean more and more toward him, tilting, ready to topple. The swirling spirals of the disk left him dizzy.

Cardan blew out a cloud of smoke, tore his gaze from the device, and was rewarded by a nervous strain that strengthened as he approached. He seemed to have walked a long distance when he reached Donovan and Maclane.

Donovan's voice sounded slightly unnatural. "What do you think of Doc's Folly?"

"I begin to see Kenzie's viewpoint."

Maclane said dryly, "We couldn't subcontract it to someone else, could we?"

"The thought has its attractions. But the idea was to keep *our* people busy."

Maclane nodded toward a nearby table. "Take a look at Doc's notes."

A mottled black-and-white bound notebook lay on the table. Cardan leafed slowly through pages of equations interspersed with lines of unreadable symbols. "Did Griswell keep his notes in Arabic?"

Donovan said, "According to Beasley, one of Doc's assistants, that's the Graham version of Pitman shorthand."

"How do we decipher this?"

"We've got an expert coming. That's the least of our worries."

"What else?"

"Beasley. And Allan, another of Doc's assistants."

"Still nervous?"

"Scared witless. But they won't say why."

Cardan looked up at the looming bulk. "Are the pivots on that thing strong enough?"

Donovan nodded. "It's all strongly made. But we don't feel comfortable in the same building with it."

Cardan cleared his throat. "You got it together faster than I expected."

"Faster than *we* expected," said Maclane.

Donovan said, "It practically fell together."

Cardan glanced from Donovan to Maclane.

Donovan said, "All we're doing now, though, is checking the mount."

"Once you've checked it," said Cardan, "let's stop there till we're sure what's in that notebook."

"That's our idea."

Maclane said, "I'll show you one thing that's not in that notebook." He opened it past the last of the pages on which anything was written, and bent the pages back. The cut edge of another page was visible, sliced off close to the spine.

Cardan tilted the notebook, to see faint impressions indented on the blank page following.

"You might try a strong light crosswise on this page."

Maclane nodded.

"Somehow," said Donovan, "I begin to think we'll earn our keep on this job."

***

Cardan, at his desk the following day, considered Doc's bound notebook which lay opened to a page of incomprehensible calculations. About two-thirds of the way down the page, there was a square root of negative one, circled, with a line drawn to a question mark and some unreadable symbols.

Across the desk, Maclane and Donovan were leafing through typed pages. "Here we are," said Maclane. "That comment near the question mark reads, 'Why this? What's the significance?'"

"Doc didn't understand his own calculations?"

"Evidently not when he wrote that."

Donovan said, "We worked out what was on the missing page."

"What?"

"A handwritten note:

"Eli—The times match. Marius."

"That's all?"

"That's all."

" 'The times match'?"

"Right."

"Whose writing?"

"Doc's."

"No date?"

"Nothing."

Cardan sat frowning. "Supposedly, that note was to Doc's boss, Eli Kenzie. But suppose you wrote someone a note. What would you do?"

"If," said Maclane, "the only paper handy was a notebook like Doc's?"

"Yes."

"I'd tear out a sheet, then write the note."

"Doc evidently wrote the note *first*, since it left an impression. *Afterward*, the note was cut out."

Donovan said, "You think Doc meant the note to be in the book? Then, before passing the book on to us, Kenzie cut out that page?"

"I'm wondering. Now, what are those 'times' Doc mentions? Could they be times mentioned in the notebook?"

"Very possibly," said Maclane, "but they '*match*.' Match what?"

Cardan picked up the notebook, and examined the page. "Kenzie isn't stupid. And I don't suppose he thinks we're stupid."

Donovan nodded. "He must have known that as soon as we saw that cut page, we'd examine the next page. It follows he left it for us to find."

Cardan said, "Suppose Doc gave Kenzie information Kenzie wants to be able to deny knowledge of, but that he thinks we'll need."

"He leaves us enough to piece it together?"

Cardan nodded. "There's something here he's washing his hands of. What's in this notebook, now that your short-hand expert has it transcribed?"

"Aside from the math," said Maclane, "which we can follow only to a point, there are various comments, plus a record of asterator trials."

"And their *times*?"

"Yes. But what do the times match *with*?"

"Well, let's see what's in there."

Donovan handed over the typed transcript.

Cardan leafed through it, reading the entries carefully: "October 30: Thirty-one second run, started at 10:30 this morning. Deuterons against the liner of chamber forty-two ended it. We do get cascade. But, again, there's no power. Yet there's helium-3 in the effluent. We must have fusion. But still, we haven't got it . . . November 9: Forty-eight seconds, starting around 10:17 a.m. The longest yet. But she shut down for deuterons in chamber forty-two. Again, no heat. Power goes *in*, not out. There's a sizeable power consumption in this thing. All we have to do is fix chamber forty-two, and we have workable fusion. *But where's the energy?*"

Cardan looked up. "Was it working?"

Donovan and Maclane shrugged helplessly.

Cardan read on, to the final entry: "December 9: Seventy-two seconds! Almost a minute and a quarter! Started a little after 10:00 a.m., and everything worked like a dream. Still this damned chamber forty-two wrecked us. We've done all we can by field control, positioning the frame, and tension on the shell. Best replace the whole track. Still no detectable output. Yet the energy has to go somewhere. Could the process induce some form of transparency in the apparatus? Why that imaginary factor? Is there a connection?'"

Cardan sat back. " 'Cascade'? What does that mean?"

Donovan said, "There are a great many paired 'tracks,' leading to 'coincidence chambers' near the rim. At any given instant, up each track comes a deuteron—a stripped nucleus of heavy hydrogen—moving in response to applied fields, operated under computer control. Two deuterons reach the chamber—"

"One deuteron from each track?"

"Right. By Doc's process, they are supposedly in the 'proper condition to fuse.' They come together—"

"What is the 'proper condition to fuse'?"

As Donovan hesitated, Maclane said, "There are quite a few things about this process we don't understand. Doc assumes that there *is* such an ideal condition, and he tries to attain it by a process that is partly clear and partly very obscure. There's a little note in there somewhere, 'Would they try to mate two cats by just throwing them at each other?' Doc's reasoning on control of the applied fields is another thing that's only partly clear to us. He evidently has his computer compare results in the different sets of tracks as well as successive performances in each pair, considered over time. The computer then adjusts the fields to 'optimize' performance. But the details aren't clear. He apparently set down just enough to remind himself of points he wanted to remember or to think about further. We can follow it only so far."

"At any rate, there is a deuteron from each track?"

"Right."

"And you say he controls the relative positions of the deuterons?"

"With applied fields, adjusted by feedback from each deuteron, whose fields affect the applied fields in ways which depend on the aspect and position in space of the deuterons."

"And the details you don't understand?"

Maclane shook his head. "Among other things, I can't follow his math. I'm not sure just how the feedback works. The details of the computer control are an enigma. I have only a hazy picture of how this device actually works."

"The deuteron," said Cardan, "has a proton and a neutron. Is the idea to get them lined up so they collide with the two neutrons closest, or slightly at an angle, or what?"

"Doc," said Maclane slowly, "represents this ideal condition for fusion by the Greek letter *omega*. He refers to it as 'the omega condition.' But to exactly picture it . . . It seems to me he is making further assumptions."

"He has a more detailed mental picture of the deuteron?"

"Or of the fields associated with it. Or, who knows?"

Donovan said, "I think that has to be it, Mac. The fields associated with it."

Cardan sat back. Then he shook his head.

Donovan said, "What is it?"

"There's something here I can't put my finger on. Something aside from what we're talking about."

Maclane said, "I have the same sensation. On top of everything else, there's something I can't pin down. I have the sensation of playing chess while I've got a bad case of flu. There are things I don't grasp."

Donovan said to Cardan, "What do we do? Test it? Or try to figure it out? We ought to be able to learn something from operating it."

"I'm still in the dark about this 'cascade' Doc mentions."

Maclane said, "To begin with, a deuteron test-stream is sent through each set of tracks in turn. If there's a malfunction, the asterator stops. If every set works, the asterator 'goes into cascade'—that is, all the tracks work, and build up to maximum capacities."

"Can you keep the asterator from going into cascade?"

"We could test each set of tracks separately."

"Why don't you, tomorrow, test each set once. That would normally precede cascade, wouldn't it?"

"Yes," said Maclane.

"But don't let it go into cascade."

"Why not?"

Cardan didn't smile. "I've got a hunch."

Cardan that afternoon bought a small world globe and that evening installed himself with the globe, a long extension cord, a lamp, a card table, a metal ashtray, a folding chair, a pocket calculator, and an electric heater, in a small windowless shed built onto the hangar during an earlier project. The shed, covered with corrugated metal siding, had no telephone or electrical outlets. Free of buggable surfaces, the shed's rough new construction had provided reassurance at a time when they had wanted a place to talk openly without fear of electronic eavesdropping. The shed's metal siding was backed with thick insulation and, as the temperature dropped outside, Cardan was conscious only of the calculations he was making. At length, he looked up.

He was now almost certain. But almost, of course, wasn't good enough.

***

In late afternoon of the following day, after the asterator test, Maclane and Donovan came to Cardan's office.

Donovan said wearily, "No wonder Doc ran his car into that wall."

Cardan said, "You only *tested*?"

"Yes, and every track functioned. But there was no energy release. There has *got* to be an energy release!"

Maclane said exasperatedly, "This is really *cold* fusion. What the devil happens?"

At the door, there was a soft rap and Cardan called, "Come in."

His secretary stepped into the office, looking pale and shaken. "You asked me specially to listen to the news."

"Go ahead."

"They reported a scare at the Scoville nuclear power plant."

"A scare?"

"They're shutting down the reactor."

"Did the report say when it happened?"

"A little after three, at Scoville."

"Any details?"

"Not in the news."

Cardan nodded, and sat back. "Thanks."

She swallowed, and went out.

"A friend of mine," said Donovan uneasily, "works at Scoville." He frowned. "A little after three?"

Maclane nodded. "It happened just an hour before we tried the asterator."

"Scoville," said Donovan, "is *in the next time zone*. It happened *when* we tried the asterator."

Cardan exhaled carefully. "As Doc said, 'The times match.' You didn't move the asterator after the test?"

"No."

"We'll have to try it again. Whatever you do, don't let it go into cascade."

***

Cardan, a cigar jutting from the corner of his mouth, stood behind Maclane, who sat at a small panel, and methodically tapped a yellow button labeled "TEST." On a little oblong screen, the red digits "083" lit up, followed by "084," then "085."

At a small table to the side, Donovan was talking on the phone to his friend at the Scoville plant. Suddenly Donovan gestured. "Scoville! More trouble!"

Maclane sat staring at the glowing numerals: 085. Cardan tapped him on the shoulder. Maclane wrote briefly in his notebook, shut off the asterator, and came to his feet. Cardan led the way to the windowless shed, unsnapped the padlock, and shut the door behind them. In the darkness, they could hear the whir of the heater fan. Cardan felt along the extension cord and snapped the light switch. The papers were lying on the card table as he had left them. He turned two of them face up, for Donovan and Maclane to read:

Asterator Runs

Date	Length of Run	Apprx. Time Run Started
9/29	30 sec.	10:25 a.m.
10/11	22 sec.	10:22 a.m.
10/24	41 sec	10:24 a.m.
10/27	24 sec.	10:14 a.m.
10/31	31 sec.	10:30 a.m.
11/9	48 sec.	10:17 a.m.
11/17	46 sec.	10:19 a.m.
11/26	54 sec.	10:08 a.m.
12/2	29 sec.	10:11 a.m.
12/9	76 sec.	10:01 a.m.

Nuclear Accidents

Date	Place	Local Time	Corresponding Time at Asterator
9/29	Britain	3:26 p.m.	10:26 a.m.
10/24	China	10:24 p.m.	10:24 a.m.
11/9	U.S.	7:17 a.m.	10:17 a.m.
11/17	U.S.	9:19 a.m.	10:19 a.m.
11/26	France	3:09 p.m.	10:09 a.m.
12/9	Russia	6:02 p.m.	10:02 a.m.

Maclane said, "No wonder Doc killed himself!"

"It's obvious," said Cardan, "once we get over the idea it's impossible. Eight of the twelve times that asterator has been run, there's been a nuclear accident somewhere.

And, since this string of disasters started, there have been no nuclear accidents reported except when the asterator has been run."

Donovan and Maclane stared at the papers. Then Donovan turned, to look at Cardan. "But, how?" said Donovan.

Cardan shook his head. "I can't imagine. But if every time I snap on a flashlight the object it's aimed at blows up, then I am going to be very careful with that flashlight."

Maclane shook his head. "This is totally impossible."

"It happened," said Cardan. He raised his cigar, discovered he was holding a dead stub, and tossed it into the ashtray. "If something happens that is impossible, we've got only two explanations that I can see. First, we're wrong about what's impossible. Second, what happened is different from what we thought."

Donovan straightened. "Mac—"

Maclane glanced at him.

Donovan said, "That asterator has its fields controlled by a computer, the intent being to 'optimize the ease of fusion.' There's a whole sequence of operations right there that we don't understand, that Doc's notes don't explain, and that his assistants couldn't clear up for us."

Maclane's eyes narrowed. "That's true."

Cardan frowned, felt his pockets, located a fresh cigar, and absently stripped off the wrapper. "The computer is intended to adjust the fields to 'optimize the ease of fusion?' Not to 'achieve the necessary conditions' for fusion? *Optimize* the ease of fusion?"

Maclane nodded. "There's a difference in viewpoint involved. I think Doc expected first to get a partial success, and the computer was then to vary conditions, trying for a better result."

"By stages, he'd arrive at perfection?"

"As close to it as possible. And each set of tracks, having slightly different conditions to start with, would supposedly have a slight difference in the number of successful fusions of deuterons. The computer apparently compares the results, draws conclusions from them, varies the conditions further, and then brings all the tracks to the optimal condition—to equal the best results achieved by the best set of tracks. If some one set can't closely equal the results of the others, something is wrong, and the asterator shuts down."

"But," said Cardan, tossing the crumpled cigar wrapper into the ashtray, "when does the computer stop trying to optimize conditions? When there is one hundred percent fusion of deuterons?"

"Not necessarily. There may be a better approach with the same result, say a more efficient use of the energy to generate the fields. So the computer keeps varying conditions."

"Supposedly," said Donovan, "this will stop when every possible change produces a falling off in efficiency."

Cardan, scowling, felt in his pockets for matches. "How does the computer judge the proportion of deuteron pairs that fuse?"

Maclane glanced at Donovan who shrugged helplessly. Maclane looked back at Cardan. "We don't know. Doc knew, of course. But he had a lot of leeway at Hanwell. He just gave instructions, and he didn't always explain them. These so-called experts sent along with the asterator couldn't tell us. In time, we should be able to work it out. But we can't do much if, every time we turn it on, there's an atomic scare."

Cardan struck a match, and puffed his cigar alight. He shook out the match, and said, "There's nothing like strict logic for getting from the sublime to the ridiculous, and a computer is strictly logical. All right, suppose we just imagine that we've turned on the asterator for the first time. A proportion of deuterons fuse. What happens?"

Maclane said, "The computer tries field alterations, and keeps bringing the lowest tracks up to the levels of the more successful tracks. That, at least, is our understanding of it."

"So, now, finally one set of tracks achieves one hundred percent successful fusion. Then what?"

"The computer brings all the others to the same state, and varies conditions further to see if some approach uses less energy. It then brings every track to the same condition, so far as possible."

Cardan frowned. "Mac, *where* will fusion take place?"

"Somewhere in the coincidence chamber."

"At different places? Or—"

Donovan gave a low exclamation. "We've been assuming fusion at random locations within the chamber, with the deuterons in slightly varying relative positions. But what if there are quantum effects that limit the possibilities? Or if there is one *optimal* location and attitude, and finally all the deuterons fuse at that one location and in that one attitude?"

"And," said Maclane, "each pair of fusing deuterons

in any given chamber expels its neutron in the same direction, and with the same energy, as every other deuteron pair in the chamber?"

"Yes," said Donovan. "Mac, that would give us a ray of neutrons!"

"Wait, now. In cascade, the numbers of fusing deuterons will be enormous!"

Cardan said, "Meaning?"

"Meaning," said Maclane, "that if this *does* happen, we could end up with—" He paused, his eyes widened, and he glanced at Donovan.

Donovan let his breath out in a hiss. "It could produce a ray of closely packed neutrons possibly turned to identical attitudes with respect to one another, identically spaced, with God alone knows what possible linking of forces, or, perhaps, breakdown into smaller particles."

Cardan, for a brief instant, saw a thin compact ray hurtling through space, straight toward a complex nucleus. The ray, stretching far back, was, along its length, packed, dense, and massive. Its influence reached ahead of it, and. . . . Abruptly, the vivid mental picture vanished, and Cardan said, "When it approaches an atomic nucleus, what will happen?"

Donovan shook his head. "We've got no basis for comparison."

Maclane said, "That's the problem. It's almost like a long thin sliver of neutron star."

"Maybe worse," said Donovan. "Along its axis, this ray could involve a lineup of neutrons a hundred or a thousand times in length the diameter of a neutron star. There's no way to predict the forces involved."

"Then," said Cardan, "for a rough approximation, take something worse than a neutron star."

Maclane began to object, but Donovan, frowning, said, "The only thing I can think of would be a black hole."

Maclane shook his head. "That would take us beyond speculation into the realm of speculation squared. We're trying to understand one unknown by comparison with another unknown. Then we have to apply a correction to make up for the lack of the main characteristic of a black hole—an enormous gravitational field. It won't work."

Cardan, frowning, recalled all that he had heard of black holes, shook his head, and was about to agree with Maclane that this was too strong a comparison. But Donovan was nodding, and said, "I think that's it. The comparison doesn't have to give us the guaranteed answer. What we need here are ideas, and this analogy suggests one. Near a black hole, space-time is warped, due to the enormous mass involved. To an external observer, an object falling into a black hole will seem to fall *for an infinity of time*. Now, I'm no expert on black holes, but there is one difference between stable nuclei—which in effect must be transparent to the ray emitted by the asterator, or it could never affect nuclear installations at such a distance—and unstable nuclei, which are decomposed by it."

Maclane said, "I can imagine a ray like this penetrating a stable nucleus. After all, a sufficiently energetic neutron may strike a nucleus, and pass through unaffected. If the neutron's wavelength is short enough, it has a measurable chance to pass between the nucleons—the protons and neutrons that make up the nucleus itself. But, why should this ray decompose an *unstable* nucleus? Where's the difference, as far as penetration by the ray is concerned?"

Cardan glanced at Donovan, and asked, "The asterator ray would pass through the stable nucleus like a rod pushed through a bunch of grapes?"

"Yes."

Maclane said, "Why wouldn't it do the same with an unstable nucleus?"

"Because," said Donovan, "the instability—"

"Some of these 'unstable' nuclei have half-lives of over a billion years."

Donovan nodded. "But the instability means that, given sufficient time, the nucleus will spontaneously decompose. All that's necessary is sufficient time. No out-side energy needs to be supplied. The unstable nucleus will decompose by itself, in time. And," added Donovan, "we are in the position of external observers, watching as this dense ray approaches the successive nuclei. It must penetrate normal matter with no noticeable effect. From what we observe, it also must decompose radioactive nuclei. How? In front of this long dense ray, it's natural to expect a terrific field-distortion, roughly the kind of thing we'd expect with a very long, powerful magnet. But what kind of field-distortion? Is it a linking of strong nuclear forces? We have no way to know. But, take the black hole, just for comparison. To the external observer, there are time-related effects. An infinity of time seems to pass before an external object falls out of sight. Suppose we have a similar thing. The ray approaches a stable nucleus. The intense distortion at the head of the ray impinges on the nucleus. The nucleus experiences the equivalent, for it, of the passage of an *infinity of time*. What does the observer see?"

"Nothing," said Maclane, frowning.

"Right. Which is exactly what we would expect to see in an infinity of time, since the stable nucleus is outwardly unaffected by time. But the *un*stable nucleus, exposed to what, for it, is the equivalent of the passage of infinite time? Even if the half-life of that kind of atom is enormous, what of it? In infinite time, *it will decompose*. All radioactive nuclei in the path of the ray will decompose."

Maclane, frowning, said, "Let's get back to this field-distortion at the head of the ray. You don't say it *is* time?"

"Equivalent, for the nucleus, as the ray approaches, to the passage of infinite time."

"How," said Maclane, and then he paused. "The nucleus of an unstable atom supposedly is unstable because its components—protons and neutrons—are not in the right proportions to stay permanently linked together. There is a configuration—a relative position within the nucleus— in which the protons and neutrons no longer hold each other together, and sooner or later they come into that configuration. Then time, for the nucleus, is *the opportunity to take different configurations*. This 'field distortion,' approaching and then passing into and through the nucleus, must have the effect on the binding forces within the nucleus of successive changes in the configuration of the nucleus. Those changes in binding force that would eventually have come about due to changes in configuration, are briefly brought about by the field-distortion. And the nucleus comes unbound."

Donovan glanced at Cardan. "There's a conceivable mechanism for it."

Cardan discovered that he was holding a dead cigar and a burnt match. He tossed the match into the ashtray and said, "So, in its effects overall this asterator is like a kind of enormous lawn sprinkler, spraying these rays in random directions. Now, let's see. Each coincidence chamber emits its own ray?"

Maclane and Donovan nodded.

"But," said Cardan, "if by chance some one ray strikes a nuclear installation, can this *one* ray affect enough nuclei to detonate, say, a reactor *that has already been shut down?*"

Maclane said, "There's another point about the ray that we have to consider. The computer optimizes the ease of fusion."

Donovan, frowning, said, "True. But we've already considered the point. I think the Chief's reservation is right. *One* ray couldn't do it."

Cardan winced at the nickname, "the Chief." Where Marius Griswell had been stuck with being called "Doc," Cardan found himself repeatedly objecting that he didn't run a fire company, or lead an Indian tribe. Still, it could be worse. One hot-tempered acquaintance had discovered he was known as "the Dragon." Cardan glanced at Maclane, who was shaking his head.

"Wait a minute, Don. If we accept this effect, then the ray directly in line with them is bound to affect the fusing deuterons."

"Yes, I suppose. Still, Mac, the ray is moving *toward* the target nuclei. It's moving away from the deuterons. So—"

"I didn't say the effect would be the same. I said there'd be an effect."

"Yes. That seems reasonable."

"This effect may for some reason finally lessen the ease of fusion noticeably. Then what?"

Donovan nodded. "Yes, I see. Well, the computer will shift its fields and after a slight delay the deuterons will fuse in a different part of the coincidence chamber. It will start a new ray. That's *it*, Mac! In cascade, the coincidence chamber will be radiating detonation-rays the way a machine-gun sprays bullets. It will be bound to hit something if it's left on long enough."

"And," said Maclane, "when some one ray does hit a series of radioactive nuclei, I wonder—how will the computer interpret the result?"

"I'd think the break up of the radioactive nucleus might well exert forces at an angle to the axis of the ray. That could have the effect of destroying the far end of the ray. Repeated often enough with other radioactive atoms, that would limit the length of the ray, and supposedly limit the effect of the ray on the fusing deuterons. That compared to rays that hit no such target would be interpreted by the computer as optimization."

"Then," said Maclane, "that would do it! The computer would try to optimize the conditions for fusion in all the other chambers by shifting the fields to make the conditions identical, as if using the position and attitude of the nuclei in the optimal chamber as a model."

Cardan said, "And this will?"

"Aim every last ray from the asterator in the direction of the nuclear target. And, if the rays don't all hit, the computer will keep making minor adjustments to optimize the conditions. Very quickly it should have every ray focused on the target."

"Then," said Cardan, "with no intent on Doc's part to do this, the asterator will, first seek a nuclear target and then, second, saturate the target with nuclear detonation rays."

"Yes. In effect."

In the bare room, the sound of the electric heater fan seemed loud, as they thought this over.

Cardan nodded slowly. "This at least gives us a mental picture. But right or wrong, it is still all theory. And however it turns out there's an actual application that may catch up with us anytime."

"What's that?"

"However this works, it *does* work. And it's no fusion reactor."

"No, it's not practical. Unless—"

"Not practical as a fusion reactor. But it's potentially one of the most brutally practical weapons ever made."

Maclane glanced at the two sheets of paper.

Cardan said, "All that's needed is an aiming mechanism and whoever has an asterator can choose whose nuclear installation gets blown up. Even now it's bad enough. If we merely turn on the asterator and keep putting it in cascade we can almost count on as many nuclear disasters between now and six o'clock tonight as the world has seen till today. In a total of two hundred and eighty seconds, Doc set off six nuclear accidents. And he wasn't trying. What would half-a-dozen more nuclear disasters do? How many A-bombs and warheads are there out there, waiting to be set off? How do you stop a ray that can penetrate matter?"

Donovan said, "And Kenzie knew it!"

Cardan raised his cigar, found it was out, considered relighting it, and waited thoughtfully while Donovan and Maclane said what they thought of Eli Kenzie. When the worst had passed, Cardan said, "Kenzie probably got Doc's note when it was too late to save Doc. He was stuck with the asterator, with no one he trusted to work on it. He didn't dare tell us why he was hiring us. But I never heard a more fake explanation. And he must have known I'd know it was fake."

"You're saying he warned us?"

"And offered to sell us the device. My guess is, he's willing to pay for some kind of decent outcome to this mess. I think we should take him up on it."

"What? Buy the asterator?"

"A part interest. Given Doc's reputation, and the obviousness of those lists, we can't tell who may know about this. We're even responsible ourselves for two near-disasters. We *can't* quit. We may as well make something out of it."

Maclane stared. "You're not thinking of a commercial application?"

"What else?" said Cardan.

***

Eli Kenzie glanced around the shed, folded his overcoat, seated himself at the card table, and moved his briefcase closer. He took out a monogrammed handkerchief and wiped his forehead, his upper lip, and the back of his neck. He glanced at Cardan. "Mind if I adjust the eavesdropping environment?"

"Go ahead."

Kenzie opened his briefcase, took out three flat boxes, put one on the table, one on the floor, and one on the seat of an empty chair. He flipped switches, and each box gave out its own mixture of conversation, offbeat music, and apparently random sound effects. He produced two lightweight headsets, connected by a cord, and tossed one to Cardan. Cardan slid it on, and Kenzie's voice spoke in his ears: "Let anyone try to decipher this garble. You said on the phone you want a part of the asterator?"

Cardan adjusted the mouthpiece. "Right."

"You know what it does?"

"We know one of its little effects."

"We'll sell you the whole thing, cheap. How's that?"

"We'd like fifty percent even better."

"You want help financing what you've got in mind?"

"Right."

"What arrangements?"

"We turn it into a commercially practical setup with your backing. You then get fifty percent of the profits."

"Where's the profit in this sackful of cobras?"

"Do you agree?"

"Sure. We'll sell you half, keep half for ourselves, and take fifty percent of the profits as the payment. But before we put any more money in this thing you have to convince us it makes sense."

Cardan nodded, signed two prepared copies of a briefly worded agreement and slid them across to Kenzie who read them carefully, signed, folded one copy into his pocket and sat back.

"You understand, we can't hope to just develop this as

a nuclear-missile defense. Once word gets out, we've got an instantaneous international crisis. There has to be an answer for that, too."

Cardan slid a thick sheaf of papers across the table, and said dryly, "Our plans are fairly wide-ranging."

Kenzie examined the papers. His eyes widened. He cast a sharp glance at Cardan, and slowly nodded.

✱✱✱

Cardan, as the weather grew bleaker, continued to buy his accustomed newspaper each morning and found the news no worse than usual until that time of the year when road crews begin to wonder where to put the next snowfall. That morning Cardan climbed over the dirty gray snowbank at the curb, crunched across the salted ice on the sidewalk and found himself looking at a headline that read:

NEW ATOM BLAST!
ANOTHER ACCIDENT!
NUKE RESPITE ENDS!

In his office, Cardan questioned Donovan and Maclane, who stared at the map in the paper, and shook their heads. "There is no way we could be responsible this time for that blast."

"Then someone else has one. Whether they realize what it is or not."

The next morning's headlines read:

A-BLASTS IN RUSSIA
AND CHINA! PANIC
SWEEPS THE WORLD!

Cardan read this in a Washington D. C., restaurant at breakfast with Kenzie. At ten they were talking to a fear-paralyzed Secretary of Commerce. By ten forty-five they were describing the situation to the President, who listened wide-eyed. "Why didn't you tell me sooner?"

Kenzie said, "We didn't want to hand you this basket of snakes until we felt sure we had an answer."

"What is it?"

Cardan handed over a sheaf of neatly typed papers and diagrams clipped together at the top. He and Kenzie waited. The quiet in the room was broken only by the crackle of turning paper. Then the President took a deep breath. "We'll try it."

***

In the following months Cardan had little time to do more than glance at the headlines. Certain of these stood out:

U.S. CALLS FOR
ATOM PARLEY!

PRESIDENT USES HOT LINE,
URGES NUKE CONFERENCE

U.S. REVEALS NUKE DEFENSE!
BLOWS UP MISSILES IN FLIGHT!

RUSSIA, CHINA, ALL NUKE
POWERS AGREE TO CONFER

ATOM CONFEREES AGREE!
WEAPON LIMITS STATED!

ATOM WEAPONS BEING
PUT IN ORBIT AROUND SUN
BY U.S. COMPANY

It was about the time that last headline appeared that Cardan found himself on a program known as "Face the Press," grimly answering questions nicely slanted to make him squirm.

Mr. Skinner: Now, you are removing these warheads for profit? Do you actually think you have a right to make money from the potential destruction of the human race?

Mr. Cardan: We're on the edge of nuclear disaster. Putting all these excess warheads far from Earth costs money. Naturally, we expect to get paid for the job.

Mr. Kauldron: Are you aware that the Soviet Bloc possesses a vast military superiority to the United States and our allies in conventional weapons? Suppose all this unilateral nuclear disarmament strikes the Soviet Bloc as an invitation to conventional attack?

Mr. Cardan: If—

Mr. Kauldron: And the next part of my question is, are you the one who's responsible for all the deaths in nuclear accidents?

Mr. Cardan: Who said it's unilateral disarmament? There have even been reports of—

Mr. Kauldron: How do you defend against an attack by overwhelming forces using conventional weapons, in which they have a huge advantage?

Mr. Cardan: If it comes to that you plaster them with rocks from space.

Moderator Cooke: Ah, I believe, Mr. Cardan, you just said that there 'even were reports'—reports of what?

Mr. Cardan: 'Nukeleg blackmail.'

Moderator Cooke: What . . .

Mr. Cardan: A large nuclear power makes a secret trade with a developing resource-rich nation, A-bombs for raw materials, at a time when the small nation hasn't yet heard of asterators.

Mr. Boyle: The big nuclear power smuggles the warheads in?

Mr. Cardan: Yes.

Mr. Boyle: Then I see the nukeleg part. Where does the blackmail—?

Mr. Cardan: After the warhead has been delivered, what do you suppose happens next?

Mr. Boyle: I . . . Ah—

Mr. Cardan: Suppose a ray from an asterator should happen to hit that warhead?

Moderator Cooke: The seller threatens to blow up the warhead he just sold?

Mr. Cardan: He explains that his asterator might, just accidentally, sweep a ray across that warhead. To avoid that, he will have to attach special expensive devices to the asterator. There'll have to be more payment—more raw material.

Moderator Cooke: Incredible!

Mr. Kauldron: Mr. Cardan, you said we could drop rocks if we're conventionally attacked.

Mr. Cardan: Small captive asteroids, in orbits we control. In effect, man-made meteors. The result would be as bad as getting hit with a hydrogen bomb.

Mr. Kauldron: What's to prevent any opponent from doing the same to us?

Mr. Cardan: Right now, there are more of us up there.

Mr. Boyle: If I'm not mistaken, you're using the Hi-Lift Super-Booster and the Hi-Sky Modular Transport System, to move these warheads. These are Hanwell Industries projects that were rejected by the government for use in the space program. Is that right?

Mr. Cardan: Yes.

Mr. Boyle: Why were they rejected?

Mr. Cardan: Too expensive.

Mr. Boyle: Then—correct me if I'm wrong—in this series of nuclear disasters, Hanwell Industries has invented a reason for the government to buy their system.

Mr. Cardan: The government hasn't bought them. We use them to move the warheads. The government just pays a fee for warhead removal.

Mr. Boyle: Why do you use this government-rejected system?

Mr. Cardan: It's big enough to do the job.

Mr. Boyle: You have to admit, it looks like some sort of scheme to get the Hanwell Industries systems in commercial use.

Mr. Cardan: Well, maybe. But, gin and water look alike. If you see a man drink a pint of water, does that make him a drunk?

Mr. Kauldron: Some time ago I asked if you should be blamed for the death of people killed in nuclear accidents. You haven't answered the question.

Mr. Cardan: Doc Griswell apparently thought he was

responsible, but that involves a question you might have trouble answering.

Mr. Kauldron: What question?

Mr. Cardan: If you're driving on a curving mountain road in winter, and sunlight reflects from your windshield momentarily blinding a skier going down a tricky slope and the skier gets killed, are you responsible?

Mr. Kauldron: I—Ah—

Mr. Cardan: The asterator beam was even less foreseeable.

Mr. Skinner: Is the beam dissipated or dispersed after a certain distance or length of time?

Mr. Cardan: We've assumed that it may be. We've found nothing to prove it yet.

Moderator Cooke: Mr. Cardan, your Planetary Freight Corporation is a business, not a government-subsidized agency. What do you sell?

Mr. Cardan: Nuclear transport and storage. There is a safe-delivery charge to put the warheads in storage, a small rental fee while in storage, and a charge to withdraw warheads from storage, if anyone ever wants to do that.

Mr. Boyle: Where are the storage sites?

Mr. Cardan: On the far side of the Earth's orbit beyond the sun, keeping pace with the Earth.

Mr. Boyle: Why there?

Mr. Cardan: The asterator can't be accurately aimed at a target no one can see. And we find that the beam can't penetrate a mass of radioactive nuclei; it's apparently dissipated when the nuclei decompose. The sun contains an enormous mass of radioactive nuclei, and therefore should stop any asterator from hitting the warheads.

Mr. Kauldron: And if you blow up the sun? That's an improvement?

Mr. Cardan: The asterator ray is puny compared to the mass of the sun. It should have less effect than tossing a kitchen match into a roaring bonfire.

Mr. Boyle: Until asterators are put in space, away from the Earth the warheads are safe?

Mr. Cardan: That's our belief.

Mr. Kauldron: Why should a communist country pay a capitalist company to freight their warheads into space? They could make equally effective equipment themselves, couldn't they?

Mr. Cardan: When a crocodile has you in its teeth, do you take time to argue ideology?

Mr. Skinner: How do we protect our nuclear power plants? We can't put them in orbit.

Mr. Cardan: To protect them, we've developed the Dust Shield and the Whirlpool.

Mr. Skinner: What are—

Mr. Cardan: The Dust Shield is a set of shells surrounding the reactor. Blasts of gas through the shells circulate a dense, mildly radioactive dust. An asterator ray aimed at the reactor is absorbed by, and decomposes, the dust in line with it. More dust is constantly swept around, so the ray can't get through. The Whirlpool is based on the same idea but uses a liquid.

Mr. Skinner: You make the asterator, which causes the need for these devices. Then you sell the devices. You're really working both sides of the street, aren't you?

Mr. Cardan: If you'll think this over, I think you'll agree that there are worse things to do than protect the reactors and put the bombs on the far side of the sun.

Moderator Cooke: Is there any other development related to the asterator?

Mr. Cardan: The Asterator Drive which is a spaceship drive.

Moderator Cooke: How does that work?

Mr. Cardan: Picture a pencil made of lithium deuteride around a core of a radioactive material. When the asterator beam strikes the core, the radioactive material disintegrates causing fusion of the lithium deuteride with a tremendous release of energy which can be used to drive a spaceship.

Mr. Kauldron: Does that mean you're now polluting space itself with radioactive waste?

Mr. Cardan: The details are secret, but the current model also decomposes the radioactive waste.

Mr. Skinner: But . . . That drive is controlled hydrogen fusion! Isn't it?

Mr. Cardan: Yes.

Mr. Boyle: Is this apparatus subject to being blown up by the asterator?

Mr. Cardan: Certain parts could be, but they are heavily shielded.

Mr. Kauldron: So, why can't a shield be used to protect atomic weapons?

Mr. Cardan: It can be. But there's a continuous expense in running the shield. Then to use a warhead the shield has to be taken out. To deliver the warhead you need a delivery shield. None of this makes for quick and easy delivery of nuclear warheads. Incidentally, if the shield fails, the warheads may get blown up while you've still got them.

Moderator Cooke: Gentlemen, our time—

Mr. Kauldron: I have just one short question. First—

Moderator Cooke: —is up. Thank you, Mr. Cardan, for being with us on 'Face the Press.'

***

It was some months later that Cardan sat considering the handsome painting lying on his desk. Neat grids of warheads moved through space with a watch station in view in the background. Cardan didn't care to think how much nervous sweat had gone into this job. But most of the rough part, happily, was finished.

Donovan, looking at the painting, shook his head. "I'd never have believed any country would volunteer for nuclear disarmament, much less all of them."

Maclane said, "I wonder what the moral of this experience might be? 'Every sword has two hilts'?"

"'A thousand bombs in the distance,'" suggested Donovan, " 'are better than one underfoot.'"

Cardan said, smiling, "You're both philosophers. It's also possible to find a research and business moral in this."

"What's that?"

"There are," said Cardan, "two well-known kinds of gold mines. The first yields a heavy yellow metal. The second is the mine Galileo opened up, and that Newton, Edison, Goddard, and Doc Griswell—each in his own way—worked in. There are a lot of differences between those two mines, but there's one little thing they have in common."

"Which is?"

"Neither mine has to yield 100% solid nuggets to be worth working. A fraction of a percent is enough. So however unpromising an ore may look, if what you want is there at all, things may still work out: *The secret of the work is in the refining.*"

The Day the Machines Stopped

Brian Philips hated fights. He was strong and capable enough, but the experience of his twenty-nine years suggested that justice didn't always win. Often enough, nobody won; both sides were losers. But experience also told him there were times when it was better even to lose than to back down.

Brian braked his car in the company parking lot, shut off the engine, and looked at his watch. 7:25. He was twenty minutes earlier than usual, and that, he thought, ought to be enough. He glanced around. Although the offices and laboratories of Research East didn't start work till 8:00, according to the schedule, in actual fact the parking lot was even now more than a quarter filled.

The big black car of the corporation president, James Cardan, was already in its usual spot near the door, and the window of Cardan's fourth-floor office was lighted against the dimness of the overcast, early-spring morning. Here and there, Brian noted, other offices and labs were lit up, but not the windows of the lab where he worked as a chemist. That probably meant that he'd arrived before his blond assistant, Anne Cermak. He hoped he'd gotten there about the same time as Carl Jackson.

Brian remembered Carl's comment when for a few moments they'd found themselves alone in the lab some days before:

"This is supposed to be an age of sophistication," Carl had said. "Everyone is supposed to be very civilized with everyone else. But I'm going to make an exception. I want Anne. Stay away from her."

For a moment, Brian didn't speak.

Carl said flatly, "Just so you understand."

Brian said, "Maybe I could just say that's up to Anne. But I've already spent too much time getting run over by people who knew what they wanted."

"Sorry to hear it."

"So I'll make an exception. *I* want Anne. I'm not staying away from her, either here or outside."

They'd been interrupted then. What would have happened if they hadn't been interrupted, Brian didn't know . . .

He slid out of the car, locked it, and crossed the lot toward the building. A very light drizzle was in his face, and the air felt cold and damp. Here it might be warm by noon, but coming in on the short cut through the wooded hills, the snowbanks had still been piled beside the road. Winter hung on despite the fact that tomorrow would be the first day of April.

As he reached the building and walked up the single broad step, he turned sidewise to shove open the outer door. He noted, as he turned, the mud spattered across the front of Cardan's car, and smiled. Cardan believed in saving time. The ruts, potholes and dizzy horseshoe curves of the short cuts through the surrounding hill country made no difference to Cardan. Beside his car was another equally mud-spattered, with a small Roman Numeral I bolted to the grille. This, Brian knew, was one of the company's experimental cars, with the gasoline engine taken out and another power plant put in.

He pushed open the building's inner door, felt the steady, steam-heated warmth, crossed to the elevator, pressed a button marked 4, and a few moments later was walking down the hall to his lab.

As he snapped on the lights he was aware of the familiar sense of pleasure that two years of work at Research East had only made more real. He glanced at the soap-stone-topped lab benches, with cabinets underneath for apparatus, that ran down two sides of the small room. He noted the chemical balances in their glass cases, the shelves of reagents in bottles and jars, and, at the far end of the room, the two cubicles with their partitions of wavy glass. He went into the right-hand cubicle, fitted out as a small office, and hung up his coat. Beside his desk, in a low bookcase holding chemical texts and handbooks, was a portable transistor radio that incidentally served as a book end. He glanced at his watch. Almost 7:30. He snapped on the radio for the news summary he usually listened to in his car on the way in.

The sound came on loud, and as Brian turned down the volume, he saw near the leg of his desk, beneath the cord from the phone, a pale-blue square of cloth. He picked it up—a girl's small, clean handkerchief with the letter "A" in one corner. He breathed in the pleasant scent and shut his eyes. For a moment it seemed that Anne was right there before him, a blond girl with dark-blue eyes, a straight nose, a firm chin, and a figure disguised but not hidden by the gray lab coat.

The radio announcer finished an ad for a local bank and started to give the news.

There was a quiet knock on the lab door.

Brian turned up the news a little louder and walked to the door. He was reasonably sure who would be there. Carl Jackson was in the habit of dropping in to talk to Anne before Brian, who had farther to drive, got in in the morning.

Brian opened the door. Carl Jackson blinked, then stepped in and shut the door. He glanced around, scowling. "Where's Anne?"

"Not here yet."

The two men looked at each other. Brian could feel the intensity of Carl's gaze as they measured themselves against each other. Brian stood a fraction under six feet. Carl was about six feet two. Brian weighed a little less than a hundred and eighty. Carl, equally muscular and athletic, weighed over a hundred and ninety. In addition, there was something about Carl's light-blue eyes that suggested sudden anger and lightning reflexes. With his close-cropped pale-blond hair, tanned lean face, and powerful build, Carl presented the appearance of a formidable athlete. Brian felt the sense of oppression of a man physically outclassed by his opponent.

The mutual inspection had lasted only a few seconds, but at the end, Brian could feel his own disadvantage, tinged by a brief sadness, because only a few weeks ago, before Anne had arrived on the scene, he and Carl had been almost friends.

Carl broke into his thoughts abruptly. "How old are you, Brian? About thirty?"

"Twenty-nine," said Brian.

"When's your birthday?"

Brian frowned. "In a few months."

"How much do you make?"

Brian now caught the drift of Carl's questions. There was a chill in his voice as he said, "Why do you ask?"

"About five thousand," said Carl. "Isn't it?"

Brian said nothing, not bothering to volunteer the information that Carl's figure was out of date. Cardan had quickly raised Brian's pay to six thousand five hundred, and Brian had no feeling of being cramped on his salary. A few years ago he would have thought himself lucky to earn half as much.

Carl, his eyes slightly narrowed and glowing an electric blue, said, "I make eleven thousand. Twice what you make. I'm twenty-seven, not almost thirty years old. You've got a dead-end job in a dead-end field. I'm in electronics, the fastest growing field there is." He paused for a moment, then said, "Which of us has the most to offer?"

Brian, feeling the pressure of Carl's physical superiority, and the strain of looking unflinchingly into the hard, confident blue eyes, had the feeling of a man cut off and besieged on every side. Carl's manner showed his awareness of what Brian must be going through. But there was a little quirk in Brian's character that Carl wasn't aware of.

Carl went on. "I've been doing some research on you, Brian. I know in detail just what a mess you made of your life till you finally settled down." He looked Brian up and down, still unaware that Brian functioned a little differently than he did himself, and added, "Just forget about Anne. If you're honest, you'll see you aren't good enough." He paused, then added deliberately, "If you've got any guts at all, that is."

And that did it. All through this torrent of abuse Brian had said nothing in his own defense, had made no angry accusations of his own. He had even been able to see a certain one-sided truth and logic in what Carl said. He had stood perfectly still while Carl filled the cup of insult to the brim, seeking to break Brian's spirit by words. And Brian had done nothing. The pressure had built up in silence.

Before iron melts, it glows red, then white. It is possible to detect, by watching it, just how hot iron is. Dynamite is different.

Brian felt the blow as a heavy impact on his right fist. That was all. His vision cleared, and Carl was back against the doorframe, bent nearly double, his hands over the lower part of his chest. Time stretched out as he leaned there, unable to move.

Into the silence came the voice of the radio announcer, giving the news summary:

". . . disturbing report from Pakistan, where border patrols have picked up a defector who claims to be a Soviet scientist assigned to work at a secret Soviet base in the mountains of Afghanistan. According to the scientist, the work being done in Afghanistan could destroy overnight much of man's accumulated progress for several thousand years."

Brian frowned and glanced at Carl. Carl slowly straightened, murmuring, as if talking to himself, "*One punch.*"

The announcer went on, "Unrest in the Middle East flared up again . . ."

Carl was looking at Brian with an expression of dazed wonder, and then of respect.

Brian watched Carl warily, conscious that if he were in Carl's place, he would have to fight. Carl, however, didn't work that way. He grinned and said, "Sorry I jumped on you so hard. But you've got an unfair advantage. You work with Anne all day."

This was so different from what Brian expected that he couldn't seem to get hold of it. Finally he said, "What choice does that leave me? I could either quit working here or get a new assistant. *Naturally*, I work with her. She's a chemist. Why don't you go find yourself a girl electronics technician?"

Carl said apologetically, "I like Anne."

"I don't blame you. But I like Anne."

They looked at each other in exasperated bafflement.

In the quiet, they could hear the radio announcer summing up the news headlines.

Carl scowled. "What was that about research in Afghanistan?"

"One of their scientists is supposed to have defected," Brian explained. "He claims they were doing work that could set progress back several thousand years."

"What kind of work?"

"I don't know."

The announcer said, "For further details, listen to our regular newscast at eight . . ."

Carl glanced at Brian. "Were you planning to listen to that?"

"No. Why? Do you think there's something in it?"

"I don't know. There have been rumors of a Russian cryogenics lab in Afghanistan. The rumor is that the Russians and Afghans made a deal. The Russians would put up a dam and hydroelectric project, and the Afghans would let them put up a cryogenics lab and supply it with power from the hydroelectric project."

Brian thought it over. Cryogenics involved the study of extreme cold. At temperatures well below zero, familiar substances acted far differently than usual. Liquid mercury froze solid and could be used to hammer tacks. Hot dogs snapped like sticks. And when the temperature was made low enough—hundreds of degrees below freezing— there were very strange effects. At these extremely low temperatures an electric current had been started in a lead ring, and two years later, it was still flowing. The helium ordinarily used to fill balloons became a liquid that could slip through tiny cracks, and showed strange properties not shared by other substances. In addition, there was a rare variety of helium that didn't show the strange properties. Brian could see why anyone might be interested in such research.

"Why put the lab in Afghanistan?" Brian inquired.

Carl smiled. "To get it out of Russia."

"Explosive?"

"Apparently."

"I wonder what they were doing?"

"That's the question."

"Well, I guess I will listen to the news," Brian mused.

"Would you mind if I listened with you? The chief is in and out of our lab and I don't care to be listening to the radio when he comes through." Nearly all the men called Cardan "chief," to Cardan's occasional exasperation.

"Come on over. But it will probably all boil down to the fact that nobody really knows anything about it."

"Probably." Carl turned to the door. "I'll see you."

"Okay."

Brian scowled. He and Carl were now apparently back on good terms, but none of their problems had been resolved.

Out in the hallway, there was a brisk tap of heels. Brian smiled. The room suddenly seemed brighter, the objects in it clearer. Brian even imagined that the air was scented with the faint fragrance of the handkerchief he'd found earlier.

✸
Chapter 1

Anne Cermak was wearing a white cotton blouse and a black skirt, and the fragrance Brian had only detected on the handkerchief was now subtly pervasive. She was carrying her short navy-blue coat, and with her free hand reached for the light switch as she came in. She looked at Brian in surprise.

The almost painful longing Brian felt when she was away suddenly became pure pleasure; then he noticed that she'd been crying.

She turned away as she closed the door and tried to speak lightly. "You scared me. I'm used to getting here first."

Brian put his hand gently on her shoulder. "What's wrong, Anne?"

For a moment she stood intensely still. Then Brian noticed the faint trembling. Carefully, he turned her toward him. She was trying to hold her head straight, but tears were streaming from her tightly shut eyes.

"Anne—" He held her close, and suddenly her face pressed against his shoulder. She cried desperately for a moment, then gently pulled away. "I'm sorry."

"What is it?" he asked, still holding on to her.

Her face twisted. She began to sob, and clung tightly to him. "Oh, Brian, it's Daddy."

Brian had met the elder Cermak, a gaunt, gray-haired man with a surprisingly direct gaze.

"His heart?"

She shook her head and pulled away. She opened her small blue purse, took out a handkerchief, and dried her eyes.

"I don't know what it is. I woke up last night and he was crying. It was the first time in my life I ever heard him do that. And then he thanked me for being a good daughter, and wished we could have had more time together—" She shut her eyes.

Brian frowned, thinking of the several thousand dollars in his bank account. "Anne, can I help? I make fairly good pay, I've had little to spend it on."

"It isn't—" She shook her head. "You'd have to know him. His heart is bad, and maybe that's part of it. They say sometimes there's a strong feeling of anxiety. But this is different. He said he'd had a dream; and he *believed* this dream! It was like a prophecy, and he could see into the future. He told me what would happen, and then he became so deeply depressed he wasn't like the same man. Oh, Brian, what can I *do*?"

For a moment he could think of nothing to say. Then he remembered the talk he'd had with Anne's father one night, on the porch of the old frame house the two had rented on the outskirts of town. Remembering the straightforward conversation, Brian mused, "He seems a sensible, hard-headed man—wait, this happened at *night*?"

"It was dark out. I think it must have been about four."

Brian thought it over. "Sometimes in the middle of the night things seem a lot worse than after the sun is up. He's had an awful lot of hardship, hasn't he?"

She nodded. "But things have been better lately. This is a good job. I make enough for both of us."

Brian remembered Anne saying once that her mother had died when she was very young, and her father had raised her. That must have been no easy job. The elder Cermak had been a coal miner in the mountains of West Virginia, where mechanization and the competition of gas and oil had eliminated many jobs. Without special skills, he could now find little to do. Yet Anne had told Brian that it had not been a scholarship or a loan that had put her through college; her father had done it.

Brian frowned. Maybe the older man was feeling useless now that he was unemployed. Of course, he didn't mope around the house. He had painted the inside, room by room, keeping himself busy during the winter between trips to the employment office. As he jokingly told Brian while showing him the living room he'd just finished painting, "I have to keep myself busy and earn my board." He grinned at his daughter. "I don't want to be a kept man." There had been no resentment in the comment— and yet his inability to earn money had to rankle.

"I can't believe it's anything but a bad night," he assured her. "Possibly he's coming down with some sickness. There's been a lot of flu around. If you want to take the day off and stay with him, I'm sure Mr. Cardan would—"

She shook her head. "It wouldn't help. He all but threw

me out of the house, shouting me down when I tried to say I'd stay with him. I got ready for work and went back in to argue with him; he took me by the arms and walked me right to the door. I *couldn't* stay with him."

"Do you want me to drive you out this noon?" Anne usually rode back and forth, in the morning and at night, with a woman neighbor who had a job in a nearby factory.

"No," she said, "he wouldn't like that. But, Brian, could you—if I invited you to dinner tonight—?"

"I'd like to come." He smiled. "You ought to know that."

She said, "If I could only get him to thinking about something else. And he likes you." She looked at Brian with a warm smile and started to say something, but at that moment there was a rap at the door.

Brian remembered that Carl had asked to listen to the news with him. The news was the last thing Brian wanted to listen to at that moment, and Carl was about the last person he wanted to see. But there was nothing to do about it now.

Anne had gathered her things together, and now said to Brian, "Thank you." They smiled at each other for a moment.

The knock at the door was repeated, a little louder and more insistent.

Anne went into the left-hand cubicle to hang her things up, closing the door of the cubicle quietly behind her. Brian glanced at the lab door, and said, "Come in." He looked at his watch. It was a few seconds before eight. Brian could scarcely believe it. He seemed to have lived several weeks since he'd pulled into the parking lot. Actually, a little over half an hour had passed.

Then the lab door opened and a frowning Carl came in. "Anne here?"

"She got in a few minutes ago. Sure you don't want to listen to that news down in your lab? I don't think anyone would hang you for it."

Carl shook his head. "This would be the wrong morning. The chief's in a terrible frame of mind."

"What's wrong?"

"As nearly as I can figure it out, he had a bad dream."

Brian blinked.

Carl said defensively, "I know. It sounds crazy. But he's got Donovan and Maclane tearing around like wild tigers. Come on, let's listen to that news and then I can get back to work."

They went into Brian's cubicle and turned up the volume of the radio. For a moment they were treated to an unctuous voice describing the wisdom of a local firm of stockbrokers. Then there was a news item neither of them were interested in. Brian by this time had lost interest in the news about the Afghanistan cryogenics lab, and walked out to see what he had to do today. He had a check list thumbtacked to a small bulletin board and was glancing at it when he heard the announcer say, "Dr. Wienko said the low-temperature research into the relationship of the structure of Helium Four with its strange properties was only one aspect of the Helmand laboratory's work. Here is a portion of the interview."

". . . Would you say, then, Doctor, that the researches are a danger to the world at large?"

"Not a danger to the world, no. But to civilization as we know it, yes."

"This isn't a question of a great explosion, a great deal of destruction?"

"You don't need a great explosion to create a great deal of destruction. Take modern industry and break the wires that bring electricity to the factories. That is all you need to do. If you can keep the wires broken, the industry is as useless as if you blew it up with a hydrogen explosion. No, this is not a question of an explosion. It is an entirely different kind of thing."

"How is it different?"

"Well, past research has discovered for us the laws of nature. Then we have built on these laws of nature."

"And this is different from that?"

"Yes."

"But all science can do, Doctor, is to discover facts, deduce theories, find out which theories are true laws of nature. Isn't that so? How can there be anything different?"

"Because science is not standing still. As we work down closer to the core of things, we discover that our first conclusions were naïve. We did not know as much as we thought we knew. We assumed that when we found a law of nature, it was invariable. That was ignorance on our part."

"Do you mean that a law of nature is—that it can be changed?"

"That is right. We have here the key to persuade nature to do things differently, in a limited region of space. But this is dangerous. It is like undermining the ground on which you have your house."

"Might this be a key to antigravity, as it's called?"

"It might, but that is a comparatively constructive use. What I speak of are certain processes in nature that are more vulnerable to interference than we realized. On some of these processes, we have built our present civilization. And as we have built, we have cast aside what went before. Consider the position of electricity at present. If electricity should fail, what would happen to our civilization?"

"And you believe that these experiments could cause electrical trouble?"

"I have no doubt of it. It has happened before. On one occasion, we had already a temporary failure of electrical power in an approximately circular region with a radius of more than nine kilometers."

"Did you object at that time to the experiments?"

"Not at all. The experiments are very necessary."

"Then why do you object now?"

"We have made improvements and refinements in the apparatus. The vacuum is harder, the temperatures lower, the materials purer. My colleagues feel that this will make a noticeable but not large change. My studies convince me that, on the contrary, there will be a marked and decisive change. The radius of the surface area affected will be on the order of one thousand times as great. Possibly the effect will show new characteristics when it occurs on so large a scale. In any event, the result will be the destruction of civilization as we know it. Modern industrial civilization is in great danger at this moment."

The voice cut off, and the announcer said, "That report came from Pakistan, where a Soviet scientist has just defected to the West. There was fresh trouble in the Middle East last night—"

Brian turned off the radio.

Carl said, "He claims that their experiment is likely to cause widespread power failure? Is that right?"

"As nearly as I could tell, he claims it will cause widespread *irreparable* power failure."

"Then I guess we wasted time listening to it," Carl countered. "There *is* no irreparable power failure."

Carl looked around, obviously wondering where Anne was. A pounding of heavy heels going past in the hall outside attracted their attention.

"Oh-oh," said Carl. "It sounds like something is going on out there. I'd better get back in circulation."

The minute he'd hurried out, Anne opened the door of her little office. Her face was very pale.

Brian, alarmed, said, "What is it, Anne?"

For a moment she seemed unable to speak, then she said, "Brian, that's what Daddy's dream was about."

It took Brian a few moments to realize what she meant. "Listen," he said, "does your father have a radio in his room?"

"Yes, he has a little portable I got him last Christmas."

"Could he have left it on last night?"

"I suppose so. Why?"

"Suppose he were lying there, slightly feverish, and the radio wasn't turned all the way off. Then, suppose this report came on and he heard it just as he fell asleep. He could very well have imagined he dreamed it."

She said, "That *could* be it. He might have turned the volume control way down without remembering to actually turn the switch." She sounded relieved. "That *could* have happened."

Brian said, "I don't claim to know much about electronics, but according to Carl there is no way to permanently cut off electrical power."

Anne smiled. "That's a relief to me. I'm sorry I made such a fuss."

Brian smiled. "Is my dinner invitation still good?"

"You know it is."

"Well, let's see what we have to do today." He crossed the room to study his check list. Anne came over to stand beside him. Brian felt the sense of deep contentment that rarely comes to a man, and seldom lasts long even then. He had a job that he enjoyed, in a company that he wanted to work for, and Anne, he realized with a wonderful certainty, liked him—just as he liked her. For a moment, everything seemed perfect.

And then, overhead, the lights went out.

Anne's hand gripped his arm. Brian frowned, opened the door, and glanced out in the hall. The hall lights were out.

Anne said, "Oh, Brian. I'm afraid."

"It may be just a local power failure. Let's see if there's anything about it on the radio."

He snapped on the portable radio. Nothing happened. He turned the volume control high and swung the tuning knob from one end of the dial to the other.

There was no sound.

He clicked the radio off, then on again. Still no sound. He picked up the phone that sat on his desk. There was no hum, buzz, or sound of any kind.

He dialed the operator. Nothing. He realized that his heart was hammering, and that he was on the edge of panic.

With an effort, he compelled himself to breathe slowly and steadily, calmly, and to sit down and methodically think things over.

Anne was watching him tensely.

Merely looking at her was such a pleasure to Brian that abruptly his sense of tension snapped, and he could think clearly. He said, "Don't you have a little flashlight you carry in your purse?"

"Yes," she said.

"Would you get it? And I should have a big one here in this desk, somewhere."

Brian was thinking that lights could be cut off by a power failure, and so could a number of broadcasting stations, if the failure were widespread enough, but flashlights carried their own power with them.

He slid open the drawers of his desk, looking for his flashlight.

Anne came back from her cubicle, a stricken look on her face. She was holding a little pocket flashlight. "It doesn't work. The light doesn't work any more."

Brian suddenly realized that the anguish in her voice was not for the bulb that didn't light. She was undoubtedly thinking of her father's dream.

Brian found his flashlight, tipped it so he could see the bulb, and pressed the switch forward. The bulb remained dark.

Brian took the batteries out. He remembered putting them in, fresh, not long before. He hadn't used the light enough for the batteries to grow weak, and so far as he could tell from looking at them, there was nothing wrong. He tried the flashlight using an extra bulb; it still didn't work. He was putting it back in the desk drawer when he realized that, for some reason, the flashlight felt strange.

Puzzled, Brian took it out and looked at it. The finish looked somewhat dull and lusterless, but then, though the batteries and bulb were new, he'd had the flashlight itself for several years. He felt the smooth surface of the metal, couldn't pin down what was wrong, and impatiently put the flashlight back in the drawer.

Anne still stood in the doorway, holding the little pocket flashlight. Her face showed concern.

Before Brian could say anything, the lab door opened.

Carl, his face tense, said, "Brian, Anne, the chief wants you."

***

Cardan, a powerfully built man who looked to be in his middle forties, was seated at his desk, a smoldering stub of cigar clenched in one corner of his mouth. On the desk were a couple of dry cells, cut open; a flashlight, taken apart; and a glass jar with two metal strips immersed in a clear solution, a wire running from each of the metal strips to connect with a meter lying on the desk.

Donovan, a tall blond-haired man, was leaning across the desk, examining the connections. A slender, sharp-featured man named Maclane, standing beside Donovan, said to Cardan, "You *dreamed* this would happen?"

Cardan put the smoldering stub of his cigar in the ash tray, and, scowling, pulled open a desk drawer and selected a fresh cigar. He lit it from the stub, sat for a moment blowing out a cloud of smoke, then shook his head.

"What I dreamt was this nightmare, all right. Electricity vanished from the face of the earth—" He seemed bewildered. "We've got to find out what's going on." He glanced up, nodded to Brian and Anne, then glanced back at Maclane.

"Mac, suppose you get some men started checking every form of electricity. Try every electrical power source— battery, generator, magneto—whatever you can think of. If that doesn't work, try generating static electricity. Go at it from every angle conceivable."

"I'll get right to it," Maclane said on his way out.

Cardan glanced at Donovan. "Don, suppose you circulate around and find out about *other* energy sources. You might start by checking our experimental cars down in the lot. That lightweight gas turbine and the new steam engine ought to be down there. See how they work."

"Okay, Chief."

Carl, Anne and Brian came in as Donovan went out. Cardan glanced at Anne, his expression softening slightly. "Can you run a series of standard chemical reactions to see if, from a chemist's viewpoint, everything is apparently normal and as it should be?"

Anne nodded.

Cardan said, "Good. Go to it."

Anne hurried out of the room. Cardan eyed Brian and Carl for a moment. "You two feel tough?"

Carl grinned. "Hard as nails, Chief."

Brian noticed the glint in Cardan's eyes. There was something about the way Cardan sat there, speculatively watching them, the smoking cigar in his raised hand, that was a challenge.

"What," said Brian, "did you have in mind?"

Cardan drew on the cigar, and blew out a cloud of smoke.

"The news this morning told of a Russian lab in Afghanistan, and of one of their men who quit, claiming what they were doing in the lab might knock out electricity a long distance away. Not too long after that, our lights, phone, and radio went off, and we haven't been able to raise so much as a dull glow in any piece of electrical apparatus since. It's natural to put two and two together and conclude the Russian lab is responsible. But Afghanistan is a long distance from here. Before we jump to conclusions, we want to know what it's like *outside*. We need to know if the electricity has been knocked out all over the city. If it is, what things will be like out there after this goes on for a while is hard to say. I want a pair of men to go out there and see what's going on. Are you willing?"

"I'm willing," Brian agreed.

Carl said, "Sure."

"Okay," said Cardan. "Look around and see if you can get some idea just how far this lack of electricity extends. There are bound to be effects we wouldn't think of offhand. Find out all you can. See how people are reacting. Then get back and let us know."

Brian and Carl nodded their agreement at the same time, and turned toward the door.

Cardan called, "Wait a minute."

They turned around.

Cardan said, "Stick together out there. Don't get separated. We don't know yet what it may be like."

Carl said, "If we split up, we could cover ground twice as fast."

"Sure," said Cardan, "but my idea was to get you both back afterwards."

"I don't think there'd be any trouble," Carl said. "At least, not yet."

"How are you going to get around?"

Brian said, "That's right. If electricity is knocked out, there goes the ignition system of cars."

"Yeah," Carl agreed. "But I know a place where we can rent bicycles."

Cardan said, "Assuming cars *are* stopped, and the view out the window over there looks like it, there are going to be a lot of people on foot, and some of them aren't going to like it."

"Hm," said Carl. "Yes, I see what you mean. Maybe the two of us *had* better stick together."

"I think so. And keep your eyes open." He smiled. "Good luck."

"Thanks, Chief." They turned, nodded to a wiry man with black hair combed straight back, and went out. Behind them, they could hear Cardan say exasperatedly, "Smitty, do I look like an Indian, or the head of a fire department?"

"I don't know, Chief," said Smitty. "Why do you ask?"

Carl and Brian glanced at each other and grinned. But in the dim hall, lit only by the light coming from the open doors of occasional labs, their faces had a shadowy, sinister look. It occurred to Brian that the situation wasn't yet real to either of them. As they walked by the closed door of the lab where he and Anne worked, it occurred to Brian that if electricity *was* gone, so was his job. So much of the work done by Research East involved electronics that, without that work, the company couldn't survive.

And then Brian realized that it was a lot worse than that, that this thought only began to scratch the surface. It was with a vague feeling of dread that he followed Carl into the dark interior of the elevator.

Carl stopped abruptly. "My mistake." The elevator, being electric, obviously could no longer run.

Brian said, "Let's try it anyway."

Carl felt through his pockets, found a book of matches, and struck a light. Brian held his breath, and punched the button to take them to the ground floor.

Nothing happened.

Carl shrugged. "Worth a try."

"Yeah. Well, the stairs are around the corner there."

They walked around the bend in the hall; the box over the door that usually glowed red, spelling "Exit," was dark now. Carl pulled open the door and Brian followed him quickly down the steps. At the ground floor, where the door opened out into the parking lot, Carl hesitated.

"Somehow, I'm not anxious to go out there," he said, his usually pugnacious face bleak.

Brian paused before the closed door. "By the time we get back, things may seem a lot different."

For a moment they both stood silent, then Brian said, "But things are going to change whether we go out there or not."

"I suppose so."

Then, as if by common consent, they pushed open the door.

Chapter 2

Cool spring air chilled their faces as they stepped out onto the parking lot. A gust of wind blew several pages of a newspaper, folding and unfolding, across the blacktop, to press them flat against the link fence. Then they were out of the shadow of the building and the sun was warm as they walked toward the gate.

Donovan's voice came to them from a car backed part way out in the lot. "Mind trying your cars before you leave?"

Brian thought for an instant that perhaps they'd been mistaken, and it *was* only a local power failure. Then he saw the puff of steam blow away in the cool air as the car glided forward. That was the experimental steam car, and all it used electricity for was lights, accessories, and a device that could be used to ignite the pilot which, in turn, lit the main burner. But a match would do the job just as well.

Carl and Brian waved their assent to Donovan and split up to go to their own cars.

Brian slid into his car, put the key in the ignition and turned it. Ordinarily there was a faint noise from somewhere in the machinery as he turned on the ignition. But now there was silence.

Brian turned the key further, to switch on the starting motor. The only sound was of the wind blowing past. The car remained silent.

Brian tried again, and then once more. Nothing happened.

He looked at the clock on the dashboard, stopped at nineteen after eight. He tried the dome light without success, then glanced at the ammeter and turned the headlight switch on. The ammeter needle stayed dead on zero. He snapped on the radio and the only sound was the click of the pushbutton. Habit led him to turn off the useless switches before he got out. Then he stood, one hand on the door, the cold wind whipping his trouser legs about his ankles, and abruptly he asked himself: *How could all these things stop working?* The car battery was self-contained, and as long as the generator kept the battery charged, it, in turn, would supply current to start the motor and run all the car's accessories. How *could* anything affect this self-contained power supply?

Scowling, Brian opened the hood and checked the connections of the battery cables. They were tight and clean. He got out a pair of pliers, spread their handles wide, wrapped his handkerchief around the wide-open jaws, and pressed the end of one handle to the positive terminal of the battery. Cautiously, he swung the pliers to touch the tip of the other handle to the battery's negative terminal.

Nothing happened.

Brian rubbed and pressed the bare metal against the

battery terminals. There was no spark, no sign of life from the battery.

He put the pliers away, took a last look under the hood, lowered it, and locked the car door.

Across the lot, Carl slammed down the hood of his car, tossed about eight feet of cable with clamps on both ends into the trunk, and crossed the lot, the sun glinting on his blond hair, his pale blue eyes narrowed in exasperation.

"Any luck?" he called.

"All bad," said Brian.

Carl nodded dispiritedly.

Donovan was just climbing out of another car. He called to them, "How did it go?"

Carl held both hands up with his thumbs down.

Donovan waved his hand in thanks. Brian and Carl headed toward the gate.

"It acts," said Carl, "exactly like a dead battery. The question is, *is* it a dead battery?"

"I couldn't raise a spark," said Brian.

"Me either. But what could make the charge leak away that fast?"

"Ionized air?"

"Maybe. Or a conducting surface layer on the battery. But where would *that* come from?"

"According to the news—what was it?—a law of nature can be changed."

Carl's lips tightened. "Something like that. I think he said, 'We have here the key to lead nature to do things another way, in a limited region of space.' That was the sense of it."

"Yes," said Brian. "There was more, too. Something

about, if you could break the wires that carry electricity to factories, and keep the wires broken, the factories would be just as useless as if you blew them up with an H-bomb."

"Break the wires," said Carl. "Did he mean make actual breaks in the wires, or was it just a figure of speech?"

"The trouble is," Brian said, "we don't have enough to go on."

They were through the gate now, on the sidewalk. In front of them, in the street, opposite the entrance to the parking lot, sat a motionless car. About twenty feet behind it was another motionless car, its hood raised. Both vehicles were empty. People were hurrying along the sidewalk, their faces baffled or angry. At a curbside phone booth, a well-dressed man irritably jiggled the hook of the dead phone. "Hello? Hello! *Operator!*" The traffic light over the intersection ahead swayed in the wind, its three lenses dark.

Snatches of conversation flew past like the bits of paper that blew along the sidewalk.

". . . have to get there by ten, but am I going to *do* it?"

". . . place is going to be a disaster area by this time tomorrow if this goes on . . ."

". . . So? It's a vacation. How *could* I get to work? I'll watch TV . . ."

At the corner, two lines of cars, headed in opposite directions, were drawn up as if waiting for the light. On the intersecting street, the cars were spread out, one halfway through the intersection, another making a right turn, just outside the crosswalk, as if waiting for a pedestrian. Most of the cars were empty, but here and there stood one with its hood up, the exasperated owner leaning in to check connections or tighten wires.

Carl led the way around the corner and they walked up a few blocks, through a district of small stores. Here the owners, wearing aprons or suitcoats, stood in the doorways of the darkened shops. Outside a small tavern, a burly bartender was frowning heavily and talking with several customers sipping beer.

"Sure," he was saying, as Brian and Carl passed. "This isn't the first time the lights went out on me. Or the TV. But what about the traffic? How do you explain that?"

A few doors away they sighted a store with new bicycles out on the sidewalk.

Carl said, "Here we are," and they went inside. A thin, gray-haired man joked with Carl for a few minutes, then agreed to rent them two bicycles for seventy-five cents each, till early afternoon. The owner grinned. "Seeing it's you, Carl. For anyone else, I'd charge a buck and a half, at least. I've got the only wheels in town that work."

"Better not charge me a buck and a half," said Carl. "Or the next time your TV quits—" He drew a finger across his throat.

The proprietor laughed. "Okay. Bring them back in good shape. Speaking of TV, have *you* got any idea what's wrong?"

"Beyond me. Maybe a sudden ionization of the air let the charge flash out of car batteries and grounded a lot of wires." He glanced at the battered bicycles. "What do you mean, bring them back in good shape? You want us to do a repair job?"

The proprietor responded with a cheerful insult and then they were out in the street.

The scene, as they pedaled toward the river and the bridge leading out of town, remained about the same; but, seen on a larger scale, because they were going faster, it became alarming. Endlessly, they raced past cars to their left, while to their right the people mingled on the sidewalks, some hurriedly trying to keep appointments, others milling aimlessly. As they passed through the main shopping district, pedestrians overflowed the sidewalks, and Brian and Carl swerved to flash down the white line in the center, passing stalled cars and trucks on either side of them. Then they were pedaling up the gently arching bridge over the river.

Brian had let Carl lead the way, but now he pedaled harder and pulled up beside him.

"North Hill?"

Carl thought a moment, then nodded. "Good view from there."

They shot down a little-traveled side street and raced down comparatively deserted roads where only a few cars were stalled, and only a few puzzled people walked, frowning, beside low buildings and wooden fences. Then they were on a road that led into town from the hills outside.

Carl, leaning forward, his blond hair blown back by the wind, big hands gripping the handle bars, grinned at Brian suddenly.

"Race?" he challenged.

Something about the fresh country air, the brisk wind, the bright sun, and invigorating exercise after the tensions of the morning, gave Brian a sense of boyish pleasure.

"Why not?"

"To the overpass."

"Okay."

Carl spurted forward. Brian, grinning, raced after him. Using a trick that had served him well in the past, Brian began to breathe hard, well before he needed to.

Carl glanced back over his shoulder. "What's the matter, Grandpop? Out of shape?"

Brian, the exhilarating extra oxygen pouring through his system, began to pedal harder. Carl glanced ahead, then glanced back, surprised. Brian was edging up on him. Already the front wheel of Brian's bicycle was level with the rear wheel of Carl's.

Carl fixed his gaze on the bridge coming into view a half mile up the road, and pedaled mercilessly.

Brian, his attention fastened on the front wheel of Carl's bike, willed the distance to shorten, then focused his thoughts on the rhythm of his legs and lungs. For a moment he was conscious of nothing but the wind hard on his face, then vaguely conscious that he was drawing forward, moving slowly and steadily ahead of the man and the bicycle beside him. Carl became aware of this, too, and for a moment he began to pull away.

It seemed to Brian that there was nothing more he could do, but from somewhere inside him came an unexpected determination that brought him forward again, and then side by side, the two of them flashed over the overpass and up the first rise of the road that branched off to lead up the side of North Hill.

After a hard uphill climb, Brian and Carl, breathing heavily, leaned the bicycles against two trees at the edge of a graveled parking place where in the summer cars often stopped to look south over the city. Among the trees were green-painted picnic benches and stone fireplaces, and Brian and Carl, each casting secret yearning glances at the benches, yet neither willing to admit to the other how worn, weak, and tired he felt, walked unsteadily through the picnic grounds, past occasional patches of grainy snow that lay in hollows and behind fallen logs, where the sun couldn't reach till it rose so high that the branches of the thick hemlocks no longer intervened. Underfoot, the ground felt soft and springy, and Brian was afraid that if he stepped a little too abruptly, both knees might give way and he would land flat in the snow.

"Ah," said Carl, his mouth opened only slightly in order to disguise the sound of heavy breathing, "here we are."

Brian made his own voice as steady as he could. "Yes. Here we are."

Spread out below them was a wide, clear view of the city, the highway curving into view from the side, sweeping across in front of them, then swinging away in a wide, gentle circle to disappear on the other side. The scene was clear, and so plainly different from what either of them had ever seen from this vantage point, they both forgot the need to appear invincible, and sank down on a large, gently sloping granite rock on the edge of the hill.

From here they could see the city, the river curving through it, shining here and there in the bright sun, and the railroad tracks between road and river.

This much, they'd both seen before.

But the motionless cars and trucks dotted endlessly

along the highways, the people trudging along the side of the road, the long freight train dead still on the tracks, the thick pall of smoke pouring from the factory chimneys, the tail of a crashed plane just visible in the wreckage of a burning house near the edge of town—all this was different.

After a few minutes Brian and Carl had both recovered their breath, and they were both still staring at the scene. All through town, and as far as the eye could see, no single car or truck, large or small, was moving.

Brian said, "There's nothing local about this."

"No. And seeing it all at once, it looks worse."

Brian glanced at the smoke pouring from the factory chimneys.

"Why so much smoke?"

"They use electric precipitators to collect the smoke particles. With the electricity out, the precipitators don't work."

Brian looked from the chimneys to the highway. Unlike the situation in a traffic jam, the cars were well spread out. Some few were pulled to the side, but most were still in the traffic lanes.

Carl got to his feet a trifle unsteadily.

"Well, we've seen what we came for."

"Wait a minute," said Brian. "Let's be sure we understand what we see."

"The main thing is, nothing's moving. No motors work. That's what the chief wanted to know."

"Maybe," said Brian, trying to keep the sarcasm out of his voice, "*you* can see and digest the whole thing without thinking it over, but *I* can't."

"What is it," said Carl, sarcasm creeping into his voice, "that you'd like explained to you?"

"To begin with," said Brian, "that train—" He paused, startled, as he saw something out of the corner of his eye.

Down on the highway, at the extreme right, something large was moving. "Forget the train. Take that for a starter. Explain *that* to me."

Carl, on his feet a few paces back from Brian, stepped forward and bent to see under the low limb of a nearby hemlock.

"I don't see—" He paused, blank-faced.

Down on the highway, a huge truck was steadily weaving its way in and out amongst the stalled cars. It slowed, edged up to two cars abreast, shoved the left-hand one well forward out of the way, then backed and came ahead again to weave through between them. A puff of black smoke drifted up from its vertical exhaust. The sun shone in a brief flash on the lettering giving the trucking company's name.

The truck slowed, stopped, and one of the drivers jumped out to take the wheel of a car slewed across the road. The grind of gears was plainly audible as the truck eased forward, pushed the car to the edge of the road, backed and filled, picked up the driver who'd gotten out, then eased ahead again.

Carl nodded slowly. "It's a diesel. That explains it."

Brian said, "The compression of the fuel and air fires it, and they don't use spark plugs?"

"Right. I think some of them use a spark at the beginning, when the engine's cold, but after it heats up they don't need that. And, of course, the engine's hot now."

The truck was creeping past. People at the side of the road were shouting to the driver, apparently asking for rides to the nearest town, but the driver shook his head and kept going down the highway.

"How," said Brian, puzzled, "do they start those things?"

Carl thought for a moment. "I *think* they start the same as any other car, with an electric starting motor."

"In that case, as long as the engine runs, they're all right. But if they turn it off, it's dead, and that's the end of it?"

Carl ran a hand through his yellow hair. It was plain from his look of chagrin that Carl was remembering his own confident statement that they'd seen everything they needed to know.

Brian, wrestling with the problem the truck presented, was only vaguely aware of Carl's discomfort. As far as Brian was concerned, the only thing that mattered was to get the clear picture of the situation as Cardan had requested. And as far as Brian was concerned, he knew that *his* picture wasn't clear yet.

"How about that train?" he said. "That's a diesel, isn't it?"

"Yes, it is."

"Would it fire by compression, the same as the truck?"

"Yes, but they're actually electric trains. The diesel engines turn generators, and the electricity that's generated runs the electric motors which turn the wheels."

Brian looked at the trucks stalled here and there along the road. He could see at least one of them, close behind a small foreign-made car, that hid the upright stack of a diesel.

Carl, his expression alert, had noticed the same thing. "Looks like that one almost ran into the car in front."

Brian nodded. "He probably stopped in a hurry, took one look around—"

"And he'd naturally be dumbfounded to see all the cars stopped at once," Carl continued. "No doubt, people would start getting out. If he'd had his radio on, all of a sudden all the stations would go off."

"He might think it was an atomic attack."

"He'd yank on the brake, turn off the ignition, and take a flying dive for the nearest ditch."

"Then, when nothing happened and he came back, the engine wouldn't start."

Carl looked at Brian with a puzzled expression, then frowned and looked down again at the highway. The diesel that was still running was out of sight now. The people were still walking along the edge of the highway, a few scrambling up the bank to the overpass Brian and Carl had crossed, and heading into town.

"*Now* have we seen everything?" Carl asked.

Brian looked around and spotted a medium-sized white oak about fifty feet away. "If we climb that tree over there, couldn't we see over these evergreens?"

"Sure, but—you mean, so we could see further down the road?"

"Yes."

"What's the point of that? We'll just see more of the same."

"How do we know?"

Carl started to speak, then changed his mind. Scowling, he led the way to the oak. He turned to say something, then shrugged, took hold of a low limb, and pulled himself up into the tree.

Brian waited till Carl was up in the tree and out of the way, then took hold of a small limb, feeling the rough bark under his fingers, pulled himself up, got his feet onto a limb nearby, stood up to grip another limb overhead. The dead, brown, violet-tinged leaves still clinging to the limbs rustled around him as he climbed.

At last they were above the level of the young hemlocks and could look out onto a stretch of highway that reached far out into the distance. As far as the eye could see, the sun shone on the smooth hoods, roofs, and front windows of stalled cars spread out along the highway.

"See," said Carl. "What did I tell you?"

"Yes," said Brian. "You were right. But now we *know* it."

Carl flushed slightly, started angrily to speak, then stopped. Ruefully, he said, "You've got a point there. I *do* go off half-cocked sometimes."

"I didn't mean—"

"Maybe not, but it's so. That's something in your favor."

Brian failed to get the point, but Carl reminded him, "Remember, we both want the same girl."

"Sure, but can't we leave that up to her?"

"Suppose you thought *I* was going to get her?"

"I wouldn't be happy. But—she could do worse."

Carl looked blank for an instant, then grinned. "Thanks. But how does that help *you*? You like her, don't you?"

"Of course I like her."

"Then how," said Carl, looking puzzled, "could you give her up?"

Brian exasperatedly started to speak. He was going to say: *I don't own her. Neither of us do. How do I give up something I don't have?* But he saw this wasn't what Carl meant. Slowly, Brian said, "I've lost things before."

For a brief instant, Carl looked sympathetic. Then he shook his head. "That's the difference between you and me. I always get what I want."

"Even—" Brian began.

"By hook or by crook," said Carl positively, his light-blue eyes frank and clear. "I *win*. I've *got* to."

Brian looked off in the distance for a moment. He, too, had an outlook on life, picked up in the bruising punishment that had come about before he learned it, and he could put it in a few words, just as Carl could put *his* philosophy in a few words. But something warned Brian that this wasn't the time. Instead, he smiled suddenly and looked at Carl.

"What happens if two guys like you meet head-on? Something gets broken?"

Carl grinned. "We try to avoid each other."

Brian laughed. They took a final look around, then climbed down the tree, dropped to the ground, wincing as the impact put strain on their sore legs, and headed back for the bicycles.

Brian, smiling, said, "Race back?"

"Ouch," said Carl. "Let's just see how far we can coast."

"I wonder if we could put the bikes out of sight by the side of the road on that last curve, then walk down and ask some of those people about the cars. You know, what it was like when they stalled?"

Carl thought a long moment. "Worth a try."

They left the bikes in the trees by the road and asked the people coming up from the highway about what had happened. The answer was always the same:

"The engine just *stopped*, that's all. And then *nothing* worked. Starter, lights, horn, radio—the whole business was dead. So we got out and walked."

Brian and Carl got their bicycles and went back into town.

On the way through town they could see the trouble building up.

In the streets, with their motionless cars and dead traffic signals, without the usual faint sounds of radios playing, and of juke boxes in the background, with the television sets dark, the lights and electricity gone, and the phones dead, with the novelty of the thing starting to wear off, and the fact that it was going to have to be lived with beginning to dawn, with the familiar tools and comforts missing, and uncertainties and vague horrors beginning to loom, people were instinctively gathering together.

The little groups Brian and Carl had seen earlier were big groups now. They stood about on the sidewalks, some staring glumly and others talking excitedly while they looked around at the dead neon signs, really noticing for the first time the gray untended structures that rose up behind the shiny storefronts. They looked down the streets where no cars or buses ran, for the first time seeing a mile as a mile, not as a vague distance to be overcome via a token handed to the driver, a few steps to an empty seat, and a five-minute wait. Other little mobs of people had taken over neighborhood grills or soda fountains, invited in by special prices as worried proprietors cut down the stocks of food and ice-cream that wouldn't keep with electric refrigerators and freezers off. And once the crowds gathered, they stayed there, no one anxious to leave his own, now-familiar group to walk down the nearly empty sidewalk. In a crowd, there was warmth, companionship. Outside, the silent city, with its main life-current cut off, seemed strange and alien, and the atmosphere had the stillness that came before a thunderstorm.

Past these uneasy, tentatively waiting groups of people, Brian and Carl pedaled with casual slowness, their expressions unconcerned. No one made any hostile gesture toward them. A few people called, "Hey, taxi!" or "Pretty good, no battery." Brian and Carl grinned back and said nothing, but the perspiration on their brows wasn't just from the exertion of pedaling the bikes.

The tension of potential trouble was growing in the air, though the people in those groups waiting in occasional stores might not know it. They saw only each other, whereas Brian and Carl saw the city. So far, nothing really irreversible had happened. Let the power come on again in a few hours, and it would just be an event that stood out, like Hurricane Hazel, or The Blizzard. It would be referred to in later days as The Power Failure, an event more unusual than natural disasters, but on the whole less harmful. It would be made into a joke by entertainers on TV. Magazine articles would be written to describe the way it came about, and how it ended.

But what if the power failure *didn't* end in a few hours?

From somewhere came the smell of smoke, and up ahead Brian saw perspiring men in firemen's uniforms carry past a long ladder, axes, and a length of hose. In a moment, they vanished up a side street.

When the fire trucks won't run, what can the fireman do? Who has more power then, the fire company, or the man with a match?

Brian and Carl glanced at each other, their faces deadly serious. Then they forced smiles, and kept pedaling slowly, casually, back toward the Research East building.

Around them in the city, the pent-up hysteria slowly mounted.

☀ Chapter 3

Brian and Carl left the bicycles where they'd rented them and started back on foot to the Research East building. The crowds in the doorways watched them in blank or speculative silence, and once they were stopped by men anxious for news—any news—who listened avidly as Brian and Carl told of cars stalled far up the highway.

At the Research East entrance, the gate was shut, with an ominous black cable looped and coiled inside, and a sign, "Danger—High Voltage," warning off people who might drift in and cause trouble later on.

Smitty, his black hair combed straight back as usual, opened the gate for them and grinned. "Maybe we can't do anything else with electricity, but it'll still scare people. Go right up, the chief's waiting for you."

Wearily they climbed the four flights of steps to the top floor, and the last flight of steps seemed as long as the other three put together.

"All it used to take," said Carl wonderingly, "was to push a button."

"That was just this morning."

"It seems like years ago—in another world."

Brian said, "Maybe Maclane and Donovan have figured something out."

"Maybe. But taking electricity away from civilization is like taking the framework out of a building. You have to find a substitute awful fast or the whole thing will collapse on top of you, and that's the end of that."

They shoved open the doors at the head of the stairs, walked into the corridor, and a few moments later were staggered to see the piles of rifles, shotguns, ammunition in boxes and bandoliers, hunting knives, knapsacks, pack baskets, skis, snowshoes, heavy blankets, axes, canteens, ponchos, coils of rope, gasoline lanterns, kerosene lanterns, cans of meat, heavy paper sacks of flour and sugar, a stack of cigar boxes and cigarette cartons, gasoline and kerosene cans in a long row against the wall, a box two feet deep and about three feet long containing nothing but gloves and mittens in assorted sizes, another containing heavy socks.

Brian and Carl looked at the supplies and whistled.

"Looks like the chief plans on clearing out."

The sound of many voices came, slightly muffled, from the office ahead.

They knocked and Cardan's voice called, "Come in."

They pushed open the door of the office. Cardan sat at his desk, a smoldering cigar jutting from one corner of his mouth, a .45 Colt automatic flat on the desk beside him. Maclane was standing in front of the desk, and Donovan was at a table to one side, using a hydrometer to test several six-volt and twelve-volt batteries sitting on the table. Donovan looked up as Carl and Brian came in, Maclane kept talking, and Cardan nodded abstractedly.

Maclane was saying, "Batteries, magnetos and generators just don't work, that's all. The only kind of electricity left, so far as I can see, is static electricity. You can still take a glass rod, rub it with a cloth, touch two pith balls hung close by on threads, and they'll spring apart. But try to pass a current through a wire, and you get nowhere."

"Take a look at this," suggested Donovan. He was using the hydrometer on one of the cells of a six-volt battery. The fluid from this battery tested out as "fully charged."

"Almost thirteen hundred," said Donovan. "But now look."

He took a flat metal bar, laid it across the clean shiny terminals of the battery—and nothing happened.

"It's not a question of the charge leaking away, after all. If it were, that battery would be dead," mused Brian.

Carl agreed, staring at the battery, then looking at the hydrometer. "Mind if I try that?"

"Go ahead."

Carl repeated Donovan's procedure and got the same result.

Maclane was saying, ". . . no *conduction*. The trouble seems to be that, for some reason, the electrons are more firmly bound to the metal atoms, so the 'electron gas' that ordinarily carries an electric current in a wire just doesn't exist any more. Or, perhaps, it exists but it's nowhere near as free-moving as it used to be. It's as if that damned Helmand lab sent out a signal that threw a switch inside the atoms—made a minute rearrangement of some kind."

There was a knock at the door. Cardan called "Come in," and Anne Cermak, wearing a light-gray lab coat, stepped into the room. Brian crossed to her immediately and she welcomed him with a smile.

Carl looked up from the battery, saw Brian and Anne talking, and he studied Brian intently for a moment, his eyes lit with a pale glow. Abruptly, he blanked his face and looked back at the battery.

Brian was conscious only of Anne, whose smile faded as she asked, "Is it bad out there?"

"Not yet," said Brian. "But it's getting bad." He realized why she was worried, and said, "Anne, I'll try to get out to see your father after we're through here."

She started to speak but was interrupted by Cardan. "How did things turn out? Notice any changes in chemical tests or reactions?"

"No," said Anne, "everything seemed the same. Except— sometimes the color of a reagent seemed slightly different. But it could have been the lack of electric light in the lab."

"But the reactions themselves seemed the same?"

"Yes, sir."

"If you hadn't been particularly watching for differences, would you have noticed any?"

Anne thought a moment. "No, I don't think I would have."

Cardan turned to Brian. "What's it like out there?"

"Getting bad," said Brian. He described much of what they'd seen. He told of the silent, waiting groups, the ominous quiet of the city, and the growing tension. "It looks like a powder keg waiting for a match."

"That's the same impression we've had," Cardan said, "even though we've stayed fairly close. Any sign of electricity?"

"None that we could see." Brian described the firemen headed for the fire, on foot. "And as far as we could see from North Hill, no cars were moving."

Carl cut in. "There was a diesel truck moving."

Cardan looked at the smoking tip of his cigar, and there was a moment's silence which contained a distinct suggestion of a rebuff. Carl drew his breath in as if to speak, then hesitated.

"Where was this?" Cardan wanted to know.

"On the highway." Carl described it in careful and accurate detail.

Brian, listening closely, remembered that he, Brian, had seen this truck after Carl had insisted that they might as well go back, and that there was nothing more to be seen. Brian now listened to Carl describe it very much as if he, Carl, had been the only one to see the truck.

Cardan and the others were listening intently. Maclane looked interested, and Donovan seemed a little excited. Cardan's face remained expressionless.

"So," Carl concluded, "it seems clear that diesel engines are all right while they're running, but I imagine if once they stop, then the electric starting motor won't work."

Maclane straightened up and glanced at Donovan with a faint grin.

Donovan said, "That could be the answer. Rig the engine to start on compressed air."

Cardan's face was still expressionless. Carl cleared his throat, but didn't speak. Cardan looked at Carl, a thin wisp of smoke drifting from the cigar he held in one hand.

"Did you see anything else that moved?" There was a faint emphasis on the word "you."

Carl stammered a little as he said, "N-no. We did see a diesel locomotive, but it was stopped."

"What," said Cardan, "did you decide was the reason for that?" Again there was the faintest emphasis on the word "you."

Carl said, "I—we thought it was because the generators and electric driving motors wouldn't work."

Brian suppressed a grin. Carl had taken credit that belonged to Brian, and now, to avoid looking egotistical, Carl was forced to give up credit that really was his own. Brian had forgotten the quickness with which Cardan detected any false note in a man's report.

Cardan had turned to Maclane and Donovan. "Can we fix diesel trucks to start on air?"

"Be a problem," said Donovan. "For one thing, because of the lack of electric power tools. But we've got that portable steam turbine Hooper dreamed up, along with fourteen different sizes of the same thing. Some of them run on LP gas. You remember, Chief, we were trying to sell them as self-powered tools for use away from power lines, up on roofs and so on? And when we had a manufacturer lined up, the mechanic demonstrating the thing got it set up wrong, almost burned his arm off, and before we could get that mess straightened out, self-contained battery-operated tools were on the market."

"The main trouble," said Cardan, "was that the things were bulky."

"That doesn't matter now. And then there's that shuttle-hammer gimmick he worked out, with the little self-contained, reciprocating steam-engine and all the attachments."

Maclane grinned. "That one will really keep your hands warm in cold weather. If it doesn't shake your arm off first."

"Who cares?" said Donovan. "They work."

Cardan blew out a cloud of smoke, smiled, and said, "Steam engines and diesels started by compressed air. Will that do it?"

"Ought to," said Donovan.

"And," said Cardan, "oil and gasoline mantle-lanterns for light?"

Maclane said, "They give a light that can compete for brightness with electricity. But those mantles are fragile. We'd better be sure we've got plenty of spares."

Cardan nodded in agreement, studied the glowing tip of his cigar for a moment, blew out a cloud of smoke, and said, "Good. Now the question is, what do we do? Do we stick around here or do we clear out now?"

"Wait maybe three days," Donovan said, "and this town is going to blow wide-open. Transportation, power and light are gone. To a large extent, heat is knocked out. All of a sudden we've got less capability for actual work and haulage than they had in seventeen-sixty, because then, at least, they had horses and oxen. With this new setup, all of a sudden we just aren't in any shape to care for anywhere near the number of people that are going to have to be cared for. It's going to be every man for himself. And there are a lot of people in this part of the country."

"Don's right," Maclane agreed. "If we could do any good by staying here, we should stay. But this thing is too big. This isn't a question of a man putting his finger in a hole in the dike and keeping out the flood. It's a question of the whole dike collapsing at once. Anything we might do wouldn't have time to have any effect. We'd just be drowned."

Donovan said, "Let's head for Montana, Chief. That's less-settled country; they're used to rough conditions there, and we've got our test site there—plenty of buildings and equipment."

Cardan glanced questioningly at Brian and Carl. Brian said, "It's a long trip, but that diesel truck we saw *did* get through. The only thing is, what if, at some section of the road, there was a traffic jam at the time the cars' ignition systems were knocked out?"

"So that," said Cardan, "there is, for instance, one solid mass of cars half a mile long?"

"Yes," said Brian. "Then what do we do?"

Donovan said, "We'll either have to drag them out of the way, or shove them off the road. If we can't get by on the mall or shoulder. We'll want to travel on superhighways, away from the cities, as far as possible."

Maclane said, "It's better than staying here and winding up in a siege."

There was a knock at the door and one of the men from a lab downstairs, his face cut and bleeding, was in the doorway with half a dozen others setting down cartons outside.

"I thought you'd want to know, Chief. They're getting into an ugly mood out there. The idea got around that the electric company is behind all this. It seems they put in an atomic reactor, and it shorted out all the electricity somehow. Everybody went to his car, because the reactor was going to be fixed, and then the cars would start. When it didn't happen, the frustration was too much for some of those guys. They're out there smashing windows and threatening to beat in the brains of anybody in reach. Meanwhile, there's a kind of migration going on—people trying to get home on foot in different directions. Naturally, after they get shoved around a few times by these soreheads, they're in no mood to be even so much as sneezed at the next time. You can still get through out there, but you've got to keep your eyes open."

"There's another thing to think of," Cardan said. "Did you ever read that story about the lady and the tiger?"

"What do you mean, Chief?"

"A man is taken prisoner and put in an arena that has two doors. If he opens one door, a beautiful woman will be waiting inside. If he opens the other, a hungry tiger will rip him to shreds. He doesn't know which door has the tiger behind it, but he's got to open one of the doors."

"How does that apply to us?"

"For all we know," said Cardan, "the electricity *may* come back on again."

"In which case," said Maclane, "if we've done anything really effective to take care of ourselves—"

Donovan finished it for him. "We'll appear to be selfish criminals."

Cardan said, "How are we going to get these diesel trucks? If the phones worked, we could try making arrangements that way. But they *don't* work. To find someone who can sell them to us is going to take time."

"Sure," said Maclane, "and if we pussyfoot around trying to do everything strictly according to the rules, we'll never get done. And if the current doesn't come back on, we'll get swallowed up in the chaos that follows. That isn't going to help anybody."

"And aren't we pretty damn certain the current *isn't* coming back on?" Cardan inquired.

"It certainly looks that way to me," Carl said.

"Okay," Cardan said, "here's what we do. On the other end of this block there's a parking lot that belongs to a large trucking company. They use quite a few diesels. If we knock out the fences between here and there, we can bring those diesels in here without going into the street. First, we must get something that will supply the power to start the engines. Second, we have got to do everything possible to make this legal, and to give the trucking company a fair deal. Third, we've got to be sure we keep a good grip on this building till we've got the trucks equipped, loaded and ready to leave. Fourth, *then* we can start out, taking a route that will let us pick up the families of our own people. That means they're going to have to be notified in advance, and told where to be when we pick them up. Don, ask Miss Bowen if there isn't a map of the city in the files."

Donovan was back in a few minutes, the two men spread the map on the desk, and Cardan said, "Railroad Avenue is wide, and there's not too much traffic on it. Fourteenth Street runs out here through the southwest part of town. Suppose we have our people from that part of town at the intersection of Fourteenth and Railroad Ave?" The two men discussed details.

"Are you prepared to risk your necks again this afternoon?" Cardan asked.

"Yes," said Brian.

"Sure," said Carl.

"We'll have Miss Bowen make a list of the addresses of the families that live in the southwest part of town. While she's doing that, we'll canvass the men to make sure they go along with the idea. You go out and tell the people to be at the intersection of Fourteenth and Railroad Avenue at three in the morning."

"Three in the morning," Brian repeated.

"Right," said Cardan, getting up. "By that time we should be ready, and I hope the mobs will have worn themselves out and be sleeping it off. Now Miss Bowen will get you that list."

***

Half an hour later, Brian and Carl found themselves on bicycles, riding through a part of town that had been filled with people earlier, but was deserted now. The windows of the cars in the streets were smashed, and a man was lying against the base of a fence, either dead or unconscious. Carl and Brian were both quiet, thinking of the bicycle shop, where they'd found the windows smashed, the bicycles gone, and the owner on a cot in a back room, blood seeping from under a bandage on his head, a .32 revolver in his hand as he lay facing the door.

"Ah," he'd murmured, smiling faintly as Carl came in. "For you, I have a bicycle." He felt in his pockets and pulled out a key. "Here, open up that closet. They cleaned me out, but already I had put away those bikes." He'd explained to the dumbfounded Carl how the mob had burst in, shoving and fighting, and flattened him when he'd tried to stop them. But, having thought there might be a heavy demand for bicycles, new or used, when people realized there was no other reasonably quick way to get around, he had already put the battered bicycles Carl and Brian had rented out of sight.

"Big civilized men we are," he'd said sarcastically. "The first time the juice goes off, we have a riot. You give us a week like this and we'll be eating rats and mice and smashing each other's heads in for a can of soup."

"Listen," said Carl, "are you hurt bad?"

"I'll be all right. It's just a smack on the head. But it makes me mad. This civilization we got is like a set of stilts. We think we're high up, big men, but it's only the stilts, not us. As soon as one of them catches in a hole, over we go, and when we get up, we're just little men. It's only the stilts that were big . . ."

They had left the old man, still grumbling his disappointment in people, and pedaled briskly toward Anne's father's place, but when they got there he was nowhere to be seen. They called, but the house was empty. Brian finally turned to go, then suggested leaving a note.

"Wait," said Carl, as they stood in the kitchen, where the only sound was the tick of a kitchen clock. "Listen, I thought I heard somebody moving downstairs."

Brian opened the cellar door, looked down into the darkness, and felt a chill premonition.

He called. "Mr. Cermak?"

Behind him, there was the soft scuff of Carl's foot on the kitchen floor.

The back of Brian's head seemed to explode in a burst of lights.

Chapter 4

Brian came to to find Anne's father bathing his face with a cold wet towel. As the older man's tough, workworn face showed concern, Brian sat up dizzily and felt the large tender bump at the back of his head. He had a violent headache, but it seemed to be something he could get over. Then he thought of the time and glanced at his watch. The crystal and face of the watch were smashed.

Steve Cermak noticed Brian's gesture and turned to the kitchen clock on the shelf near the stove. "Twenty-five after two," he said. "What happened?"

Brian told him. Cermak shook his head sorrowfully. "I was out for groceries. I thought of going into town after Anne, but on foot it's a long walk, and I was afraid I'd go in one way while she came out another way. Then she'd be worried and go looking for *me*. I went upstairs and stretched out for a nap; I woke up a few moments ago, certain I had heard a moan. That's when I came down and found you."

"Yeah, thanks to good old Carl." Brian was reminded that because of his colleague's double-cross, he was now pressed for time. "Listen, I'll have to go ahead on the bicycle and get them to send a truck for you." Brian got to his feet, wincing at the furious headache, and went out to get the bicycle he'd left leaned against the porch steps. Anne's father followed, picking up an oil lantern from the kitchen table.

The bicycle wasn't by the porch steps.

They descended the steps, the lantern casting long swinging shadows on the frost that whitened the lawn and crunched stiffly underfoot. They looked briefly under the porch and behind a nearby hedge, then Cermak said, "While we look, time passes."

"Yes," said Brian, "we'll have to make it on foot."

Cermak went inside and came out carrying two jackets. He tossed one to Brian. "We're about the same size."

"Thanks."

Cermak blew out the lantern and shut the door. They slid down a low bank in front of the house and walked along the road.

Brian said, "We've got a long walk ahead of us—and not too much time to do it in. I'm afraid we'll have to run—"

"Young man, don't you worry about me. If you think we need to run, let's run."

They alternated running and walking down the road, their frosty breath drifting slowly up in the cold air that chilled their faces and made Brian's throat feel raw. Every step he took made his head throb, and the muscles of his thighs, because of the race with Carl, rebelled against further activity. It occurred to Brian that the idea of the race might not have been a spontaneous one. Perhaps Carl had already been planning to leave Brian behind, to be swallowed up in the collapse of civilization, while he, Carl, got away to make a fresh start with Anne. Brian remembered Carl saying, "I always get what I want. By hook or by crook, I *win*."

They rounded a bend in the road. The smell of smoke was suddenly strong in Brian's nostrils. There was the pressure of a hand at his arm.

"Wait," said Anne's father. "What's this?"

Ahead of them was a downhill slope, at the bottom of which were two burning houses, facing each other across the road. A little knot of people was struggling in the road, and to the right, a lone woman was sobbing by a pile of furniture near the curb, where an old car was parked.

It seemed clear to Brian that here was the miserable end of somebody's hopes, but all he felt was exasperation at the thought that their way might be blocked.

"Maybe we can run past them when we get close."

"Okay."

They walked downhill, and when they came near the little knot of struggling people, Brian and Cermak started to race past, well to one side.

As they came abreast, a girl's voice cried, "Help! Oh, *help*!"

Brian had a brief glimpse of a girl's face in the glare of the fire, her eyes wide with terror. Then she was slammed back against the car, and the only sound was the roar and crackle of the flames. One of the men rocked the girl's head to one side with an open-handed slap. The other grabbed the cloth of her jacket.

Cermak and Brian whirled at the same time. Cermak shot his right arm around the neck of the nearer of the two men, yanked him back, getting his left arm around the man's waist. There was a brief pinwheeling motion against the glare of the fire, and the second man's hand shot forward, a glint of steel sparkling momentarily.

Brian slammed the knife-hand aside, pivoted on his heel, and smashed his antagonist on the point of the chin. There was a grunt as the man's head snapped back and he slammed against the fender of the car, off balance, near Cermak. Cermak promptly sank a terrific left-handed blow in the knife-man's midsection and the fight was all over.

The dark-haired girl, still wide-eyed, trembled with relief. Brian said, "Do you live here?"

"No, I was just passing through."

"Which way are you going?"

She pointed down the road toward the city.

"Then you'd better stick with us, if you can." Brian picked up the knife and handed it to her. "Keep this. You may need it. You close it like this, and press this stud to open it."

"I don't know how to thank—"

"Don't. Let's get out of here. We're in a hurry." Brian spoke more sharply than he'd intended. He wanted to help the girl, but the momentary delay could already have made them late at the rendezvous. A few minutes' polite talk could cost them a two-thousand-mile hike.

A few moments later Brian and the older man were going down the road, alternately running and walking, the girl coming along behind them, when abruptly Cermak stopped.

"Oh-oh," he murmured. "Wait."

Brian stopped. Ahead of them, from a peculiarly dark

place where a row of tall hemlocks cast their shadows across the moonlit road, came a grunting, struggling noise, and Brian could make out the dim outlines of a group of men, some moving around among the trees, others standing around watching two of them fight.

Cermak murmured, "Better go around this," and they made their way off to the side, guiding the girl by the arm, around to the rear of the houses. Then they were back on the road again, but now a cloud covered the moon, making their progress slower. Here the girl thanked them profusely and disappeared up an intersecting road.

Brian and Cermak were now in a more settled part of town. Encounters with people became more frequent; the roads were more often blocked with cars, and once Brian took a bad fall from a child's roller skate lying on the sidewalk in the dark. When they finally reached the corner of Fourteenth Street and Railroad Avenue, the trucks were gone.

By then, the sky over the city was lit with a red glow. Off to the east, it was just starting to get light.

Anne's father, studying a layer of thin mud at the corner where a large puddle had partly dried up, said, "They've been here, Brian. Even in this light, you can see the marks of big truck tires."

Brian looked around, thinking that Cardan might have left some sign for anyone who reached the spot late. Then he saw the paper tacked to the telephone pole. In the poor light, it took Brian at moment to read it:

Supplies
At R. E.

Anne's father said, "Could we catch up to them at another place in town?"

"I'm afraid not. We'll have to get some supplies, and hope they're held up on the road."

They started out through the city, detouring large groups of people and narrow places, but having to scare off occasional individuals and small groups which made menacing gestures, took a closer look, and generally moved on quickly. By now, their clothes had been torn and dirtied in a number of scuffles. Anne's father had picked up a short length of black-painted pipe after one of those fights, and he carried it jutting forward so that in the poor light it looked like the end of a sawed-off shotgun. Brian, after falling over the child's roller skate, had gotten up only to have a bat turn under his foot. This was small, but solid, and Brian had taken it along with him. Brian didn't know how he looked himself, but the dirtied face of Anne's father, lit by the red glow and with eyes in shadow, was not one to encourage troublemakers.

They were crossing the bridge over the river when Brian suddenly thought how calmly Cermak was taking it all. "I thought all this would be a terrible blow to you."

"So did I. Why, did Anne say something to you?"

"She said you foresaw it."

Cermak was quiet a moment, studying a car stalled just ahead. He shifted his length of pipe to cover it, and Brian dropped back a little, as if to give a clear field of fire.

Nothing moved in the car as they went past, but afterwards Brian thought he heard a very faint creak of the springs. They both stiffened and turned. After a time they moved in closer. The car was deserted.

Cermak grunted. "What a stupid business this is. You get to suspect your own shadow." He clucked disapprovingly. "And people going around robbing others. For what? What does money mean now?" He glanced ahead, where all was clear to the bridge.

"Yes," he said, going back to the question Brian had asked him. "I *did* foresee it. But it's no credit to me. I just had a dream. I saw the lights go out, and the cars stop, and people rush out shouting, 'What's happened to the power?' I could see the whole thing, and when I woke up, I was near to being crazy. All my life I've worked underground, envying people who worked in the sunlight. Someone with more brains or better luck could have got out of the spot I was in. Until I was almost thirty, I never woke up to the fact that, first off, I was in the wrong part of the country, trying to get work where too many were out of a job. Then I had sense enough to get out of there. Twenty-nine years it took for this to dawn on me.

"All my life, I've been that way. Thrifty and hard-working, but stupid. The trouble is, it's not how hard you work that they pay you for, it's what you accomplish. A man could chip rock all his life with a sledge hammer, ten hours a day, and get less done in his whole life than another man could do in half an hour with a few sticks of dynamite. Which man deserves the more money? Another ten years it took me to see that. I was stupid, because I thought I could get ahead on hard work and always putting my money away, but finally it came to me a man has got to think, too. By then, I was in the rut it took me all those years to dig while I was being smart, working hard for pennies and putting the pennies in the savings bank.

Finally it dawned on me that hard work was good, but you had to have hard thought, too. By this time it was a little late for me, but I could still help Anne. And it worked out. She had a good job, with good people. She could hold her head up. But a man still needs to work."

They crossed the street. No one bothered them.

Anne's father said, "It's hard to waste most of your life, finally see what's wrong, help your daughter to do things right, have things finally start to go right, and just then have everything smashed. I was almost ready to do away with myself this morning, but it dawned on me that that was wrong. Why do that when maybe my heart will finish me anyway? Besides, this awful thing at least has made people equal again. No one is going to be asking me how many grades I went in school. All those paper requirements don't mean a thing any more. I'm not happy about this mess, but somehow I feel useful again."

They went on in silence till they reached the Research East building. They climbed the stairs wearily to the fourth floor, found food, clothing, blankets, canteens, several .30-06 Springfield rifles, a box containing bandoliers of ammunition, and a map showing the route Cardan intended to follow. Brian copied the map, he and Cermak fell into exhausted sleep, and then, somewhat rested, they each took a canteen, rifle, a hundred and twenty rounds of ammunition, and as many supplies as they could pack on their backs, and went cautiously down to the street.

"Where now?" said Cermak. "Two thousand miles is a long trip on foot."

"Down the street and several blocks to the left, there's

a bicycle shop. If Cardan gets held up getting fuel, or runs into a jam of cars and trucks, we may catch up yet."

They made their way to the shop, saw no bicycles in sight, but found several cartons containing partly assembled bikes. Half an hour later they had assembled two of them and were out of the city and on the highway. No one stopped them. Apparently, after the nightmarish day and night that had gone before, the city had fallen into a stupor of exhaustion. Brian was grateful that they wouldn't be there when it woke up.

Then he thought of Carl, riding comfortably down the road ahead.

A murderous anger gripped Brian, and he settled down to a steady, mile-eating pace.

✺ Chapter 5

The highway stretched ahead of them, a long unending track reaching to the horizon, dotted with an endless succession of cars. Pedaling steadily, they went past dazed people torn loose from civilization and not yet drawn into any other pattern, drifting along uncertainly. Here and there they passed cars and trucks that had been pushed to one side, and occasionally they saw fresh signs of big truck tires to the side of the road, or on the grassy mall in the center. On the level or going downhill, they made good time. But going uphill was another matter. Brian estimated that they averaged about two miles an hour uphill, pushing the bicycles. This quickly became a serious matter.

The first day or two Brian and Steve Cermak traveled by day and slept at night, making use of the cars that were always nearby on the road. But as day followed day, the situation changed. Though the superhighway was designed to avoid passing directly through heavily populated cities, it often came close to them, leading Brian and Anne's father into clouds of smoke from burning cities, where the fire trucks couldn't run, the water pressure was down, and the firemen had to struggle like everyone else to save their own lives.

As the highway passed supermarkets and shopping centers, they saw rioting mobs, heard the crash of the big plate-glass windows, and the screams of trampled people. But out of this chaos, a new pattern began to emerge. Now they began to hear the sound of gunfire, saw men spring from car to car, working their way along curbs and gutters and ditches, and race in small groups toward the sides and rear of chosen buildings. Now the battles were beginning to rage for control of the stocks of food and manufactured goods. More and more often, the people they passed were armed, and the whine of bullets missing them narrowly warned them that they could easily join the bodies ever more thickly strewn along the road, lying motionless face-down, or on their backs, terrible eyes staring at the sky.

They crouched one day near a pine tree by the side of the road, hearing the bang and rattle of gunfire ahead, with the gloom of late afternoon deepened by heavy clouds of smoke, and lit by a towering pillar of flame rising from a large service station down the highway.

Cermak said, "We can't go on like this. Through these places, and when we're walking the bikes, it's too dangerous."

"We'd better keep out of sight by day, and travel at night," Brian said. He glanced at the road. "And right there is something else we'd better look out for."

Cermak followed his gaze, to look at the crouching figures bending over the prostrate bodies, briefly and expertly robbing them, then gliding on.

Cermak involuntarily raised his gun, then slowly lowered it.

Brian watched them warily. "Worse yet, there are traps and ambushes being set. That close call we had today was just a sample."

Brian and Cermak had been going downhill on the right side of the highway when Brian noticed the odd fact that, on both sides of the road, the lanes were blocked, the cars lined up almost abreast. Then he noticed another thing. In the right-hand lane, straight ahead, the front wheels of the car toward the side of the road were turned sharply to the left. If the car had been driving with the wheels in that position, it would have swung in front of the car to its left and been wrecked. Obviously, the car had been moved, steered downhill and parked in line with the other car. Brian glanced around. It was too late for him to brake. He leaned to his left, and the bike shot across the grass. Simultaneously, the door of a car to his right opened up and there was the loud report of a gun going off.

Brian glanced back, worried about Anne's father. There was no time for Brian to help him, but one quick glance was enough. Steve Cermak was forty feet behind, gripping the handle bars with his right hand, the big Springfield resting across his right forearm, his left hand gripping the small of the stock, and his left forefinger on the trigger. As Cermak passed the open door, he squeezed the trigger; there was a second, much louder, report, and that was the end of the trouble.

"Yes," said Cermak, looking down the road at the shopping plaza, where guns flashed in the twilight, and where the tall shadows of dark light poles wavered across the face of the buildings, lit by flames of fires burning out of control. "Yes, now honest people have the least chance, so we'll meet only human wolves, rats, and vultures." He looked at the shadowy figures flitting down the road from body to body, glanced around and gripped his gun tighter. Brian, too, unconsciously checked his gun, his thumb feeling to be sure the gun was cocked and the magazine cutoff turned up.

Brian and Cermak had suddenly become conscious that even if they escaped the other dangers, their food would soon run out. They were sparing it, and they still hoped to catch Cardan before they needed more. But their packs were lightening steadily.

In time they were away from the worst of the heavily populated districts, traveling through country that was almost wild in places, and very hilly. They still saw signs of the trucks that had gone before, and twice they had run into massive traffic jams that must have delayed Cardan and his men, but they hadn't caught up. Then, in a stretch of desolate country, they ran out of food, and there followed a day when their only refreshment was a drink from the canteens they filled at the numerous streams they passed.

The next day, while searching for food, they came to the third traffic jam. Here the pile-up of cars reached through a complicated cloverleaf at the base of a hill where a wide blacktopped road, almost jammed with cars, passed under the superhighway. Farther down the super-highway, a line of toll gates stretched across the road. Huge signs told of a service station to the right, and food and lodging to the left. Down below, they could see people moving along past the cars, and disappearing under the overpass. Ahead, the cars were thick on the road, but on the other side, across the grass, where the cars had been leaving the toll gate, they were more spread out.

"Well?" said Cermak.

Brian shrugged. "We've got to have food."

"What about Cardan and your friend Carl?"

Brian drew a slow deep breath and checked their map. "That's it," he said. "They went down this ramp, and came up that one."

Off in the distance, to the left, there was a brief burst of gunfire. Cermak nodded. "There's food there—and trouble."

"Okay. Let's go, fast. If we want food, we can't avoid trouble."

They bent over the bikes, and, one behind the other, swooped down the hill, through the tollgates, and walked their bikes up a moderately steep hill.

They hid the bicycles in a kind of small oblong concrete room under the grassy center strip at the middle of a long culvert, the handle bars hooked through a set of bent pipes that made a ladder from a manhole overhead. They looked back in from outside, saw the bicycles were not conspicuous, and went on, taking only their empty packs, their guns, and a bandolier apiece of ammunition.

They climbed the bank by the road, pushed through the low trees, and found themselves in a soggy place where the water stood in thin puddles on gray muck, with the bare brush as thick as a hedge around them, and trees rising here and there, many of them dead, and reaching out before them into the distance.

It took several hours to get around this place, and by

then the sun had climbed high overhead. But spread out below them, at the foot of a long gentle slope, was a shopping plaza.

Cermak grinned and nodded, then lost the grin as he studied the plaza.

The sound of gunfire was now loud and clear, and almost continuous. From amongst the cars jammed in the front of a parking lot, they could see an occasional dull flash, and many wisps of blowing smoke. Across the front and on both sides of the long block of buildings there seemed to be one continuous fight. Only to the rear was there no sign of fighting. There, sawhorses blocked off the parking lot where some repair work was being done on a drainage system. Just beyond the line of sawhorses, there was a long ditch, and nearby, several bodies stretched out awkwardly, where they had tried to make it around the side to the rear, and failed.

Cermak said, "They're coming from both directions along that road. See there?"

From along the road to the right, Brian could see a slow trickling of armed men, hidden from the buildings by the lines of cars.

Brian watched intently. "They work in close to the front of the buildings, by the cars in that lot. If they leave the cars, they've got a hundred feet of dirt and asphalt to cross, and a ditch, before they get around in back."

"You see those little holes knocked in the side, high up in that blank wall back of the show window?" Cermak asked.

"Yes," Brian said, his eyes pinpointing on the occasional flashes appearing at these holes. "Yes, I see. They can shoot across the lot and straight into the ditch from there."

"It's a deathtrap," Cermak said. "But from down there, you wouldn't know it till it was too late."

"I wonder if anyone's watching the back."

The two men studied the apparently bare dirt at the back of the plaza. On closer examination, it looked like blacktop tracked over with dirt from the excavation. There was a drainage ditch around the lot, and beyond that, empty fields. To one side, the ditch ran back straight across the foot of the slope where Brian and Cermak looked out from behind a screen of thick brush. From where they sat in relation to this ditch, there was scattered cover. From the ditch to the rear of the stores there wasn't enough cover to hide a mouse.

They studied the buildings carefully. Cermak cleared his throat. "They should have someone covering the rear. But there's a lot of shooting down there."

"They could be hard pressed."

There was a moment's silence as they looked over the bare fields to either side. No one down there was trying to get across those bare fields to the rear. Everyone was coming along the road, where the jammed cars offered cover.

Again they studied the empty parking lot at the rear, the ditches leading to it, and the empty space that had to be crossed to get to the back door.

Finally Cermak said, "Well, I've seen bear traps I'd rather walk into than this thing. But if we don't go down there, what do we eat?"

Carefully, stealthily, they eased down the slope toward the ditch.

***

It seemed to take them forever as they worked their way along the slippery, steep-banked ditch with the sucking-mud bottom under slow-flowing icy water, then they were peering out through the dead grass at the stretch of dusty, empty parking lot at the rear of the stores. They lay still there for long minutes, studying the doors, ventilators, trash cans, and the cement-block wall of the building.

Not moving, Cermak murmured, "See anything?"

"Not a thing." Brian very carefully tilted his head sidewise to study the roof, then slowly and carefully glanced around to either side.

"Funny nobody at all tries to get around this way."

"They've got wide-open fields on either side. There's no cover. But it stands to reason they ought to have a guard inside, watching this way, just in case."

"I don't see any."

"I don't either."

Brian was looking at the vacant parking lot. He'd seen empty spaces in his life, but nothing that compared with this. From his low ground-level viewpoint, it appeared to stretch out, flat and bare, for a hundred yards in front of them.

Cermak laughed suddenly. "Looks like a damned airfield, doesn't it? Well, if we wait, someone else may get the same idea. Ready?"

Brian braced himself. "Ready as I'll ever be."

Cermak's voice was low and hoarse. "We'll head for the red door of that supermarket. When I count three. One—two—"

Brian cautiously eased himself a little farther up the bank.

"Three," said Cermak.

They scrambled up the bank and sprinted across the parking lot.

Brian was pumping his legs as fast as they could go, but he had the feeling of crossing a mile-wide flat at a leisurely crawl.

Then abruptly the cement-block wall at the rear of the building was right in front of him, and slowing down was just as hard as running had been. He whirled at the last minute to lightly bang the wall with his upper arms and back, and looked quickly around, the gun raised. But no guard was in sight on the roof of the building. He took hold of the red-painted door and, a moment later, he and Cermak were in a bare whitewashed room with a few empty crates on the floor. They went through an open door to one side, and found themselves in a room about twenty feet wide, apparently running the full depth of the store, with boxes and cardboard cartons stacked from one end to the other.

At the far end of the room, high up, was a small irregular patch of light, where someone looked out and fired. No one else was in sight, but the firing from the front of the store was rising to a crescendo.

Using their pocketknives, they tore open nearby cartons, finding baby food, big jars of pickles, mustard, relish, bottles of ketchup—all the things they didn't care to find themselves living on for the next week. Warily, they eased up the aisle, in clear view of the man at the hole, if he merely turned around. They reached a pair of swinging doors with small diamond-shaped windows and Brian cautiously glanced out. A barricade of food cartons, bales of garden mulch, and overturned shopping carts blocked the aisles where the row of checkout counters faced the long, smashed front window of the store. Behind the barricade, men crouched and fired in a haze of smoke, while outside in the parking lot, a row of cars rolled forward slowly, the front wheels climbing over the outstretched bodies that lay there in the smashed glass.

Behind the cars, there had to be people pushing, and when the cars reached the front of the building, then it would be possible for them to gather in numbers, right next to the building, for one final rush.

Cermak quickly loaded Brian's pack. The cars were coming steadily on, almost to the curb, and now one of the men in the store glanced back nervously over his shoulder.

Brian loaded Cermak's pack, his fingers feeling thick and clumsy, and fastened down the flap. They went quickly down the aisle, then something *whanged* over Brian's head as he turned, and a stinging shower of bits of cement hit him on the side of the face. Then they were at the back door. On the other side was that stretch of parking lot, and Brian could see its empty flat bareness from the doorway. Behind them, the firing rose to a new height, and now there were yells, curses, and the pound of feet.

"Come on," Cermak whispered. He threw the door back and they bolted onto the lot.

This time fast motion was more difficult than before. The goods in Brian's pack bounced around as he ran, the pack itself bounced on its frame, the frame started to shift as a fastening loosened, and the lot seemed to stretch out forever. When they were halfway across, something whined past Brian's head, and an instant later there was a puff of dust ahead and a black groove appeared, showing the asphalt through the accumulated dirt.

Something plucked lightly at Brian's pack, what sounded like a swarm of yellow jackets whined past overhead, and then the ditch was at his feet. Brian hit the opposite bank of it hard, slid, and landed calf-deep in the icy slop and ooze.

Cermak was in the same situation to Brian's left. "Keep low," he muttered, and began working his way along the bank. Brian followed.

Behind them, the firing was intense and continuous.

It had taken them a long time to get to the shopping plaza along the ditch and, because of their load, it took them longer to get back. At intervals, bullets whined overhead, and when they finally scrambled thankfully up the bank through the brush on the hill overlooking the shopping plaza, they were worn out. They took a look back, eyeing the bodies strewn over the lot in the rear of the supermarket. There was still an almost continuous firing, but Brian, looking down, was unable to see who was fighting whom.

Cermak said, "We got out of there just in time. We were lucky, but it isn't over yet."

They paused to eat the first food they'd had in a day and a half, then wearily made their way around the swampy stretch and back down toward where they'd hidden the bikes.

They'd scarcely gotten the bikes out when there was a rattle of gunfire, increasing in intensity and then gradually dying away again.

"Better get going," said Brian. "We can sleep when we put this place well behind us."

They coasted down the hill. Brian was just beginning to breathe easily as the bike glided swiftly ahead, when there was the faint dull glint of something stretched across the road, then the bike twisted and slid fast to the right, spilling him to land heavily on the pavement.

A dark figure scrambled out of the ditch, there was the flash of an upraised knife, and a deafening roar as Cermak fired across Brian's shoulder.

An instant later Brian had his own gun unslung and was firing at a dim figure that raced toward them from a nearby car. Then Brian and Cermak were working their bolts as rapidly as possible, and the shadowy figures were coming at them from all sides, outlined now in a white light that rose over the hill.

Brian's bolt stuck wide-open, warning him that the magazine was empty, and he knew he had no time to reload. He waited, the gun muzzle drawn back, ready to slam into the chest of the first attacker to come in reach.

Then two of these attackers spun around and slammed to the earth, and the rest ran down the hill to stagger in midstride and fall.

A blinding glare moved down the road and, through the ringing in his ears, Brian could hear Cardan's roar, "Stop the trucks! Those men are ours!"

At the sound of Cardan's voice, Brian walked to the cab of the truck. Cermak, frowning, stepped to the side of the road.

Then the big trucks were stopped, and Cardan, a .45 automatic in his right hand, jumped out, grinned, gripped

Brian by the left hand, turned, and shouted, "Shove those cars out of the way! Scouts out! And make sure of these bodies here!" He looked at Brian and smiled. "You not only caught up—you got ahead of us. Are you all right?"

"By the grace of God," said Brian fervently. "Another minute would have been too late."

"That's all it takes." Cardan turned away to answer the shouted question of a man who came running over, and then Brian saw someone else.

The athletic build and blond hair were familiar, and so was the intent, calculating expression.

And then Carl sauntered toward the two men.

Chapter 6

Brian looked at Carl's clean-shaven, well-rested face. He appeared to be in good shape, looking as if he'd been sleeping at night and eating regularly in the daytime. Moreover, he appeared to know it. His head was tilted slightly, with something of the look of superiority with which the son of a wealthy man might look at the sweaty child of a ditchdigger.

Beside Cardan, someone said, "Chief, there's quite a roadblock up ahead. The cars are too close to get by, and they're clear across the mall in the center. This gang here must have set it up so that no-one could rush them and get away."

"Clear it out," said Cardan. "Keep your eyes open, and use the chains. It may be like that setup we ran into the first time we stopped for fuel."

"We'll be careful."

Cardan glanced at Brian. "It's good to have you back." He smiled suddenly. "Here's someone else who feels the same way."

Anne, her blond hair brushed and shining in the light of the gasoline lanterns, started to run to Brian, and caught herself at the last moment, a mixture of emotions struggling on her face.

"Oh, Brian," she said at last, smiling happily, "I'm so glad you're here!" She frowned. "But why did you—?"

Carl's voice cut in. "We've found your father, Anne."

Anne turned, to cry out, like a child, "Daddy!"

She ran to the elder Cermak, who, unnecessarily steadied by one of Cardan's men, was coming toward them, his Springfield rifle gripped firmly in his right hand. Cermak smiled as he saw Anne, but his eyes narrowed intently when he looked at Carl.

Carl stood about six feet from Brian, a look of satisfaction on his face. A little louder than was necessary, Carl said, "Decide you couldn't make it on your own, Brian?"

Through a layer of gathering weakness from the hundreds of miles covered on the bicycle, lack of sleep and food, and the two narrow escapes of the day, Brian became aware of an ugly sensation, deep down inside himself. He remembered Carl's footsteps behind him, the blow on the back of the head. Out of the corner of his eye, Brian could see several of the men watching him and Carl.

Cermak had returned his daughter's kiss, and now spoke briefly to her. She shook her head. Cermak spoke more forcibly, and then thrust her aside. He jerked open the bolt of his rifle; an empty cartridge flashed in the light as it flew out, then in one blur of motion Cermak stuffed a fresh clip into the magazine and slammed home the bolt. He watched Brian and Carl without expression.

Carl was looking down at Brian. "Afraid to speak?"

Brian was aware of a steady dull ache in his left arm, where he had landed when the bike overturned, a slow throb at the back of his neck, and a multitude of aches and stiffnesses, all felt through a haze of weariness. Something told Brian that his chance of beating Carl now was nonexistent. The only thing to do was to put off the fight till he had some rest. But how?

Carl's eyes glinted. "You don't look very good, Brian. You'd have done better to come with us in the first place."

No one else said anything. But it became obvious to Brian, despite his weariness, that Carl was speaking for the benefit of the others.

Carl said, "I don't like a guy that runs out. You're here now, and I suppose we'll have to take care of you, but I think you need a lesson."

From several of the men came an approving murmur.

Carl stepped forward. There was a flash, a deafening roar, and the pungent smell of burned nitrocellulose. Something lightly ruffled Carl's hair.

There was a dead silence for an instant after the shot, and then Carl very slowly turned his head.

Cermak handed his gun to his daughter, and grinned at Carl.

"Fight *me*, why don't you?"

Carl blinked.

"*Daddy!*" cried Anne.

"No, no," said Cermak, holding her back with one hand. "He's tough. He and Brian go off together and only Carl comes back. Carl tells his story, and Brian isn't there, so of course only one side gets told. Carl's side. Then Carl rides along protected by everyone else, while Brian has to fight his way for hundreds of miles, on his own muscle. After he's worn out, Big Carl shows up riding in a truck and he's going to teach Brian a lesson for being so cowardly as to fight his way across hundreds of miles of territory, by himself, with an old man to lug on his back. This Carl is a big fellow. If someone else does something brave, that makes Carl a hero."

There was a motionless stillness in which the hiss and roar of the gas lanterns sounded loud and clear, and all the men in sight were frowning at Carl and glancing in puzzlement from Carl to Brian to Anne's father.

Brian kept his face from showing the grin he felt at Cermak's sarcasm. The only flaw in the argument was that Carl, from what Brian had seen, was no coward. He would lie and misrepresent whenever it suited his advantage, but Brian had seen no sign of cowardice. The men who were with Carl must have had time to find this out by now.

"Oh," said Carl, a look of relief crossing his face as he saw a way out. "I forgot he's had time to fill you full of lies."

He turned to face Brian, a look of genuine anger on his face. It was anger at the spot he found himself in. "You'd stoop to anything, wouldn't you?" He glanced at Anne. "Take care of your father, Anne. He's tired, and this rat has been pumping him full of lies. And keep that gun away from him. We can't have anyone around who shoots at his friends."

He glanced at Brian. "Don't have much to say for yourself, do you?" He glanced to one side, saw that several men were holding the smiling Cermak, and immediately took one long step forward, reaching out a big hand and knocked loose the gun Brian had been absently holding since the trucks had shown up.

Brian still stood unmoving, the accumulated fatigue

combining with the unfairness of the attack to create a feeling of unreality, as if he were watching someone else rather than experiencing it himself.

"This," said Carl, "is for running out on me." His open hand struck Brian jarringly across the side of the head. His other hand slapped Brian's face in a stinging explosion from the other side. "And *that's* for telling my girl's father lies."

Carl landed a lightning blow to the stomach that left Brian gasping, and then Carl had him by the cloth at the throat, holding him up as he said, "I don't like to do it, Brian, but you've got to learn if you're going with us. You don't leave your friends to do all the work. And you don't lie about it afterwards. *You hear me?*"

From somewhere to the side, Cermak's voice reached them.

"You tell him, Carl hero. You've had the sleep."

There was a murmur that might have meant anything, but Brian, out on his feet before Carl had ever touched him, felt Carl's hand tighten and lift brutally.

For one blinding instant, Brian saw himself held like a rag doll while Carl taunted him, hoping for Brian to struggle a little, giving Carl further excuse to slap him around.

Brian was suddenly wide-awake. He let go a crushing blow to Carl's jaw, and saw him stagger back. He caught up with him in three swift steps, yanked him upright, and struck him a blow that came up from the ground. An instant later, Brian's open left hand lashed out twice, repaying the slaps in the face, then his right buried itself deep in Carl's midsection, doubling Carl up as if he'd been hit with a telephone pole.

Carl was on the ground, his eyes glazed, and Brian was standing over him, his mind running back through the things Carl had said and done, aching for the justification to land one more blow, but vaguely aware that the accounts had been evened up and anything more would place the discredit on his side.

Then the anger was gone, and he was breathing hard, aware of a dizziness and a tiredness, of the pain in his left arm, and of aches, stiffnesses, sore muscles, and a throbbing head.

Men were crowded around and someone was shouting for water. Someone gripped Brian's shoulder, and he turned to see Steve Cermak, grinning broadly.

"That punk has been filling Anne with lies." He glanced at the prostrate Carl; a bucket of water was being emptied in his face. "I never saw anything so pretty in my life. Come on."

They started toward the trucks, then Brian remembered the gun Carl had knocked from his hands, found it, carried the gun toward the truck that someone pointed out as a place where he and Cermak could sleep, and then he remembered the bicycles. With someone else carrying a gas lantern, they found the bikes, one smashed out of shape and the other perfectly usable, and put them in the truck. With these safely on board, they crawled into the roomy interior, and found places to settle down in the soft hay.

***

After a long, dreamless sleep, Brian stirred to the rumble of the truck. Daylight was seeping in around the door at the far end. But it was warm nestled in the soft hay, and Brian drifted off to sleep again. He woke the next time with someone gently shaking his shoulder. Light was streaming in at the open back of the truck, and Brian woke, stretched, winced at his swollen knuckles, and scrambled to his feet.

Smitty, clean-shaven, grinned at Brian.

"I let you sleep through breakfast, but I figured you'd want lunch. There's a stream back in the trees to the right of the road if you want to wash up. The cook-truck has hot water, soap, and some mirrors for shaving. You can take your time. We're broken down again."

"What's wrong?"

"The usual. Apparently when the binding of the electrons to the metal atoms was increased it wasn't only the conduction of the electricity that suffered. Brightness and *heat* conductivity are off, too. The metal of the pistons and cylinders in the engines doesn't get cooled as well as it should; it overheats, and just what goes on in there is hard to say, but we've had cracked blocks, pitting, spalling off of bits of metal, pistons stuck tight in the cylinders. I don't know what it is this time, but we were due for it. We get a breakdown every few hundred miles. At least it didn't happen at night."

Brian followed Smitty past a number of bed rolls he hadn't noticed the night before, and dropped out of the truck.

"Hard to work on at night?"

"Unless you've already cleaned out the place, you don't know who's going to take a pot shot at you. Moreover, if a truck stops all of a sudden, there's a chance of two trucks slamming into each other. In the daytime, we run further apart."

"At night, it's dangerous to get separated?"

Smitty nodded. "The highway is bad enough, but when you go off it to get fuel, food, or anything else, all hell breaks loose. Either some bunch of thugs has already grabbed what you want, or else there's a vigilance committee, citizens' protective association, or something just as good, right there to see the thugs *don't* grab the place. Either way, you're an outsider, and they don't want you. Then there're setups like what you ran into last night. If you hadn't set them off first, they'd have hit us later when we stopped to get the roadblock out of the way. *They* wait for somebody to rob a place like that shopping center, then they, in turn, ambush the robbers."

"Nice," said Brian ironically.

"Isn't it? The trouble is, everybody has to eat."

They were walking along past the trucks, and Smitty said, "Here's the cook-truck. 'Morning, Barbara, Anne."

Anne Cermak and Barbara Bowen smiled at Smitty and then at Brian. Brian was suddenly conscious of his dirty clothes and unshaven face. But he was also hungry. There was a large kettle of stew cooking slowly on a bottled-gas stove inside the truck, and a pile of bowls of unbreakable plastic, and a tray of stainless-steel spoons.

Brian took a bowl of stew off to one side, ate hungrily, then went off to the stream to wash up. He came back shaved, and by now the small, cursing crowd at the front of one of the trucks had subsided, the hood was down again, the women and children on the grass at the center of the road were going back to the trucks, and the men were coming out of the woods and back from up and down the road where they'd been serving as guards and lookouts.

Brian hunted up Cardan, who put him on one of the trucks as a guard. Anne's father volunteered as the driver, but Anne herself was in another truck with Barbara Bowen.

The days passed pleasantly enough—by comparison with what it had been like when Brian and Cermak were traveling by bicycle—but Brian couldn't help noticing that every day the going got tougher.

The cars were getting thicker along the roads, which meant many more obstacles to go around, or to get out of the way. The trucks were already carrying a number of cans of extra fuel, which they stopped to refill at every opportunity. But they were low on food, and as Cardan was determined to get more before they ran out, the result was a carefully planned raid on a shopping center. This took an entire day, and was immediately followed by an ambush worse than any they'd run into before.

Brian had looked forward to being with Anne, but they were in separate trucks while traveling, and when they were stopped there was a desperate need for guards and lookouts.

At every stop Cardan now had some of the men bolting tight more big oblongs of the galvanized iron roofing he'd loaded up with after the last raid on a shopping center, and which now, in several layers of thickness, served to armor the trucks against the fire of most light hand-weapons. The extra protection was needed, since they were now being fired on by people who apparently shot for fun as well as plunder. They were getting into a section like a suburb of hell. Cars and trucks were burnt out, the roads were strewn with broken bottles, barbed wire, and spike-studded boards; the ditches were dug into trench systems, and an explosion had knocked out a wide section of overpass. From all sides there was continuous firing, with leaping flames devouring the buildings in the background, and a pall of smoke blotting out what lay beyond. Cardan pulled back out of it, sent the steam car on a brief reconnaissance to the south, learned that it was no better that way, tried a wider detour, and ran into another mess. Before they were through, they'd gone a hundred miles out of their way, suffered painful wounds, and repaired half a dozen tires. It took the better part of a week to get back on the highway.

"Well," said Smitty, studying a map, "I think that was Cleveland. One of these days, if we last long enough, we'll hit Chicago. I'm not looking forward to it."

Once again they were making good time. They were well stocked with provisions, and at every stop the men were strengthening the protection of the trucks. Now more of the rear tires were shielded, and metal disks were fitted to the front wheels. Small-caliber bullets striking from the side would do little damage unless very well aimed. "But," as Cardan pointed out, "a few gasoline bombs heaved at us out of a ditch could end the whole thing." He decided on a wide detour to avoid Chicago, at the same time staying well north of Indianapolis. By now, no city looked attractive to them.

Several days later, they seemed to be in the clear again, traveling along a wide, deserted road, weaving occasionally to pass the inevitable cars, when Brian, traveling this time in the steam car that raced in front of the trucks to see what was up ahead, saw a cloud of dust far ahead as they swooped over a low rise.

"Now," said Brian, pointing out the dust cloud, "what do you suppose makes that?"

"Either a lot of animals," said Cermak, frowning, "or a lot of people."

Smitty, driving, said, "Whichever it is, that's a sizable migration."

He slowed the steam car. They studied the dust cloud for a moment, then they raced ahead for a closer look.

Cermak cleared his throat. "If that's a migration, it's got a leader. If he's got any sense, he'll have flank guards watching this road."

Smitty slowed to a stop. Ahead and to either side was a gentle rise covered on the left with small trees now starting to leaf out. Most of the rest of the land they'd passed was open farm country, the fields already plowed and ready to be planted by the tractors that no longer ran.

Smitty swung the car around and they reported back to Cardan, who nodded thoughtfully. "We'll keep going, but stop short of that place. From what you say, they're headed south, and we're going west. We'll wait till the column, whatever it is, goes past."

A little while later they were there, the head of the dust cloud now perceptibly further to the south. But the tail of the cloud was still out of sight to the north.

"If," Smitty suggested, "we could get through those woods beside the road, we could look down on whatever it is that's going past on the other side."

"Go ahead," said Cardan. "But be careful. This is a bad setup, and there's no telling what you may run into."

Smitty, Brian and Steve Cermak walked up into the woods. It was a cool day, but the ground was soft underfoot, and the small leaves just coming out gave the forest a misty, delicate appearance. The sky overhead was a clear blue, with only a few high clouds. There was a light breeze, and it carried the sound of voices.

Then Brian was near the edge of a low steep bank, looking down through the trees, seeing, on a wide dirt road below, a column of men.

Brian glanced back over his shoulders to where Smitty and Cermak, further back in amongst the trees, covered him from either side.

As he turned to look back, he saw, about forty feet away, three men standing in the shadow of a tall evergreen. They were watching him, their guns not quite aimed at him, but requiring only a slight shift to be centered on him. One of them called out in a low voice, "What you doing, man?"

"Looking," said Brian, all his senses alert.

"You alone?"

"My friends are covering me."

"We don't see them."

"They'd be careless if you did."

"What you planning?"

"We wanted to go past. But we can wait."

"Which way you headed?"

"West."

"And you're sure your friends have got us covered?" the man asked slyly.

"Make a false move, and you'll find out," Brian said amiably.

"How many of them?" the man wanted to know.

"Only a dozen," said Brian, "but all good shots."

The man hesitated, his gun hand itching to swing his

weapon around. For a moment there was a deathly silence as uncertainty plagued the man. Abruptly he relaxed, grinned from ear to ear, let out a bellow of a laugh, and commented, "I believe you."

Almost nonchalantly, he motioned to his companions and they took off to join their column. Brian heaved a deep sigh of relief and walked back to where Smitty and Cermak were waiting.

"What was all that about?" asked Cermak.

"I tried a bluff," Brian said. "And it worked. But for a moment there it was touch and go." He wiped the perspiration off his forehead.

Their release from extreme tension made them feel almost hilarious, and Smitty and Cermak congratulated Brian on his handling of the situation.

"Well," said Brian, "I couldn't have pulled it off if you two weren't there to back me up. How were they to know whether there were two of you or a dozen?"

Sudden gunfire erupted in the direction where they had left the trucks. Obviously, they weren't in the clear yet.

As one, they moved through the woods toward the firing.

Long before they got back, the gunfire had ended.

Chapter 7

Brian, Smitty and Cermak looked cautiously on one burning truck. The other trucks and the steam car were gone. On the road lay one of Cardan's men, a long hunting arrow jutting from his back. On a hill nearby was another man dead, an arrow embedded in the base of his neck. A dead stranger, still holding a bow and a quiver of hunting arrows had been shot through the chest.

Anne, smeared with mud and dirt, climbed from a ditch by the side of the road. She explained that Cardan had been talking to her when the trouble started, and he had thrown her down out of sight and told her to crawl into a nearby culvert. There she had heard the fight, but had seen nothing of what happened.

As they were trying to reconstruct what had taken place, Carl, fully dressed, his hair wet, and unarmed save for the knife at his belt, walked down the gentle, sparsely wooded slope on the opposite side of the road, carrying a towel in one hand. He had a sick weary look, and for once paid no attention to Anne.

Brian and the others waited silently. Carl walked over, drew a ragged breath, and looked at them steadily.

"I saw it all," he said dazedly. "And I couldn't do a thing."

There was a silence, and Brian said, "Where were you?"

"Up the slope, washing in the stream. The scouts checked the woods on both sides and sent word that everything was all clear. Cardan didn't like the spot, but finally let the women and kids get out for some air. I felt sweaty and dirty because I'd been on guard at that last place and didn't have a chance to wash. I found a stream, followed it uphill, and didn't bother to take my gun because I wasn't going far. The stream wound across this open field, and I had to go way up to find a place that was out of sight. I'd no sooner started to wash than there was the bang of Cardan's .45, and there went our two guards on this side, running down the hill. The thing was over before I could do anything. About a dozen guys in camouflage suits, armed with bows and arrows, came out of the woods across the road, covered the women and children, made the men start up the trucks, and took off. They apparently knocked over a portable stove Barbara Bowen had lit to heat some coffee, and that set one truck on fire. They took the rest of the trucks and the steam car."

They looked at him silently, seeing the attack in their minds.

Carl took the silence for censure, and said almost pleadingly, "I couldn't do a thing. When they left, I made it up to the top of the slope east there, saw them turn off onto a dirt road headed north. That's all I know."

Smitty finally said, "Did they kill Cardan?"

"I don't think so. But I think he got one of them."

"Then they'll regret this—if they live long enough."

Cermak was frowning. "Where did they come from? What were they doing here?"

Brian said, "They could have planned to attack that column we ran into, decided it was too much, turned back this way and heard the children. The guards could have been watching the other way at the wrong moment, and those arrows would have made no sound that would warn people down here."

Smitty looked around at the desolate scene. "I wish the chief had had one of his hunches about this."

"Maybe he did," said Carl. "Miss Bowen had to beg him to let the women and kids get out of the trucks."

"If the woods and the road had already been checked, and there were guards watching, what did he see he didn't like?" asked Cermak.

"The chief works on hunches more than you'd think," Smitty informed them. "It sounds crazy, but when you get right down to it, he's *got* to. He's used to dealing with things that aren't known well enough yet to handle precisely. I think what he sees is the sum total of a whole lot of things, each too small to mean much by itself. When he's uneasy like that, there's generally a reason."

Carl said, "Like the dream he had before all this started. He was in a terrible mood, and we thought it was all for nothing. *Now* look."

Cermak said, "He had a dream?"

Smitty nodded. "He didn't exactly foresee what would happen. He was just uneasy about the general trend in certain kinds of research. And he was right."

They stood still for a minute, looking around and wondering what to do now.

Brian glanced at Carl. "One of the scouts is on that hill back there, dead. His gun is still with him. And there's one of their men, with a bow and some arrows."

Carl nodded his head in thanks, crossed the road, and climbed up the bank into the woods and out of sight.

Smitty watched him go. "He seems to be telling the truth. But I'm not enthusiastic about having him with us."

Cermak checked his gun. "I'd trust him as far as I could spit a mouthful of fishhooks."

Brian had given little heed to Carl since their fight, but now he thought the situation over carefully. "I think he'll be all right—provided we keep our eyes open if we get in a spot where it would pay him to stab us in the back."

Cermak cradled his gun. "It's never going to pay him to stab us in the back." He said to his daughter, "If he talks to you about going off with him or anything like that, let us know." He turned to Brian. "If he's going with us, Anne had better stick with me. The more Carl sees you and Anne together, the more likely we are to have trouble."

Brian agreed, but he was galled at the realization that once again Carl was keeping Brian and Anne apart.

Across the road, Carl slid down the hill, the bow and quiver slung across his back, a bandolier of ammunition over his shoulder, a rifle in his hand.

That night, they camped near where the trucks had been. The night was cold, they had no blankets, didn't want to show a fire, and woke early feeling cramped and stiff. And now they had no food. Since there was nothing else to do, they started walking. They kept going to the west, hoping to find some farm where they might get food.

Early that morning they found a farm, but a fusillade of shots greeted them when they got near it. They walked on. The same thing happened at the next farm. The third time it happened, Smitty shouted, "We want to buy food!"

A bullet screamed close overhead in answer.

They lay on the ground studying the building. It was a two-story frame structure, with one bare tree about forty feet from it on the far side. Save for the ruins of a burned-down barn, and shrubs to either side of the front door, there was no cover, and the land all around was flat.

Brian shouted, "Trade you bullets for food!"

There was a silence, then a deep male shout. "What size gun?"

"Springfield thirty."

"Wrong size!"

There was a moment's quiet, then a shouted warning, "Don't come any closer! We'll shoot to kill! We've been burnt out once and we're taking no chances!"

Brian looked at the blackened ruins of the barn.

He shouted, "Know any place we could get food?"

"Can't tell you. Everybody's in the same spot we're in."

Cermak growled, "I see his point. But I'm still hungry."

Brian lay flat, and said in a low voice, "How many guns fired at us that first time?"

"I'd say there were at least three of them," Carl volunteered. "Two downstairs, and I think there was a flash from that upstairs window to the left of the door."

Smitty said, "Better clear out. We haven't got any

advantage, and it might just occur to them to shoot us and have our guns and bullets for themselves."

Brian called, "Thanks, anyway."

"Sorry we can't help you. Could give you water."

"Thanks. We've got that." Brian glanced around. "Let's get out of here."

Carl said, "One at a time. We'd better cover each other on the way."

They got away from the house without trouble, though when it was clear that they were leaving, the people at the house started calling questions as to what conditions were like along the road, when they'd eaten last, and whether they were sure they had plenty of water.

Smitty said, looking back, "Well, they *wanted* to help."

"There's not many calories in that," Carl commented wryly. "And we'll probably get the same business at the next place."

Toward noon, they reached another farmhouse, and except for a different voice, their greeting was the same. The people would have liked to help them, but they couldn't.

Later Brian and the others halted as another farmhouse, a two-story frame structure like the others, came into sight.

Cermak said dryly, "We could get very hungry this way."

"Well," said Brian, "let's think it over. We've got four guns, plenty of bullets, a bow, arrows, and a quiver. We need food, blankets, and it wouldn't hurt if we had a pack to carry more food in. Is that right?"

"That about covers it," said Smitty.

"Okay," said Brian. "With this much firepower, we

ought to be able either to trade something for food, or else make it worth somebody's while to at least give us enough to get on to the next place."

"Now we're talking," Cermak said. "A bullet from one of our guns would probably go right through these houses, from one side to the other."

"Only," said Smitty, "it might kill somebody on the way. Say there's a man, wife, and three sons in one of those houses. The men are armed, and we accidentally shoot the mother. Not only does that make us murderers, but very shortly we're going to have something on our hands that won't be easy to end."

Brian said, "Why don't we be reasonable, like we have been, only this time insist on something to keep us going to the next place where they might have food. They ought to be able to spare us that much. If they won't, we could offer to trade, maybe, one gun and bullets, or the bow and arrows, for food, blankets and something to carry things in. If that doesn't work, we could warn them we'd fight, and give them a demonstration."

"If they wanted to trade for the bow and arrows, all right," Cermak agreed grudgingly, "but we may need every bullet and gun we've got."

Carl said, "In time, this bow is going to be worth much more than it's worth now. You can make your own arrows, with practice. And after you shoot them, you can go get them and shoot them again. Once we run out of bullets, the guns will be useless."

Smitty said, "Let's go to the next farmhouse and see what happens."

This time, after they'd made a careful reconnaissance

and crept up by way of the barn and outbuildings, the house turned out to be empty. The livestock was gone, most of the cooking utensils and part of the bedding were gone, and in the cellar were wide shelves where rings in the dust showed that many dozens of jars of canned goods had been removed. There remained a few odd jars of vegetables, pickles and fruit, dated several years before. In the pantry that adjoined the kitchen were a few potatoes and onions, and a large box of oatmeal.

While Anne did the best she could to turn this into a meal, the men made up blanket rolls. Late that afternoon they were on the move again, fortified with boiled potatoes and onions, bread-and-butter pickles, and stewed tomatoes, followed by a dessert of canned peaches. With them they carried the bedrolls, a few pans, and the box of oatmeal. They wore improvised packs, and as the cloth straps dug into their shoulders, they wished they had never thought of that idea.

The next farm they passed was a large one, where men were working in the fields with horse-drawn, seed-sowing machines. Brian, Anne and the others were scarcely in sight when the bullets began to fly over their heads.

This became a pattern they gradually got used to. A few isolated farms, held by small groups of people; other farms abandoned. At the abandoned farms there were usually some odd scraps of food to be found, and the buildings provided shelter. But there was seldom enough food, and often they had to sleep out during cold, wet, miserable nights.

Brian was aware that as the days passed they were gradually getting weaker. Worse yet, they were now well

into a section of the country that had been visited by too
many outsiders and didn't care to see more. Many of the
farms were completely burned out. The people in those
that still stood didn't talk, but opened fire on sight. The
larger farms resorted to more drastic action, and parties of
men charged out on horseback, only to hurriedly change
their minds when the long-range accuracy of the four
Springfields began picking off horses and men before they
could get close.

Brian and the others found themselves near a small
town where, they felt, there must be supplies, but the
occasional sounds of guns from the town made their
approach cautious, and the sight of lone figures sprinting
from one building to another amidst a fusillade of shots
changed their minds entirely.

Smitty shook his head. "The whole country's gone
crazy."

Cermak shrugged. "They've got to eat."

Carl said wearily, "It's the same thing as back home: no
power, no lights, no communications, no transport. The
country was run on electricity and now that's gone."

To the northeast, and far off to the south, Brian could
see pillars of smoke. From somewhere toward the
southwest came the sound of continuous gunfire, clearly
audible now that the shots from the nearby town had died
away. Wherever there was any sign of people, there was
trouble in one form or another. The convulsion was
coming to a climax, and Brian knew the motivation. As
Cermak had said, people had to eat.

The next day, from a low hill, they looked off to the south
on a moderately large shopping center. From the tall dead

electric sign over the center, snipers were picking off the attackers who crept toward them through the flat fields nearby. Cars had been rolled off the roads leading to the center and burned. At the center itself, the cars in the parking lot had been pushed into a tight circle around the buildings, and the air let out of the tires so that no one could crawl underneath. From behind the cars, the defenders had a clear field of fire at anyone trying to cross the wide sweep of parking lot, where the only cover was the isolated light poles, dominated by the huge electric sign overhead. Plainly enough, the people outside couldn't get at the food without killing the defenders, while the people inside couldn't keep the food without killing whoever tried to force his way in. Meanwhile, the people inside would have no reliable way to get water. It looked bad enough in the daytime, but what neither Brian nor the others could visualize was what happened on a dark night when no one could tell friend from foe, and hungry men and women crept desperately across the parking lot, knives and guns in hand, toward the buildings.

As they looked at the building, it began to come home to them.

Smitty cleared his throat. "Let's move on."

One afternoon, tired, hungry and sick of the endless burning, looting and killing, Brian and the others lay down to rest in a clump of trees near a narrow blacktopped road by a stream. It was still broad daylight, and after they had rested they hoped to go on several miles more before nightfall.

They had scarcely begun to settle down when there was the bang of guns close by.

✳ Chapter 8

Brian sprang to his feet and worked his way carefully through the trees. In a moment he was peering out at a stream where several farmers were guiding two teams of rearing horses as they drew wagons through the water toward a narrow blacktopped road. From a patch of brush atop a nearby embankment there came the flash of guns.

After what he had seen in the last few weeks, the situation was crystal clear at a glance. Brian took a quick look at the farmers, their honest, hard-working faces twisted in despair, then he dropped behind a thick log and slammed roaring shot after shot into the brush. As he stripped a fresh clip into the magazine, he shouted, "Carl! Smitty! Steve! Hurry up and we can get the lot of them!"

There was a wild scramble in the brush and three men were desperately pumping their bicycles in a mad race to get away down the road. Guns and belts of bullets were strewn over the road in their haste. Brian sent a final shot close above their heads. There was an additional clatter on the blacktop, and they streaked off at an even higher speed.

In the stream, the horses splashed and plunged, but

with the end of the gunfire, the farmers managed to lead them up the low bank to the road.

Cermak was at Brian's elbow.

"What was that?"

"Ambush," said Brian. "They were hidden in the brush along the road down there."

"Ah," said Cermak, "kill the farmers and take the horses."

Brian took a careful look around, then walked down toward the farmers.

There were, he saw, four of them. Two were ripping up shirts to bandage a man who was wounded. The other farmer, a burly man of about sixty, smiled broadly and walked over to Brian with outthrust hand.

"Friend, I'll never be happier to see anybody if I live to be a hundred! That gun of yours was the sweetest music I've ever heard."

Brian gripped his hand. "For the last week we've been shot at from about every farmhouse we've passed. Now I see the reason."

The farmer nodded. "It's gotten so a man can't turn his back without getting a bullet in it. You can't live unless there's enough of you to stand guard day and night." He shook his head. "That's why people shoot at strangers. My name's Ed Barnaby. You and your friends move in with me till you're rested up, and maybe you'll think better of us."

Cermak and the others came down and the wagons made their way along the road. With the addition of the guns and ammunition left behind by the ambushers, they made a formidable party.

Ed Barnaby explained that they'd taken the wagons to

get grain left behind at the farm of his friend, Dave Schmidt, who had moved in with him.

"You see," he said as they traveled slowly through the gathering dusk, "we've got plenty of room. It's a big house, and there's just me, my wife, my three boys and two girls; and now my neighbor Dave Schmidt and his family. That sounds like a lot, but when you see the house, you'll see there's plenty of room."

The house was a dazzling white in the moonlight, standing among tall trees that arched above its steep, black-painted metal roof. It stood three full stories high, with tall windows, and a porch that ran around two sides on the ground and second floor. A two-story, L-shaped addition, apparently added as an afterthought, was itself as large as an ordinary house.

"My Granddad wanted lots of room," Ed Barnaby said with a broad, appreciative grin. "He had fourteen children, ten of them boys."

Brian slept that night in a room with delicately flowered, silvery wallpaper, on a soft bed with crisp clean sheets and light warm covers. The next day they had pancakes and sausages for breakfast, and Ed Barnaby showed them the springhouse, dairy barn, chicken coop, smokehouse, hog pen, stable, icehouse, pond, and a small blacksmith shop.

"Grandfather," said Barnaby, "believed in being self-sufficient. I think we can make out all right, so long, that is, as we can keep from being shot dead or burned alive. Grandfather could probably have handled that problem, too, but I'm not so sure Dave Schmidt and me have the right idea. If we'd known what we were doing, we'd never have got caught in that stream bed the way we did. Now, I've watched you boys, and it seems to me you know how to handle yourselves. If you'd care to rest a little before going on west, we'd be glad to board you, if you'd guard the place for us."

Brian and the others liked the idea. While Barnaby and his people worked in the fields, Brian, Carl, Smitty and Steve Cermak made sure no one raided the farm. They studied the layout of the buildings and showed Barnaby the places where it was easiest to get in. Barnaby had two of his sons drive in several lines of fence posts, and Brian and Carl put up barbed wire. They cut down one of the trees, and several bushes that obscured the view from the house. Now, from the cover of the big building, those inside could fire on anyone who tried to tamper with the fences. Then they built a small, sturdy platform around the trap door opening on the roof of the house, and they had a view out over the barn and outbuildings, where one man or woman could serve as a lookout while the others worked.

They'd been there a week when they began to feel well rested and ready to move on.

"I hate to see you go," said Barnaby as they were eating a big dinner. "We've been getting our work done for the first time since this trouble started. We've been getting our sleep, too. I used to jump awake two or three times a night thinking I'd heard somebody out in the barn. I hope you won't leave unless you've got to."

The others eagerly joined in, offering to help stand guard at night, and then a shrill whistle, the prearranged signal for trouble, interrupted the meal.

Carl, who'd been on watch on the roof, came down the stairs fast.

Ed Barnaby said, "What is it? Should we get our guns?"

"Yes, but stay hidden and don't shoot unless the other side shoots first! There are hundreds of them!"

**

While the others took up their positions inside the house, Brian and Ed Barnaby, each carrying their guns, went out on the porch.

Dozens of armed men, their guns at the ready, stood at the line of fence posts that stretched across the front lawn. The barbed wire lay in lengths on the grass, each strand cut off where it had been stapled to the posts. The men waiting by the fence posts watched the house and buildings alertly. At the center of the lawn stood a man with a whistle raised to his lips, watching the house and waiting.

Back of this line, men trudged past on the road, in a long column, four abreast. The men carried guns, and, watching closely, Brian began to notice significant details.

Every twelve men, there was a break in the column. The men at the head of each file were armed with semi-automatic weapons—often M1 rifles or carbines. The second men carried rifles, usually Springfields or American Enfields. The third men carried shotguns. After that, there was a miscellany of sporting rifles, shotguns, and foreign weapons, until at the end of the line, the third men from the end carried shotguns, the second men from the end carried rifles, often Springfields or Enfields, and the last men carried semi-automatic weapons.

Now, as they marched past, Brian could see that at the

head and tail of each section another man walked at the head of the files on the left side of the column.

Barnaby murmured, "Look businesslike, don't they?"

"There's a break every so often when they go by. What's that for?" Brian wondered.

"They're formed in units. Apparently there are four twelve-man squads, the squad leaders marching in front, the assistant squad leaders in the rear. The four squads make up a platoon, with the platoon leaders marching on the far side of the columns."

"What's this coming now?"

Down the road came four men abreast, carrying heavier guns than any they'd seen till now. Behind them came four men carrying light loads of ammunition, and behind them four more men heavily loaded with ammunition.

"Those," said Brian, "are automatic rifles. Whoever's running this has it all organized."

Next came four men pulling a light cart carrying a water-cooled thirty-caliber machine gun, and four more men pulling another light cart loaded with ammunition. Behind that came a man leading a saddle horse, and beside him a tall, dreamy-looking man wearing on his dark-brown hair a thin band of silver ornamented with slightly raised crests that flashed and glittered in the sunlight. As Brian watched in astonishment, this man raised his right hand; there was a barked command and a single blast on a trumpet. The column came to an abrupt halt. Another shouted command followed, the armed men turned to face the farm buildings, the officers came through the intervals of the line, and the tall man with the band of silver flashing on his head stepped to the horse and swung into the saddle.

For an instant Brian expected the whole line to come forward in a rush, but then the high, clear, carrying voice of the man in the saddle reached out, its tone reasonable, appealing.

"Farmers, just a word before we march on. If the crops are to be planted in good season, they have to be planted now. But no man can work in the fields and stand guard with a gun at the same time. If we're to avoid starvation later, we have to get rid of these killers and arsonists *now!*

"We all know that for weeks you've had to fight off these human rats. You've been held back and slowed down because you had to struggle with the vermin. That's over with. Now you can put away your guns and plow and plant to your heart's content. The Day of the Rat is over." He beamed and swept his hand to indicate the men around him, then he raised his clenched fist. "Right here is the Cat!"

There was an involuntary murmur of approval from the house, and then a roaring cheer from the men in the road.

The farmers were out on the porch, talking excitedly, and the armed men on the road had broken formation and were on the lawn opening boxes of dry rations and taking mugs of steaming coffee and cocoa from men who carried trays from a wagon in the road.

Schmidt, the neighbor who lived with Barnaby, said excitedly, "Sounds like they mean business."

Barnaby looked at the guns and grinned. "They're equipped to *do* business!" He glanced at Brian. "What do you think?"

The best Brian could manage was to say, "It could be."

Brian was looking at the flashing silver circlet on the tall man's head.

Carl had come out on the porch, to be followed by a dubious-looking Smitty and an expressionless Cermak. Carl glanced around, noting the way the men were spreading out in the shade under the trees, then went back in the house.

Cermak glanced at Brian, and said dryly, "What do you think of that guy, Brian?"

"What he *said* was all right. But what's that crown for?"

Smitty was watching the corner of the house where the porch ran around the other side. "I don't know if you noticed, but one of those people just came up onto the porch with a sheet of paper and a stapler. It looks to me like he tacked up some kind of notice."

Brian saw the man go down the steps. "Let's take a look."

They walked around the corner, to find, stapled to the wall, a large oblong of heavy white paper bearing in small black print a long series of paragraphs. Brian's eye skimmed rapidly over large sections of print as he read the more outstanding points:

NOTICE

Owing to the disastrous failure of electric power throughout this region, be it resolved:

1) That this country, and those districts contiguous to it, shall unite for common defense and be known hereafter as the Districts United.

2) That the inhabitants of these Districts United shall act toward the creation of conditions in which unlawful elements shall be eliminated.

Toward these desirable ends, the following measures are hereby set in motion:

1) Since outside criminal elements are carrying out their practices of killing, arson, robbery, and bushwhacking, a new crime has come into existence, which shall hereinafter he known as "karb," from the initial letters of the criminal acts referred to. Therefore a Defense Force is hereby created. This Defense Force shall eliminate all criminals practicing karb, by hanging, shooting, decapitation, or whatever other method.

2) To facilitate swift and purposeful action in eliminating karb, a commander of the Defense Force is appointed, who shall be known hereafter as the Districts United Karb Eliminator, or, from the initial letters of the words, D.U.K.E., which may be shortened to DUKE or Duke.

3) The duties of the D.U.K.E. shall be to care for and control the Defense Force, restrict and eliminate karb, and endeavor to create those conditions in which work can be carried on without unlawful interruption.

4) Toward this end, the following rules are hereby put into effect . . .

There followed a long list. By order of the D.U.K.E., any foreclosure of mortgages or other sale or exchange of farm properties was suspended. By order of the DUKE, all money taxes on land were revoked. By order of the Duke, all money taxes on income or property were revoked. There then followed a list of taxes payable in storable foods of various kinds, in firewood and in hay, grain, and livestock. To avoid the wrong persons being shot or hanged, and to make things easier for the flying squads of karb-eliminators, no one might travel without a permit from the Duke's local representative. At the end was a paragraph to the effect that any grievance or complaint could be taken to the Duke.

"Nice," said Cermak, dryly. "The Duke is everything."

Smitty said, "Look how the notice is signed."

Brian and Cermak studied the imperious scrawl at the bottom of the paper. The signature itself was impossible to decipher but below it were the printed words, "Charles, Duke of the Districts United."

"He's got the thing organized, justified, and explained," Smitty said, "so if you read it sentence by sentence it seems almost reasonable. And, of course, the Duke himself forbids mortgage foreclosures and taxes, and will punish karb and right wrongs. The food taxes are put in sort of anonymously—just some unavoidable thing that had to be done."

"What he's setting up is a feudal system," Brian commented. "The farmers are tied to their land, and pay part of their crops in return for protection. The ruler controls the armed force, makes the laws himself, and administers justice. Same thing as the Middle Ages."

Cermak shook his head. "They say the government is still holding out in the northwest—in Montana and

Oregon. I think we should head there the first chance we get."

"Yes," said Brian. "And we'd better move fast. It won't be long till they have the lid nailed down tight."

Smitty glanced at several of the Duke's men who were heavily bandaged. "Evidently there are a few people around who don't like being boxed up."

Brian studied them. "It might be worthwhile to know what happened." He moved down the steps, past several of the Duke's men who were joking with the girls of the family, and crossed the lawn to the group of bandaged men. He bumped one of them with his elbow, turned to say "Excuse me," then blinked as if in surprise.

"*You* must have run into trouble."

The man's head was heavily and neatly bandaged, and his left arm was in a sling. But he grinned. "Run into a gang of scientists."

Brian said, "Scientists can't fight, can they?"

One of the other men, his right hand covered by bandages, gave a groan. There were about half a dozen of them, all badly beaten up, and they all glanced at each other. One took a bite out of a loaf of bread sliced lengthwise, a chunk of meat in the middle. Around this mouthful, he said, "I never knowed they could fight, myself. But they learned us a lesson."

Another said, "They hit us with everything. To begin with, they weren't on foot or on horseback. They were driving *trucks*."

Brian looked blank. "Special kind of engine?"

"Diesels. They started them on compressed air. And when old Duke seen them trucks coming toward the crossroads, he like to run us into the ground getting there first to throw up a roadblock. But that was only the start of the fun. We must have outnumbered them . . . anyway, ten to one, but they had machine guns, hand grenades, and flame-throwers, and just for variety every now and then an arrow would fly out of one of them trucks and somebody'd get skewered. I'd have let them go, myself. We were all getting kind of tired of them. But not old Duke. He was all over us, telling us we *had* to get this bunch, and pretty soon they run low on ammunition, and that flame-thrower of theirs give out, and we got them.

"They had their women and kids with them and everything. Bunch of scientists, headed west. Planned to join up with the Federals up in Montana, near as we could figure. Duke made a deal with them, so now we got the only crew of scientists around here. Duke figures we can use them to make steam cars, fix up locomotives, make gunpowder—lots of things. Only trouble is, they wouldn't strictly promise not to try to get away. Got to be careful they don't sneak out on us."

Brian and the Duke's man were still talking when Carl came up, looking worried, and drew Brian aside.

"Listen," said Carl, "Anne's gone."

"*Gone!* Where?"

Carl kept his voice low. "We think the Duke's got her."

***

There was the blast of a whistle, and the Duke's men started back to the road. In a few minutes they were again in formation, and the cooks' helpers were picking up the coffee and cocoa mugs, pieces of waxed paper, and empty ration boxes that were left piled at the base of trees and shrubs. Quickly, Carl explained what had happened.

"Schmidt saw Anne go outside. She wanted to ask her father about something, and said she thought she'd seen him go outside near the fence. She was going to come right back in, but this Duke saw her and called her over. That's the last anyone's seen of her."

Brian looked at the column of troops just starting to move past. Far down the column was a truck, which he recognized as one of Cardan's. He climbed up on the porch, then onto the porch rail, and carefully scanned the marching column.

"There's only one place she could be, Carl. That's in the truck."

Carl bit his lip.

Smitty came over, followed their gaze, and stared at the truck. "That's one of ours!"

Brian jumped down and told him what the Duke's men had said.

"Then," said Smitty, relieved, "they must have gotten away from that crew with the bows and arrows."

"That doesn't help us any if Anne's in that truck."

Cermak had come around the corner of the porch and stopped abruptly. "*Who's* in the truck?"

Brian said, "Carl thinks Anne is gone. We both figure if she's in that column anywhere, it's inside the truck."

Cermak stared at the passing truck. "Yes. He is the Duke. She is the peasant's daughter. If he wants her he will *take* her. Wait a minute while I go inside and make sure."

"Damn it," said Carl, looking at the two guards armed

with Tommy guns at the rear of the truck, "how are we going to get her out of there?"

Smitty looked at the platoon coming along behind the truck. They looked particularly well armed and tough.

Slowly the troops moved by.

Cermak, his face carefully blank, came out of the house. "She's gone, all right."

"Whatever we do," said Carl, "we're going to have to do it fast."

Cermak said bitterly, "There isn't a thing we *can* do, and that Duke knows it."

"We *can't* just let her go!" Carl insisted.

"You think she means more to you than she means to me?" Cermak asked. "But I've run my head into too many stone walls not to know another when I see it. Count their guns, then count yours. Go read the notice on the porch. We won't get anywhere against him. But they say the government is still holding out in Montana and a few other states, and sooner or later they're going to have to finish this Duke. Maybe, if I tell them what he's doing, they'll do it now."

Brian said, "I think I see how we could get close enough to keep an eye on her, and maybe get her free later."

Carl said tensely, "How?"

"Join up with them."

Anne's father said angrily, "Don't you think he'll know enough to suspect your reasons, and put you where you can't do anything?"

Brian again described what he'd learned about the Duke and Cardan.

Carl snapped his fingers. "He wants *scientists!*"

Brian nodded.

Smitty said hesitantly, "*That* might work."

"You do what you want," Cermak said. "I'm going to find what's left of the United States and tell them what's going on here. I know you're doing this for Anne, Brian, but be careful this Duke doesn't suck you in. He'll be clever."

Fifteen minutes later Brian, Carl and Smitty had said good-bye to Cermak and their farmer friends, and were on the road, walking steadily and fast toward the tail of the column on the road ahead.

Before long, they caught up, explained what they wanted, and a tall benevolent figure with glittering ducal coronet greeted them cheerfully, quizzed them briefly on their specialties, and then rubbed his hands together.

"This is a splendid day, gentlemen. I've already captured a number of men scientists, and a woman scientist who was staying at a farm along the way. But you are the first to join me voluntarily." He beamed upon them paternally, then told them where to get shelter halves, blankets, and food when they camped that night. Then he sent for someone to help them get acquainted.

The next day, following stops at several more farms, the Duke and his men set out for their base.

Chapter 9

Built on a low bluff, near the place where a smaller stream joined a river, the Duke's base presented a number of problems to an attacker. Its location made approach tricky from any direction but one, while an impressive tangle of barbed wire blocked the way in that direction. A tall watchtower looked far out over the countryside, making surprise more difficult. The buildings in the camp were completely surrounded by an earth wall and an outer ditch. Like all of the Duke's arrangements that Brian had seen so far, the base had a solid look, as if it were very unlikely to fold up at the first blow.

Brian and his companions had been unable even to catch sight of Anne. They had hoped for better luck at the base, but what they'd seen so far looked unpromising.

Inside, Brian, Carl and Smitty were given quarters in a one-story building about forty feet long. At one end was a small room containing two double bunks. Across the short hall was a lavatory. The rest of the building was empty. Shortly after they'd gotten there, several of the Duke's men carried in a box containing an assortment of books, most of them high school texts in chemistry, physics and biology, and a plain wooden table.

Smitty said dryly, "Now we're all set."

Brian said, "Well, the main thing is to find Anne, then get in touch with Cardan."

"We'll have a swell time doing it. Did you notice the layout on the way in?"

Brian nodded. There had been half a dozen worn, two-story wooden structures side by side in a straight line, with another two-story building placed well back of one end of the line, and the low one-story building they were in now, set well back of the other end. These buildings were rectangular, and had apparently all been there long before the Duke. In addition, there was a newer-looking, large, square central mess hall, with another square building and the watchtower in a line back of it. The original rectangular buildings and the mess hall, seen from the air, would form sort of jack-o'-lantern's face, the straight line of six buildings, side by side, forming the mouth, the square mess-hall the nose, and the two separated buildings further back, the eyes. The other square building was at a point midway between and slightly above the eyes, with the watchtower in line further above it. In addition, a number of smaller buildings were scattered around without visible pattern. But what Brian and Smitty were thinking about was the particular way these buildings were split up.

When they'd marched in with the others through the gate, they'd found themselves between two lines of strong fence topped with barbed wire. This led directly through a second gate into a large circular yard with the mess hall in the center, and five additional gates leading to the five separated sections of the base. The row of six side-by-side buildings was split in half by the two lines of fence leading in from the outside. The two other widely separated buildings that sat back from the ends of this line were cut off from it by two more fences. The watchtower and the square building back of the mess hall were separated from the other buildings by double lines of fence topped with barbed wire. Each of these separated sections was connected to the others only by a gate to the yard around the mess hall. When they marched in, half the troops promptly turned right through one gate, while the other half went left through another gate. The line of six two-story buildings were evidently barracks. The Duke and certain of his officers and men went to the square building back of the mess hall. That must be the headquarters building.

Brian, Carl and Smitty had been shown into the small building they were now in. There remained only one place on the Duke's base that might house Cardan and his men. That was four fences away, on the opposite side of the Duke's headquarters and watchtower. Anne, if she was actually on the base, was apparently inside the heavily fenced headquarters building.

As Brian was contemplating these obstacles, there was a knock on the door at the end of the large room. A man came in carrying a covered tray and a wicker basket.

"Eats," he said cheerfully. He set the tray and basket on the table. "Duke says to start studying up on steam engines. You want to earn your pay and water, you're going to have to repair one we're bringing in."

Smitty said promptly, "For that, we'll need tools."

"Sure. You'll get tools." He grinned broadly and went out.

Carl said, "What was that about earning our pay *and water*?"

Brain scowled and raised the lid of the tray. The odor of roast beef, boiled onions and baked potatoes drifted out into the room. In the basket were three fresh rolls, split open, butter melting on them.

"There's plenty of food here," he said, "but no water."

Smitty came back into the room from the direction of the washroom. "There are four sinks, a shower, and a variety of other fittings in there. The only thing in the pipes is air."

They looked at the food a moment, then glanced at each other. Smitty said, "Well, we may die of thirst, but I don't plan to die of starvation." He pulled out a roll.

They were finishing a highly satisfying meal when there was a rumble and a clank outside. Brian opened the door and saw a collection of rusty scrap metal being unloaded from a wagon.

Carl came over. "What's *that*?"

Brian swallowed the last of his roll with a dry mouth.

The men on the wagon dropped off a couple of rods with large fittings at one end, swung the wagon around and went out. The gate clanged shut behind them.

Carl turned around and leaned back into the building. "Hey, Smitty!"

Smitty mopped his plate with his roll. "I'll be out in a minute. Look things over and see what you think."

Brian and Carl walked around the pile of parts, but were no wiser at the end than at the beginning. There were, among other things, a large, heavy cast-iron base, a heavy spoked wheel, rods of different shapes and sizes, a cylindrical piece of metal, a good-sized piston, a little tank, odd lengths of pipe, and assorted loose bolts and cap screws. To one side lay a greasy cloth with a hammer and a variety of wrenches and other tools wrapped up in it.

Smitty came out the door of the building wearing a look of contentment, and walked around the pile. He bent over, pulled out one of the rods and examined the large end carefully, got up, and leaned over to pull out another part.

On the far side of the fence, a good dozen of the Duke's men lounged around, grinning and watching the obvious discomfiture of Brian and Carl.

Smitty straightened up. "It's all here. In fact, some joker has thrown in some extra pieces to foul us up."

"Great," said Carl. "What is it?"

Smitty looked surprised. "It's a low horsepower, side-crank, slide-valve steam engine. See, here's the crosshead, this is the connecting rod, and there's the crankshaft. The whole thing has already been put together and then disassembled. You see the grease here, and the way this rust has been scraped away so the metal is shiny where the parts have been fitted together?"

Carl shook his head. "I'm just manual labor on this job."

Brian was struggling to remember what little he'd ever learned about steam engines.

Smitty said, "Do just as I say. First, bring that table out so we can get some of these parts up out of the dirt. Then we'd better start putting it together. I'm thirsty already."

Under Smitty's directions, they began assembling the engine. At dusk, one of the Duke's men carried out a gasoline lantern which cast its white glare and hard shadows on the scene. Around midnight, the three men, covered with perspiration and dizzy with thirst, stood back from the finished job. They were through.

The piston was connected to the piston rod, the piston rod to the crosshead, the crosshead to the connecting rod, the connecting rod to the crankshaft. The valve gear was all connected up. If they had a source of steam, the thing should work.

There was a clang as the gate opened and three men came in carrying buckets of water, while a fourth man looked over the engine, grinned, and said, "Okay, you'll do. The Duke'll see you tomorrow morning at eight." He nodded to the others, who set down the water.

Brian, Carl and Smitty drank the cool water cautiously, like men who have crossed the desert and are afraid to take too much at once. They fell into their bunks, exhausted— only to be blasted out of bed by a bugle thrust in the nearest doorway. They were sure they'd slept about an hour; it turned out to be six a.m. The roar of a megaphone invited them out for half an hour of violent calisthenics. A tray containing three steaming bowls of corn-meal mush was delivered to them at seven ten, followed by another six buckets of water. A small wood stove was lugged into the room, and several men were connecting it up as Brian, Carl and Smitty trudged sleepily out to the gate and said, "We're supposed to see the Duke at eight. Where do we find him?"

"At the palace. Through that gate to the left."

The "palace" turned out to be the large square headquarters building near the watchtower. This had a porch completely around the base and the second floor, with several business places, namely the Palace Barber Shop, the Palace Refreshment Stand, and the Palace Clothes and Equipment Mart, on the first floor. Beside a broad flight of stairs to the second floor was a sign in the shape of an arrow, with the letters D.U.K.E.

The second-floor porch, running completely around the building, had a variety of doors opening off it. To Brian's right as he left the steps was a door marked D.U.K.E. Against the wall nearby was a large grandfather clock, plainly put there as a hint to people to come and leave on time. The clock now said three minutes before eight. On the other side of the door from the clock stood a guard, who watched them with no particular expression.

"We're early," Brian commented. "If we go in now, he'll be mad. Let's walk around for a few minutes."

Smitty grunted. "Good idea."

The guard paid no special attention as they took the lucky opportunity to walk around to the opposite side of the building, where the porch looked down over the two-story building that they thought must house Cardan and his men. As they watched, a broad, powerfully built man with a frayed cigar stub clenched in the corner of his mouth opened the door at the end of the building, and nodded to someone within.

Unnecessarily, Carl murmured, "That's Cardan."

From within, a tall blond man, and a sharp-featured man with dark hair, stepped out carrying a box containing dull whitish oblongs about four inches long by three wide.

Smitty said in a low voice, "Soap."

Brian caught his breath.

Just then, there was the sound of a door closing around the corner of the building, and the Duke's voice was low but clear.

"My dear," said the Duke, "I could end your resistance very easily. But I want your decision to be freely made."

Anne's voice carried a trace of exasperation. "I've already told you my decision."

"But that's the *wrong* decision. You don't know what you're trying to throw away. I offer you position which no one else in this world can offer. Don't smile. Already I control this base and the outlying camps. I have brought peace and order to a region that would have been lost to starvation and murder. This is only the beginning. Through the entire country, there's a crying need for peace, order and central direction. There is a need, and I supply the lack. What you see now is just the beginning of a snowball."

The voices were coming closer.

Brian and his companions went quietly down the porch in the opposite direction, and were waiting outside the Duke's office when, looking exasperated but stubborn, he walked in and was immediately all cordiality as he invited them inside and congratulated them on putting the steam engine together. He pulled aside a curtain on the wall to reveal a map of the roads and railroads of the state. The eastern part of the map was thickly crisscrossed with lines indicating tracks.

"As of now," said the Duke, "there are three means of rapid transportation here: horse, bicycle, and diesel truck started by compressed air. The horse has a top speed of, say, thirty-five miles an hour, and can't sustain it for more than a few minutes. The bicycle can go fifty miles an hour downhill, and up the same hill it goes one mile an hour with the rider pushing. Neither can carry much of anything as baggage, and in a storm the rider is fully exposed to the weather. The diesel truck can go fifty or sixty miles an hour over a long distance, carrying a considerable load, but we have a certain amount of difficulty supplying suitable fuel, and this will get worse before it gets better.

"In addition, the same thing that now blocks electricity seems to weaken the metal itself, and this engine relies for power on a rapid series of violent explosions inside the cylinders. As a result, the engines have to be pulled apart every few days. In short, we have nothing but unreliable means of rapid transportation at our disposal. This limits the radius of effective control of any military force we can form. It means that the only practical defense against anarchy is the creation of many small independent units, each self-sufficient and capable of defense against roving gangs of arsonists and murderers."

The Duke's fist banged on the desk. His eyes flashed. As Brian and the others waited alertly for an explosion of temper, the Duke beamed upon them.

"It won't do. I visualize in its place a mighty organization of steam locomotives, each capable of fueling by coal or wood, knitting together a network of armed camps under my own control, devoted to keeping order, eliminating karb, and bringing in supplies and recruits throughout a continuously expanding region. Such locomotives, pulling short trains, could average between forty and forty-five miles an hour, and travel, if need be, a thousand miles a day. They could do it without excessive strain or wear on the metal, and they could easily carry loads that would be too heavy for transportation by road. They would enable me to switch troops from one place to another very rapidly, and to unite a large region under one centralized control." He leaned back and beamed upon them. "The people who did the work that put this tool at my disposal would be very liberally rewarded."

Brian and the others went back to their little building with a clear picture of what the Duke had in mind.

"That So-and-So," said Smitty, "sees himself as a dictator, with a fleet of locomotives carrying his private army around the country from one place to another."

"Sure," said Carl. "And he can do it, too. People will be so glad to get the gangs off their necks that they won't realize they've been taken over till it's too late."

Brian said, "Anne's father was right. We've got to find out if there's some piece of America left somewhere, and join up with it."

"Remember, he's got Anne," Carl reminded.

"We know where she is, anyway—and where Cardan is," said Smitty.

Brian glanced out the window at the double fence, "We've got to find some way to get in touch with them."

Outside their door, there was the crash of metal.

Smitty swore.

The door opened. One of the Duke's men said, "This came out of an old lumber mill. Duke wants it working again. You get your water when she works. Let us know if you need anything."

Outside was a formidable heap of scrap that made what they'd worked on the night before look brand-new.

In the next few weeks, Brian, Carl and Smitty repaired eight old steam engines. Food, fuel, clothing, special privileges—and water—were their rewards. The first thing any of them knew of a new job was the sound of its being unloaded and the announcement that they would get water when they had it finished. They took to hoarding water in the sinks and washtubs, but there was a limit to the amount they could store, while there was no limit to the rusted, stuck, cracked, corroded antique engines they were supposed to repair.

At night, when they were between jobs, Brian, Smitty and Carl tested the fences around their part of the camp, and discovered an ingenious system of spring-loaded bells that immediately announced any attempt to get over the top. They could not cut the fence itself without it being discovered the next day, and the bottom of the fence turned out to be set in concrete. After a great deal of nighttime exploration, they finally found a weak place under the fence leading to a space between the outer wall and the fence surrounding the Duke's "palace." At the other end of this narrow passage was the place where Brian had seen Cardan, Maclane and Donovan; and here, too, was a spot where the fence could be burrowed under. While Smitty stayed behind in case a guard should come on one of the infrequent checks, Brian and Carl succeeded one cloudy night in getting under both fences, making their way through the darkness to Cardan's building, easing open the door, and getting in, only to be immediately knocked senseless for their pains.

Brian opened his eyes in a room lighted brightly by a kerosene lamp, with blankets over the windows, and the harsh flat planes of a man's face regarding him through a cloud of cigar smoke.

Brian recognized Cardan and, behind him, the sharp features of Maclane.

Brian dizzily sat up. His voice came out in a croak. "Hello, Chief."

Cardan answered with a bare grunt and glanced at Carl, who was looking around dazedly.

Brian sniffed, aware, through the smell of cigar smoke, of a complex of faint odors that might conceivably come from glycerin and a mixture of nitric and sulfuric acids at work.

He risked a guess. "I hope you're keeping it cool."

Cardan looked at him, then glanced at Donovan. "How's this batch coming?"

"Slow, as usual. We don't want any accidental reactions."

"When are you planning to get out?" Brian asked.

Cardan looked thoughtfully at the glowing tip of his cigar and considered the question. "Possibly next week. Do *you* have any plans?"

"First we wanted to get in touch with you. We're too worn out pounding on antique steam engines to plan very far ahead."

"That explains why the pressure on us has let up a little," Cardan said.

Brian asked, "What can we do to help?"

"There isn't much you can do," said Cardan, "except to keep caught up on your work and do nothing to make them suspicious. As for how we're going to get out, you may have noticed a big piece of wheeled machinery on your way in."

Brian shook his head. "It's black as pitch out there."

"Well," said Cardan, "there's an antique steam tractor out there. This so-called Duke wants it rebuilt and fitted with a blade—to make a kind of steam-powered bulldozer. We plan to distract attention with several dynamite blasts on the far side of the camp, use the bulldozer to shove the wall into the ditch, and get away in the steam cars and diesel trucks that are in for repairs at the time. We can't tell just what night will be right, but we'll let you know when it comes."

"What about Anne?"

Cardan took the cigar out of his mouth. "Is she here?"

Brian told what had happened, and Cardan thought a moment. "We could rig up something to immobilize the stretched wires that work that alarm system, then we could cut the fence, put a ladder up the side of that building and get her out that way. First, we'll have to find out what room she's in, but I'm sure we can do that."

Brian didn't like the idea of standing aside while the others did the work, but Cardan insisted.

"This has been planned for a long time, and we can't change it now. Don't worry. Just keep on as you have been. Don't do anything to arouse suspicion. We want to keep them happy till we blast our way out of this place. Just go on as you are till our man crawls in and tells you to clear out."

***

Doing as Cardan said and sticking to their usual routine was maddening, and to avoid thinking of the escape, they worked harder than ever. The Duke was delighted with them.

Soon they were at work in a large machinery shed, newly built between the palace and the watchtower. Here everything seemed to go wrong. Boilers were clogged, mechanical power-transmission lines tore themselves loose, engines vibrated, safety valves stuck, then let go with a roar and refused to close, governors ran the engines fast, then slow, then fast again, in a maddening rhythm that drove them to distraction; and in the midst of this chaos, the Duke came in covered with soot and dragged them outside for a look at their half-collapsed smokepipe. Only gradually did they begin to straighten out the chaos. And then one night Brian woke to hear Carl say urgently, "Come on, Brian! The chief says we're leaving!"

Brian stumbled to his feet, dressed rapidly, and stepped to the door. As he went out, there was a dull impact at the back of his head, a burst of dazzling lights, and he felt himself falling.

His last conscious thought as he spiraled into blackness was the realization that Carl had done it again . . .

***

Somewhere, there was a heavy explosion, shouts, and the sound of running feet. Then there was another explosion, the sound of shouts, a raining of dirt, pebbles, the thud of falling rocks, shouted orders, and a blast that seemed to go on forever.

A glare of light appeared, and a rough voice said, "There's one, Duke! There's one that didn't get away!"

Rough hands gripped Brian by the arms.

An open hand slapped him stingingly across the face.

The light glared in his eyes, and the Duke was looking at him with a cold intensity.

Chapter 10

Brian, seeing the spot he was in, groped for some way out. Before the Duke had the chance to speak, Brian said angrily, "Did that yellow-haired Judas get away?"

The Duke looked puzzled, then turned as two of his men came over, supporting a battered and swearing Smitty.

A look of perfect mutual understanding passed between Brian and Smitty. If Smitty had had any lingering doubt as to what had caused Brian's original delay in joining the rest of Cardan's men, it was gone now. Angrily, he said to Brian, "I tried to catch him, but he got away."

Brian said, "He smashed me over the head and knocked me senseless."

"I know. Then I chased him, and he cracked *me* over the head. He jumped into some kind of truck and a whole bunch of people went right out through the wall."

Smitty was obviously trying the same gambit that had occurred to Brian. The only trouble was that, first, it all rang slightly false to Brian's ears; and second, if the Duke separated them, they would have no chance to get together on a story. Brian might say one thing and

Smitty something else. The only chance they had seemed to come from the unmistakable indignation in their voices. The men around the Duke looked puzzled. The Duke himself glanced first at Brian, then at Smitty, as if urging them to go on.

But Brian, who'd had very little practice in misrepresenting things, was afraid of the fantastic and transparent web of lies he might spin if he once got started. Smitty, on the other hand, had no way to know what Brian might already have said, and was afraid to go on for fear he might contradict him.

The Duke was glancing impatiently from one to the other when Brian realized Smitty's predicament.

With silence now stretched to the breaking point, there rose from the depths of Brian's subconscious a liar's credo that he had heard somewhere: *Always stick as close to the truth as possible—only change what has to be changed.*

With this for a guide, Brian said, "Something woke me up. I said, 'Carl?' Then he said something like 'The chief wants us outside.' So I got dressed and came out. The instant I opened the door there was a blinding flash, and the next thing I remember there were rocks and dirt raining down around me."

The Duke remained silent, but one of the Duke's men said, "How come you knew it was Carl? It was dark in the room, wasn't it?"

Brian perspired. He had uttered only four sentences and already he was trapped.

Smitty got him out of it. "Carl would get up and prowl around at night." This was true enough, as, before Cardan's warning, all three of them had prowled around at night.

The Duke glanced at Brian. "Carl said, 'The chief wants us outside.' And you thought he meant me?"

Brian realized that this had been another mistake, but he managed a convincing shrug. "Who else?"

One of the Duke's men said, "That's what the rest of the scientists called the head scientist who smokes the cigars—chief."

"Then," said the Duke, "evidently Carl found some way to get to the others, and threw in with them. Just as he was leaving, someone called him, and he was nervous and afraid he'd be followed, so—" The Duke glanced at Brian. "Let's feel that bump." Brian winced as the Duke's fingers probed the tender spot, and then the Duke said, "Obviously, these two were fighting on our side. Let them go so they can check the machine shed for us."

Brian and Smitty were greatly relieved by the Duke's leniency with them, but not by the change that came over the base as the Duke pointed out to his shame-faced followers what could have happened if this had been an attack instead of an escape. Discipline was tightened up, and Brian and Smitty found themselves constantly guarded—not, apparently, because the Duke really distrusted them, but just to be on the safe side. In the next few weeks the new and stricter routine became solidly established, and Brian and Smitty couldn't see the slightest possibility for escape.

The Duke's most distant patrols reported the successful escape of Cardan's men, Anne, and Carl. Anne, the Duke never mentioned, but he determinedly put his energies into repairing the damage done to his base and his plans.

By now, the Duke had acquired more old steam

engines and steam cars. Some he wanted made very light and fast. Some he wanted made into the equivalent of armored tanks. Others were to be shielded around the engine and part of the cargo section, and equipped to carry heavy loads of water and fuel. Gradually, a steam-powered armored force came into existence, capable of moving over the roads in a body at thirty or forty miles an hour by day.

The steam-powered workshop in the shed was now equipped with power lathes, drills, saws, and a blacksmith shop. The Duke was selecting the best-fitted of his men to do skilled work, and the competition was keen because of the relief from the continuous exercises and drills.

By now, the Duke's men had regular ranks and insignia, and a standard uniform to be worn at all times except when off duty. But the men were busy and off-duty hours were rare. Flying squads of cavalry roamed the countryside hunting for "karbists." The Duke's armored force prowled the roads and highways, spotting towns that had been taken over by gangs, sending word back to the base by fast steam-car, and often by their mere appearance overawing and demoralizing the gangs before the infantry arrived in short trains of steam-drawn wagons.

Brian went along on one of these trips, huddled between the driver and the gunner, sucking in oven-hot air and feeling his nerve-ends tingle at the thought of what could happen if a high-velocity bullet should slam through the improvised armor and pierce the boiler. His experiences led him to provide heavier armor for selected parts of the steam cars, relocate the boilers, and put in a device to provide ventilation for the men.

He and Smitty now had in mind what they could do if they could only get one of the faster steam cars fueled and ready, and a half-hour's head start. But now the Duke's guards were perpetually alert, kept that way by special exercises, by a squad of daredevil "guard-catchers" whose job it was to get past careless guards, and by a merit system that brought extra privileges to guards who halted the "guard-catchers" with a shouted warning, and extra kitchen-duty to those who failed to spot them in time.

The Duke's men were gradually becoming an elite corps, with the pride of such an organization, and while they regarded Brian as one of themselves, he could not get out because he lacked the proper pass, and the Duke saw to it that either he or Smitty was always on strenuous duty at the base when the other was out.

Late spring turned to summer. The Duke's territory expanded, and his army grew with the volunteer sons of farmers and town dwellers, eager for the chance to rid the country of outlaws and parasites.

As the summer passed, the Duke's control reached farther, and became stronger at the same time. Brian and Smitty were kept working on steam locomotives, and they now had a trained crew to help them. By fall, the crew was doing all the maintenance work, and Brian and Smitty had a combined laboratory and office in a workshop that had grown to the size of a small factory.

One day in late fall, Brian looked up from a new chemical bench, and realized that he was no nearer to Montana than he had been that spring. He was here. Anne—and Carl—were there. And the chances of escape were worsening. It was no longer possible to escape the

Duke's grasp by going thirty miles away. His control now stretched out for well over a hundred miles, with the fast steam-cars providing a delivery and messenger service that knit the whole together. Brian himself had helped work out the compound for the signal flares and design the mirrors that soon would be used to flash warnings and messages from one end of the Duke's domain to the other, along a special chain of stations centering at his headquarters. At a word of command, the roads could be blocked and the guard posts alerted for fugitives. If Brian was going to escape, he should do it now.

But Brian was determined to escape with Smitty, and the Duke chose this time to send Smitty out with a crew to repair a steam locomotive that had just been found by a scouting party.

Time passed.

The chain of signal stations was completed, the guards remained as alert as ever, and then the countryside was deep in snow, the streams iced over, and the mercury hovering around zero.

One evening in the pit of winter, when the temperature had plunged deeper yet, the Duke sent for Brian. After questioning Brian closely on the progress of his work, the Duke leaned back in his big chair and put his feet on the shiny bumper of a cast-iron stove that radiated a steady comforting warmth.

"You've done well, Brian," said the Duke expansively. "You don't mind if I call you Brian, do you?"

"No, of course not," said Brian, puzzled by the sudden friendliness.

"I've watched you," said the Duke, beaming, and

pulling over a kind of humidor on wheels. "You've done good work."

"Thank you, sir."

"Even though," said the Duke, opening the lid of the container and taking out some cheese crackers, "you've wasted a certain amount of time trying to find some chance to get away."

Brian started to protest.

The Duke paused with the crackers and smiled. "People become leaders, not because they understand test tubes or bank balances, but because they understand *people*."

Brian looked at him a moment, then said, "How long have you known this?"

"Since the night the others got away. I'd suspected it before that time. Of course, I knew Cardan and the others wanted to get away. What I didn't appreciate was their ingenuity. You see, I lacked the technical knowledge to realize what they could do. It was the soap, wasn't it?"

"The soap?"

"A by-product of soap manufacture," said the Duke, "is glycerin." He waved to a small shelf of books nearby. "I've been more careful since that experience. They made soap for us, and glycerin for themselves. From the glycerin, by the proper procedure, nitroglycerin can be prepared. And from nitroglycerin can be made dynamite. Just what the exact steps they followed were, I don't know." He was watching Brian alertly, with an expression of good humor. "I'm surprised to see that you're interested rather than uneasy. Apparently, *you* didn't make it for them, after all."

Brian shook his head. "I suspected the whole thing

when I saw the soap carried out—that is, I suspected they were making explosive, and could use it to get away—but I was too busy working on steam engines to have helped them, even if I'd wanted to."

"Nevertheless, you'd planned to leave with them." It wasn't a question but a statement.

"Anything I might say," said Brian, forcing a smile, "would tend to incriminate me. But if you knew this then, why did you accept our story?"

"Why not? I needed you. And it was obvious that you'd missed the opportunity to get away. The only question was, would the men believe you? If not, I would have to devise a punishment that would satisfy their anger, while still enabling you to recover and be of use. I've never seen a worse liar, but with my help, luckily you convinced the men that you were innocent."

Brian speechlessly accepted the dish of crackers the Duke held out to him.

The Duke peered into his box on wheels, extracted two mugs and a large Thermos bottle, and filled the mugs with steaming cocoa. "There's nothing like a fire and a cup of good hot cocoa when it's twenty below outside. Yes, the situation was very bad that night, and the best I could make of it didn't correct it entirely."

"Certainly discipline was tightened up. You've gained a lot of territory since then."

"True, but against the petty opponents I've had to contend with, territory is easy to gain. It can be lost just as quickly to superior opponents. It's necessary to look ahead and consider the caliber of the opposition. In that light, the loss of Cardan and his men was very possibly fatal. Our organization here is primitive, and we need everything we can get in the form of scientific and engineering skill to strengthen us against the opposition."

Brian was puzzled. "What *is* the opposition?"

"The old habits and patterns of thought from before the disaster. New organizations, I can deal with. But to the northwest, the old pattern still holds. I thought for a time that it would die out, be extinguished in the disorder. But it has survived, and now it extends itself with lightning rapidity. When the old trumpet sounds with all its power, then the people rally to the old flag, and the banners of the new look cheap and shoddy. People obey me now because they judge me against a background of ruin and chaos. Let them see me for a time in comparison with things as they were before the disaster, and I will appear little. Let there be a choice between me and the old flag, and I will be lucky if my own men stick with me. *That* is why the loss of Cardan was a possible deathblow. He went to the northwest, and when he went, that block of scientific and engineering skill was transferred from me to them."

The Duke paused, the cocoa cup half raised, and his eyes gazing off as if he looked into a different world that Brian couldn't see.

"Before the escape of Cardan, the Federals were going under. Only one state and parts of two others still flew the old flag and held to the old ways. And the chaos was spreading, threatening to submerge them even there. Then it was as if the old way, in its death struggle, sent out a call for whoever was still faithful. Cardan heard that call, and he went. He wasn't the only one. For weeks around that time there was a flow of men, young and old, leaving here for the northwest. We stopped some, but we couldn't stop all. And it wasn't only hands and guns that went north. Brains went north, too. A few months later their crisis was broken. And that is the opposition I'll be measured against someday."

Brian listened in astonished silence, noting a strange shine in the Duke's eyes as he spoke of the old flag.

"Why," said Brian, "if you feel that way—?"

The Duke raised his hand. "I came into the world from a direction that gave me a poor perspective on the old ways. Let's not talk of that. Let's talk of what we have here. Everyone in my organization is looked after. There is no graft, no crookedness. Karbists are destroyed on sight, not left to burden and poison the rest. Child-killers and dope-runners lead a short life here. Every man is honest, because he knows that in his honesty he has the full power of the organization behind him. You've seen order brought out of chaos, and the countryside made safe for honest men who are willing to work."

The Duke talked on, and what he said seemed true. Brian felt his personal power, and, somewhere in the background of his mind, he was always aware that the man could snap his fingers, say, "Kill this man," and Brian would be killed.

"What I've done," the Duke went on, "I've been able to do because I understand people. But I need someone who understands *things*. I need a right-hand man who can run the mines and factories, who can knit the broken bits into a smooth-running system. I need someone like that, and so does the whole country. I offer you this job, and with it, authority and power second only to my own."

For an instant, Brian wavered. Then abruptly he saw the fallacy in the Duke's position. As in other dictatorships, the power was concentrated in one man. But even if one man survived the power without delusions of grandeur, what happened if he was shot, died of heart failure, or fell down a staircase? Immediately, everything would be thrown into chaos. In this case, Brian would be second in command, but he would have been put there by the Duke, and his power would rest on the Duke, who would be gone. Inevitably, there would be a power struggle. Granted that the Duke had shown skill and restraint in the use of his power, what assurance was there that the next man would do the same?

The Duke, seeing Brian's hesitation, smiled. "I can understand your hesitation. But I wouldn't offer you this if I weren't sure that you could do the job, and that you wouldn't misuse the power. But there's no need to decide right now. Think it over."

That discussion was the first of many that Brian had as the subzero cold held military operations to a standstill, and the Duke craved companionship and conversation in the long winter evenings. One night, he raised the question of the disaster that had caused the trouble.

"A clever device," said the Duke. "It has us hamstrung, tied in knots. I wonder how fast the Russians are progressing while we are still trying to get back on our feet?"

Brian, convinced that the Russians had been hurt as much as anyone, argued that the disaster had resulted from an accident. The Duke nodded. "Maybe. But it so nearly collapsed our whole structure that it's hard to think it could have been *entirely* accidental."

"I don't know," said Brian. "We'd gotten so that any delay anywhere tended to paralyze the system. A short circuit could knock out power in a whole district. A shipping strike could stop whole industries. Everything was so knit together and interdependent that a failure in any part reacted on the whole."

Another night, toward spring, Brian excused himself on the grounds that he was worn out. The Duke smiled. "You're doing the work. You should have the rank and reward." The next night, the Duke sent for Smitty, who came back close to midnight and said, "I wish I was back with Cardan. This bird is out of his mind. He asked me how I'd like to be a marquis and have everybody bang his head on the floor for me. I think that's what he was talking about. How is a man supposed to do his work when he has to be up half the night talking nonsense?"

It occurred to Brian that the Duke was sending a gentle hint that he was growing impatient. Brian would have to decide soon, one way or the other. This little push decided Brian. He sat up and swung his feet over the edge of the bed. Smitty was by the stove, warming his hands after the icy trip back from the Duke's palace. The room was barely warm, but the floorboards were icy under Brian's bare feet.

"Listen," he said, "are those guards outside again tonight?"

"They're huddled in the anteroom, feeding chunks to the fire. Nobody's *outside*. Out there, you can feel your nostrils congeal and your nose turn blue every time you take a breath."

"I wonder about the guards at the gate."

"They're there, no doubt, and just as cold as everyone else." Smitty turned to thaw himself on another side. "What are you thinking?"

"I noticed on the work sheets that a fast steam car got repaired today. It's ready to go out tomorrow."

Smitty was silent an instant, then he gave a low whistle.

"Ye gods, Brian! Tonight is no night for that. No one in his right mind would go out tonight!"

"That's the point."

"You mean, they wouldn't be expecting it?"

"Of course they wouldn't. You just said so yourself."

Smitty looked out the window, where the icicles dangled five feet long. "I wish I'd kept my mouth shut."

Brian got up and looked out.

A full moon shone on the snow-covered roof and icy ground. Everywhere he could see, the windows were dark and the walks and roadways empty.

Excitedly, he said, "This is our chance. We've been working all this time for the Duke because we had no *chance* to get away. Now is the chance!"

"Brian, *listen*—"

Brian was already taking the blankets from the bed.

Smitty said anxiously, "What are you going to do with them?"

"We're going to rip one into strips and knot them to make a rope. When I'm down there, you throw the other blankets down to me, because we're going to need them in the steam car. But first I'm going to see if I can't write the Duke's signature."

The next forty minutes saw them make their way, fingers stiff with cold, down the improvised rope to the ground, then slip and teeter over the uneven ice to the entrance door of the repair garage.

From the guardroom inside, a voice said, "Come on, Ed, throw in another piece. What ails you?"

"Hit this chunk a crack with your rifle butt, will you? It's froze to the ground."

Smitty, shivering, murmured, "We can break a window in back."

"No," whispered Brian. "They'd hear when we opened the big door."

He knocked on the door. "Open up! Duke's orders!"

The door came open and two rough figures looked out. "My God! What could bring anyone out on a night like this?"

"Fire in the oil field," said Brian. "It came in on the flasher an hour ago. Duke wants it out, and no one there knows how." Brian spread his hands at the stove. "We can blast it out, I hope. First we've got to figure out some way to get near the thing."

"What's the trouble?"

Brian grimaced. "Too hot."

This brought a round of laughter, and if there had been any trace of suspicion, it was gone now.

The guards helped them check the steam car. Oil, water, and gas gauges showed full, the chains were on the wheels, and the fabric top and side-curtains were as tight as they could be made. When steam pressure was built up, the guards folded back the building's heavy doors, Brian advanced the speed lever, and the car rolled out smoothly, skidded, crabbed along sidewise on the ice, then straightened out again.

At the gate, Brian thrust out an oblong of paper bearing the date and the printed words, *Give these men every possible assistance*, with a fair imitation of the Duke's scrawl beneath it.

The men in the gatehouse turned up the oil lamp and, in the glow from the smoked-up lamp chimney, huddled over the little piece of paper, then asked, "What's broke loose that he sends you out on a night like this?"

Brian told the same story he'd told the other guards. It brought the same laugh, then the paper was handed back.

Brian eased the car forward as a powerful crank raised the gate, to the sound of a heavy snap as the base of the gate broke loose from the ice. Then they were outside.

Already, as they pulled their blankets around them, they could feel their feet growing numb.

But behind them, the Duke's base was fading into a dim shadow in the moonlight.

And ahead of them, the frozen road was wide-open, stretching out unguarded into the far distance.

***

It was daylight when they reached the first of the rare fuel and water stations that dotted the roads at long intervals. To Brian's astonishment, the place was a smoking shambles.

"Chimney caught fire," said one of the men who turned as Brian came over. "The damned fool didn't have the sense to clean the soot out." He looked at Brian's car. "What brings you out in this weather? You after those escapees?"

Brian kept his face straight, nodding. "No chance you'd have noticed them?"

"An army could have gone past and we wouldn't have seen it. We had our hands full with this thing."

"When did you get the word?"

"Came over the flasher two hours ago. I wouldn't break my neck if I were you. With the stations closed to all traffic, they'll run out of steam soon enough, or get nailed when they come in for fuel."

Brian went back to the car and told Smitty the bad news. Then they drove in silence till Smitty said, "Look, this country is familiar. This is where we were earlier, before the Duke showed up."

Brian looked around in surprise. "I think you're right."

Twenty minutes later they were in the yard of the Barnaby farm.

"Yes," said the elder Barnaby, "you don't have to say a thing. We know all about it. They had messengers going from house to house on horseback not an hour ago. Now you take the four horses we're raising for the Duke's service, my eldest boy and Ed Schmidt's son, and knock me over the head before you go so I can tell the Cols you took the horses by force and the two boys for hostages."

" 'Cols'?" said Brian.

"Citizen's Obedience League. I don't know if the Duke planned that or it just grew up naturally, like toadstools where the ground is rotten. If you make it to America, tell them to come as soon as they can. The teaching in the schools here is changed; all the children swear allegiance to the Duke, and the secret police plant spies in every town and every house. My own daughter is in it, and she'd turn me in as soon as she'd spit, except that this morning she's away at a group meeting."

Brian stared at him. "That bad? But what do you mean, 'If you make it to America'? This *is* America."

Barnaby shook his head. "No, it isn't. I mean, where they still fly the flag. Where they still *vote*. Tell them the Duke's neat system. First, he ends karb. Everybody's happy, and everybody goes along with his rules. But his rules never end. By the time the karb is wiped out, his representatives have moved in, and everything is split up into compartments. Nobody can move off his place without permission. If you do, you're hanged for a karbist. All it takes is a piece of paper, and your property is redistributed—Duke's orders."

"But you can complain to the Duke!"

"When first you have to go to the local representative for a travel permit?"

Brian shook his head. He looked around and saw two strong boys leading horses that were saddled and ready.

"Smitty," said Brian, "would you see if there are guns in the back of that car? The work sheet said it was a patrol, not a courier car."

Smitty climbed inside and came out carrying two rifles by the slings. Brian saw that they were Springfields. The Duke's choice of weapons coincided with that of Cardan, especially in cold weather, when a complicated action might make trouble. Smitty handed one gun to Brian and one to one of the boys. A moment later he was out with two more rifles, and with bandoliers of ammunition.

"We may have to fight," Brian said. "You can say I told the boys that once I got them out of here they could never turn back. They'd be hanged for violating the no-travel law. That will explain why they fight, if we have to fight."

Barnaby agreed.

The women came out with water and sandwiches, and put small bags in the pockets of the men's coats. Then Barnaby said, "Now, don't waste any more time. And leave a bump I can use for proof, and a bruise to show where I hit the ground."

Ed Schmidt finally stepped forward. There was a quiet thud, and Barnaby crumpled to the ground.

"On your way," said Schmidt. He glanced at his son. "And mind you, boy, when you shoot, don't waste bullets firing over their heads! Aim for the chest, and leave it to Providence to save the vermin if it's God's Will."

The boy nodded, tears streaming down his cheeks.

The women reached up to kiss their sons good-by, and Schmidt said, "Hurry. We've got to report this."

And then Brian and the others were on their way.

The sun was up now, and with it as they rode came a day as unbelievably hot as the night had been cold. To their astonishment, the pleasant warmth of the early morning turned into summerlike heat by noon. The glare of the sun on the snow all but blinded them, and ground, heaved up by frost, gave way under their horses' hoofs. Their progress was maddeningly slow.

That night, it was warm, and they could hear the rushing of streams filling up with the run-off from the melted snow. They fed the horses at roofed-over sheds where hay was piled to feed cattle. They slept in the hay, and for food, they added water to some of the mixture of ground dried corn and sugar that the women had put in their pockets. The next day dawned sunny and hot, and that night the two boys "karbed it" at a farmer's smokehouse, returning with enough meat to keep them contented for a few days of travel. Then days and nights blurred together until all they knew was that they were headed north and west, and finally they were out of the Duke's territory. No identifiable sign told them that, but there seemed to be something in the air—a feeling of freedom that Brian had forgotten existed.

It was a little later that they crossed the brow of a hill, and Smitty said, "Look back there."

Brian turned around.

Behind them, far back, were a dozen little dots, spread out over the country in two staggered files, and coming toward them fast.

The Duke's men had found the trail.

Chapter 11

After studying the distance between themselves and their pursuers, and the speed at which the pursuers came, young Barnaby made a suggestion. Instead of a desperate attempt to gain distance, they went at a pace that would spare the horses, moving fast and easily as the Duke's men drove their mounts to ever greater exertions and steadily whittled down the distance. The country was more broken now, and here and there were rocky stretches where a trail was hard to follow. At one of these places, the Duke's men thundered off in the wrong direction, and when they discovered their mistake and turned back, their winded horses began to give out. By nightfall, Brian and the others had more than their lead. The next day, they saw only occasional distant signs of pursuit, and that night, they were confident.

The next morning, the Duke's men were right behind them, and there was nothing to do but make a run for it. But the Duke's men had faster horses. Ahead of them, as they plunged down a hillside, Brian could see a pair of shining railroad tracks, and, off in the distance, a peculiar towerlike structure. Something moved at its peak, and swung back. What it was, he didn't know and then there was no time to think of it.

Now they were part way up the side of the mountain, and a tumble of rocks offered some refuge so they sprang off to crouch behind the rocks and the four Springfields brought two of their pursuers from the saddles. The others split and raced right and left, swinging up the hill to come at them from opposite sides.

Smitty said, "We could go downhill, while they're split—"

"No future in it," said Brian. "We've got to shoot the horses. It'll be hard to get us out of here then."

A few minutes later the Duke's men were rushing them, racing downhill from left and right. The bullets zinged off the rocks and over their heads, fortunately missing them, but they, in turn, hit nothing. As they half rose to fire at the retiring horsemen, the bullets filled the air around them like angry bees.

"They're uphill of us!" shouted young Schmidt, and Brian saw the trick that almost finished them. A few of the Duke's men were armed with semi-automatic weapons, and two of these men had dropped off uphill when the charge started. There they'd waited for their opponents to turn their backs, and only good luck had saved Brian and the others. And now, the siege began.

The sun glared down as the Duke's men crept from cover to cover, a few of them always on horseback, ready to rush in if the chance presented itself. The enemy's ammunition seemed inexhaustible. Young Barnaby got a bullet through the arm. Sharp fragments of rocks brought the blood streaming from Smitty's forehead. Schmidt, crazed by thirst as the afternoon wore on, rose up screaming at the Duke's men, and a steel-jacketed bullet went in one cheek and out the other, leaving him suddenly sober and glaringly conscious that the next piece of insanity would be his last. Brian, deaf from the incessant gunfire, was still unhurt, but aware of his dwindling stock of ammunition and of a growing sense of detachment from reality. The afternoon slid by, and the white sun blazed down from a declining angle. The Duke's men began to work around to take advantage of that angle, knowing that just at sunset, Brian and the others would be blinded from that direction.

Brian, roasted by the still-hot sun, his throat parched, lay in the waves of heat reflected from the rocks, and breathed in the odor of gunsmoke and hot horseflesh. He counted his ammunition again. He had three clips left. That was fifteen rounds, plus two shots in his gun. He thought he'd done well to have that much left. But it wasn't going to be enough. And the enemy's ammunition seemed endless.

Somewhere through the heat and the ringing in his ears came a distant wail. The Duke's men pointed, and those more distant squirmed away from the fight and ran to get their horses.

Brian twisted to look out between two rocks.

Down the mountainside, a locomotive thundered around the bend, drawing three freight cars. Atop the front engine fluttered an oblong of cloth, its red and white stripes, and white stars against a blue background, bringing a sudden lump to Brian's throat.

Then the Duke's men were racing on horseback toward the engine, waving their guns and firing warning shots.

The train slowed, came to a stop. The whine of a bullet over Brian's head warned him that some of the Duke's men were still on hand to keep Brian and the others pinned down. Brian crouched lower, determined to do what he could for the helpless train.

To his astonishment, several of the Duke's men lifted in their saddles, twisted and fell. A machine-gun rattle drifted up from the train.

The remaining horsemen returned the fire.

The sides of the freight cars slammed up and in. There was one concerted motion, and mounted cavalrymen were beside the train. The remainder of the Duke's men fell from their horses, and now the cavalry came up the hill, in two wide arcs, and the pair of the Duke's men who had stayed to pin Brian and the others down were on their feet and running. Brian, Smitty and the two farm boys saw one of their tormentors fall, and the other stagger, then throw up his hands as suddenly the cavalrymen caught up. Then the cavalry turned and rode to where Brian and the others stood up, swaying with exhaustion and still clutching their guns. The leader of the cavalry, a thin dark man with captain's bars and "U.S." at his lapel, said something to Brian.

Brian heard a faint sound, but pointed to the guns, the rocks, and his deafened ears. The captain spoke again, louder.

"Where are you from? The Duchy?"

Brian nodded, tried to speak, and couldn't. He saw the world begin to sway, and reached out to steady himself against a boulder. The captain turned to one of his men, who dismounted and gave Brian a drink from his canteen.

"You were," said the captain, his face expressionless, "in the Duke's service?"

Brian didn't move, studying the captain's expressionless face. He tried his voice, and the captain said, "Just nod for 'yes.'"

"We were prisoners," said Brian hoarsely. "These two boys were forced labor on a farm. My friend and I were at the Duke's headquarters under guard."

"Doing what?"

"Whatever the Duke told us. We did it or we died of thirst."

"What did he tell you to do?"

"Repair steam engines and steam cars, armor them, work on signals systems and factory repair."

"How long were you there?"

"Since last spring."

"And this was your first chance to escape?"

"We tried once before and didn't make it."

The captain studied them. "Raise your right hands. Face the flag on the locomotive. Repeat after me. 'Before God, I swear allegiance to the flag—'"

Brian and the others steadily repeated the words.

When the oath was completed, the captain relaxed and took out a small leatherbound book, and said, "Names?"

Brian said, "Brian Philips."

Smitty and the others gave their names, then the captain blinked. "Brian Philips," he murmured, flipped back through the book, and said, "Lieutenant, take charge of the burial and prisoner-interrogation details. Stay alert and in view of the lookout station. Troopers Quincy and Howe, dismount and help these two gentlemen into the saddle. All right, Mr. Philips, you and Mr. Smith follow me."

Brian, with no idea what was happening, barely able to cling to the saddle, was rushed to the train and he and Smitty put aboard. The captain called to the trainmen. With a clank of couplings, the train began to back. It reached the base of the embankment below the tall tower Brian had seen from a distance. The captain sprang from the locomotive to a ladder up the bank, climbing a ladder up the heavy timbers and vanished into the tower. At its peak, big semaphore arms swung up to attention, dropped wide, then swung up again. Then the tower was out of sight as the locomotive backed around a curve onto a track connecting at an angle, dropped off the two rear cars, pulled forward on a second track that curved to rejoin the line they'd been on originally, then backed up again to the ladder. A few minutes later the captain climbed down and shouted, "Take them all the way to Butte! We'll clear the track in front of you!"

The engineer waved his hand and the train began to move.

A trainman climbed back, heaved on the lever that slammed the long side door shut, then gave each several drinks from a canteen. Brian and Smitty, exhausted, found a pile of loose hay in a wooden pen, sank down in it and immediately were sound asleep.

A loud wailing blast, repeated again and again, woke Brian up sometime after dark. From somewhere far ahead, the blast was answered in kind, a distant wail that was repeated over and over. The engine picked up speed, the heavy *chuffs* becoming faster and faster, weaving a rhythmic pattern that sent Brian off to sleep again. When he next woke up, the engine was silent, and men were shining the beam of acetylene hand-lamps around the car.

Still half awake, Brian was rushed out into a street lit by widely spaced, soft gaslights, into a big building that trembled continuously underfoot. From somewhere came the scream and grind of machinery, then they went through a huge room where piles of coal glistened in the dim light. They passed a door from behind which came a clang and scrape of metal, walked along beside huge, asbestos-wrapped steam pipes, and then again were in a hallway, then rattling up in an elevator to a hall, high up in the building. Here the tremble and shake was less pronounced, the throb of coal-fed steam power just a murmur in the background, and one of the guards was knocking at a door lettered: "James Cardan, President."

"Come in," said the musical voice of Cardan's receptionist, Barbara Bowen.

Brian looked at her as in a dream, saw her smile, heard her say, "The chief's waiting," and a moment later saw the familiar broad, rugged figure behind the desk. The guards left, and Brian was abruptly wide-awake. He glanced around. Smitty was gone. A cigar rested in a tray on Cardan's desk, a thin wisp of smoke climbing up in the lamplight.

Cardan eyed Brian in silence for a moment. "What kept you from leaving with the rest of us?"

"A crack on the head."

Cardan's eyes seemed to drill into his, boring, seeking, probing. It occurred to Brian that he might not be believed. Suddenly angry, Brian glared back.

Cardan, his voice without intonation, said, "That's the story you told before."

"It's a story I'll never tell a third time."

Cardan looked at him a long moment, searching out his meaning, then suddenly he began to smile. He picked up the cigar, grinned, drew on it, and blew out a long puff of smoke.

"How did it happen this time?"

Brian described it.

Cardan shook his head.

"What happened then? What did you do?"

Brian told him the whole story. Before it was over, Cardan had gotten out a map and was checking the location of the Duke's installations. By the time they'd finished, the sky was growing light in the east, and Cardan said, "I guess it's time I gave *you* some information now."

He drew a rough outline map of the North American continent, penciled in several small ovals along the Eastern Seaboard, and marked the rest of the coastal area with heavy black strokes.

"The heavily settled places are gone—starvation, riots, epidemics, chaos. There are just a few enclaves here and there that held out. Canada came through pretty well, though Quebec split off on its own—it's New France now. The central part of the U.S., we don't know much about, but there's talk of a seaborne expedition through the Panama Canal—which we still hold—and up the Mississippi to find out."

Cardan drew several large ovals. "To the south, there's a colored state called 'Freedom Land,' and a lopsided Texas sandwiched between the 'Apache Nation' and a sort of bandit empire called 'Herrero's Kingdom.' Further north, taking in parts of half a dozen Western and Middlewestern states, we have this damned Duchy. It blocks us off the others. It threatens to lock us up west of the Rockies. When I say 'us,' I mean what nearly everyone calls 'America.' That's Montana, Idaho, Washington, Oregon, large parts of the six adjoining states, and a section of Colorado." He glanced at Brian. "You want to hear this?"

Brian nodded. He had a vague feeling of letdown now that he was finally here, but there was a sense of grim satisfaction, too. He said curiously, "Do we know anything about the rest of the world?"

"Quite a bit. A lot of ocean vessels are steam powered, and armed steamships can travel comparatively unharmed by the loss of electricity. We sent an expedition to try to reach the source of all the trouble, in Afghanistan. They crossed the oceans. But they weren't able to make it all the way."

"Why not?"

"It's not very nice there. Starting at about one hundred eighty miles from the site of the Helmand laboratory, metal becomes increasingly brittle. At about one hundred fifty miles, metal cracks and shatters, and the same effect becomes noticeable with other materials. A heavy leather belt, for instance, can be snapped between the fingers. At around one hundred twenty miles, the same weaknesses noticeably affect the human body. A stumble can mean a broken leg. The bones are brittle. The hands and feet become numb, as if from cold, thought is slow, and the release of energy by the chemistry of the body is slower yet. At a hundred miles, there's a sort of desert. Vegetation is dead or stunted. There's bare dirty sand, and crumbling rocks. The body has become exceptionally fragile, fatigue is continuous and breathing is very difficult—apparently because the body just can't assimilate the oxygen.

"All these difficulties seem traceable ultimately to a closer binding of electrons. If this effect extends all the way to the Helmand laboratory itself, it's hard to see why the lab hasn't been destroyed by it. Maclane thinks there may be a belt of interference around the lab, in which the effects are less severe than they are further away. We don't know. But distance makes a difference, and if you'll look on the opposite side of the globe from Afghanistan, you'll find a stretch of the South Pacific containing, among other little bits of real estate, Easter Island. This is about as far away from the Helmand project as you can get on Earth. There, electricity still works. America has taken those islands and heavily fortified them. Quite a few of our men are there. The hope is that we can work out a missile capable of traveling a large part of its flight without benefit of electrical devices, and land it on the Helmand lab. But it's quite a problem."

There was a soft bonging noise, a rattle of wires, and a cylindrical capsule about six inches long and two and a half in diameter traveled along a track and came to rest back of Cardan's desk. He reached out, flipped it open, and sat back to very carefully look through several typewritten sheets of paper. He wrote rapidly on a note pad, tore off the top sheet, folded it in the little capsule, and started it on its way back along the track.

"Donovan and Maclane," said Cardan, "have been grilling Smitty. He tells substantially the same story you do. With this 'Duke,' we have to be careful." Cardan put his cigar in the tray and leaned back, his hands clasped behind his neck. He blew out a cloud of smoke.

"I can offer you a job here or on Easter Island. They need another chemist out there. We need one here. The salary there is higher. But—" He smiled. "—There are other compensations here."

He got up, opened the door to the next room, and spoke quietly to Miss Bowen. He came back, sat down, and knocked the ash off the cigar.

A few minutes later, the door opened.

"Excuse me," said Cardan, getting up. "I have something to say to Miss Bowen."

Brian turned around. Standing in the doorway, her blond hair shining in the early morning sunlight slanting through the window, her blue eyes smiling, stood Anne Cermak.

Brian stood up, looking deep into her clear smiling eyes. Then the eyes changed.

"Oh, Brian," she said, and abruptly he was holding her close.

Long moments later, she said, "Let me—let me show you around the building. We can't stay here like this. Come on." She took his hand, and then Brian was looking at ingenious devices being developed to substitute for electricity. There were miniature steam engines and turbines, flexible insulated lines for conveying steam from central boilers, oil lamps with improved mantles that gave a clear white light and refused to break, unlike the usual fragile mantles. A little device to partially replace the flashlight drew a multitude of flints across a rough steel surface, the many sparks creating a pale white light that an eager technician had Brian try out in a nearby darkroom. There were mechanical phonographs brought to a high state of refinement, and a signal system that relied on fluctuations of hydraulic pressure in a long thin tube. To his astonishment, Brian saw substitutes for nearly every one of the simpler electrical devices he was used to. But the very number of substitutes, and the ingenuity that had had to go into them, showed what a pillar of civilization electricity had been.

"It's fine," he said when they were in Anne's small lab at last, "but it will be a lot better if we can get electricity to work again."

Anne nodded, then smiled suddenly, "We've forgotten something. Dad's on the railroad here, and he's off duty tonight."

Brian looked puzzled.

She laughed. "Don't you remember our dinner date?"

"Oh," he said, smiling. "Am I still invited?"

"Just try to get out of it."

"Well—" He'd forgotten that invitation made what seemed like years ago, just before the electricity went off and Carl came in to tell them Cardan wanted to see them—

And then Brian remembered other things.

"Carl. Where is he?"

"Carl? Why, he has a job here. He used to be on this floor, but Mr. Cardan moved him. I don't know just where—"

"Excuse me a minute." Brian's fists tingled. He was thinking of that last crack on the head, of all the insults and underhanded blows he'd experienced from Carl. He was remembering the difference between Carl and himself. As Carl had said, that difference was that Carl always won. The room around Brian seemed to grow momentarily lighter, then darker. Then his emotions were wrapped in cotton wool, and everything else in his life was put away to wait until he had a chance to settle with Carl.

He went down the hall to Cardan's office. "I'm looking for Carl," he said.

"You're just in time." Cardan turned to the window. "If you're quick enough, you might just manage to see him."

Brian threw the window up and looked out.

Down far below was the open platform of the train station. A long passenger train was starting to move, and just springing aboard was a tall, blond, athletic figure, the suitcase gripped in one hand showing bits of hastily packed shirts sticking out.

Brian studied the distance to the ground. The train gathered speed. It was obvious insanity to try to make the jump to the ground and run a race with a steam locomotive capable of seventy or eighty miles an hour.

But it took a distinct effort for Brian to pull his head back in the window.

"That train is headed for the coast," Cardan told him. "Carl just volunteered for the trip to Easter Island. All I did was tell him you were back."

Brian drew a deep breath, and Cardan watched him, smiling. Cardan had watched the struggle, and he knew what actuated the two men. And Carl's philosophy that he must always win was no defense against someone who always did his best, once that best reached a certain level.

Brian could feel himself gradually readjust to the situation.

If Carl had stayed there, Brian would have had no choice. But now Carl was gone. Brian gradually relaxed, and pulled down the window. He looked at Cardan and grinned.

"I have some questions I'd like to ask—about terms of employment."

Cardan sucked on his cigar. His face took on the shrewdly innocent look of a businessman determined to make a profitable arrangement, but who knew that the arrangement had to be truly profitable to both sides if he was to get the best work.

Then Brian was shaking hands, and was on the way down the hall to see Anne Cermak and make arrangements for their long-delayed dinner date.

Brian's body ached, and his skin felt dry and hot from yesterday's sunburn. He was wearing the same clothes in which he'd been chased across two states and spent the afternoon in a rock pile with a Springfield rifle and four dead horses. He'd been ambushed, shot at, driven through ice and smoke, forced to pillage for his food, turned into a steam-engine rebuilder by endless drudgery, and had only narrowly escaped the job of assistant dictator in one of the cleverest tyrannies since Nazi Germany. It came to Brian that he was a wreck, a shambles, and no woman would want him.

He pushed open the lab door. Anne smiled up at him and came into his arms.

It had been a rough two thousand miles, but at last he'd made it.

Brian was home.

PART II

SOLVER OF PROBLEMS

The Missile Smasher

The night air was warm and almost still, the only sound the faint lapping of the lake, far below, against the rocks. Long after sundown, the parapet atop the tower still felt warm. Richard Verner, crouched beside it, looked across the water at the dark, tree-lined shore, then down at the shadowy buildings below the tower. Nowhere could he see a guard.

The faint moonlight, diffused through high clouds, lit the stone floor that formed the top of the tower, to show a small metal table bearing several empty glasses, an ashtray and a half-empty bottle of suntan oil. Nearby, on the floor, was a thin mattress covered with a large beach towel. Beyond that was a dark bulky shape that in daylight could be seen to be a gaily-striped tent, like a tent at the beach where people might change their clothes.

In the faint moonlight, Verner quietly crossed the stone floor, to very gently draw open the rough canvas flap of the tent.

Inside, it was pitch dark. A current of heated air drifted

out past him. Then, as he carefully moved inside, he touched something hard and round, angled up from the stone floor toward the interior of the tent. In that instant, he knew that what he was here for was real, and not a fantasy after all.

The general who had brought the problem to him the week before had warned him it would seem unreal. Straight and spare, with a craggy face and tarnished pilot's wings above a triple row of ribbons, the general had said, "Mr. Verner, I understand you're a heuristician—that it's your business to help solve problems other experts alone can't handle. I suppose you must have seen many strange problems. But I doubt that you've ever seen one as strange as mine. I'd like you to look at this photograph, and then listen to me very carefully."

Verner took the slightly foggy color photo, and saw a gray stone tower, rising above thick green forest against a deep-blue sky. Atop the tower was a nearly flat-roofed tent, gaily striped. Just visible through the opening of the tent was a thing that looked like the end of a large telescope.

The general said, "My problem, Mr. Verner, involves our newest rocket-launching facility. Of the first six important launches from this site, one was successful, three went off-course so wildly that they had to be destroyed, and two were satellites that went into very unsatisfactory orbits. This is a record of one success and five failures. The trouble has been traced to a fantastically rapid build-up of heat at the base of the rocket. We are convinced that we have had, among other things, exceptional erosion of the nozzle through which the exhaust gases pass. These rockets are very carefully checked before launch. Nothing has been found wrong with them. Yet without something wrong, this heat buildup is impossible. The only explanation of these failures is *sabotage after the rocket is launched.*"

Verner sat back, eyes narrowed in concentration, the photograph in his hands.

The general said tensely, "We are at a crucial point in space research. These continued failures could give our adversaries a lead we might never overcome. They have every reason to sabotage our rockets. But how? How could they possibly sabotage a rocket *after it is launched?*"

Verner listened intently. The general's urgency gave his words added weight as he said, "There seems to be only one possible way. Some years ago, a method of forming light into a very intensely coherent beam was invented. This device was called the 'laser.' Since then, much highly-classified work has been done on it, here and abroad. We are satisfied that very intense bursts of coherent light, focused on our rockets as they reached a given altitude, could create the very heat effects that have caused us so much trouble."

"And this photograph?"

"That was taken by accident from a handling tower by one of our technicians. He didn't think anything of it till he noticed the thing inside the tent."

"What looks like a telescope?"

"Yes. But why mount a telescope inside a tent? One technician thought it was a telephoto camera lens. *We* think it's the end of a highly advanced projector of intense bursts of laser light. This is the exact kind of thing, Mr.

Verner, that we would have laughed at a few years ago. But a few years ago, we would have laughed at the idea of sending a man to the moon. We don't laugh at these things any more."

"Wouldn't a beam of *light* be seen?"

"The unsuccessful launches were carried out in full daylight, and the rocket, of course, makes a very dazzling glare by itself. The laser light would be focused in short intense bursts at the base of the rocket. In these circumstances, I doubt that we would see anything at all, except the final results of the heat buildup."

Verner thought about it in silence, his eyes half-closed, and then said, "The problem isn't just to stop the sabotage, is it?"

The general smiled. "I can see you're the man we need. No, we could end this sabotage in a number of ways. But think what would happen. To begin with, these saboteurs have set the device up in this tower, built years ago by a rich man who wanted his own castle, and started it on an island near what is now our launching site. His money ran out, but he got the tower finished, and it has walls several feet thick. The grounds there are so overgrown they're almost a jungle. The men who operate this device must *expect* us to rush out there, as soon as we discover it. They will methodically destroy the device, put their hands up, and get ready for eventual trial and prison sentence. They have already cost the country hundreds of millions of dollars worth of damage, but that's only the beginning.

"During the trial, this laser beam, which has worked only on a slowly-rising rocket lifting off from a fixed location, will be magnified into a new communist superweapon, to create an international scare. Next, we will be accused of Gestapo methods in capturing these people. They've undoubtedly got it all figured out, our move, then their move. We've considered every move we can make, and there isn't one that really pays us back for the damage they've already done the country. But we've studied some of the work you've done, and we're convinced you can find a way to hit them where they don't expect it, without our being directly involved, and throw them off balance."

Verner said, "You realize I often have to call on experts of every conceivable kind, for facts and for the use of their special skills?"

The general nodded. "Get whoever you need. We'll help, too."

Now, inside the dark canvas tent atop the tower, Verner carefully felt of the massive pipe-shaped brace, and cautiously ran his hand along the cool metal, to where the brace joined a second and a third brace. He could feel at the center a kind of heavy metal platform around a vertical pin, but the actual laser-device was not there. Next he ran his hand along the metal to the floor, felt the hollow where the heavy pipe of the brace was bolted to a flattened metal bar cemented into the floor. He straightened, and examined the rest of the tent.

To one side was a large dark blot on the stone floor, and he knelt beside it to find a hole leading down into the tower, the trapdoor opened back against the parapet. Several minutes of careful exploration disclosed, directly above the hole, a frame of heavy lumber supporting a large pulley, whose rope was coiled up in a corner of the tent.

Somewhere down in the tower was the laser device. When the time came, it would be hoisted on the rope and mounted. For now, it was out of reach.

Verner stepped out of the tent, and looked up at the large silent shadow, drifting overhead. He aimed a tiny shielded flashlight upward, blinked it twice, then twice again.

A smaller shadow detached itself from the larger, dropped down onto the tower, and turned uncertainly.

Verner reached out, took the soft cloth of the camouflage suit, and tugged gently. The shadow became a man of middle height, breathing a trifle hard from exertion and excitement. In a quiet whisper, Verner described the situation. The man nodded, and slipped into the tent.

Uneasily, Verner waited. Down on the ground below the tower, two large dim forms slipped in and out of the shrubbery and the deep shadows of the trees. Dogs, searching for any intruder.

From the tent came an occasional faint glint of light, too dim to reflect down into the tower, but bright enough so that Verner carefully drew the tent flap shut.

Overhead, the dark shadow moved a little aside, then back, and once a dim reflection showed for an instant a long line curving away toward higher ground in the distance, and a bar-taut line and dangling release-cord leading down to the tower.

Then there was a quiet rustle of cloth, and a murmur. "It's done."

Again, Verner flashed his light upward, and this time a long knotted rope swung across the tower. He caught it, waited till the other man climbed awkwardly up, then followed. As he pulled himself into the man-carrying basket of the balloon, it was the tower that took on a look of shadowy unreality. Then it was drifting away into the night, and Verner knew that they had either won or lost, but they wouldn't know the answer till the next day.

Early the next morning, the general stood beside Verner, watching the tower through binoculars.

"I don't see," he said, "how you will even know when that laser device is in place, much less hope to put them out of action. Remember, the mere sound of a helicopter will warn them, and then they'll destroy the laser."

In the binoculars, the striped tent stood out sharp and clear atop the tower—and suddenly blurred in a puff of dirty yellow smoke that billowed out from beneath it, burst out in a cloud past the flap—and then two men staggered out, the yellow cloud swirling around them.

From one side, fast and low, a helicopter shot across the treetops, whirled over the tower, climbed sharply, and the canvas tent, caught in a trailing net embedded with hooks, ripped up and off its frame, showing a thick stubby cylinder looming through the yellow smoke.

Already, a second helicopter was streaking in, to pause for an instant as a man wearing a gas mask dropped to the flat top of the tower, threw a bundle down the hole, bent intently at the cylinder, then lifted it and a cone fixed beside it, put them in a large net lowered from the helicopter, caught a rope and swung up.

The helicopter lifted, gained speed, and was gone.

Verner said, "Several cameras have already taken pictures of that device, from long distance, and from the helicopters. The man who took it from its base is an expert at defusing bombs and detecting booby traps. The large bundle he dropped into the tower was a little something extra—part payment for the damage these people have done. It may persuade them to be cooperative. Who knows?"

The general smiled. "Now we will proceed with the launch."

***

The rocket was a tiny dot high in the sky, and the engineers were grinning at each other, when the general said, "How did you manage to gas them from long distance, and how did you know when they had the laser in place?"

"We got a specialist in there who laid down a thin transparent insulating film where the laser was to rest, and who then, as I understand it, *sprayed* a thin circuit on the film. As soon as the laser was in place, it changed the electrical characteristics of the circuit. That activated a relay that touched off small gas cartridges packed into the hollow legs of the support."

"And what was that bundle that was dropped into the tower?" the general asked.

"To even up the damage the saboteurs have done, we have to do more than get the laser. Our own research people may already have a similar device. So the saboteurs need to be cooperative and answer a few questions."

The general smiled. "How did you propose to manage that? These men are tough."

Verner nodded. "The trouble at the top of the tower would be pretty sure to bring the others up in a hurry. And those on top would go down as soon as possible. It follows that both sets of them would pass through the room directly below the top of the tower."

A phone began to ring, and as someone reached for it, the general frowned and said, "How—"

"That room," said Verner, "is where the bundle went."

The technician holding the phone turned in astonishment to the general. "Sir, some self-confessed saboteurs are out at the gate. They want medical aid."

The general blinked. "What for?"

"Among other things they claim to have been attacked by swarms of hornets and a number of scorpions. But their main difficulty seems to be that they got unexpectedly tangled up with half-a-dozen rattlesnakes."

Verner said quietly, "There's an ambulance truck standing by with everything they'll need. But it would be ordinary courtesy for those saboteurs to answer a few questions first."

The general gave a low whistle.

"That," said Verner gravely, "should solve the problem."

The general grinned suddenly and turned to the technician.

"Send them in."

The Problem Solver and the Killer

The dead man lay face down on the polished board floor beside the bunk, the stag-handled hilt of a hunting knife jutting from his back. Blood had soaked his blue woolen bathrobe, and spread out in a dark pool on the bare floor. His arms were stretched forward so that he lay almost in a straight line, his hands near the night-table by the head of the bunk, his feet pointed to a window whose panes were heaped with snow.

Low on his left wrist, just above the place where the hand broadens out, was a stainless-steel watch with the face cracked; but the hands were pointing to the correct time—8:01. Nearby, glinting dully in the morning light, lay a pair of bent, broken rimless glasses.

Richard Verner rose from a crouch beside the body and glanced around the room. He had come to this isolated hunting resort on the advice of his friend, Bartlett, who assured him that a week-end in the fresh air would be a healthy change from the city, and from the clients who, having never heard of a heuristician when Verner desperately needed clients, now swamped him when he already had too many.

"The fresh air," Bartlett had insisted, "will do you good, Dick. It's a beautiful place, easy to reach, with detached cabins, and a central Lodge. You can cook your own meals, or eat at the Lodge if you like. The hunting is good, the atmosphere relaxed, and there isn't a problem or a client for miles around. The weather now would be just perfect—fresh and crisp, but not cold."

Late the night before, Verner had slid, spun, and shoveled his way into this vacation paradise through a record-breaking snowstorm. This morning, he had been jarred awake by Bartlett's urgent, "Wake up, Dick! Lew Phipps has been murdered!"

Now Bartlett stood, square-built and stocky, by the night-table, and set the phone back in its cradle.

"No use," he said. "The line's down between here and the village. We can call the other cabins or the Lodge, but that's all."

At the window, where more and more snow drifted steadily down, a powerfully built man in the uniform of a brigadier general turned to look worriedly at Bartlett.

"Can anyone get through on foot?"

"Not for hours. The snow is too deep."

"Damn it, this is the *fifth* of these killings. And this is the only one we can prove is an actual murder. We've got to get the police here before the killer has a chance to escape."

Bartlett shook his head. "I don't know how. Once the snowplow opens up that road, everyone here is going to want to leave. This deep snow has ruined the hunting."

The General gnawed his lip, and his face took on the intent look that Verner had seen many times in his career. It was the look of a man who has a problem that *has* to be solved, but who is baffled as to how to solve it. Abruptly the General turned to Verner, and a speculative, faintly hopeful expression crossed his face.

"Bart here tells me you're a heuristician—a professional problem solver. Could *you* track down the killer?"

"I'm not a detective."

"I don't ask you to take fingerprints or question suspects. Mr. Verner, Lew Phipps was one of our best men in the field of submarine detection. We *can't* let the killer get away. When a key scientist is killed, thousands of other men may die later because of the scientist's unfinished work."

Verner looked at the General with sudden interest. "You're saying Phipps was killed because he was a key scientist?"

"Let me give you the facts, and see what you think. A couple of months ago an immigrant German specialist named Kupfer went out in his sailboat on a nice fall day, after telling his wife he'd be back in an hour. A week later he was washed ashore on Long Island, drowned. He'd been working in our submarine detection project. Last month Horn and Gabert, two of the best electronics men in this field, went out on a camping trip, and wound up under a rock slide, both dead. About two weeks ago Commander Jack Howells, one of the Navy's top antisubmarine men, took a few days off, and managed to electrocute himself in the bathroom of a motel where he was staying overnight."

The General glanced at the body on the floor. "And now we have this."

"The other four deaths were considered accidental?"

"There was no *proof* that they weren't. Whoever did it covered his tracks neatly, until now. This time we've got a clear-cut murder."

"And the problem—" said Verner.

"Is to get this killer before the snowplow comes through. Otherwise he'll get away—and more good men will die."

"How do we know the killer is still here? Why couldn't he have left last night?"

The General glanced out the window at the falling snow. "Bart talked to Lew on the phone about eleven last night. So Lew was still alive then. At about eleven fifteen I was turning onto the ridge road that leads in here. I think you'll agree that in the fifteen minutes between Bart's phone call and my turning onto that road, the killer couldn't have murdered Lew and gotten away down that road."

Verner nodded. "Not last night. I turned onto it around ten, and all across the ridge there was a blizzard of flying snow, and deep drifts. It took me over an hour to get through."

The General nodded. "Later on it was even worse. I started into it at eleven fifteen, and shoveled my way out around two in the morning. I didn't meet anyone on the way, so if a car left here, it must have been after two. But with the snow that heavy, and that wind on the ridge, the road was solidly drifted in by two. No one could have gotten through there. And there's no other way out."

Verner nodded. "Then the killer must be trapped here. And as you say, he can leave in the exodus before the police learn about this. But couldn't we stop everyone from leaving?"

The General shrugged. "A lot of these people are from out of state. They won't want to be tied up in the investigation. We could *try* to keep them here, but I don't think it would work. One or two would pull out, and the rest would follow."

Verner nodded. "All right," he said. "I'll try to get your man for you. But bear in mind, I'm not a detective. I don't have a detective's special skills. I'll have to work at it my own way."

The General nodded. "I don't care how you do it—just get him."

* * *

Verner spent the next half hour carefully looking over the cabin. There was a lot to see. The cracks in the floor, several yards from the body, showed distinct traces of blood. Next to the kerosene heater, its sheet-metal side dented, lay a white chip of tooth. The floor near the sink, in the tiny bathroom, looked clean, but smelled of vomit. There was a scattered trail of blood droplets from near the outside door to the small compact kitchen, where a single strip of cloth damp with kerosene lay in an opened wooden storage cabinet that was filled with empty cardboard cereal and dried-milk boxes. Beside the cloth was a drop of wax.

There was another trail of blood droplets from the outer door almost to the body of the dead man. Near the outer door was a small pool of blood. Most of the furniture in the main room of the cabin was overturned, and the leg of one of the chairs was broken. The dead man's deer gun was in the closet, and his hunting knife was in his suitcase, but his .22 target pistol was missing from its holster in the suitcase.

The three men considered this mass of information in silence. Bartlett looked up from examining the body, and said apologetically, "The left lens of these glasses of Lew's isn't broken quite as you'd expect. Part of the lens is crushed in a semicircle. What does that mean?"

Verner said exasperatedly, "I suppose there are some murders without a single clue, but in this one we have too many."

The General said, "But what the devil does it all add up to?"

"With a thing like this," said Verner, "the idea is to get hold of a loose end somewhere and pull." He frowned for a moment, then said, "For instance, that rag smelling of kerosene is suggestive, and so is the drop of wax."

Bartlett said, "That's right. There could have been a pile of kerosene-soaked rags in that cupboard, and a lighted candle. The killer could have planned to have Lew die in an 'accidental fire'."

Verner nodded, and glanced around. "There's that small pool of blood near the outer door, and the trail of scattered droplets that leads from there into the kitchen. For the blood to accumulate in a pool suggests that some-one lay motionless there, bleeding. Then this person apparently came to, perhaps saw the flickering glow of the candle, and as the droplets show, went out to the kitchen. Since the rags and candle aren't there now, he evidently threw them outside."

The General nodded. "That makes sense. But who *was* this third person?"

Verner frowned, and glanced at the body, with the stag-handled knife jutting from its back. "*That* knife didn't belong to Phipps, did it?"

The General shook his head. "Lew's hunting knife is in the suitcase. He never carried a knife like that one."

Bartlett looked puzzled. "Wouldn't that be the killer's knife?"

Verner said, "The difficulty with that is, why should a cold-blooded killer leave *his* knife, which could possibly be traced?"

The General massaged his jaw. "That brings us back to this third person who was lying near the door, and came to, and put out the candle."

Verner said, "Perhaps we can check this line of reasoning. Bart, would you call the Lodge and see if anyone's missing."

Bartlett picked up the phone on the night-table. As he made the call, Verner crouched to study the body. He was still looking at it when Bartlett set down the phone and said, "A guide named Gordon Lecour hasn't been seen since he went out for a walk before turning in last night. He was a big man, wearing a hunting jacket, boots, heavy trousers, and he carried a stag-handled hunting knife in a sheath on his belt."

Verner stood up. "That explains it. Suppose that while the guide was out on his walk, he overheard the struggle in this cabin, and came in. At that precise instant he'd find three men pinning a fourth to the floor."

The General looked at Verner in surprise. "How can you know that?"

"Look at Phipps's body. Arms stretched straight out, his watch far down on his wrist, his legs straight back, and his socks shoved down around the ankles. Body face down and flat on the floor. How did he get into this position? How did his watch get almost down onto his hand unless it was shoved there, and how could that come about unless someone held him by the wrists? A second person, lying or kneeling across his legs and gripping Phipps's ankles, would account for the socks shoved so far down. Now, neither of those men would have a hand free. So it would take a *third* man to use the knife."

The General stared at the body. "And yet stabbing him was a fool's play. It completely ended the chain of 'accidental deaths'."

"Yes. But there's one situation in which they might have to kill him quickly. Suppose the guide *did* burst in on the killers as they were holding Phipps pinned to the floor with, say, his head shoved in a pillow?"

The General swallowed, turned, walked across the room, and then came back again. "That's what must have happened! And then all hell broke loose."

Verner's gray eyes glinted. "The guide was a big man, and we can roughly gauge his physical condition from the fact that he walked out into a record-breaking snowstorm on a frigid night just to get a little fresh air before turning in. And from the violence that's been done to this room, and the vomit and blood that have evidently been wiped up, he must have exacted quite a toll before they finally overpowered him."

The General said, "What of Lew, meanwhile?"

"When the guide first came in, the killers would have had no way of knowing if he had anyone else with him. They couldn't take the chance of letting Phipps revive and either getting away or joining in a finish fight. They must have stabbed him right then."

The General nodded slowly. "After they had the guide down, they could have put *his* knife in Lew's wound, to try to make it appear as if the guide had killed Lew. There'd have been little enough evidence to disprove it once the cabin had burned down."

Verner nodded. "And here we come to one last fact. The killers left Lecour here, with his knife in Phipps's back. The faint traces of blood and vomit suggest that they cleaned up most signs of their own presence, perhaps with the thought that, for instance, some remnant of the blood might be analyzed and prove that someone beside Phipps and Lecour had been here. They did that much, but by the time they'd hunted through the cabin and located a suitable weapon—Phipps's target pistol—they'd apparently run out of steam."

The General frowned. "How do you figure that?"

"It would have been natural to pose the body to suggest a fight. But it wasn't done. These droplets from the door to near the body suggest that after the killers shot Lecour, they just threw the gun on the floor near Phipps, and went out. Lecour, recovering consciousness later, prevented the fire, then apparently looked around for some weapon, saw the gun, picked it up, and went out with it."

"Yes," said the General, "it all fits. But why—" He paused. "Yes, *now* I see why they ran out of steam. A knife wound can be a lot more serious than it seems at first. There's internal bleeding."

Verner nodded. "One or more of them very suddenly had to be gotten back to their cabin."

"If only we could follow them!" said the General. "The guide may have been able to follow them, because of their tracks through the snow. But it's too late for us to do that."

Bartlett nodded. "There wasn't a track in the snow anywhere when I came over to call Lew. Any tracks have long since been covered up."

Verner said, "If we could think as they thought, we might have a chance. Let's see, now. We know they did this late at night, because Phipps talked to Bart on the phone at eleven, and so Phipps was still alive then. Yet they didn't do it too close to daylight, since it must have taken time for the snow to fill up their tracks."

Frowning in thought Verner went on, "Now, let's see. The simple and obvious way to get here would be down the walk from the Lodge. But that walk is kept lighted at night. By coming that way, any chance meeting on the walk would mean that someone had seen them. And *that* could make trouble the next day, *if* they came by the walk."

The General said, "Okay, so they didn't come by the walk. But the way these cabins are set, with random spacing, it would be hard enough to get from one to another cross-country on an ordinary night. Last night you couldn't see a cabin ten feet away. If they'd tried to come cross-country, these killers would have floundered around half the night, and probably ended up in a ravine."

"Nevertheless," said Verner, "there's just a chance that they were very clever." He glanced at Bartlett. "When you talked to Phipps on the phone, did he seem worried?"

Bartlett shook his head. "He was just afraid that the

General might have trouble getting in along the ridge road, because of the snow. By then the forecasters were predicting a record snowfall."

Verner nodded. "He didn't mention any unusual sound?"

"No."

"Of course," said Verner, "they might have done it while he was out." He shrugged on his heavy, fur-lined coat. "We'll have to go out and see."

"What are we looking for?" said the General.

"A nail," said Verner, "or a hook, driven or screwed into the outside wall of this cabin."

✷✷✷

Outside, the snow was still falling steadily as they separated to examine the back and the two side walls of the cabin. A little under five minutes had passed when the General's voice carried around the corner of the cabin. "Now, what in the Sam Hill is this?"

Verner and Bartlett joined him to study two tiny holes, less than half an inch apart, high up at the back wall of the cabin.

Bartlett said, "A fence staple, driven in and later pulled out, would leave just that kind of mark. But why would a staple be driven in here?"

Verner said dryly, "To hold the other end of the string."

Bartlett looked at him with a blank expression.

The General swore.

Verner said, "Where they have frequent blizzards, the farmers run a rope from the house to the barn, so they can go from one place to the other without getting lost in the snow."

Bartlett straightened up slowly. "Good Lord! They could have put that there while Lew was over at the Lodge eating dinner. It was dark enough by then, and no one would have had any reason to come back here and find it."

The General said grimly, "With a length of cord passed through that staple they could come straight through the snow and darkness without anyone seeing them. And they could leave the same way."

Verner nodded. "But," he said, "by doing that, they left tracks."

"Under the snow," said the General ruefully.

Verner peered around and saw the slender slip of a seedling that grew straight up out of the snow. He reached down with his knife, cut the seedling off at the base, trimmed it, then passed the small end down through the light deep snow. He then pulled it out, and pressed it in his own footprints. He spilled snow over the footprint, and tried again. Then he put the seedling down through the snow where none of them had stepped.

Bartlett and the General watched blankly.

"Yes," said Verner. "The bare grass and weeds, under the snow, feel springy, resilient. But when you press down on a place where the snow has been walked on, compacted, there's a sticky sensation."

He handed the seedling to Bartlett, who thrust it down through the light snow, and felt, out of sight, the springy vegetation. He pressed the tip into his own footprint, and felt it stick in the heavy compacted snow. He looked at Verner with respect, returning the seedling.

Verner probed down through the snow again and

again, then slowly moved out in almost a straight line, away from the cabin. When he turned to look back, his gray eyes glinted.

"Before we go any farther, we'd better get our guns."

Several minutes later, probing carefully to find the trail of hidden, compacted footprints, they were moving slowly out through the snow till there was nothing in sight before or behind them, on either side, overhead or underfoot, but snow—snow lying on the ground or falling, seemingly endlessly . . .

***

When the cabin loomed into view ahead of them Verner turned to the General.

"There we are. They went straight from their cabin to Phipps's cabin."

The General studied the cabin. "We want to be sure we've got the right people."

"We can be sure by their physical condition. The killers have been through a tough fight."

Bartlett said, "Suppose I knock on the door. I can say a guide is missing, and the management wants to know if anyone has seen him. When they first come to the door, I'll say it's cold, and shove my way inside. If I'm not out in three minutes, you'll know we have the right cabin."

Verner nodded. "If you think they're not the ones, call out loud and clear when you come out. Otherwise, we're coming in."

Bartlett nodded and started out.

The General looked at the cabin. "That window in back looks good. Boost me up, and I can smash in the glass when we go through."

"You boost *me* up. I think I can work the latch from the outside."

"Good. That won't warn them."

They moved close to the cabin.

A loud knock, followed by a mingling of voices, came from the front. There was the sound of the door closing.

Verner glanced at his watch, slipped off his heavy coat, and leaned his gun against the cabin wall. The General boosted him up to the window. Verner glanced into the small empty kitchen, then worked intently at the catch.

When the third minute had just ticked past, with no sound from Bartlett, he eased the catch loose with a faint snap, and pulled the window open. Carefully he climbed through into a room with a sink, a small refrigerator, a bottled-gas stove, and a door, slightly ajar.

From beyond the door came a male voice. "You better make up a better lie than that, and fast."

Verner reached down. The General handed up the guns. Verner helped the General through the window.

Bartlett's voice came through the door. "What the devil *is* this?"

"I think you know what it is. Babs, check the back."

Verner flattened himself against the wall as the kitchen door swung abruptly open.

A blonde girl, a livid bruise across the side of her face, stepped in carrying a machine pistol.

The General slammed her across the head with his gun barrel. Verner stepped through the door.

On the other side Bartlett stood with hands raised before a man with his right arm in an improvised sling, and a small black pistol held awkwardly in his left hand. As

Verner's fingers tightened on the trigger, the man shut his eyes in weary disgust, and dropped his gun.

Across the room a heavily bandaged man in an armchair raised an automatic.

There was a deafening roar as the General fired. The bandaged man jerked violently, then slid forward onto the floor.

In the ringing silence Verner, Bartlett, and the General looked around.

There were two cots in the room, and on each cot a motionless figure was covered with blankets.

Bartlett picked up the automatic, checked the bathroom, then the closet, and found nothing.

The General leaned his captive against the wall, feet far out. Verner pulled back the blankets on the cots and found the badly mauled bodies of the guide and one of the killers.

The General looked around with grim satisfaction, then gripped Verner by the hand. "The next time we have an insoluble problem we'll know where to take it."

A few moments later, with their prisoners securely tied in strips of sheet, the General was searching through the kitchen while Verner and Bartlett stood guard in the main room of the cabin.

Verner looked around at the bodies, the snow-heaped windows, and the bound captives. He glanced quizzically at Bartlett.

Bartlett shook his head apologetically.

"Well," he said, "I *thought* it would be a vacation."

The Hand
From the Past

The police lieutenant, tall, well-built, his face unshaved and eyes red from lack of sleep, leaned across the desk.

"You've helped us before. Now we need your help again. We're up against a blank wall, with nothing to go on but this note!"

Richard Verner glanced at the slip of paper torn from a pad, with small circles and scratch marks in the corner, where someone had worked a ball-point pen to start it writing; the note itself was in clear, angular handwriting.

"We got this note," said the lieutenant, "in this afternoon's mail. This is the first we've heard of Judge Cabe since hoodlums entered the courtroom yesterday morning and shot their way out, with him as a prisoner. Since then, we've scoured the city, but there is no trace whatever. We've got to find where they're holding him, but we don't know where to look next. And now we get this note."

"This is the judge's handwriting?"

"Yes. I recognize it myself, and Mrs. Cabe is positive it's his handwriting."

"But it's an odd note."

"That's another thing that bothers us. The hoods' purpose was to get a hostage in return for a prisoner. That adds up. But Judge Cabe would never have written a note like that unless he was either out of his head or badly scared—and I've never seen him scared."

Verner, frowning, read the note:

> To Whom It May Concern:
>
> I, John R. Cabe, do hereby order, on my authority as an Officer of the Court, that the prisoner Roger Maynard be unconditionally released no later than six o'clock p.m. Thursday, the day of receipt of this Court Order.
>
> The prisoner is not to be tried, but is to be released in return for my own safe release.
>
> I must warn that my captors are heavily armed, resourceful, and utterly ruthless, and if this mandamus is not obeyed by six p.m. Thursday, I shall be executed.
>
> By order,
> Judge John R. Cabe, C.S.R.

Verner looked up, frowning, glanced again at the note, and then settled back.

The lieutenant looked at the intent expression on the face of Richard Verner, then watched in amazement as Verner turned the note around, to look at it from all angles. The lieutenant glanced at his watch: 4:00 p.m.

Again Verner turned the paper. The lieutenant, scowling, began to speak, then shut his mouth, swallowed, and took out his wallet.

Verner glanced briefly at the back of the note, then put the note faceup on his desk, and again turned it, to examine it from various angles.

The lieutenant, remaining silent, took a calling card from his wallet. Under a piece of clear plastic was a newspaper clipping held to the card by transparent tape. It was this newspaper article that had first attracted the lieutenant's attention to Verner, and he had kept it as a souvenir. Across the top of the card was printed, "When Desperate, Call—" Under that, was the clipping itself:

". . . instrumental in unraveling the mystery was Richard Verner, a new kind of specialist known as a 'heuristician.' Verner explained that a heuristician is a professional problem solver, who works with other experts. Nearly all problems, he said, can be cleared up by much the same techniques, provided the necessary expert knowledge is available."

The lieutenant put the card away, and observed that Verner had the note now at about a forty-degree angle. He was no longer reading the note but was now examining the marks where the judge had scratched his ball-point pen to start writing.

Suddenly the lieutenant could stand it no longer. "Listen," he said, "I didn't come here to ask you to figure out what kind of *pen* he used. We've *somehow* got to figure out *where he is being held*!"

Verner reached out to snap on the intercom. "Jean?"

A pleasant feminine voice replied, "Yes, Mr. Verner?"

"Could you come in here for a minute?"

"I'll be right there."

Verner glanced thoughtfully at the lieutenant. "You say the judge doesn't scare easily?"

"I've never seen him scared. He's tried some cases where every trick has been used—bribed jurors, 'bought' experts, political pressure, grandstand scenes in the court-room, threatening phone calls to witnesses, and finally crank letters to Judge Cabe himself. He's never wavered. The harder the pressure, the harder he concentrates on doing his job."

"How did he start out? That is, before he *was* a judge?" he asked.

"He worked his way through law school as a court reporter, to begin with." The lieutenant glanced at his watch. It was now a little after four. "How does this help us *find* him? At six they kill him."

"Is it likely that the people who abducted him would have *moved* him to another location? Or would he still be where they had him when he wrote this note?"

The lieutenant shook his head. "They wouldn't have wanted to take the risk of moving him. Besides, they had this well planned, and they don't *need* to move him. They won't leave us any opening to catch them that way."

There was a tap on the door, then Verner's secretary, Jean Benedict, stepped into the room. Verner glanced at the lieutenant and said, "What you need is his *location*? The address of the place where he is?"

"Yes!"

"But the only chance he had to get in touch with you is by this letter?"

"Such as it is, that's all."

Verner motioned to his secretary, who crossed the room with a swift tap of heels. Verner lifted the blotter on his desk, and put the note underneath, at a slight angle, leaving only the part showing where the pen had been started. "Read that," he said, watching her carefully.

She leaned over the desk, tilted her head, and there was a moment of silence.

"East," she said, frowning in concentration. "East—side . . . East-side. Now, is this 'okay'? No, *oak*. Eastside . . . Oak. Total? No . . . Oh, this is at an angle, and in the old style . . . *corner*." She looked up. "Some of these marks don't mean anything. They're just where someone started his pen. But this mark here is written twice, and it means *eastside*, and this means *oak*. This mark is at an angle to the others, but it means 'corner.' If this is an address, it must be 'corner of Eastside and Oak.'"

The lieutenant stared at the paper. "Do you mean those little scratches that would fit under your thumbnail make up a message? He said, *Corner of Eastside and Oak*—is that right?"

Eyes wide, Jean Benedict nodded, and the lieutenant whirled and went out. She glanced at Verner. "What—?"

He lifted the blotter to show her the rest of the paper, with its handwritten message.

That night, Verner was in his office when the phone rang, and the lieutenant said, "Still there? I'll be right over."

He came in with a tall white-haired man, who stretched out his hand and beamed.

"I'm John Cabe. I'm grateful *someone* could read my hen-scratches."

Verner smiled. "It was my secretary who read it. All I did was to realize there was something there *to* read."

"But," asked the lieutenant, "*how*? How did you know that? It was just a little scribble at the side, what anyone might do to start the pen flowing."

"Yes," said Verner, "but the longhand message didn't fit the judge's character, didn't fit legal procedure as I understand it, and must not be the message he was actually *trying* to send. But how could he send any other message? They would have been watching. How could anyone write a message while he was being watched, without being detected? Only by using something the other person would never glance at twice, and could not recognize as a message if he did see it. Well, as a hint, there were those initials the judge must have earned a long time ago, and had written after his name. They told us what to look for."

"C.S.R?" said the lieutenant.

The judge smiled. "Certified Shorthand Reporter."

The Problem Solver and the Hostage

Richard Verner sat back in his desk chair, his right hand at his chin. His faintly red-Indian features were intent as he listened to the tall, well-built police officer across the desk.

"We had to get this man," said the Lieutenant, "before he did any more damage. He's been responsible for more than twenty robberies in the last six months, and he's trigger-happy—a mad dog. If anyone hesitates, he shoots them. Our trouble was, he hit different parts of the city, apparently at random, and we couldn't find any useful pattern. Well, by sheer persistence, trudging around the city with a drawing the witnesses agreed on, we finally learned of someone who looked like the man, living in a room on Fraley Street. This morning we went over to get him."

"What happened?"

The Lieutenant sighed wearily. "He must have spotted us. Just before we got there, he grabbed a little girl walking down the hall, yanked her into his room, locked the door, and shoved a couple of pieces of heavy furniture against it. Then he yelled, 'Try and come in, cops, and this kid gets it through the head.'"

Verner sat motionless for an instant. "You mean, if *you* went in, he'd shoot the *girl?*"

The Lieutenant gave an ironic nod. "That's where we were early this morning. That's where we are now."

Verner glanced at his watch. It was a little before noon. "What did you do?"

"We finally offered to clear out and let him go, if he'd let the little girl come out unharmed. But he says he's too smart to trust a cop. The instant he comes out, he says, we'll shoot him. He's holding on to the girl."

"This can't go on forever."

"No, but what can we do? We've got to get him fast, to save the girl. But he's in a third-floor room with just one door, and that's locked and barricaded. He's got Venetian blinds at both windows. He can watch the street, but we can't see into the room. The thing is no bluff, either. He's a killer—take my word for it."

Verner glanced off at a corner of the room for an instant, then back to the Lieutenant. "Why bring this to me? I'm not a detective."

"Detectives," said the Lieutenant glumly. "I've already got detectives—they're running out my ears. And they're all up against the same blank wall I'm up against." He felt through his pockets. "We need detectives, but every now and then we also need a different point of view." He smoothed a newspaper clipping, and held it out.

Verner took the clipping and read: ". . . instrumental in

unraveling the mystery was Richard Verner, a new kind of specialist known as a 'heuristician.' Mr. Verner explained that a heuristician is a professional problem solver, who works with other experts. Nearly all problems, he said, can be cleared up by much the same technique, provided the necessary expert knowledge is available."

The Lieutenant said doggedly, "Any expert knowledge you need in this problem, either we've got it or we'll get it for you. You just solve the problem. Get the little girl out of there alive. Get us out of this terrible mess."

***

The building was old, of dirty red brick, and stood on a street corner in a small shopping center. It was long and narrow, four stories high, with a flat roof. The narrow end of the building fronted on Fraley Street.

Verner and the Lieutenant stood well back in a vacant room across the street, looking out the window.

"That's his room," said the Lieutenant, "on the third floor, in the corner. He's got two windows. The front one looks out on Fraley Street. The other looks out to the side, over Meacham Street."

Across the way, in both windows on the third floor, dirty Venetian blinds swayed gently, as if moved by a faint breeze.

"Thanks to those blinds," said the Lieutenant, "he can watch both streets, and we can't see into his room from either street."

Verner studied the blinds. "But he can't see *up*."

"No. Little good that does us."

"Let's go over."

They went out into a back alley, emerged farther up the

block, crossed Fraley Street, and approached a side door of the building, on Meacham Street.

The Lieutenant cleared his throat. "With minor exceptions, each floor is a carbon copy of the others." He led the way inside the old building, with its dark halls, high ceilings, long stairways, and moderately large rooms with heavy paneled doors and tall windows. The woodwork was scarred and dark, the walls were papered with long-faded patterns, and the plaster ceilings were stained and cobwebbed. When they reached the second floor, the Lieutenant said quietly, "Here's an exact duplicate of his room. His is directly overhead."

The room had a large sagging bed in the far corner, between the two windows. A heavy dark dresser stood against the wall to their right, a dark chest of drawers to their left, and beyond that, the door to a shallow closet. The Fraley Street window was in a direct line with the hall door.

Verner looked over the two heavy dark pieces of furniture, then glanced at the dark paneled door. He said quietly, "You say everything is the same above?"

"Except that his furniture's against the door."

They went up to the third floor, where a police sergeant and two uniformed policemen stood with their backs against the wall, guns in hand, and listened to threats that the girl could "die any minute." The sergeant shouted back that if anything happened to the girl, the police were coming in, their guns blazing.

As the Lieutenant watched uneasily, Verner methodically examined the door and its frame; then, frowning, Verner glanced up and down the hall at the narrow windows that supplied the light in the hallway.

From within the room came the sudden cry of a frightened child, a slap, silence, then muffled sobbing.

Verner and the Lieutenant moved grimly down the hall.

"Well," said the Lieutenant, "what do you think?"

"How much help can you get?"

"As much as I need."

"Can you get pneumatic drills working in that alley?"

"To cover the sound of whatever we do? Yes."

"Can you get a loudspeaker set up in that building across the street, to draw his attention away from the door?"

"Sure." The Lieutenant frowned. "But we've already thought of tear gas, pressure hoses, or a sharp-shooter across the street. Remember, what we do has to be sure and fast."

Verner nodded.

"We've got one other little problem."

"What's that?"

"While the drills are working and the loudspeaker blaring, somebody has to be lowered headfirst down to the side window on Meacham Street."

Involuntarily, the Lieutenant glanced out toward the hard cement sidewalk.

"What's the point? We can't get in fast enough that way. And we can't risk a shot by somebody three stories up, hanging upside down by his feet."

"No, but if he goes down upright, his feet can be seen from inside before his head is down far enough for him to see anything through those slanted blinds. If he's upside down, he'll be able to see in almost as soon as he can be seen from inside. And if he's lowered along the edge of the side window, while the loudspeaker attracts the killer's attention to the front window on Fraley Street, he'll be able to see how that furniture is arranged against the door, without being seen himself."

"Who's going to perform this feat?"

"I think either you or I should do it. We've got to find out first-hand what I want to know."

The Lieutenant's eyes narrowed. He cast a brief but searching look at his companion. At first glance, Verner's tall frame gave a somewhat catlike appearance of lithe quick strength. His waist was narrow, and his face lean. A closer look, however, revealed something deceptive in his appearance—as of a building so proportioned that it seemed more strongly built close to than from a distance.

The Lieutenant shrugged. "I think whichever one of us is lighter ought to do it." The Lieutenant had the muscular build of a light-heavyweight boxer. "It's going to be hard hanging onto the ankles while he's lowered outside." He cleared his throat. "I weigh 175, myself."

Verner said, "You're elected—I weigh 184."

***

The pneumatic drills sent their racket reverberating between the buildings, and the boom of the loudspeaker urged the killer to release the little girl unharmed, as Verner, himself far out of the window, gripped the Lieutenant's ankles. Two burly policemen clung to Verner with bruising strength, but the Lieutenant kept motioning to be lowered even more.

For an instant it seemed as if they'd gone too far, and would all slide out the window to the pavement below. But then the Lieutenant signaled to be pulled up. They scraped him with painful slowness up the wall, got the red-faced, perspiring Lieutenant safely in, eased him to his feet, and moved back into the room. The Lieutenant drew a deep breath.

"The chest of drawers and the dresser," he said in a low voice, "are dark, like the door. They're the same size as the furniture downstairs. They're both pushed endwise against the door, about four inches apart."

Verner nodded. "Let's go down and get the blankets over the hall windows."

***

The trapped killer had turned hysterical and begun wildly to threaten the little girl's life.

The loudspeaker projected an earnest voice, "We've told you, as long as the girl isn't hurt—"

"Yeah, you told me! But you can never trust a cop!"

"If you won't believe us—"

"All right, but I warn you—you'll never save this kid! I'm going to—"

From the shadows between the dark dresser and the dark chest of drawers standing side by side, there was a brief flash. As the shot echoed in the room, the killer's gun clattered to the floor. Dazed, his hand clasped at his shoulder, the impact threw him against the blinds and the frame of the front window facing on Fraley Street.

There was a silence that seemed deafening.

Outside, the pneumatic drills abruptly stopped. The loudspeaker was suddenly still.

"Stay right where you are," said a voice from outside the door, as clear and unmuffled as if it were inside the room. "Don't move, or you're a dead man."

Blinking, the killer glanced around the room, then

back to the heavy dark dresser and bureau standing side by side against the dark, closed door. The voice seemed to have come from there, but the door was still shut. It couldn't be opened without shoving the furniture aside, and the furniture hadn't been moved. Feverishly, the killer glanced at his gun on the floor, then quickly all around the room.

Before he could move, there was the brief slap of a rope against the building, the side window on Meacham Street shot up, and the Venetian blinds were thrust back. A big catlike man with a faintly red-Indian profile was suddenly in the room; he scooped up the gun, carried the little girl out of the way, and yanked the heavy pieces of furniture aside.

Then the door was open, to show the pitch-black hall outside. Policemen burst in, there was the snap of handcuffs, and the sobbing mother rushed inside, snatched up her little girl, and hugged her. The door was pulled shut by a police sergeant who, having stepped out, shouted down the hall, "Take those blankets off the windows! We want it light when we bring him out!"

The prisoner gave an angry exclamation.

In the hall the blankets came off the windows, and now the light shone through the closed door where one narrow panel had been sawed away while the killer had stood at the front window, looking out onto Fraley Street and shouting threats. Now, too late, he could see how he had been trapped by a loudspeaker, some noisy drills, and four inches of space between a bureau and a dresser.

The Lieutenant glanced at Verner. "It seems simple enough. It looked impossible before."

Verner nodded. "That's the way it often is. But a problem can nearly always be solved, given time, exact knowledge, and—"

The Lieutenant smiled, "—and, Richard Verner, heuristician."

The Problem Solver
and the Defector

The wail of the siren died away as the police car pulled onto the shoulder of the superhighway and slammed to a stop. Hodge, the C.I.A. man, slid out of the car and held open the door.

Just ahead, the traffic police, outlined by the late afternoon sun, waved on the interminable stream of motorists. By the roadside was a ripped guard rail where twin streaks through the dirt and grass swerved off toward the granite face of a steep bank. Near the bank an ambulance was parked, and men were working purposefully at the wreck of a smashed automobile.

Hodge glanced around as his companion, a tall well-built man with intent gray eyes, followed him out of the police car. Hodge's glance was worried, since on this man, Richard Verner, rested his hopes of retrieving a disastrous day. Verner was a heuristician—his business was to take the facts of the most baffling problem, put them together, and find the only possible solution. And Hodge, like the men working around the wrecked car, was thoroughly baffled.

"Several hours ago," Hodge had explained to Verner, "an official of an East European embassy, a man I'd met at a New Year's party, called me from a roadside phone booth. He said he wanted political asylum, and to prove his earnestness he was bringing along a key diagram of 'Shower,' a foreign missile we're anxious to learn about. He said he had hidden this vital piece of paper in his car.

"While he was talking to us on the phone, he got nervous about a black sedan he saw cruising past, said something about a 'death squad,' hung up, and left the booth. He'd already described his own car, and we'd suggested the best road, so we thought we could get to him. Incidentally, we'd also notified the State Police, the State Department, and the F.B.I. But before any of us could reach him, he was run off the road and killed."

Verner shook his head. "And the vital diagram?"

"That's the problem. On the phone he'd said, 'I am a good amateur mechanic. I have this paper well hidden.' We're sure no one else had time to search that car for it. But we can't find the piece of paper. The worst of it is, we've learned that high officials of the man's embassy are burning up the roads to get here. We can't prove he'd already changed sides. They'll impound his property— they have the legal right to do it. So *we've simply got to find that piece of paper*."

The two men watched the mechanics work feverishly on the wrecked car. Sections of trim were unscrewed, hollow knobs and the underside of chrome strips were examined, and the fabric was carefully cut away. Large canvas sheets had been staked down, and parts of the car were spread over the sheets in orderly rows.

But the hiding place still eluded them.

Verner glanced at the canvas sheets and thoughtfully considered the spread-out contents of the trunk compartment—jack, tire iron, suitcase, brief case, several paperback novels, a worn car-repair manual, a red two-gallon gas can, and a large gray-enameled metal chest open to show shiny tools of all kinds.

"What are those things?" Verner asked.

Hodge shrugged. "They've all been searched. The suitcase lining has been pulled out, the handle slit, the clothes examined. The books have all been carefully leafed through and the covers cut open. The tool kit has been checked for a false bottom or double layers. The tool handles have been drilled through, to be sure there's no hollow where a tightly rolled piece of paper could have been hidden. We didn't find anything—not a sign or trace of the blasted thing."

"And the man's body?"

"The doctors say the paper isn't there, either."

Verner nodded, and watched the mechanics, who had the rear end of the car hoisted up and were now draining the gas tank. Soon they had the tank out and cut open. One mechanic crawled under the car to look at the differential. Around the car there was unceasing activity—but the diagram remained hidden.

Hodge shook his head, and glanced uneasily at his watch. The minutes were slipping past quickly—too quickly.

Soon the rear end of the car was up on blocks, while at the front the engine was being lifted out.

Hodge said exasperatedly, "We've already looked in every conceivable hiding place. Now we're looking in places that are inconceivable."

Verner nodded sympathetically.

Hodge said, "Aren't you going to carry out an investigation?"

"What do you think I'm doing?"

Hodge frowned, but said nothing.

The minutes ticked steadily by.

At last the car was spread out like a child's mechanical toy, and the men who'd been working at it stood around helplessly.

Verner suddenly seemed to relax. "Hodge, what's harder than finding a needle in a haystack?"

Hodge looked blank. "What's that?"

"It's even harder," said Verner, "to find a *particular piece of hay* hidden in a haystack."

Hodge said shortly, "Riddles won't help us." He looked ready to say more, but just then a mechanic walked over, frowning.

"That paper isn't there—not a sign of it," the mechanic reported.

"It's *got* to be there," Hodge exclaimed.

"It isn't. You can reduce that car to powder and you won't find any piece of paper."

Hodge stood still for a long moment, then drew a deep breath and glanced at Verner. "Your job is to solve problems. All right, let's see you solve this one."

Without hesitation Verner walked past the car to the canvas sheets where the contents of the trunk compartment were spread out. He picked up the worn, grease-smeared repair manual. He leafed past pages of text, past photographs and diagrams of engines, transmissions, power-steering units, the connections of vacuum lines in power brakes, and then he paused to study a worn-looking diagram.

He handed the book to the mechanic. "What part of a car is this?"

The mechanic frowned at the grease-smeared page, turned the book around, looked at it closely, then shook his head. "No part I ever saw before."

Verner handed the book to Hodge, who examined it in astonishment, then pressed back the pages. "Evidently he cut out the original page, trimmed the diagram to fit the size of the manual, glued it in so close to the binding that it's hard to see the glued edge, then made it look like one more worn, grease-smeared page."

Hodge carefully worked the diagram out and slipped it into an inside pocket. He motioned the mechanics to look busy, and glanced at Verner.

"How did you know?"

"Once we were sure it wasn't in the car itself, I asked myself: Where would a diagram be *least noticeable?* And the answer is: Obviously among *other* diagrams."

Hodge nodded slowly. "And the only place where there were other diagrams was in the car-repair manual. We must have looked right at it, but we were so sure it was just another car diagram that we didn't recognize it."

The two men turned as, from the road, they heard a screech of brakes, and a burly well-dressed man, his face pale with mingled fear and anger, loudly claimed diplomatic immunity and thrust past the police.

Hodge smiled and said quietly, "His problem is a little harder than finding a particular piece of hay hidden in a haystack."

Verner watched the East European diplomat and his staff shove their way toward the wrecked car.

"Yes," said Verner. "It's even more difficult to hunt through a haystack for something that isn't there."

Key To The Crime

The dead man lay on his back in the damp leaves, shot through the temple. His cheap tan business suit was ripped and torn in a dozen places, front and back, as if by thorns. A nickel-plated revolver lay beside him on the leaves.

Looking down on him was a man of roughly his own build, but dressed in new leather high-laced boots, rough brown trousers, checked jacket and hunter's bright-red outer vest and cap, with an expensive shotgun under his arm and a look of bewilderment on his face.

At the dead man's head, a man in his late twenties, a silver sheriff's star on his own leather jacket, knelt to study the body. A little back from the others stood a fourth man, tall, dark-haired, dressed in a business suit and a gray all-weather coat, who looked with alert gray eyes at the body, at the bewildered-looking hunter, the thick low-growing green pine in the surrounding forest of bare maples and beeches, and the nearby moss-covered ruin of an old cabin, where four cars were parked on the edge of the graveled road.

The sheriff glanced up at the man in the business suit and gray coat.

"The description matches, Mr. Verner. Black hair, gray at the temples. Brown eyes. About five feet eight. Spare build. Brown business suit and shoes. There's no wallet on the body, but this must be the man."

Verner looked at the body noncommittally and said nothing.

The hunter cleared his throat nervously.

"I thought he was lost, officer. I wasn't going to shoot him. He stumbled out of the woods, and he looked as if he were going to fall. I hurried over toward him. I completely forgot that I was carrying this shotgun. I shouted to him, he glanced around, saw me, and said, 'You won't take me alive.' I think then that I must have raised my own gun. It went through my head that the man must be crazy. I didn't know what he might do. Then he shot himself."

***

It had been only some four hours earlier that the phone had rung in Richard Verner's office, and a man's worried voice had said, "Mr. Verner, this is Brian Darrell. I'm the sheriff of Rockland County. Is it true, Mr. Verner, that you make your living by solving problems?"

"That's right. Why?"

"Because I've just had one hell of a problem dumped in my lap, and I need help to solve it."

"What's the problem?"

"Late last night, a car went through here, rounded a curve, hit a patch of ice, and went off the road. It smashed through the guard rail and down into the ravine. This morning, a farmer noticed the smashed guard rail, and called me up. I got out there, and found that the car had gone all the way to the bottom of the ravine. The driver had apparently switched off the engine as soon as the car slid off the road, but that hadn't helped him any. He was dead. Shot through the back of the head."

Verner frowned. "*Shot?*"

"That's right, Mr. Verner. There were three men in the car. Two in the front seat and one in the back. Both men in front had been shot through the back of the head. The man in back had been shot twice through the chest. They were all dead."

Verner said nothing for a moment, and the phone hummed quietly in his ear. Then he said, "Were these men armed?"

"The two in front were. The man in back wore a shoulder holster but had no gun."

"Gangsters?"

"Far from it. They were F.B.I."

Verner gave a low exclamation. "You're sure of that?"

"As sure as their identification would let me be."

"No sign of any fourth man?"

"Yes, there was. A pair of handcuffs on the floor of the car, and an open right rear window. This car was a four-door sedan. It ended up jammed between the bank and a fallen tree. You couldn't open any of the doors enough to get through."

"So that this fourth man would have had to open the window to get out?"

"Yes. And the window was wide open. There'd have been no other reason to open the window. It's cold today, and it was colder yet last night."

"How do you know it went over at night?"

"The headlight switch was turned on, for one thing. For another, we had a light snow last night. It covered the car tracks, and there's no snow under the car. You see what must have happened?"

"You think the F.B.I. was transporting a prisoner, the car slowed, the prisoner threw himself against the man beside him, grabbed his gun, shot him while he was off-balance and momentarily distracted, and did the same to the two men in the front seat. The car slid down into the ravine and smashed to a stop. The prisoner crawled out a window and escaped."

"That's it. Now, here's my problem, Mr. Verner. I don't know if Rockland County is the poorest county in the U.S., but I'd hate to see one that was poorer. I'm the sheriff, and for practical purposes, I'm the whole sheriff's department, too. The coal mines here are shut down; what lumbering there is, is done by a few men with chain saws, bulldozers, and so on; if you've already got a farm, you can maybe make enough money to eat, but that's all. But we've got good hunting here, and we're trying to attract sportsmen and campers. For the first time, this year it looks as if we may be able to manage it."

Verner was scowling. "What's that got to do with this escaped prisoner?"

"That prisoner escaped on a pretty good road that has next to no traffic on it at night. I've deputized enough men to man roadblocks to stop him getting out on that highway, and I've notified the state police and the F.B.I. I don't think he got away from here last night. I think he's still here. Now, he's already killed three men. He's armed, and he's loose in some of the ruggedest country there is around here.

"We've got deer hunters camped out here and there in the middle of nowhere, completely out of touch with everyone else. If this killer walks in on them unexpectedly, he can kill as often as he wants to squeeze the trigger. We've got no way to warn them. We can't possibly protect everyone. We've got to get this murderer, and put him out fast. But how? We don't know where he is."

"Yes, I see the problem."

"He's out in that forest somewhere, but the ground is cut up, uneven. There are patches of thick brush, stretches of pine woods, ravines, and places where you can't see fifty feet in any direction but straight up. Listen, could you possibly get out here?"

In a little over three hours, Verner found himself stepping down from a light plane, whose pilot looked around at the stretch of grassy field where they'd landed, and shook his head.

At the near end of the field, a white car bearing a gold sheriff's star was parked. The door opened, and a powerfully-built man with a sheriff's star on his jacket and a forty-five revolver on his hip, walked over to shake Verner's hand.

"We've had word from the F.B.I. about our man. They say he's a psychopathic killer, and as clever as they come."

"Any more sign of him?"

"No. Nothing."

"Are the roads blocked?"

"Yes. Every motorist who goes through is checked. The

state police are out in force. The F.B.I. has a team of men headed here. We've warned everyone we could reach, and we've gotten a posse together to go through the woods from one end to the other to warn the hunters. But that's easier said than done." He looked at Verner, and said, "I've heard you solve problems that are too tricky for other experts. I hope you can solve this one."

The sheriff slid into his car, and pushed open the door on the other side. Verner got in, and said, "Could we retrace the route the F.B.I. car traveled—and go in the same direction as that car was going?"

"Sure. What do you have in mind?"

"To overcome three highly-trained men so quickly, the killer had to be fully alert *before* the car skidded. Why was he any more alert than the men with him, *unless he had just seen something that suggested a plan?* If we follow the same route the car followed, we may see whatever it was that suggested the plan."

The sheriff looked doubtful, frowned, started to speak, then slammed on the brakes. The car, coming down a steep muddy hill road toward the blacktopped highway, slowed abruptly as a rabbit bounded across in front of it. The sheriff let up on the brakes, and stopped the car at the highway.

A state police car dashed by. Then the sheriff, glancing carefully in both directions, pulled out.

"How far did you want to go?"

"At least ten miles from the spot where the accident happened."

They drove in silence for a while, then the sheriff said, "I heard about you at a convention of sheriffs, Mr. Verner.

As I heard it, you captured a gang of spies single-handed after tracking them for several miles through fresh snow three feet deep."

Verner looked startled, then grinned. "If I'd known that, I'd have stayed home."

"Why?" The sheriff cast a quick doubtful glance at him. "Isn't it true?"

"No, it isn't." Verner looked around. "I think this is far enough."

The sheriff glanced at his mileage meter. "Eight point two miles from where we pulled out. And the car went off the road about two miles further back. Good enough." He slowed, glanced up and down the road, and swung the car around in a tight U-turn.

For a little while, they rode in silence, and the dreary hills flowed past, with occasional brown bare fields to the left, and a forest of bare trees to the right, brightened here and there by the green of a pine or occasional hemlock.

With a forced effort at cheerfulness, the sheriff asked, "See anything?"

"Not yet," said Verner, his voice noncommittal.

There was another silence, and the sheriff asked, "Seen anything yet?"

"Not yet," said Verner coolly.

Obviously uneasy, the sheriff cast a quick glance at his watch.

"The posse should have made about two-and-a-half miles by now. Of course, I could join them when they cross the Peters road. Look, do you think—"

Verner didn't answer. He was watching a series of small

cabins set back from the road, with a huge neon sign out front, reading: HUNTER'S HAVEN.

"Slow down," said Verner.

The sheriff slowed the car, frowning.

"Look," he said, "that was one of the first places we checked."

Verner looked at the sheriff as a man looks at a fly swimming in his coffee.

"Are you under the impression that I came all this distance, at your request, because I thought you were too stupid to do your job?"

"No, but—"

"Good. I never try to beat the expert at his own job. It never entered my head that you hadn't checked that motel. Keep going slowly. Where does this road go to?"

On the right, a wide rutted dirt road led up into the hills. At the base of the hill, on the corner by the road, was a small store, its clapboards painted yellow. Two weathered gas pumps stood outside.

"There's an abandoned coal mine back there. They used to bring the coal out down that road. When the mine closed, most of the people who lived up there moved out. About all that road leads to now is a fine stretch of deer country."

"Was there much moonlight last night?"

"There was a full moon, but it wasn't clear. Yes, it was fairly bright out last night."

"Where do these hunters you speak of stay at night?"

"Some stay at the motel, The Hunters' Haven, down the road. Some camp out in tents. A few sleep in the backs of their station wagons, or in campers on the backs of pickup trucks."

"What do they use for light?"

"Lanterns, mostly. Usually gasoline mantle-lanterns. They give a good white light."

"From this road, would it be possible to see any of these lights at night?"

"That depends on the hunters. Sometimes they're tired and go to bed early. At other times, it may have been raining off and on all day, with them getting ready to go out, and then getting driven back in, and they may be pretty fed up, wide-awake, and stay up late playing cards. Yesterday was a good day. When I went down this road around ten o'clock, I only saw three lights back in there, fairly close together."

"When do you think the F.B.I. men came through?"

"As nearly as we can judge, it was sometime around eleven. They probably expected to go through a lot sooner, but there was a rock slide that blocked the road about forty miles from here. If they came to that before it was cleared away, they may have decided to detour through the hills. A man who's not familiar with those dirt roads could lose half a day in there."

"Why so?"

"Well, the back roads aren't predictable. They wind all over through those hills. And they aren't well kept up. I know one spot where there's always a foot of mud and water on the road in wet weather. You can't go around it, because the ground is soft and marshy to either side. You either get stuck in it, back out of it and try another road, or else you fight your way through it and then you're on the other side. Now, no matter where the road goes, you don't dare to go back that way for fear you'll end up axle-deep in the mess. You have to drive those roads for a while to appreciate them, and to know what to do."

The sheriff slowed the car.

"Now, you see where that guard rail is bent back? That's where the car went off the road."

Verner nodded.

The sheriff pulled to the side of the road.

"If you want to examine the car—"

"No."

"But—"

"That's your job, Sheriff, and the job of the state police. I trust you to do it better than I could do it. No, unless you want to stop here for some reason, let's go back up the road."

"Back up the *same road* we just came down on?"

"Exactly."

The sheriff glanced around, and with no sign of enthusiasm swung the car back up the highway.

Verner said, "How do we know this killer didn't leave the car, go through the woods to the nearest light, shoot some hunter, steal his car and leave? He could have been gone long before the wrecked car was found."

The sheriff nodded. "We've thought of that. But I don't think he did. I think he was dazed by the time he got out of that car. When we looked at it, we could see the marks in the mud where someone slipped and scrambled up the steep bank at the bottom of the ravine. That was the *wrong* bank, to get back to the road. Of course, he may not have wanted to go back to the road, anyway. But at the top of this ravine, you eventually get into a tangle of trees, low pines, and a gas pipe-line right-of-way that's been cleared of timber and is overgrown with blackberries.

"No one would care to tackle that mess at night. You could break your neck among those fallen trees. Some of those blackberry bushes are six and eight feet high, branched, and thick with thorns from one end to the other. If he got into that, he didn't go anywhere till daylight."

Verner nodded. "In that case, we've got a chance. Turn up this road, past this little store."

The sheriff, frowning, swung past the yellow-clapboarded store with its two gas pumps. He waved to a parked state-police car, then glanced at Verner.

"How do we know," said the sheriff, "that he came back this way?"

"I don't claim to know," said Verner. "But this man is supposed to be smart. What is there to attract him if he goes further down the road?"

"Nothing. It's just empty woods, like this."

"The difference is that he's *seen* something of these woods."

"You mean, when they drove past?"

"Yes, of course. You said you saw three bright gasoline lanterns lit up here. He may have, too. Earlier, he passed the Hunters' Haven motel. Wouldn't this suggest to him that if he could get free, he'd find men and cars, split up out in the woods, protected by nothing more than a tent or the wall of a truck camper, and not expected home for several days or a week?"

The sheriff nodded. "That's true."

"If this man wasn't familiar with the woods, he would

have had no idea what he was getting into. After smashing to the bottom of that ravine, he may very well have been stunned, dazed. But what would he do today? He would still head for the most likely place he knew of to find a hunter and catch him unawares and then take his car."

The sheriff said exasperatedly, "If we *only* could warn them! We told them at the Hunters' Haven, and we warned the few we could find, but a lot of them are out deep in the woods, and there just hasn't been time—Let's see now—" He slowed the car where a graveled road, thickly but not deeply rutted, led off to the right. "That's a favorite spot for hunters. There's an old ruined cabin in there, and a flat level spot to park. Anyone who hit this road early this morning could see these fresh ruts, realize that that road is used a lot, and go back there."

The sheriff swung the car in the side road, jounced a little in the ruts, then pulled into a little clearing with a fallen-down cabin, and three cars parked side-by-side near the road. Beside the cabin grew a thickly-branched pine, its low boughs brushing the wall of the cabin.

In front of the cabin, a man in hunter's bright red cap and scarlet vest waved excitedly.

"Sheriff! Come here!"

It was then that they found the body on the leaves, the revolver close beside it.

The sheriff straightened from examining the dead man. The hunter shifted his gun, keeping the muzzle carefully pointed down, and reached in his hip pocket, to pull out a wallet.

"My name's Foster, Harold Foster. I don't know this

man. I can't understand what happened here. Did he think I was attacking him?"

The sheriff shook his head. "It wasn't your fault, Mr. Foster. This man was an escaped murderer. He killed three men last night to get away, then got lost in the woods. He was probably out of his head by morning. He must have known he'd be hunted down by a posse, and when he saw you, he thought you were one of them."

"Good Lord! If he'd shot at me, instead of—"

"We were doing our best to get word to everyone. This is the only time anything like this has ever happened here."

"Well, here's my wallet if you need my license. Here's one of my business cards. It has my address and phone number. If you need me to testify to anything, I'll certainly be happy to cooperate in every way."

The sheriff nodded and smiled. "I don't think we'll need to bother you, Mr. Foster. We're grateful no one was hurt. I can repeat what you've said to the F.B.I. men when they get here. The men he killed last night are F.B.I. men, you see."

"Then I can see why he committed suicide." The hunter shook his head, and took the wallet as the sheriff handed it back. "My car's just over here, so if it's agreeable with you, I think my hunting is over for today." He smiled, nodded to the sheriff and Verner, and walked toward a long, dark-blue Cadillac parked at the edge of the clearing.

The sheriff glanced at Verner and smiled in relief. "You were right. Sorry if I—"

"Wait a minute."

The hunter had reached the car, shifted the gun to his other hand, pulled out a keycase, tried the car door, murmured an annoyed comment, tried again, bent momentarily at the lock and then opened the car door, leaned over, apparently to move something on the seat, then turned the key in the ignition. The engine roared.

"Quick," said Verner. "Go over there and warn him about the roadblocks."

The sheriff, frowning, strode toward the car, which was just starting to back.

Verner bent briefly over the body, his coat shielding his action, and pulled open the shirt. He straightened, to see the sheriff stop by the car window. The driver looked up, smiling. There was a flicker of window motion on opposite side of the car. Then the driver's window rolled down.

The sheriff leaned down and spoke courteously.

The driver replied, then nodded and waved.

The long car backed out and swung around, then pulled forward.

The sheriff, coming back smiling from the car, said, "Well, we were lucky. And so was he."

Verner nodded.

"Unfortunately, it just ran out."

His hand, inside his gray coat, came out holding a .45 Colt service automatic. He sighted carefully at the rear tire of the moving car.

The gun roared.

The tire blew out.

The big car swerved to the side of the road as the driver spun the wheel and whirled in his seat.

The front door was open in a flash. The hunter was out, shotgun raised.

Verner and the sheriff fired at the same time.

The shotgun flew up, and discharged with a roar.

The hunter staggered back, banged into a tree trunk, lost his balance and toppled over sidewise.

Verner and the sheriff were already running.

The hunter looked up at them in shock.

"Shoulder wound," said the sheriff. "He'll recover."

Verner bent, ripped open the clean hunting shirt, took off the red hunting cap to show black hair, gray at the temples.

"Look here," he said. "Brown eyes. Height about five feet eight. Spare build. They told you the truth when they said he was clever."

"My God!" said the sheriff. "He prowled around till he spotted a man with roughly his own build and looks?"

Verner nodded soberly. "Then his own appearance would match the description on the victim's driver's license. For some purposes it gave him a complete new identity. He could have driven that car to the Mexican border if we hadn't come in here and found him."

"But someone else in the party would have reported a hunter missing."

"Whoever else he may have been hunting with?" said Verner uneasily. "Yes, only a few hunters hunt alone. Where are the rest of his party?"

The sheriff looked around, glanced at Verner, and then across the clearing.

He looked at the ruined cabin, then back at Verner.

"Keep him covered."

Slowly, the sheriff crossed the clearing.

Verner stepped carefully to the side, and kept his complete attention on the killer till the sheriff came back.

"The cabin hasn't been touched. You couldn't move anything without those old boards coming apart anyway. But there's a spring about forty feet away, with a rock shoved over the top and one body head-down inside."

Verner nodded, and looked down at the killer.

"So," said the sheriff tonelessly, "it follows that he hid back of that ruin, got behind those two hunters, shot one, disarmed the other, shot him so it would appear to be suicide, shoved the first one into the spring, carried the second to the back of the cabin, changed clothes, and was carrying that one out when we showed up. Then he was out in the open, away from the cabin, couldn't get rid of the body, so he did the next best thing and called us over." The sheriff frowned. "Wait a minute. Why did he bother to kill the second one so it would look like suicide?"

The prisoner tired without success to sit up. He whispered, "I was going to take him in the car. If nobody had found the wreck, then I could put him in it and burn it."

Verner kept his gun ready, and his attention carefully centered on the killer.

"Then," said the sheriff wonderingly, "we'd find the four burned bodies, think their prisoner had killed the F.B.I. men, been trapped with them in the blazing car, and committed suicide?"

The prisoner shut his eyes. "Sure."

Back toward the road, there was the throb of an

engine, and the squeal of brakes, then the sound of footsteps on the wet dirt and gravel.

The sheriff turned away, and Verner, watching the prisoner closely, could hear voices, and the words, "F.B.I.," and then the snap of the card section of a wallet or pocket case. Then he heard the sheriff say, "Right over here. And you're welcome to him."

Two trim, neatly-dressed men stepped into view through the trees, followed by two more. They looked down at the killer, and one of them nodded, and said, "This is the man."

The sheriff said, "I'm turning him over to you."

"Yes. We'll take it from here."

The sheriff led Verner off to the side.

There was the sound of footsteps, the throb of an engine, the crunching of gravel, and the sticky squishing of mud, then silence.

The sheriff drew in a deep breath. "I'll have to notify the families of these two men. But at least I'm not standing here with those F.B.I. men telling me this body is the victim, and the man I made friends with was the killer."

The sheriff shook his head ruefully. "Well, we got him, thanks to you. But how on earth did you know?"

"Thanks to the car," said Verner.

"The car?"

"In some makes of car, you insert the key in the lock with the flat spine of the key down and the indentations up. Cadillac is one of the makes that has the spine up and the indentations down. When he jammed the key in the lock upside down, it seemed peculiar. Next, he had to try two or three different switches to find the right one to lower the driver's window. It followed that he wasn't familiar with the car. Of course, he could have bought it recently. But look here."

Verner knelt briefly by the body of the man shot through the head, who had seemed at first to be the killer, but was actually the killer's victim. Verner opened the dirty, sweat-stained shirt. Underneath was a clean undershirt.

The sheriff nodded slowly. "I was too busy being friends with a rich hunter to think of that. The killer naturally would switch clothes as fast as he could." He glanced at the body, then looked around. "While I take care of the rest of this, would you put the spare on that car?"

Verner glanced at the big car, where it sat across the road, with the door on the driver's side still open and the window down.

For some reason, the car had a grim contented look, as if it knew who had really trapped the escaped killer.

The Problem Solver
and the Burned Letter

The gravel crunched and the leaves rustled in the tall trees that lined the private drive. Richard Verner guided his car past the expanse of close-clipped lawn that swept on and on from the gate and the brass plate lettered *Frank G. Margate*.

Seated beside him in the front seat of the car was the younger of Frank G. Margate's two sons. Charles Margate, a short well-dressed man in his early fifties, glanced out the window as a small wooden sign saying *Service Road* came into view. "Keep to the right here, Mr. Verner. The house is up ahead."

A white-brick mansion, with a white-pillared entrance, loomed through the trees as the drive curved to the right. The building was three stories high, with large wings thrust out at both ends, and a line of tall evergreens that blocked the view past the nearer, or western, wing.

Verner slowed the car. "Your father's office isn't in the nearer wing, Mr. Margate?"

"No, that's the servants' quarters. They have the day off, so I'm particularly anxious that we be here now. Father's office, or study, as he calls it, is at the far end of the house, at the back of the east wing."

Verner pressed lightly on the accelerator. As the car rolled down the drive, he thought for a moment of Charles Margate's problem, as Margate had explained it that morning.

"Mr. Verner, I am being systematically worked into a false and dangerous position by my older brother, Bertram. As I told you, Bertram is comptroller of my father's company, Margate Mills. I am vice-president in charge of manufacturing. My father, Frank Margate, founded the business, built it up, and it seemed natural for Bert and me to go into it. I wish now that I'd gone into something else—anything else—but that's neither here nor there. About six months ago Bert suggested that Father, who is getting well along in years, be eased out. I didn't agree, and I'm afraid we had quite a violent scene over it."

Verner said, "Excuse me, Mr. Margate, but how old is your father?"

"I'm fifty-four. Bert is fifty-six. Father is eighty-two. But he's in good health, and nothing will put him out of control of the company except sheer incapacity. Bert insisted it was time we took over. In fact, that would mean Bert would run the company. I'd rather work for Father, though believe me, that's no bed of roses. Recently, I've learned that Bert has been cleverly criticizing my work to Father, and frankly I'm worried. Any executive of the company can now testify that there have been bitter clashes between Father and me, while he and Bert have apparently gotten along quite well lately."

Verner frowned. "You're afraid you'll lose your position?"

"I'm afraid something will happen to Father, and that when it happens I'll be suspected. Bert spoke pretty strongly while we were arguing. He said, 'Will he never step aside? Look at us, Charlie! We're practically old men. We've lost our chance to be independent, and where are we? It's still Frank G. Margate, President! Maybe when I'm seventy and you're sixty-eight, we'll *still* be getting these little homely lectures from the great Frank Margate, President! Well, I've waited long enough!'"

"Your brother wants to control the company?"

"He does. At the least he wants some visible sign that he *will* control the company. Over twenty years ago I was vice-president in charge of manufacturing and Bert was comptroller. Since then there's been no change. It was tacitly understood that when the time came, Father would move up to Chairman of the Board, and one of us, probably Bert, would become president, while the other became executive vice-president. This hasn't happened. Meanwhile, Father keeps a very tight grip on the family investments. Bert and I work on salary, and live as moderately well-to-do executives. Father is extremely rich. No doubt he tells himself that what he has will be all ours some day. But I'm afraid Bert has decided that 'someday' will never come."

Now, as the car rolled along the drive, Verner said, "You want me to try to get some line on exactly what plot your brother has in mind?"

Charles Margate nodded. "We can't hope to unravel it

in one afternoon. But there's got to be a start. If you can get any clue at all, it will be a help."

"Won't your father resent me as an outsider?"

"No. I'll vouch for you, and it will be all right. He likes to meet new people. You'll have to expect that he'll show you all over the place, and I'm afraid you'll be worn out before that's through. But I'm equally certain Bert will stick close to you, out of suspicion."

Verner smiled. "At any rate I'll meet the two men."

"Yes. We've got to start somewhere, Mr. Verner. I just don't like this situation. It's dangerous."

They rounded the last curve of the drive and were now traveling parallel with the front of the house. The drive widened here, to allow room for cars to park near the door. Further ahead, partly hidden by tall shrubbery, was a separate graveled parking space.

"That's Father's own parking place," said Charles Margate. "A walk leads straight back from there to his study. When he has men from the plant out here, or other people strictly on business, they park there. Stop right here, Mr. Verner, and we'll walk to the study."

Verner pulled to the side, shut off the engine, and got out. Now he could see past the tall shrubs. Two cars were parked in the space ahead. One was a new deep-blue hardtop, highly polished. The other was a police car.

Verner stood motionless. He could still hear only the rustle of the leaves overhead. But there was a faint scent in the air.

Charles Margate got out and shut the car door. The slam sounded loud in the stillness.

Verner sniffed once sharply, then sniffed again.

Now he recognized the faint odor.

Kerosene.

Charles Margate glanced uneasily at Verner, who looked around quickly.

The breeze came from the north, and now there was another faint scent, like that of hot metal.

Suddenly the front window of the west wing lit up in a reddish glow, that showed almost at once in the next window, and then in the next.

Verner opened the car door. "Get in! Quick!"

Charles Margate hesitated in confusion.

Verner turned the ignition key. The engine caught with a roar.

"Get in!"

Margate got in, then tensed. "Father—"

Verner pressed down the gas pedal. With a spray of gravel the car shot ahead, across the edge of the drive onto the walk and the lawn, past the two parked cars. He spun the wheel, rounded the eastern corner of the house, and then they were at the rear of the mansion, where a long flagstone terrace ran the full length of the house. At this side the terrace ran around the corner, almost to the line of shrubbery. In this wall, looking out on the back terrace, were two windows and a door.

"Your father's study?"

"Yes."

The door opened and a grim-faced man, helped by a uniformed policeman, was carrying out a large white-haired man, his body stiff and unnatural.

With an inarticulate cry Charles Margate jumped out of the car.

Verner got out, looked around sharply, then ran across the terrace and through the door into the elder Margate's study.

Ahead of him was a large desk, facing the rear door, and on the desk was a standard-sized typewriter. Nearby was a wastebasket, crammed nearly full with crumpled typing paper. On the floor nearby lay a small square typewriter-ribbon box. There were several filing cases below windows in the north wall of the room; a closed door and book shelves filled the west wall; in the east wall was a fireplace, where a police officer crouched, gently working a piece of fragile burned paper into a large Manila envelope. In the corner to one side of the fireplace was an open safe. Along the remaining wall was a leather sofa and two armchairs. Near the middle of the floor was a large brownish stain.

From the main part of the house came a gathering roar. Underfoot, the floor began to tremble.

Verner bent briefly and intently over the desk, then stepped around to the other side. He was acutely conscious that the evidence was about to be destroyed before his eyes. Then a second police officer burst into the room, shouting, "Get out! The whole place is on fire!"

The first policeman went out, carefully carrying his Manila envelope. The second officer glanced quickly around, stepped to the safe, pulled out a thick bundle of papers, and ran outside. Verner, half choked in the smoke that now swirled in through the open door, picked up the wastebasket and raced out across the terrace onto the clipped green lawn.

A wave of heat hit him, and then he was at the car. He

slid inside, swung the car in a wide circle, and looked back at the mansion.

Nearly every window in the lower two floors was alight. From some opening in the roof a long tongue of flame climbed into the sky.

Verner spun the car farther around, and drove back onto the graveled drive. Ahead of him the two other cars now rolled down the drive away from the house. When they stopped, Verner parked about twenty feet from the police car.

Inside the police car one officer was talking on the radio. The other was outside, his face tinged pink by the fire; he was shaking his head to the two well-dressed men who stood with tense faces to one side.

"—all we could do," the policeman was saying. "There just wasn't any time."

The shorter of the two men was Charles Margate, Verner's client. The taller must be Bertram Margate, Charles' older brother, who now said angrily, "I don't care what it costs, or who suffers. Whoever is responsible for this is going to pay for it."

Verner studied the brothers' faces, then said in an apologetic tone, "Officer—"

The policeman turned. He looked intelligent, but baffled.

Charles Margate glanced warningly at Verner. His brother, Bertram, said sharply, "Who the devil is that?"

Charles said, "A friend of mine, Bert. He drove out with me to see Father."

Verner said, his voice carefully and intentionally apologetic, "Odd what a person will do in an emergency.

I picked up the wastebasket and saved *it* from the fire."

Charles Margate looked disappointed.

The police officer shrugged. "Bring it over. You never know—it might help."

Bertram Margate gave a slight but perceptible start. For an instant his eyes seemed to glitter. Then he relaxed. "We all make mistakes."

Verner glanced at the policeman. "You'd better come with me. We'll have to check under the seats to be sure nothing has fallen under them from the wastebasket."

Once they reached his car, out of hearing of the two brothers, Verner said quietly, "You were picking something out of the fireplace. Was it the ashes of a letter?"

The policeman looked at him intently. "What do you know about it?"

"The typewriter was out on the desk. It's natural to think that Frank Margate had typed something. But there was no paper in the typewriter or on the desk."

"Keep talking."

Verner put his hand in his pocket, took out a small, square flat object, and put it in the policeman's hand. "Who first noticed the ashes in the fireplace?"

The policeman stared at his hand, hesitated only a fraction of a second. "Bertram Margate."

Verner nodded thoughtfully. He and the policeman exchanged a few more words, then the officer carried the wastebasket back to the police car in the glow of the burning house.

The next day Verner was at the police station, along with Charles and Bertram Margate, the policemen who'd been at the scene, and a chunky police Lieutenant who spoke politely to Verner's client.

"Mr. Margate, you realize that you're entitled to be represented by your lawyer?"

"Yes," said Charles Margate shortly. "But I don't need a lawyer. I want to know what you've found out."

"I'm sorry to say, Mr. Margate, that the wastebasket contained half a dozen unfinished letters—some mere openings—all addressed to Roger Pohl, your father's lawyer."

Charles Margate frowned. "What about it?"

The Lieutenant's voice grew softer. "Apparently it was a difficult letter for your father to write."

Charles Margate looked at him steadily.

The Lieutenant went on, "In the fireplace there was a burned typewritten letter. Many people believe, Mr. Margate, that if a letter is burned, the letter is completely destroyed. Not necessarily. If the ashes are not broken up, it may still be possible to reconstruct the letter. Type can often be read clearly, black against the gray of the ash, the letters shrunken but legible. I'm sorry to say, Mr. Margate, that the letter in the fireplace contained instructions to Mr. Pohl to disinherit you, as your father had discovered that you'd been tampering with company records in an attempt to shift the blame for stealing company funds onto your brother, Bertram."

Charles shut his eyes.

Bertram, tall and well-groomed, said in a voice filled with astonishment, "Good God, Charles! Why didn't you come to me?"

Charles opened his eyes and looked directly at Verner.

Then he drew a deep slow breath and turned to the Lieutenant. "Yes. Now I will need a lawyer."

The Lieutenant said coolly, "You might be interested to know that the crumpled unfinished letters in the wastebasket tie in perfectly with the contents of the burned letter."

Charles Margate thrust out his jaw and said nothing.

In another room a phone began to ring; it stopped when someone answered.

A moment later a detective looked in. "A lawyer named Pohl is on the line, Lieutenant. He wants to speak to you personally."

The Lieutenant excused himself.

There was silence in the room after he left, and his voice could be heard outside: "Yes, Mr. Pohl . . . Yes . . . Wait a minute, now. Could you read me that again? . . . Yes, I *see*. When was it postmarked? . . . You'll vouch for the signature . . . Yes, you're right. It's like a dead hand striking from the grave . . . No, we had the wrong man, Mr. Pohl. Just photostat it and the envelope, put the photostats in your office safe, then bring the original down here right away. It makes an open-and-shut case . . . Yes, Mr. Pohl. We can take him into custody at once."

Charles Margate's eyes were wide.

The two policemen, apparently intent on the voice from the other room, were turned partly away, listening.

Abruptly Bertram Margate sucked in his breath, leaned forward, and jerked the revolver from the nearest officer's holster.

"Don't move. I've killed once and if I have to, I'll kill again." He glanced at his brother. "Damn him, Charlie, he never *did* step aside. All I wanted was to be independent. That's why I took the money. It would never hurt him. It would have been mine anyway some day, but damn him, he was going to cut me off!"

Abruptly he whirled, and moving with incredible speed was out the door. Instantly there was the sound of a struggle, a click, and a heavy crash. Then the Lieutenant stepped back in, smiled at Verner, and turned to Charles Margate.

"Mr. Margate, you don't need a lawyer when you've got this fellow—" he nodded toward Verner—"You can leave anytime. You're free."

***

Charles Margate, seated in the client's chair in Richard Verner's office, said in bafflement, "Mr. Verner, I think my brother's mind has been warped for the past few months. But the only flaw I can see in his plan was the timing. He could *set* the fire, and hope the police would have time to pick up the clues he'd left. But he couldn't be sure the fire wouldn't burn too fast. Still, that's the only flaw I can see. But this letter Mr. Pohl received from Father—why, Father would never have revealed such a family scandal, even to his lawyer—not until he had decided exactly what to do. And to be certain of that he would have to see Bert first. He might *write* the letter—but it would remain unmailed till he'd spoken to Bert. And I know he hadn't spoken to Bert about this before the day of the fire. Mr. Verner, *Father never mailed that letter to Pohl.*"

Verner nodded. "However, he did *write* it."

"But how did it reach Pohl?"

"When I went into your father's office, there was a

small square typewriter-ribbon box on the floor by the desk. I looked at the typewriter, and saw that a fresh ribbon had very recently been put in it."

Margate looked puzzled.

Verner said, "Each time a key, any letter or punctuation mark, was struck on the typewriter, it left its imprint on that fresh ribbon."

Margate sat up. "You mean, by studying the ribbon, you could reconstruct the letter?"

"Exactly—and we're lucky the fire left the ribbon in the typewriter intact. Now, the first thing typed on the fresh ribbon was a letter accusing your brother. That was followed by the various openings found in the wastebasket, and finally by the finished letter accusing you—the one burned in the fireplace but only partially destroyed. All the letters, incidentally, had the same date."

"How could you tell which letter was genuine?—that is, written by Father."

"People rarely put a fresh ribbon in a typewriter and then put the typewriter away. Usually they put the fresh ribbon in just before typing something, and that something naturally appears *first* on the new ribbon. So whoever put in the new ribbon also typed the first letter—which accused your brother. Now, would someone else be likely to put a fresh ribbon in your father's typewriter while he was alive?"

"No. Father would have noticed the fresh ribbon the next time he used it, and known that someone else had been using his typewriter."

"Then, you see, we have to conclude either that the murder had already taken place—in which case we'd have *two* sets of fake letters—or that the first letter was typed by your father. As for the later letters, they could only be genuinely your father's if he had changed his mind completely in a very short time—maybe minutes. And then we have to explain all those later unfinished letters in the wastebasket. Having already written a complete letter disinheriting your brother, why should your father have any difficulty whatever phrasing the opening of an identical letter disinheriting you instead?

"The only explanation that covers all the facts is that the first letter is the genuine one, and the others are false. In that case *you* are innocent and *your brother* is guilty. That solution led the police to set up their trap."

Charles Margate shook his head. "It would have been too bad if Father hadn't changed ribbons, if his letter had been typed on old ribbon. Or if you hadn't noticed that this one was brand-new."

Verner nodded. "Or if your brother had realized it. But he didn't. So when he typed that letter to disinherit you, he condemned himself."

Charles Margate looked at Verner quizzically. "What is it you call yourself? Not a crime consultant or a detective, but a—"

"Heuristician." Verner smiled. "A problem solver."

PART III

PROBLEMS, SNAFUS, AND FUBARS

* For anyone unfamiliar with these words: A Snafu is a situation that's normal (i.e. we've had plenty like it) but plainly all fouled up. Fubars, thankfully less common, are fouled up beyond all recognition, but still turn up often enough in politics, war, and finance.

Warped Clue

Diana sat on the narrow cot with her pretty head in her hands and sobbed. Dave Welch watched her, his back against the bars of the cell door.

"Di," he said, "I'm going up to Tod's cabin this afternoon to look around. Can you think of anything I should watch for?"

She sat still for a moment, trembling. Dave knelt beside her, and took her by the shoulders. She looked up, her eyes dark and shiny with tears.

"I've told you all I know," she said. "It was a hot night and I felt like going for a drive. My car stalled on the hill. The temperature gauge was way up, and the car wouldn't start again. I went for help, but the gas station at the foot of the hill was closed for the night. When I got back to the car, it was pouring, and the police were there. They took me to the cabin, and I identified Tod's body. That's all I know."

"You had no idea Tod was going with your sister?" Dave asked her.

Diana looked down. "I didn't even know Jean knew him. At least they can't accuse her. She was at a square dance miles away."

Dave nodded and signaled the jailer. There was a rattle of keys, and Dave stepped out into the corridor. Diana looked up at him.

"If I had known," she said, "maybe I would have killed Tod. But I didn't."

A half hour later, Dave Welch swung his car up the hill road, rounded a curve, and went up a steep grade till he saw a spot where several cars had parked, crushing down the sparse weeds by the edge of the road. He pulled over, yanked on the brake, and glanced at the heat indicator. The engine was hot. Di's story, so far, was perfectly reasonable. He put the car keys in his pocket and got out.

By the roadside, the white pines grew thick and close. The forest floor was a mat of fallen needles. The air was hot and faintly moist. Dave ducked the stiffly-branching lower limbs of the pines, which were just high enough so he could pass between them for several hundred feet. He stepped out into a brightly sunlit clearing.

A big cabin with a stone chimney, unscreened porch, and a shingled roof charred black on one side, was perched on the summit of the slope. A gravel driveway ran downhill from the left, and curved around in front of the dwelling. To reach the cabin by car, it was necessary to drive far up the hill, turn right onto a winding road, then come down this gravel driveway.

Dave was sure that Di could never have gone so far on foot, and reached her car by the time the police found her there. But the distance through the woods was only a few hundred feet, and from the woods to the cabin the open stretch she would have had to cross was no wider. The police argued that Diana had gone through the woods, killed Tod Holmes, and returned through the woods to a place below her car, where they had seen her on the road. Except for the accident of a neighbor hearing a still-unexplained shot and phoning the police, Diana would, the police argued, have gotten away unnoticed.

Dave Welch shook his head. The best way to disprove this was to show that Diana had not gone through the woods at all. But there were no witnesses, and Dave had just seen that the woods were not impassible.

He looked down at the cabin. Sunlight glittered on its roof and a black police car was parked on the roadway directly in front of it. Dave walked across the field above the cabin, then down the drive with the sun hot on his back and the gravel crunching underfoot.

At the front of the cabin was a narrow stone terrace. A tall hard-eyed policeman walked across the terrace to stand watching as Dave approached.

The policeman gave a short laugh. "I know you," he said. "You're going with that girl. Your picture was in her handbag." He mopped his forehead, and pulled a rumpled cigarette pack from his pocket. "You can't go in." He rapped the pack, then frowned. It was empty.

Dave took out a package of Camels and extended it toward him. "I don't want to go in. I just came up to check the distances."

The policeman helped himself to a cigarette and nodded. "Thanks," he said. "Why did you go across the field above the cabin?"

"So I could walk in on the gravel, and you'd hear me coming."

"I thought you were snooping." He looked at Dave curiously a moment, then said, "Have a seat. I have to watch this place till the D. A. is sure he's got everything he wants. I can't let you go inside, but maybe I can show you what you're up against. You figure the girl didn't do it?"

"I'm sure she didn't."

The policeman shook his head. "It's open and shut. The body was right up on the porch there. Head smashed in with a medium-size rock from the wall by the porch steps. Nothing was stolen. There was eighty dollars in his wallet when we found him. What was the motive? Somebody just plain didn't like him."

"Tod Holmes had a lot of enemies."

"Sure. He was a ladies' man. There must have been a dozen husbands and boy friends who'd have been happy to swing that rock. But look at this place. There's only one road out of here. The neighbors didn't see any car go by. On the other hand, there was your girl, parked maybe two hundred yards away. Now, by good luck our first car happened to be coming down the hill when the station got the call about the shot. The car was near the side road, so they turned in, and saw the cabin roof on fire. They got here in time to find the body on the porch, and put in a call for a fire truck and some help. I came up in the second car. We came uphill just as the storm broke, and saw your girl walking through the pouring rain to her car."

Dave Welch said, "She'd just gone down to the garage. But it was closed, so she came back up here."

The policeman smiled. "I halfway believed it that

night. Sure, the woods looked too close to walk through. And we knew she couldn't have gone by the road in time. But the next day we checked, and we could walk through those woods almost as if they weren't there. That meant she could have done it. Then we found out how fond she is of her kid sister. We found out the murdered man had so many girl friends, and ditched them so fast, that his friends compared them to paper plates—'Tod's disposable women.' He was almost old enough to be the father of your girl's sister. And yet, he'd been seen taking her out lately. We figure your Diana didn't want her sister to start life as one of 'Tod's disposable women.' She came up here to tell him so. He laughed at her. Then things got rough."

"She didn't know he was going with her sister."

"That's what she'd say," the policeman said.

Dave sat back in the gathering heat of the day. Finally he said, "What about that shot?"

"His own gun. We found it in the shrubs by the porch. Either he grabbed it to protect himself, or she picked it up, and in the struggle one of them knocked it out of the other's hand."

Dave thought of Diana, her eyes large and dark, pleading with him to believe her. He did believe, but who else would?

Time stretched out, and he knew he had to find something that no one else had thought of. But what?

The policeman mopped his perspiring forehead, and moved his chair back into the dwindling shadow of the cabin. "Better get her to plead guilty. The thing is open and shut."

Dave Welch shook his head and got up. He glanced

around at the cabin with its partly-burned, warped shingle roof. He blinked. The shingles, now in the full glare of the sun, appeared more warped than earlier. He glanced around at the pine woods; the dead lower branches seemed to make a barrier around the clearing. He shrugged impatiently, and looked at the policeman.

"Isn't there anyone you'd think might have done it—if you weren't so sure about Diana?"

The policeman looked at him thoughtfully. "She was here. She had the motive. Just don't try to warp the facts, and you'll see how it had to be."

Dave stared at him. He looked at the warped shingles on the roof, then out at the thick pine woods. He whirled suddenly, and started up the drive with the sun blazing down in his face. Behind him, the policeman shouted, but Dave scarcely heard him.

He crossed the field to the woods, walked in, and a stiff dry branch poked him in the face. He ducked and another branch caught his sleeve. He pulled loose, and a branch jabbed him in the side. He backed up, tried again, and managed to work his way further in, slowly and carefully.

Behind him he heard the snap of a dead limb, and glanced back over his shoulder.

The policeman was right behind him, frowning.

Dave felt his heart beat fast. "This isn't an open-and-shut case," he said. "It's an open-and-shut woods."

"I don't get it. I've walked through and it was no trouble. You came through here yourself, didn't you?"

"Yes, but it wasn't as easy as for you—after the storm."

"The storm. Wait a minute. It started to rain after the murder. Before, the weather was dry as dust. When the white pines were wet, it was easy to walk through. Now the sun's dried things out, it's hard. Why?"

Dave Welch glanced down at the cabin. "What warps shingles? The underneath part stays damp while the upper part dries out and shrinks in the sun. With these white pines, the rain strikes the dead branches, and drains along the bottom as if you took the straw out of a soda and held it level. The liquid runs along the lower edge."

The policeman nodded slowly. "The bottom of the dead pine branch gets wetter than the top, expands, and the whole business warps up out of the way." He shook his head. "It was dry before that storm. That means the woods were like they are now, or worse. The girl couldn't have got through in time to do it."

"I told you she was innocent."

"It's a good thing you believed her. Come on."

"What are you going to do?"

"Put in a call. The fellow who called up about that shot is renting the summer place by the end of this drive. After he called up, he took his usual sleeping pills and turned in. When he gave his statement the next day, he said he'd heard the shot while walking his dog in the woods back of his place. Those woods are a continuation of these. They're the only woods like this around here, and apparently were planted when this was one big farm. My guess is, he'd never been out in them before and made that story up the next morning."

"You think he did it?"

"Well, it's guesswork, but we know his story isn't true, and we know Tod's reputation. Suppose he went down there and had a fight with Tod Holmes. Afterward, he could have set fire to the tinder-dry shingles, called the police to create a look of innocence, and gone to bed sure no one could get here before the cabin burned down."

"Sounds reasonable."

They were walking down the drive, the gravel crunching underfoot, and the sun blazing down from above. As they approached the patrol car, the policeman took out his handkerchief. "A hot day," he said.

Dave Welch nodded. "It'll be another warm night."

For the first time since Diana had been arrested, Dave smiled.

Tonight he thought they might go for a drive.

The Coward

Sergeant Gregory Jones sat on the dirt in the boiling sun, looking through the barbed wire at the jungle that bordered the far edge of the clearing, and at the mountains beyond. The heat was smothering, the air still and dead. No sound came from the jungle, and the silence was broken only by the scrape of metal as a young guerrilla took apart a U.S. Army automatic and put it back together again. Outside the barbed-wire fence, the communist guards watched their prisoners impassively.

Sergeant Jones glanced at his fellow prisoners. There were three of them, Captain Halloran, Private Vickio, and the burly civilian electronics specialist named Parker. Jones had been worried about the civilian ever since their Jeep was ambushed, but Parker had never winced. Now it was Vickio that Jones worried about.

The private was talking in a low voice to Captain Halloran, whose face was stonily cold and unresponsive.

"Honest, sir," said Vickio. "I *didn't* bug out."

Halloran didn't answer.

331

Jones looked at Vickio's earnest face. The boy had shot out of the Jeep the instant they rounded the curve and saw the long barricade across the road. An instant later, the Viet Cong showed themselves, heavily-armed and numerous, and it was obvious that while they might kill a few of the Viet Cong, they would never get out alive if they did. Vickio had halted, looked around at them, glanced back at the captain, and thrown down his gun.

Stubbornly, he now said, "I didn't. Honest, sir. I just thought we were sitting ducks in the Jeep, and I could do more good outside."

The captain's voice was cold. "What about the time Arnot got hit?"

Vickio lowered his head. "That was different."

Halloran didn't look at him.

Vickio looked up at the captain, then down at the ground, and swallowed.

Parker, the civilian electronics specialist, murmured, "Don't pay him any special attention, Captain, but that guard closest to the fence understands English."

The guard was studying Vickio with a faint look of triumph. Then he turned away, again stolid and impassive.

Vickio said tensely, "All I want is another chance."

"You've had another chance," said the captain.

Vickio got up and walked to the other end of the barbed-wire rectangle.

Parker said in a low voice, "Is it a good idea to fight amongst ourselves?"

Halloran said angrily, "No. But I'm not a good play-actor. If I can't trust a man when I turn my back, I don't want him around."

Sergeant Jones said quietly, "Sir, he just could be telling the truth."

Halloran sucked in his breath, and blew it out again slowly. When he spoke, his voice was low and controlled. "You're new in the outfit, Jones. I know what you mean. But you don't know him." The captain got up, glanced at the brooding private, and said in a kindlier tone of voice than he'd used before "Vickio—"

The private looked around hopefully, "Sir?"

"We're dying of boredom, here. Let's have mail call."

Vickio grinned. Then, with the sun beating down, and the communist guard watching blankly, Vickio used gestures and mimicry to create the illusion of a barracks full of men, a sack full of mail carried in amongst them, of eagerness, hope, disappointment, and finally the weary disgust of a homesick man reading a Dear John letter aloud to his friends.

Parker and Sergeant Jones were laughing at the end. Even the captain was smiling, and now Vickio did The New Lieutenant. Standing before a make-believe mirror, Vickio knotted his tie with elaborate care, fervently polished his bars, adjusted his cap, thrust out his chest and struck attitudes of authority so pompous and false that even the communist guards suddenly laughed, then glanced around, as if afraid to be overheard.

Parker, Jones, and Halloran clapped their hands. Vickio grinned, bowed, and turned away, then motioned to the nearest guard, who came closer, but shook his head as if he didn't understand.

In a low voice, Captain Halloran said, "That boy is a born actor. They say the best actors believe their parts. I don't know. But acting a part and living it over a long period of time are two different things. He can play the brave soldier just as easily as anything else. But it's just play-acting. It's not real. He's not a soldier." The captain looked first at Parker, then at Sergeant Jones. "I like the boy. I can't help it. But I don't *trust* him." He kept his voice very low, and glanced around. "I don't know just what we're up against here, but I wish I *could* trust him."

Jones said, "I wonder why they didn't kill us outright?"

"For some reason, they want prisoners."

Parker looked around. "There's that rumor that the Viet Cong have invited a lot of observers from other Asian countries."

"How does that fit in?"

Parker shrugged. "Maybe they want some beat-up prisoners to show that Americans aren't so tough."

Jones glanced up at the sun. There was no shade behind the wire, and they'd had no water since they'd been captured. If they were to be turned into dazed stupid specimens, all that was necessary was to just leave them here.

It was then that they heard the low swishing, murmuring sound, and looking across the clearing, saw the crowd that came to a halt there. Then they saw the Viet Cong soldiers who, with pick and shovel, began to dig halfway out across the clearing.

A thin man in olive uniform, apparently a communist Chinese, walked with several of the Viet Cong to the fence, and glanced at Captain Halloran. Speaking understandable English, he said, "It was a mistake for you foreigners to intrude in Asia."

Halloran looked at him. "You're as much a foreigner in this place as we are."

"You cannot win. We will win."

Halloran said angrily, "What's your point?"

"This is a meeting of Asians, from Thailand, Singapore, Malaya, the Philippines, Indonesia. It is important that they see just how brave is their enemy, the Americans."

"We aren't their enemy."

"Out there is a grave. You will pick one of you to die. And by the way he dies we will show all Americans are cowards."

He walked away.

Out in the clearing, the Viet Cong enlarged the hole.

Halloran sucked in his breath, then said briskly, "This is my baby."

Parker watched the communists out of sight, and swore in a low voice.

Jones looked at the pit. "Sir, you've got a wife and kids. I'm not married."

Halloran's voice grated. "I was in Korea, and they scared me. I was just a kid then. They're never going to scare me again."

Parker said, "Why play their game? When they come back, let me volunteer. They'll open the gate, I'll make a jump for a gun, and you rush them. At least, we'll have some chance."

Halloran looked around at the barbed wire, the jungle, and the guards. He shook his head.

"We'd all get killed. No. They want a propaganda victory. The only way to beat them is to take it away from them. They've got representatives from all over Asia, huh? I'll give them something to think about."

Out in the clearing, the soldiers threw dirt out of the hole.

The communist Chinese and the Viet Cong came back, and stopped outside the fence. "You have chosen?"

"Sir—" said the sergeant.

Halloran cut him off. Looking the Chinese flatly in the eye, he said, "I'm the one."

The Chinese turned and spoke rapidly to the nearest guard, who nodded toward Vickio, where he stood uncertainly apart from the rest.

The communist Chinese spoke to the guard, who stepped in past Halloran and the others and seized Vickio.

"Wait!" shouted Halloran. "I'm the one!"

The Chinese said, "America is a race of cowards. We will prove it."

Dazedly, Jones saw how they had been tricked. The Chinese communist first got them to argue amongst themselves as to who would be willing to give up his life. Meanwhile, the English-speaking guard listened, and picked out the one least willing. Then the Chinese selected this one as most likely to break down.

Without warning, Parker slammed through the guards, wrenched Vickio away from them, and spun him to the ground. For an instant, the guards looked on blankly as the two Americans thrashed on the ground, Parker's face close to Vickio's ear. Then the guards yanked them apart, slammed Parker back into the dirt, and jerked Vickio to his feet.

Parker was silent as they took Vickio out into the

clearing. Then, keeping his voice too low for the guard to overhear, he said, "I told Vickio this is a standard Chinese trick, and they'd only fire blanks and anesthetic pellets."

Halloran was watching in horror as the private, chest out and shoulders back, walked with his captors toward the edge of the open pit.

"My God," said Halloran. "Did he believe you?"

"Look at him."

Vickio stood straight and unconcerned as the Chinese, repeating his argument in several languages, harangued the assemblage, and turned to point again and again to where Vickio stood before a line of soldiers armed with rifles. Vickio smiled in contempt.

Jones looked at the barbed wire. His voice cracked. "We've got to do something!"

The nearest guard pointed his submachine gun. "You shut up."

"Look," said Parker.

Across the clearing, they blindfolded Vickio, and leaving his hands and legs free, turned him to face the pit, so that he would be shot in the back. Then they stepped away.

For a moment, Jones saw the clearing waver as his eyes blurred. His voice rough, he said, "When they fire that shot, I'm going over this fence and get one of them."

Halloran said, "You couldn't get over the wire. You'd never touch them."

"My God," said Parker.

Vickio had turned to face the firing squad. The blindfold fluttered in his outstretched hand, and fell to the ground.

There was a distinct low indrawing of breath from the watching crowd.

Halloran murmured wonderingly, "He still believes it."

Parker said, "He's making that communist Chinese look like a fool."

The guard, scowling, silenced Parker with a wave of his submachine gun, then stared at Vickio, who stood unwavering before the firing squad.

Jones looked around at the barbed wire, opened and shut his hands, then he looked up at the sky and strained his ears, praying for the sound of helicopters.

From across the clearing, came a sharp crack.

Parker sucked in his breath.

Jones wiped his forearm across his blurred eyes, and looked across the clearing. Then he swallowed hard.

Vickio, blood streaming from his left arm and shoulder, had turned, his features pale and contorted, to face the prisoners' barbed-wire cage. His right arm was raised in salute.

Halloran came stiffly erect, his eyes glittering with unshed tears as he snapped his arm up to return the salute.

For a seemingly endless moment, they faced each other.

There was a scream from the communist Chinese, and a second volley of shots.

Vickio was down.

Parker said dazedly, "He *knew*. All the time, he knew."

The crowd in the clearing was breaking up, to mill aimlessly. The communist Chinese came hurrying across the clearing, followed by blank-faced Viet Cong. For a moment, he halted, staring at the remaining prisoners.

Halloran brought his arm down sharply, to end his

lingering salute to Vickio. Side-by-side, the three prisoners looked flatly at the Chinese communist. He stood for a moment staring at them, then glanced around, and hurried on.

Halloran looked across the clearing, his jaw working, but unable to speak.

Jones said, "Sir, listen."

The prisoners stood tensely quiet.

In the distance, they could hear the gathering throb of helicopters.

A Sense of Disaster

I

Brat, as usual considerably bruised, but eyes alight with creative pleasure, sat and worried the length of broken dead limb out of the pile of kindling against the cave wall, then crawled stealthily to the fire where Ak and Rill sat gnawing on the remains of supper.

Brat shoved the splintered end of the stick into the fire.

Ak was eyeing the rolling hills visible from the cave mouth. There was a herd of something feeding there in the distance; but, in the drizzle, among the scattered low trees, with the sun about to set, it was hard to tell—

Snap!

Snap!

The resinous dry kindling caught and flared.

A bright-red coal landed on Ak's thigh. As he brushed it off, out of the corner of his eye he could see the stream of sparks and flame whip through the air.

Rill screamed and grabbed at her hair as Brat toddled past proudly waving the popping flaring length of kindling.

Ak sprang to his feet, snarling.

Brat eyed the carefully hoarded stack of kindling, back where the rain couldn't reach it. He brandished the flaming brand and headed for the pile.

Rill screamed.

Ak roared, "Nuh fla da! Nuh! *Nuh!*"

Brat scowled defiance and hurled the brand at the pile of kindling. He let go at the wrong moment, and instead of hitting the pile, the stick landed only halfway there, on the stone floor.

Rill grabbed the unlit end, and flipped it toward the front of the cave.

Brat screamed in frustration, grabbed Rill by the leg, and bit her.

Ak, eyes glittering, grabbed Brat by the hair, gave a deafening bellow, and jerked him away from Rill.

Brat screamed in outrage.

Rill, sobbing, banged into the stone wall of the cave.

Brat grabbed Ak and tried to bite *him*.

Ak, his face contorted, held Brat painfully close to the fire.

Brat screamed.

Ak listened to the scream change from rage to terror, and jerked Brat back onto the cool stone.

Brat screamed and babbled.

Ak said, his voice penetrating, "Nuh fla da! Nuh fla da! Nuh fla da!"

He punctuated his words with slaps.

Brat reeled and staggered, screamed, sobbed. Eyes flashing in terror and defiance, he stared at Rill. His eyes commanded, appealed, pleaded.

Rill, face grim and unresponsive, felt carefully of her hair, looked at the blood running down her leg, and watched grimly as Ak, with stinging slaps, continued the punishment.

"Nuh fla da! *Nuh fla da!* NUH FLA DA!"

Brat's gaze changed.

Reeling, dazed, he stared at his father.

"Nuh fla da?"

"*Nuh fla da!*" said Ak. He pointed at the pile of kindling and unleashed a torrent of words. He pointed at the fire, the kindling again, the back of the cave, with its piles of soft straw, skins, and tools, the cave mouth, the drizzle outside, then he looked back at Brat.

"NUH FLA DA!"

Brat looked sleepy.

"Nuh fla da," he said, as if considering the matter. Then, somewhat proudly, "Nuh fla da." He headed for the back of the cave, and the pile of straw there that was his own. On the way past Rill, he paused, looked at her, and spoke knowledgeably.

"Nuh fla da," he said.

"Nuh fla da," she replied.

He nodded, went past, and threw himself on his pile of straw.

"Nuh fla da," he murmured, and fell asleep.

II

Mistress Bryte finished shaping the dough into loaves as, from somewhere back toward the cow barn, the sound of screams came to an end. She let her breath out with a sigh, tucked a loose strand of hair back in place, and held her mind on mentally repeating the memorized passage of scripture, feeling calm return to her as she did so.

John Bryte's voice reached her dimly from somewhere outside, sympathetic, but with a hard unyielding quality:

"No, my lad, not then, or anytime . . . I know how it is . . . But *there is no fireplace or chimney in your little shed*. It could have set the field afire. That would have burned the barn, and the house, *and maybe us*. Once it started, we could never have stopped it. We would be driven out! We would have *no home*, do you understand? *No home!* . . . Now go clean up that mess, and never do it again or I will whip you till you cannot stand. *We can't fool with fire!*"

There came a padding of small feet past the door, and a low voice murmuring, "Wind could catch it . . . Water. Put water on it . . . Stone won't burn. Keep it in stone. Is safe in fireplace . . . Not let it get out fireplace . . ."

The voice went on past.

Mistress Bryte sighed, and got back to work.

III

Sam Markham, around in back of the woodshed, where the charred stubble reached all the way to the plowed field, had the leather strap in his hand and the screaming boy by the arm.

"Now get it through your head, *you don't play with fire!*—Do you hear me?"

The boy, tears streaming down his cheeks, looked at his father. His "*Yes!*" came out hastily, as Markham readied the strap for another blow.

"It could," said Markham, "have burned down the shed, the carriage house, and maybe the barn. And if I hadn't happened to plant this garden in a different spot this year, it *would* have! Once it starts, you can't control it! You can't burn that stubble unless the wind is right, and the ground is right, and you've run some furrows to stop it if it heads for Peters's place, and you've got somebody ready just in case, after all, it *jumps* . . . Say—Peterses are away and only the Becker boy comes over to take care of their stock. What do you think would have happened *if it had gone for Peters's?*"

IV

Mabel Lacker looked around at young Stanley, who was wandering around the kitchen at loose ends. So far today, he had dumped his toys out of his toy box, holding the box over his head so everything hit with a crash and scattered all over the floor; refused to pick things up; got up on the dining room table, where she'd put the mail, and torn the cover off of *Liberty*; tried to climb up on the chandelier in the dining room; and now she had the impression he was working up toward some horrible climax even she couldn't imagine. According to an article she'd just read, you shouldn't hit them, you should "guide the child lovingly but without coercion; violence breeds violence; to be attacked by the parent is the ultimate traumatic experience . . ." She *did* think Al was too rough sometimes, but just lately—

Little Stanley reached up on the white enameled top of the stove and took down the box of kitchen matches where she had set them after lighting the oven. He looked at her with a tentative little smile and a glint in his eye.

She took one quick step, the remembered advice to "use the superior resources of the adult to distract the child" all but blotted out by an uprush of savagery she hardly understood herself—but then the familiar position of the hands of the clock on the wall over the stove briefly caught her attention.

Five o'clock. Captain Kong came on the radio at five. Little though she cared for the captain's deep voice and the sickly piping soprano of his junior assistant, still, he *did* provide fifteen minutes of blessed relief every week-day afternoon.

"Stanley," she said craftily, "it's time for your *program*. Go turn on the radio, dear."

Stanley hesitated, then started for the living room, and she deftly wrenched the matches out of his hand on the way by.

He stopped, defiant.

"Captain *Kong* is on," she said, turning him toward the living room.

A faint look of perplexity crossed his face, then he went on out the door toward the living room.

She looked after him with a sense of relief, but also with a faint impression of something missing, something out-of-focus. She looked around, frowning.

On the stove, the water began to boil. The red needle of the thermometer in the oven door showed that the oven was hot. She shrugged, and got back to work.

From the other end of the house came the deep voice of Captain Kong:

". . . boxtops from roasted toasted Choc'm-Hulls and I will send you my exclusive official signet ring, which pops open to reveal a secret spy mirror . . ."

V

Stanley, baffled, looked at his wife.

"Richie did *what*?"

Sue Lacker said grimly, "Tried to set the draperies on fire."

"What did he try to do *that* for?"

"I don't know, but he had your lighter, and he *tried to set the drapes on fire!*"

"Uh—They didn't burn, did they?"

She stared at him. "Stanley—"

"Did they burn, Hon?"

"No. They're woven glass, or something, but *he was trying to burn them!*"

"Well—where is he now?"

"Watching the TV."

"I don't see that there's anything I can do. I mean— what *could* I do?"

She looked at him. "But what do *I* do if he grabs that lighter again and gives me the look he gave me today?"

"What look?"

"I don't know. Hellish. Defiant. *Willful*. An I'm-going-to-do-what-I-feel-like-and-you-be-damned look."

"You're overstrained, Hon. Did you—ah—did you punish him?"

"*Punish* him? I hit him as hard as I could, but he *laughed*."

For an instant, something seemed to twist inside of him, a powerful impulse that rose almost to the point of action. He took a step toward the living room, then stopped. What next? Where was the script? Who had the scenario? He paused.

She looked at him hopefully.

He shrugged.

"Look, Hon, he didn't actually do any *damage*. I'll get rid of the lighter. And—ah—you keep him watching the TV. I don't want to give him a trauma. And—uh—if he makes any trouble, I'll talk to him, try to reason it out with him *somehow*."

He went out, and she stood there, frowning.

—Just exactly what would happen if everybody tried to use unaided *reason* in a situation like this?

VI

The fascinating figure, a torch in one hand, sprang into the floodlights.

"They're unresponsive! They don't care! They don't relate! The world they have built is an evil world! There are wrongs in that world! Poverty! Want! Hunger! Coercion! They are corrupt! Their *world* is corrupt!

"I say, Burn it! *Burn* that world! Burn it down!

"Go out from here and *burn!*

"Burn!

"*Burn!*"

They glanced at each other.

Why not?

They obeyed.

VII

Adris Kammer leaned on the hoe in the hot sun, and sniffed suspiciously.

Smoke.

Eyes narrowed, he looked around. The wind was from the east. There—there came a thin wisp of it, from behind the chicken house.

After all that senseless convulsion, here he had a case of it *in his own family!*

Sandra Kammer came running at the sound of the screams, then stood by, bitterly unresponsive.

"I *told* him not to play with fire. Oh, I wish they hadn't blown up the TV station. He's driving me crazy this summer!"

VIII

As the emergency generator worked the air-conditioning to strain the smoke out of the air, General Myles looked at Senator Manx, and they both glanced at the President, who looked the professor over with the expression of a man testing one of the new coins by bite and ring to see if it was genuine.

The professor looked back stolidly, and finally the President said, "You understand, we've had a certain amount of trouble lately from theories that didn't work out?"

"I'm aware of it," said the professor dryly. "Two walls almost fell on me on the way here. The first was accidental, and the second was an ambush."

"Now, then. Let's have this theory of *yours* again."

"It's very simple. The world is a setting for a collision between man's idea of Right on the one hand, and the forces of Nature on the other. The only way a man can hope to contend at all is through discipline—self-discipline in the individual, and often discipline as a member of a group. The foundation of discipline is laid early, when the child has a collision with the parents, the child wanting something the parents *can't* allow."

Senator Manx glanced at his watch. General Myles frowned. The President said, "This is obvious."

"Certainly. It's *simple*. And in a natural state, this collision is all but inevitable. But, it can't take place if the parent can prevent it *simply by setting the child in front of a TV set.*"

The general looked around. "Then what happens?"

"You can't build on quicksand. The child grows up without discipline, can't understand the adult world, under the complexities, is *based* on discipline, sees the flaws but not the achievements, and has his collision with authority *later*." The professor gestured toward the outside.

The President said, "And what do you suggest?"

"That no entertainment shows for children be permitted. It will then, in the nature of things, be all but *impossible* to prevent the clash and the assertion of parental authority. There are three possible results. First, the parent may, theoretically, be overwhelmed by the child. Second the parent may overreact and maim the child. Third, the parent may discipline the child properly. The third response is self-strengthening, generation after generation, whereas the first two tend to destroy either the child or the family unit. We can therefore rely on the third response to regenerate the basic discipline of the race."

The President looked thoughtful, then harassed, and then smiled. "We will give this matter all the careful consideration it deserves."

The professor beamed, bowed, and went out.

The three men glanced at each other.

The President said, "General, after we get the remains of this mess cleaned up, we will have to plan a campaign against these TV stations and their children's hours."

General Myles smiled. "It might not be a bad idea, at that."

Senator Manx laughed. "But hard to maintain when the Emergency Powers Act runs out."

"H'm. Yes. Well, now, as I understand it, the situation on the Coast is finally quiet, is *that* right?"

"Yes, sir," said the general. "We have to expect a little more trouble—there's bound to be. But we finally have the upper hand, and—"

IX

Ellen Ferris dropped little Cyrus Dane into the 3-v seat.

"There, you little stinker. Shut up, and watch that until

Mommy and Daddy get home. Then if you want to burn the place down, it's *their* problem!"

X

Marcia Angio said, "Listen, Honey, this kid of yours is a firebug."

Hank Angio tossed his jacket onto a floating seat with built-in antigrav unit. The seat bobbed up and down, and drifted slowly across the room. He eyed it sourly.

"99,999,99 inflationeros for *that* thing. Was I out of my head? If you sneeze, it drifts. If a breeze blows on it, it drifts. When you sit down in it, it bobs up and down and drifts. How is that any better than if it had *legs* on it?"

"Your little boy," Marcia reminded him. "The kid built a fire under the 6v."

"It's insured. *Man*, is it hot out there today!"

"Honey, I stopped him, *but—*"

"Was the 6v *on*?"

"No-o."

"There's your answer. Put it *on*, then he'll watch it. He can't burn it up while he's watching it." He gave a little laugh. "He can't do *anything* while he's watching it."

"He needs a good licking."

"That's my idea, too." He shrugged. "But did you see that show, *The Five Hundred Days*, last night? They say the Eruption was caused by spanking the kids back then. They've got the scientific proof."

"I don't want to argue with science," she said, "but I'm

his mother, and I say he needs *something*, and *I* think it's a good licking."

"Okay, Hon. Try the 6v on him first. If that doesn't work—"

XI

Nate Mannett IV experienced the flowers, the bees, the birds fluttering gently, and the clouds drifting all about him. Ice cream cones of all flavors floated through the air, and he willed one to approach. It was strawberry, delicious, and as he ate it, he grasped a popcorn ball drifting just within reach. Happy laughter was all around him.

Nate Mannett III frowned upon him.

"I don't know, Sheil, it doesn't seem right to go out and just *leave* him here, glued to the alsens."

"If we shut it off, he'll cry. He's more and more cross, lately. He acts as if he hates the world. This is the only way I can keep him quiet. He *insists* on it."

"Well—if he *insists* on it—"

XII

Professor Weidenberg examined the class uneasily. He had a sense of having sometime lived through this same scene before, and once was enough. But he did not care to back down.

The unkempt unruly lot looked back at him with cynical disdain, as if watching a cheap performer at a sideshow.

Weidenberg said quietly, "I am recognized as an expert in two disparate fields, gentlemen. —And ladies. One is subnuclear physics."

Someone, somewhere in the room, gave a low laugh. " '*Disparate.*' Get that."

Someone else gave a lazy whistle.

The class sprawled in the chairs, watching, waiting, grinning easily.

The professor took off his jacket, revealing chest and shoulders like a gorilla, and a holster under his left shoulder. He tossed the jacket over a chair.

"The other field," he said judiciously, "is combat." The gun jumped into his hand, flashed back and forth from hand to hand as if it had a life of its own, and disappeared into the holster. "Now, gentlemen, I dislike narcotic cigarettes. They have a distracting effect. Ladies, extreme skirts and blouses, and—ah—minibikinis—also have a distracting effect, and really aren't necessary." He leered, and a kind of hair-raising lustful bestiality radiated from him.

One of the girls attempted a coy giggle, but it turned into a strangled gasp halfway through.

For an instant, there was a kind of live menacing force in the room.

The class sat up.

The professor began to teach, forcefully, demanding total attention, dominating the class.

They went out exhilarated. He sucked in a deep breath, put on his jacket. A colleague, who had come in partway through, approached him in awe.

"Charlie, with what you've got—*whatever* it is—you could do anything—go as high as you want!"

"M'm," said Weidenberg, with no special enthusiasm. "Thank you, Steve."

"I don't know what it is—you seem like anyone else until you get going, and then—I don't know—*something* happens!"

"How does this latest batch seem to you?"

"The students?"

"The students."

His colleague's eyes shifted. "Brilliant . . . Ah—but—well, to tell the truth, that's what I wanted to see you about . . . M'm . . . I'm having a little—well, I guess it's a discipline problem . . . My fault, I suppose, but—"

Weidenberg nodded moodily. Who could expect a generation weaned on electronic miracles to be thrilled by classwork? However, he listened patiently, and groped for an answer.

XIII

General Deauville led the Guard in the final attack on the Central Power Station, came through it with nothing worse than a poisoned dart through the left arm, woke up in a field dressing station that same night, and was in conference with the President the next morning.

"It was close," said Deauville. "Another twenty-five minutes, and they'd have had the cap off the regenerator, and smashed the leads to the helix. The experts don't agree on what would have happened then. At best, the whole East Coast power net would have gone out, and maybe the Midcontinent net, too. —That's the *best* that could have happened. At worse, we'd have had a hydrogen flare that might have vaporized up to thirty percent of the continent. When we got these birds, and put the facts to them, *they laughed*."

"They didn't believe it?"

"They knew it already, *and it didn't matter to them!*"

The President nodded.

"I had a visit this morning from one of our greatest sub-nuclear physicists. Last night, trying to get some perspective on this, I was reading the memoirs of a predecessor of mine, who went through a similar convulsion. I'm meeting with the legislative leaders, and certain technical experts, this afternoon. I don't know if we'll get the answer, but, personally, I am prepared to try practically anything."

XIV

Buckminster Siegel, Jr., massaged his sore hand, left his son sobbing in the bedroom, and approached his wife, who was sobbing in the kitchen.

"Well," he said angrily, "I gave him something to think about, but if I have that to go through every night when I get home, I'm getting something to do it with besides my hand. What did he do besides scorch the couch?"

"Oh," she said, "he was *awful* today! He put that New Martian lizard into the fish tank, and the lizard ate up the fish, and then drank so much water it burst, and he was screaming and howling, and kicked the dog in the ribs, ran into the rec room and dumped the alsens over the parapet into the swimming pool, with the cord still plugged in, and this greenish gas bubbled up out of the pool, and when I pulled the plug out, I got a *terrible* shock. And then he—"

"One of these short-handled fly-swatters *might* do the trick, or an initiation paddle—"

"If only," she said, "I could just sit him in front of the alsens. That's what they *used* to do, back before the Convulsion. Buck, why *can't* I?"

"Phew," he said, and looking around for something to eat.

"*Why?*" she said.

"Huh? Oh, I read about it somewhere. When they uncorked the outside cap to the Central Power Station, there was an escape of particles that did something to the ionization belt—changed the charge in it, or something. That affects the transmission. *Now* when a kid lives the alsens, he gets a terrific headache. 'Incompatible signal,' they call it. As a matter of fact, the thing gives *me* a headache every now and then. He dumped it in the pool, you said?"

She took a deep shuddering breath, and nodded.

"There's a rumor," he said, "that the higher ups figure the sets *caused* the Convulsion, and so they *made* them incompatible on purpose, by changing the signal."

"How could the *sets* have caused the trouble?"

"As I heard it, the idea was that the kid had to learn what the limits are—how far he can go—and he keeps pushing, taking more space till finally the old man just can't stand it anymore, and clobbers him, and then he knows where the limits are, the clobbering gives him an idea what happens when you go beyond the limits, and the whole thing gets stored away so when his own kid goes beyond the limits it doesn't leave him feeling helpless—he knows what to do, because he's already seen it done. But if the kid never has the collision, because the old man isn't around, or because the kid gets stuck in the alsens every time he gets mean, he doesn't get clobbered, doesn't get any idea what it's like, doesn't have it stored away when his own kid acts up, and maybe thinks there aren't any limits, anyway. He's got no idea what it feels like to go too far and have the roof fall in. Instead, he gets the idea that if he gets mean, *entertainment* will be produced for him. That's the way it's always been before."

"But is it *true?*"

"Don't ask me. Is there anything to eat in this place?"

XV

"Igor," said Marianne Fitch, her lips compressed into a thin line, "he put the cat in the matter converter."

Igor Fitch turned around slowly in the control seat, and stared at his son. "He put the *cat* in the *matter converter*."

Little Tod stuck out his lower lip and scowled belligerently. He sucked in a deep breath and his voice came out loud and clear:

"I *want* cat in verter!"

The elder Fitch swore, unbuckled the harness, and started for young Tod. "I *told* you, damn it, to be *good* to that cat! And I told you *never to get near that converter!*"

Tod felt his power flow through him, and raised his voice:

"I *want* put cat in verter! I *put* cat in verter! When I want, I go get cat *out* verter!—*No put hand on Tod!*"

The room whirled. There was a flash of pain, and another and another.

He screamed in rage, commanding the universe to yield and obey.

The stinging blows continued, one following the other in merciless succession.

He summoned his servant, the extension of his will standing there against the bulkhead, to come at once to his aid.

"You deserve it," she said.

The screams of rage become howls of pain, of mortification, shock, and a realization of disaster, then pleas for mercy. At length, he wound up in his cot, sobbing:

"Verter *eat* cat. Verter eat Tod I go near verter. Oh, I not want verter eat cat! I not go near verter. Not till I bigger. I not go near verter . . . Not go near verter . . . Not . . . Not go near verter . . ."

Out in the control room, Igor Fitch drew a deep shuddering breath.

"That cat was going to have kittens. When he killed that cat, he killed it and all the succeeding generations."

"We have more in stored embryos."

"Yes, and you know how uncertain *that* is. But we'll have to try to bring another along. Where we're going, you *need* animals to help you."

She stroked his head, said, "Are you sorry we left? I mean, left civilization?"

He snarled, "Civilization! Yes, I'm sorry to leave civilization. But connected up with it, like Siamese twins, is artificiality. Soft, easy, cunning traps. You know what some of the fools want to do now? They want to rig gravitor beams so that if somebody jumps out a window, he'll float gently to the ground. And they've come out with this thing they say corrects the distortion in the alsens signal, so the 'harassed parent' can stick the kid in it and forget him. You know the name of this thing? 'Cuddlywomb.' *Nuts!* The reason they had the last two blow-ups was that people wanted *out*. Into *reality!*"

"There, there," she said.

"*Agh*," he snarled.

She smiled at him, drew him close, but his mind was groping for a meaning just out of reach.

He nodded.

"That's it. Nobody *wants* pain. But you don't even draw breath till you get slapped. And after a long enough time without *any* pain, *any* discomfort, pleasure isn't pleasant, because there's no ground for comparison. A system aimed at *eliminating* all pain and all discomfort invites revolt, because it eliminates *enjoyment* in the process."

He looked at her, wondering why she looked so particularly alluring now, after this awful day. He checked the controls, scanned the instrument panel, then locked the board for the night. Each day, he rehearsed the approach, practiced the landing procedure, which he would need very soon, and practiced the emergency routines, which he hoped he would never need. If there should be trouble, the alarm would bring him on the run, and he hoped he would know what to do. He got up, and they left the control room.

As the ship became quiet, and the minutes ticked past and grew into hours, there swam onto the view-screen a bright pinpoint, that evolved into a dot, a silver coin, a white-and-blue sphere, and finally, a glowing world. It waited there, serene and unpredictable.

Little Tod, up and traveling around when he was supposed to be asleep, stood wide-eyed, watching the screen. Some exceptionally powerful emotion moved him.

"*Daddy!*"

Igor Fitch woke up and mumbled, but Marianne, out of long training, got there first.

"Oh, Igor, *look!*"

He arrived, half-awake, growling, "*Now* what? What did he do now?" Then he saw the screen. As he stood raptly watching, his son's urgent voice reached him.

"I *want!*"

His wife's voice said soothingly, "There, honey, Mommy and Daddy will get it for you."

Igor looked at his wife, then at his son staring wide-eyed at the screen.

"Don't let anybody fool you, Kid," he said gruffly. "There's a limit to what Mommy and Daddy can do. If you want anything like that, *you* have to get it *yourself.*"

Tod stuck out his lower lip.

On the control panel, the proximity warning woke up and went off.

Igor unlocked the board, shut off the warning, and swung into the control seat. Now, he asked himself, was there anything he *could* check that he hadn't checked at least half-a-dozen times already? Never mind what the ship-preparation experts were supposed to have done. Had *he* done it, himself?

So far as he could remember, he had covered every

item on his check-list, and had made his check-list include everything checkable. Soon now, he would find out if that was enough.

Little Todd, meanwhile, looking first at the glowing screen, and then at his father, suddenly had a look of comprehension.

"*I get*," he said sturdily. "—*Only not put cat in verter.*"

Igor smiled.

"*That's* the spirit, Kid!"

Destination Unknown

Jim Carney glanced up from the clacking teleprinter as the door slid back.

The Kid dropped into the room with a faint smile on his face. He reached back with his left hand and slid the door shut behind him.

"Hello, Carney," he said softly.

Carney took a slow even breath, and hunched slightly. The pencil gun slid down into his hand.

The Kid smiled.

"I'd like a little information, Carney."

Carney smiled back coldly. As communications technician on a Service-M, a tunneled-out asteroid hauled onto the space lanes for a supply depot, Carney could give no information without losing his job.

"Whatever you want," he said evenly, "I don't know it."

"When's Freeman Zellinger coming through?"

"I can't tell you when or if."

The Kid let the smile leave his face.

"When?"

Carney didn't answer. He kept his eyes on the Kid's hands.

The Kid's step was almost pretty as he walked across the room. His right hand drew a silky white handkerchief from his pocket. His voice was a rising falsetto.

"When—does—Freeman—Zellinger—come—through—Carney?"

Carney squeezed the stud on the pencil gun. A bright thin beam shot out in front of the Kid.

"You must want to fight," said the Kid. He took a step forward.

Carney kept his hand perfectly steady. A little more pressure on the stud and he would make himself a murderer. A little less pressure and the Kid would decide he was scared.

The Kid looked him squarely in the eyes.

"You like Freeman Zellinger?"

"Who doesn't?"

The Kid smiled.

"I like him, too," said the Kid. "I think of all those lists he's got. I'm going to get them, Carney. I'm going to be the guy that killed Freeman Zellinger."

The Kid smiled and stepped back. He walked to the door and slid it open. He looked at Carney.

"Thanks. I didn't know for sure he *was* coming through. But the way you act, now I know."

The Kid reached up, gripped the hall web, and pulled himself outside. Floating in the hall, he gave Carney a long, considering look. Then he gave a hard yank on the web and was gone.

***

Carney took a deep breath, crossed the room and slid the door shut. He went back to the teleprinter. He sorted messages till Gus Stevens came on shift, half an hour later.

Gus was short and stocky, with a thick mop of graying black hair.

"You look restrained," said Gus.

"The Kid was just in here."

"Oh. What did he do this time?"

"He wanted a little information."

"About what?"

"Look in the local tape file. Passenger list for the *City of Dallas*, refueling here about dinner time."

Gus thumbed through a number of message tapes. His eyes widened suddenly and he whistled.

"Freeman Zellinger!" Gus grinned. "Well. *Well*. Say, which way is the Kid's turret from here?"

Carney frowned, then pointed toward a corner of the room.

Gus raised his fingers to his lips and tossed a kiss toward the same corner.

"Goodbye, Kid," said Gus cheerfully.

"Goodbye, Zellinger," said Jim.

"Oh, come on. The Zell's a legend. The Kid will go out of here in deep storage."

"It takes time to get to be a legend," said Jim.

"You mean Zellinger's too old?"

"He was middle-aged when I was just a little kid."

"He's put a lot of punks and bullies under the ground since then."

"Maybe, but look where he's going."

Gus picked up the tape and frowned.

"Terra. So what?"

"He was born on Terra."

"Oh," Gus lowered the tape. "You mean he wants to spend his last few years in peace, back on the home planet. But, what's the difference? Somebody could give him the challenge there as well as anywhere."

"Oh, no, they couldn't," said Jim. "Anyone who tries that on Terra ends up behind three feet of concrete and steel. If Zellinger gets there, he can spend the rest of his life in peace."

Gus looked at the tape again, and shook his head.

"Well," he said, "I don't know. It's too bad. He's one of the good ones, too. I mean, he doesn't throw his weight around. . . . What the hell," Gus glared. "I still bet on the Zell."

"Yeah," said Jim.

"Go on, get out," said Gus. "If the Kid comes back here, I'll tell him Zellinger's coming through next week. Go on. Beat it. It's my shift. Damn it, anyway."

***

Jim went to the door, slid it open, reached up and grasped the smooth metal strands of the web. He tugged hard, and he was floating in the null-gravity of the hall. He looked back at Gus. Gus was looking gloomily at the message tape. Jim closed the door, pulled hard on the net, and shot down the hallway. He gave a quick tug to send himself flying down a cross corridor, stopped at a door, opened it and floated into his room. He set his feet carefully on the floor, switched on the gravity, and shut the door.

There was a faint rustle of cloth behind him.

"Hello, Carney," said the Kid's soft voice.

Jim turned and the rippling silky cloth snapped up. His face felt as if a swarm of bees had stung him.

The Kid's voice was a mincing falsetto. "When's—Freeman—Zellinger—coming—through—Carney?"

"I don't know."

"Come on!"

The cloth snapped up and back. It stung his cheek, his neck, his forehead.

"You want eyes to see with? When's—Freeman—Zellinger—coming—through—Carney?"

The outlines of the room wavered as if seen under water. Carney dove for the Kid and something hit him hard in the face. There was a bright explosion, then blackness.

Carney felt the hard floor under him. A bright beam was hanging in front of his face, going forward and back, forward and back, like the forked tongue flicking out of the mouth of a snake.

"When's—Freeman—Zellinger—coming—through—Carney?"

"Come on! You want me to leave you some teeth to eat with? You want some bones left to stand with?"

The beam vanished. He felt himself gripped by the collar. Something smashed across his face.

"*When?*"

Loose-lipped, Carney spat blood and clinking pieces of tooth. He felt weak and sick. But inside himself he felt a growing hardness.

"Three a.m. tomorrow," he said, his voice shaking with tension, and added silently, *Jupiter time*.

"Three a.m.," said the Kid, musing. "Thank you, Jim boy. You could have saved yourself some trouble." He went out.

Carney pulled himself to his feet and stood still till the room came into focus. He walked on trembling legs to the door and locked it. He went to the bottom drawer of his desk, pulled it out, and unstrapped a little, old-fashioned .22 revolver. He took out the shorts he used for target practice, and replaced them with explosive gougers. He looked at the gun for a long while, shook his head, and got up. He put the gun in his pocket and went to the infirmary.

The nurse on duty didn't think he should go to dinner. Jim talked to her till at last she understood. When he left, his right arm, face, neck, and part of his chest were bandaged. In his right hand, a single thin strip of gauze across its muzzle, was the gun.

***

The Kid was already at the table. He picked up three pieces of bread from a platter. The ration was one piece for a person. Carney looked around the room, then sat down. The Kid looked up.

"Is that you, Carney?" said the Kid.

"It's me," said Carney.

The Kid grinned, then suddenly looked serious.

"Say," said the Kid, "I left you some teeth to chew with, didn't I, Carn?"

"A few," said Carney.

The Kid smiled and looked relieved.

"That's good. Just don't get in my way, and I can be easy to get along with." The Kid looked around the table. "*Can't* I?" he said.

Most of the men acted as if they hadn't heard. One or two miserably nodded their heads and looked away.

"If you and me come up against each other," said the Kid cheerfully, "*you* give way. That's all there is to it." He stuffed a forkful of food in his mouth.

A lull came over the dining room. Jim Carney looked up. The station chief walked in, smiling, with several men, one a rather slender, well-knit man of slightly above average height. Carney recognized him instantly, though his hair was nearly white instead of the steel gray of his pictures.

The Kid disinterestedly glanced up and down, without stopping the tempo of his eating.

The station chief stopped at the head table, smiled, and said clearly, "Gentlemen—"

Everyone looked up.

"Men," said the station chief, "we have an unusual honor tonight. After tonight, you may say you have shared supper with Freeman Zellinger, who is our guest."

There was a momentary silence. Freeman Zellinger looked faintly surprised, then smiled pleasantly and started to sit down.

Across the table, the Kid's eyes darted back and forth from Zellinger to Carney.

"Speech!" someone shouted.

Zellinger smiled. In a calm, controlled voice that had a trace of an old man's rumble, he said, "It is a pleasure to dine with you. And it is a great pleasure to be here, so close to home."

There were cheers and clapping. Zellinger smiled and sat down.

The Kid got up. He walked down the aisle between the

tables to the table where Freeman Zellinger sat. He took hold of two men sitting across from Zellinger, slewed them around in their chairs, and jerked his thumb over his shoulder. They got up, white-faced, and left. The Kid sat down.

***

Jim Carney was on his feet, walking slowly to the table. He pulled out the chair next to the Kid and sat down, jostling him roughly.

Zellinger's eyes, Jim could see, were a clear, calm gray. Zellinger looked at Jim briefly, and it seemed to Jim that something moved deep in the back of his eyes. Then he looked back at the Kid. He reached out with a perfectly steady hand and took a long slow sip of water, as if relishing it.

Jim could feel the Kid's tenseness beside him. Suddenly the Kid relaxed and laughed.

Zellinger set the glass down gently and gratefully, as if he had partaken of a precious gift. He picked up his knife and cut a small bite of meat.

The Kid reached across with a table knife and smashed Zellinger's water glass.

Carney looked at Freeman Zellinger and saw him as an old man who had almost made it home.

Zellinger looked up, calmly chewing the little bite of meat. He swallowed, set down his fork and rested his hand on the table edge.

The Kid tossed his knife on the table.

"I challenge you—" he began.

The something that had been in the back of Freeman Zellinger's eyes was big in the front of them. His hand reached out. There was a smooth rippling snap, and the Kid's voice dragged backwards in his throat. The old man's hand rested on the edge of the table.

"Yes?" he inquired gravely.

"You son of a pig!" said the Kid. "You bastard! I'll kill you for that."

The old man waited.

The Kid's voice cut off abruptly. His hand darted back and out. There was a silky ripple.

Jim Carney clawed at the cloth and jabbed the Kid in the side with the gun.

"Fight *me*," said Carney, his voice rough.

Zellinger came to his feet.

"Give him the cloth."

The Kid snapped the cloth out of Jim's hand. He jumped up, his breath coming fast and his eyes blazing. His cheek was running blood.

"I'll kill you for that," he said.

The old man waited.

There was a little stir in the back of the room.

The Kid's hand lashed forward. The silk rippled out and snapped—in the empty air. Zellinger had moved at the last moment. He pulled the Kid's extended hand farther forward. The Kid landed with a smash in the broken glass on the tabletop, then struggled awkwardly to his feet.

Zellinger's hand blurred out and back, and the Kid was dragging in air roughly.

The Kid straightened up, blinking.

The old man waited.

The Kid made an abortive snatch in the direction of his waistband, then froze.

Zellinger smiled faintly and seemed to relax all over.

The Kid made a final small motion.

Zellinger smiled.

The Kid blinked.

"Aren't you going to go for your gun?"

"What's the hurry?" said the old man, smiling.

The Kid looked blank and frozen.

"You're too slow," said Zellinger. "You planned this so badly you had a man with a gun in your side before you even got started. With the skill and brains you've shown tonight, probably two out of five here could finish you. As for the gun, yes, when your hand reaches a certain point, I will have to kill you."

The Kid blinked. His hand edged downward and stopped. It edged a little bit farther. And stopped. A tiny bit farther.

Freeman Zellinger waited.

The Kid stood perfectly still.

Someone cleared his throat in the back of the room.

"I've had enough," the Kid blurted. He turned suddenly. He walked out rapidly with nearly a hundred eyes looking at his back.

"Two out of five," said someone musingly.

Jim Carney handed Zellinger another glass of water, from an empty place.

"Thank you," said Zellinger. He smiled and sat down, holding the glass.

Jim went back to his table. He felt worn out. He ate a little, then got up and went back to his room. He locked the door, switched off the grav, swam to the bed and snapped the blanket in place.

***

During the night he heard people drifting through the hall outside. Bits of conversation came through to him.

"Seen the Kid?"

"Scully seen him in the lounge."

"I'm going to see if I'm one of them two out of five."

"There's a lot of fives on this M. I'm coming with you."

Jim had the nightmare that he'd killed the Kid, and now he had all the lists of the people the Kid had killed, and all the lists the Kid had taken from the people he'd killed, and all the lists they'd taken from the people they'd killed, and now men were stalking Jim to kill *him* and get the lists. Jim walked around a corner and there was Freeman Zellinger, waiting. Jim clutched at his waist. A gun appeared in Zellinger's hand. There was a blast.

The blast went on. Gasping and sobbing for breath, Jim came awake. The morning buzzer was ringing in his ear. He switched it off, unsnapped the blanket and floated up. He pushed gently on the bed, drifted across the room, got his feet under him, and switched on the gravity.

He ate breakfast and went to the communications center. Gus Stevens was leaning over the clacking teleprinter, grinning broadly.

"What are you doing here?" asked Jim.

"Lefty Schultz went Kid-hunting," said Gus. "I took his shift for him. They're searching the ventilation system for the Kid right now, but I guess I better go stop them."

His grin widened.

"What's the grin for?" demanded Jim.

"Oh," said Gus, "look at this passenger list the *City of Dallas* just sent in."

Jim took the list and glanced at it. He laughed unrestrainedly.

"The Kid's retiring early," said Gus, grinning wider. The list read:

P. M. Jones	to Mars
Oscar J. Rasch	" Terra
F. R. Zellinger	" Terra
Kid Roe	" Destination Unknown

"I hope he's happy there," said Gus. He grinned some more, and blew a kiss at the wall.

High Road to the East

The Admiral moved around the bridge nervously, aware of the uselessness of the compass, the latest shift of the stars, and the ugly temper of the crew. He heard the sound of a sword loosened in its scabbard, and Alfonso Gomez plucked at his sleeve.

"Sir," said Gomez, "here are the crew's spokesmen."

The Admiral looked up angrily. A barrel-chested crewman drifted in, accompanied by a swarthy, intense-looking man and a thin, frightened individual. The barrel-chested crewman spoke with great firmness:

"We want to go home."

The Admiral glared at him.

"Go home! How, as paupers?"

"Alive. We want to go back now, while we can."

"Never," said the Admiral. "We go straight ahead."

The intense, swarthy crewman spoke up. "Sir," he said, "we're loyal. We've come with you, though all the world says this latest venture is folly. But, sir, we have limits, and you stretch our strength too far!"

"Folly!" roared the Admiral, bringing his fist down on the rail. "What did they say the first time? The truth of my idea is plain and obvious, and if you weren't frightened half to death by old women's superstitions, you'd see it!"

"Sir," said the crewman, "perhaps if you'd explain it again—?"

"It's clear as sunlight," said the Admiral, spreading his hand. "Look now, the earth's a globe." He glared at them. "Surely we don't have to go through *that* again."

"Oh, no, sir," they said in unison, "we see that."

"All right," said the Admiral. "Here's Spain, on this side. Around on the other side, here, are the Indies. And here's Cathay. If we can trade direct with them, our fortunes are made. Bring back a shipload of pepper, for instance. —Everyone wants it, and it brings a high price."

The crewmen's eyes were rapt. They nodded to show they understood so far.

"All right," said the Admiral. "Now, the Portuguese have this idea of a route around Africa. That'll work, but why bend and wind all over the surface of creation when you can go *straight!*" He brought his hand out in a straight chopping motion. "Cut off all that winding and twisting. Go *direct*. Right to the goal!" His eyes flashed.

The crewmen looked uneasy. The intense crewman coughed apologetically. "We tried that, Admiral. It didn't work."

The Admiral looked pained.

The barrel-chested crewman cleared his throat. In the manner of one treading on treacherous ground, he added, "There was land in the way."

The Admiral studied the deck. There was always this

being thrown in his face. "Well," he said irritatedly, "how was I to know that? The *idea* was right. All we had to do was make a little . . . correction."

The intense crewman nodded vigorously. "That's the part we want to hear about again. We don't understand that. Tell us about the correction again."

"Well," said the Admiral, "there we were, with that long stretch of land right in the way. It wasn't my fault. It wasn't anyone's fault. But if we went around it, we'd be winding along a length of coastline again. It'd make the journey too long. The whole idea was to go *straight!*"

The room was silent as they listened.

"All right," said the Admiral. "If you've got a gun, you don't tie the bullet on a turtle and have it crawl up and down over every little bump and rise in the ground, do you? No. You shoot it straight to the mark. And if there's an obstruction in the way, why, you just aim a little higher and loft it over the obstruction."

There was an intense silence. No-one seemed to be breathing.

"Well," said the Admiral, "so I just explained my new idea to the King, and kept after him till he finally gave me, for once, a ship that wasn't worm-eaten. And then I just—well—remodeled it a little, and got a good lot of gunpowder collected, and here we are."

"That's it," said the intense crewman. "We're here. But *where is here?*"

"Where's the bullet," said the Admiral, "before it hits the mark? We're in the air, of course."

"We've been here a long time. It seems like we ought to come down, sooner or later."

The thin, nervous-looking crewman began to whine. "I don't see why we should stand it. First, all those terrible explosions, then that wind, and nothing but float around and plug leaks twenty hours a day. Half rations, and quarter-rations, and what *good* will it do anyway? Maybe we'll never make it and we'll break to pieces on the mountains. Or maybe we're over already, *and right now we're down on the bottom of the sea and we'll* NEVER COME UP!"

"That's nonsense," snapped the Admiral. "If we were in the sea we'd feel the motion."

"Sir," said the intense crewman, moving a bit forward, "some of us have a different worry. Suppose you aimed too high? Or that freak wind that caught us—suppose it flipped us away from earth like a—a stone from a sling?"

The Admiral's face paled. Evading the issue, he said, "Don't be like the donkey."

The crewmen looked blank. "Donkey?"

The Admiral nodded. "Once there was a donkey that smelled hay over a high hill. He climbed to the top, made it over the worst places and started to descend. When he was almost there, the wind changed. He *gave up* and went back—and lost the prize."

The intense crewman frowned. "What does that have to do with us?"

"*We're* about there, too."

"But where's the proof?"

The Admiral shrugged. "It's in the log."

"Let us see. If you can show us, we'll go on."

The Admiral seemed to think it over. At last he gave an exaggerated shrug. He turned to Gomez, who was now staring out of the solitary small thick porthole the Admiral used for observations. "Gomez," said the Admiral, with a peculiar emphasis, "the *log*."

"Eh?" said Gomez absently. "Oh, yes sir. The log." He picked up the log and came forward.

"Not *that* one!" roared the Admiral, losing his temper. He glanced at the crewmen, looked guilty for a moment, then excessively innocent.

"*Two logs*," muttered the crewmen, looking dazed.

The intense crewman bared his teeth. "*Treachery!*" He whipped out a knife.

The Admiral's sword hissed from its scabbard.

"We stay on course!"

Gomez was back at the porthole. "Admiral," he said, "I think you're right. Look out here!"

Their disagreement momentarily forgotten, Admiral and crewmen pulled themselves swiftly to the porthole and stared out.

"See," said Gomez. "That's the moon, isn't it?"

"H'm," said the Admiral. He blew on the glass and wiped a sleeve across it. There seemed to be two moons out there, different sizes and in different places. The waviness of the glass added a frustrating distortion, so that it was hard to tell what was real and what was due to the glass. "Blast the fellow that made this," snapped the Admiral. "Yes, that *must* be the moon. What else can it be?" He craned his neck to squint ahead at an angle. "Ah," he breathed, "and they called this folly! Look ahead, *land!* See there, coming closer below, a cloud drifting!"

"So it is," said Gomez, awed.

"Sir," said the intense crewman, trying to see. "Let me

have a look. I was on a caravan to the East one time. Maybe I could tell where we are."

"Go ahead," said the Admiral. After a moment, he added, "What do you think?"

"H'm," said the crewman. "It's sort of red. And those lines stretching across. It can't be the Indies."

"Not the Indies?" cried the Admiral, anguished.

"It's too much like desert, sir. We must have overshot. H'm. Those lines *might* be the Great Wall. —Maybe it's Cathay."

"Well," said the Admiral, sounding relieved.

Gomez lifted a foot thoughtfully. "We're falling, sir. I don't know how I can tell, but I feel the tug of the Earth."

The Admiral squinted out the porthole again. "What goes up must come down," he said hopefully. "All right men, back you go to your posts."

"Yes, sir." The three crewmen obeyed with alacrity, relieved at the thought of land below.

The Admiral returned to the rail and bawled out, "All right now, men, get that slowmatch lit! Ready on the starboard number three fuse! But don't touch her till I give the word!"

There was a scurrying sound as his orders were obeyed. "Ready on starboard number three, sir!" Another voice called, "Slowmatch ready, sir!"

The Admiral turned and took another look out the porthole. "Awfully red," he said thoughtfully. "Well, I hope it's Cathay." He turned to shout his command and hesitated. Come to think of it, wasn't *Mars* red? He looked out again. "God, I hope I didn't discover another—" He gritted his teeth and glared out at it, whatever it was. Then he shrugged, turned away and took a deep breath.

"Starboard number three!" the Admiral shouted. "Ready now! *Light it!*"

There was a roar, and the ship turned.

"One way to find out," groaned the Admiral.

They started down.

A Tourist Named Death

Dan Redman walked swiftly and quietly down the broad hallway toward a door lettered:

A SECTION
J. KIELGAARD
DIRECTOR

As Dan opened the door, his trained glance caught the brief reflection of a strange, strong-featured face, and a lithe, powerful, and unfamiliar physique. Dan accepted this unfamiliar reflection of himself as an actor accepts makeup. What puzzled him was the peculiar silent smoothness with which his hand turned the knob, while his shoulder braced firmly and easily against the opening door. He stepped into the room in one sudden quiet motion.

The receptionist inside gave a visible start.

What kind of job, Dan asked himself, did Kielgaard have for him this time?

The receptionist recovered her poise, to usher Dan into the inner office.

Kielgaard—big, stocky, and expensively dressed—glanced up from a sheaf of glossy photographs. He said bluntly, "Sit down. We've got a mess to straighten out."

"What's wrong?"

"A few years back, Galactic Enterprises discovered a totally undeveloped planet with no inhabitants. They claimed development rights and got to work to find an economical route to the planet, which is called Triax."

Kielgaard snapped a switch on the edge of his desk and the room lights dimmed out. Three stellar maps seemed to hang in space in front of Dan, one map directly above the other.

Kielgaard's voice said, "Galactic found a route to Triax that promised to be very economical. Watch."

***

On the lowest map, the word "Earth" lit up, and a silver line grew out from it along the stellar map, then jumped up in a vertical straight line to the second map, traveled along this map almost to a place where the word "Truth" lit up. The line then jumped straight up to the third map and traveled along it to the word "Triax."

The room lighted and the maps vanished.

Kielgaard said, "In two subspace jumps and not too much normal-space traveling, Galactic can ship a cargo from Triax to Earth. That's a good, short route, but it comes too close to that planet called Truth."

Dan said, "Truth is the native name for the planet?"

"Exactly. Truth is inhabited. The inhabitants look much like us, and they're very highly developed technologically, though there is no sign that they use space travel in any form. The problem is that Galactic's cargo ships will pass close enough to Truth so that the inhabitants—call them Truthians—will eventually detect them and may or may not like the idea. Galactic's worry is that after sinking a lot of money into the development of Triax, and just as it's about to make a profit on the planet, these Truthians may blossom out with a fleet of commerce raiders, or else claim sovereignty over all contiguous space and land Galactic in a big court fight." Kielgaard glanced at Dan with a smile. "Suppose you were running Galactic and had this problem. What would you do?"

"Try to vary the route. But subspace being what it is, a mild variation of the starting point can produce an abrupt shift in the place where they come out."

Kielgaard nodded. "There's probably a usable route, but there's no telling when they'll find it. Meanwhile, the development license only runs so long before Galactic has to show proof of progress."

"What's this Truth look like?"

"Earth-type, with cities and towns scattered over its surface at random, some of the cities remarkably advanced, some antique, with forest and wilderness in between, and only haphazard communications between cities."

Dan frowned. "Well, then, I'd set down an information team, brain-spy some of the inhabitants, and ease agents into key cities and towns. At the same time, I'd go on looking for a new route, and do enough work on Triax to keep the development license. When things clear up on Truth, I'd develop Triax further."

Kielgaard nodded. "A sound and sensible plan. That is

exactly what Galactic did. And after a slow start, things began to straighten out very nicely, too. The more Truth cleared up, the more Galactic invested in Triax. And then, one day, this photograph came in."

Kielgaard held out a photograph showing a busy street corner in a city at night. A brightly clothed crowd was walking along the sidewalk past store windows showing a variety of merchandise.

Kielgaard said, "Look down that street. You see a low building, part way down the block, with a wide chimney?"

"Yes," said Dan, "I see it."

"Look just above the top of the chimney."

"You mean this arrow-shaped constellation?"

Kielgaard nodded. "There is no such arrow-shaped constellation visible from Truth."

"Then this photo is a fake?"

"They're all fakes. What apparently happened is that someone managed to get a spy into Galactic's planning division, and through him found out when and where Galactic's agents were to be set down. They grabbed the agents one by one soon after each agent landed. Since then, they've sent back reports to build up a purely synthetic picture of the planet. The only reports Galactic can rely on are the original impressions of the information team they set down to begin with."

Dan whistled. "So someone is working Galactic into position to jerk the rug out from under it."

"Exactly."

"What's Galactic doing?"

"They're trying hard to keep this quiet. But meanwhile, no one knows for sure who the spy is."

"A nice situation," said Dan. "What do we do about this planet Truth?"

***

"Well," said Kielgaard, "the first thing we do is set a man down and let him get the lay of the land. We get more agents ready to move in right behind him. We intend to use the best men available, and nothing but the latest and best equipment. If things turn out as we intend them to, whatever organization started this will come out slit up the middle, stuffed, roasted, and with an apple in its mouth."

Dan said cautiously, "Who's the first agent we set down on this planet?"

"You," said Kielgaard. "And you're going to be up against a deadly proposition. Our opponent is established on the planet, and we're going in cold. Fortunately, we've sunk a good part of our profits into research and it's about to pay off. We have, for instance, installed in your body cavity a remarkably small organo-transceiver. It uses a new type of signal which should escape detection under any circumstances you're likely to face on Truth."

***

"So I can be more or less constantly in touch with you?"

"In any period of relative calm, yes. During violent action, the interference of other currents in your brain would drown out the signal. But we've also run a series of delicate taps to your optic and auditory nerves, so we should have continuous contact by sight and sound."

"You mentioned that the cities and towns on the planet were separated by wilderness. How do I travel?"

"We have a new type of unusually small mataform transceiver." Kielgaard reached in a drawer and tossed on his desk a smooth olive-colored object little larger than a package of cigarettes. "The range is only a few hundred miles, but it uses the new type of signal I've mentioned, which eliminates the problem of orbiting a set of satellites to relay the signal. The problem of first putting the mataform transceiver in the place where you want to go is tricky, but we have a little glider that ought to do the trick."

He showed Dan how to use the glider, and several other new items of equipment, then frowned and sat back. "The worst of this is, we don't know exactly what to expect on the planet. Some big organization could even be trying to take over the planetary government. If so, a lot will depend on what stage things are in when you land. To give you as much chance as possible, your body has been carefully restructured to give you exceptional strength and endurance. The neuro-conditioning lab has recreated in your nervous system the reflexes of one of the deadliest agents ever known. Don't be surprised if you perform certain actions almost before you're aware of your own intentions. It has to be that way to cut down the risks."

Dan and Kielgaard shook hands, and Dan went out to check his equipment.

Early the next day, he was on a fast spaceship to the planet called Truth.

***

Dan was dropped low over the night side of the planet in a vaned capsule that whirled straight down, burst open on contact with the water, and sank. From this capsule, a small boat nosed out toward the coast.

In the cramped space inside, Dan checked a little gauge to be sure the boat's outer layer had adjusted to the water around it, so that there would be no sharp difference in the radiation of heat to show up on any infrared detector that might be in range. Then the boat nosed down with a *suck-swish* from the water-jet engine and began to pick up speed.

Several hours later, a thin flexible cable shot out from shallow water at the edge of the junglelike coastline. The cable whipped around the trunk of a tree well back from the water's edge, there was a faint low hum, a grating noise, and something slid up over the rocks and pebbles and came to rest among the tangled trunks and roots of the trees. A moment later, Dan was out and dragging the boat further inland.

When he was satisfied that the boat was safe, he glanced at his watch. The planet's large moon should soon be up and he intended to waste no time making his position more secure.

He broke open a carton of the little mataform transceivers, clipped several of them on small, almost completely transparent gliders, and checked to be sure the little auxiliary motors of the gliders were in working order. He slid on a helmet that fit tightly over his head and eyes, and sent up the first glider. As the faint whir of the small engine receded, Dan could see before him in the helmet a clear view of the sea, with the thin rim of the planet's moon just rising, huge and blood-red, over the horizon.

The small sensor unit on the glider sent back an image from a safe height above the forest, and Dan switched the helmet from this glider long enough to send up another.

By dawn, he had landed gliders, with their small mataform transceivers, in isolated spots outside three moderate-sized cities within range of the boat. Dan then took another of the mataform units and buried it. Standing nearby, he mentally pronounced a key word.

As he did this, the electrochemical change in a nervous tract triggered a tiny implanted device that sent its imperceptible signal to the mataform transceiver. The transceiver interpreted the signal, and for an instant Dan sensed a shift in the pattern of things around him.

Abruptly he was standing in the clearing where he had brought down the first glider. Around him were several tall wind-thrown trees. In the gray light of early dawn, he could barely make out the glider and little mataform unit clipped to it. A few minutes later, the unit was temporarily hidden, he had returned the glider to the boat, and he was picking up the second glider in a badly burned tract of forest near the second city.

***

When the three mataform units were all hidden, Dan paused for a moment to think through the next step. The three gliders, invisible to the naked eye as they passed high above the tree tops, might possibly have shown up on any of a number of detection devices, to give away both the starting point and the places where they had landed. It was now Dan's problem to outwit these detection devices.

Dan clipped another mataform transceiver to a glider, put on the control helmet, and sent the glider dodging low and carefully through the trees. He found a spot about two miles away that suited him and landed the glider. He swiftly unloaded the boat and carried its contents to the buried mataform unit, where he mentally pronounced a new key word, which triggered the unit and took him to the glider and transceiver he had just landed. In a short time, he had the contents of the boat stacked beside the glider.

Dan then disassembled boat and engine, and stacked the parts beside the boat's piled-up contents. By now, the sun was well up, and Dan was becoming aware of a thrumming drone that grew steadily louder. He quickly dug up the buried mataform unit, clipped it to a glider, and hung the glider to an overhead limb by a green string knotted so as to come undone at the first sharp pull.

Dan glanced around carefully and listened to the increasing drone. He looked up and studied a bumpy blue-green limb well overhead. This limb was so located that a spy unit on it would cover most of the place where the boat had been. Dan carefully gauged the speed with which the droning was coming closer, then went by mataform to the pile of goods he had transferred, came back with a long tube, and sighted at the overhead limb. There was a *whoosh* and a small colorless blob with a tiny bump in the center spread out on the limb. The blob gradually turned blue-gray, matching the limb, and then the spy unit was indistinguishable from the limb's other bumps and irregularities.

The droning noise was now quite loud.

Dan went by mataform to his new camp and put on the helmet he used to control the glider.

An instant later, the glider gave a whir and jerked forward. The knot came untied, and the glider, carrying the mataform unit and a length of dark-green string, flitted out of sight amid the big tree trunks.

Dan, his hand on the knob at the side of the helmet, shifted his vision rapidly back and forth from the glider to the spy unit over the spot where the boat had been.

There now came into view, in the place where the boat had been, something that looked like a cross between an oversize bloodhound and a tiger. Right behind this came a man with a rifle. Then another man, and another. The angle of vision did not let Dan see exactly where the men came from, but he supposed there was a jetcopter just overhead.

The tigerlike animal snuffled around, pawed at the ground, made trips into the jungle on all sides, and finally ran back toward the shore. The men followed close behind.

***

Dan, shifting his attention back and forth from this scene to the glider, landed the glider nearby just as the last of the men left the place where the boat had been. Dan quickly went to each of the three places near cities where he had landed mataform transceivers, and moved each of them by glider well away from the places where they had landed. He left behind in each place a small spy unit.

He had just finished doing this when several loads of heavily armed men in jetcopters came down in all three places. The men, Dan noticed, wore no uniforms, and the copters were unmarked.

Dan said mentally, "Can you hear me, Kielgaard?"

"Loud and clear," came the familiar voice. "We're getting sight and sound perfectly."

"Have you got your corps of experts working on everything that comes in?"

"Naturally," said Kielgaard. "But I wouldn't advise you to stop and chat right now. Those boys seem to mean business."

"Do they look like planetary police to you?"

"No. They don't look like anything that was born on that planet."

"That's exactly the way they strike me. Well, maybe I can make them some more trouble."

Dan got out a map and noted a long, fairly straight road from one of the cities near which he had hidden a mataform transceiver to another distant city. From this distant city, a winding river curled away to a city even more distant. That night, Dan intended to make use of road and river alike. But right now he spent an hour or so moving his goods to a place further away from the landing; then he partly reassembled the boat, and catnapped till evening. He was woken at frequent intervals by sudden drops of men and more of the tigerlike animals, at each of the four places where they had been before. Each time there was sudden activity at one of these places, a little alarm buzzed in Dan's ear, and he slid on the helmet to watch a renewed search of the ground.

He had the impression that someone had reported nothing was to be found, and that this word had been passed along to someone who had said there *must* be something there, and it had better be found or else. The search this time was much more careful. But it was not till the last place was searched that one of them came very close to the spy unit, and reached out toward it.

Dan regretfully slid back a protective cover at the lower edge of the helmet and pressed a button underneath. There was a dazzling flash, and then the scene was gone.

Dan would much rather have kept them thinking that maybe there was nothing to look for after all. But he could tell from their numbers and zeal that he was not likely to have very much his own way on this planet.

***

That night, Dan sent a glider under power down the long road to the distant city. The glider was low enough to avoid the usual detectors, but happily free of the need to dodge an endless succession of tree trunks. The river served much the same purpose, so that well before dawn, Dan had mataform transceivers planted near each of the two new cities, and also at a place right at the edge of the river. From this spot, Dan threw out into the river a heavily weighted mataform transceiver. He returned to the partly assembled boat and methodically put it together again. This time, however, he fitted sections together differently and left the heavy engine out entirely. He put his arms around one end of the thing he had put together and mentally said a key word.

The river water rushed coldly around him, gritty with silt sweeping along the bottom. There was a *chug* in his ears as the water triggered off the grab anchors around the rim of the shelter. Dan said another key word and he was inside. He snapped on a light and looked carefully around, but found no sign of a leak.

He transferred the rest of his goods, checked to see that the selective membrane panel was keeping the oxygen at the right level inside, then lay down to catch up on sleep.

The following day, he took three of his small transceivers, and went by mataform to a place outside the nearest city.

A short walk along a winding trail took Dan past a series of huts and cabins to a rough covered stand displaying combs, brooms, and other simple merchandise, along with a dusty case of what looked like soda pop, and a dust-covered carton of what appeared to be candy bars. The soda pop was labeled "GAS," and the candy had a card labeled "TOOTHROT." The girl in charge of the stand smiled and said, "Good morning, Death."

There was no one else around, and the girl spoke in a perfectly natural way, so Dan smiled back and said, "Good morning."

But as he walked on down the trail, he said mentally, "Kielgaard?"

Kielgaard's voice replied, "I heard it, Dan. We're checking at this end to see if it's some error in the vocabulary we implanted in your brain." A moment later, Kielgaard said, "As nearly as we can tell here, 'Death' is the word she used."

"Funny."

Dan rounded a bend in the trail and came to a moderately wide road, paved with smooth blocks of stone. To his right was a wall about ten feet high, with an open gate and a city street visible behind it. From somewhere came the steady beat of a drum. Dan started toward the gate, but had to jump aside as a heavily armed column of troops marched out, their faces set and their feet striking the ground in an unvarying cadence.

As the last of the troops went by, a man standing nearby turned to Dan and said, "Well, there they go. We won't be seeing some of them again in this life."

Dan nodded noncommittally, and the man looked at him sharply, then grinned and said, "Good hunting."

"Thank you," said Dan. He could hear a faint muttering somewhere in the background, which he took to be Kielgaard and his experts, trying to understand this latest exchange.

Dan followed the man through the city gates, and walked past a variety of small shops selling baked goods, meats, groceries, hand tools, books, and appliances.

Dan noted the location of the bookstore, so that on the way back he could buy some books. He wanted to transmit the contents of the books; the staff of experts could learn a great deal from a cross-section of a planet's fiction and non-fiction.

***

As Dan walked toward the center of the city, he noted that the buildings grew larger, and the shops turned into big department stores. These all looked much the same as the ones on Earth, or on many other technologically advanced planets. The merchandise showed only minor differences in design. Looking in a hardware store, for instance, Dan discovered that ordinary screwdrivers had a short curved crosspiece on the handle—apparently a thumb rest to give greater leverage in turning. Aside from such minor differences, everything seemed the same.

Dan had just decided that the planet looked almost like home when he came to a low building with a paved yard. Into the yard trundled several small carts, similar to the kind used to transfer baggage in railroad and mataform depots back home. On these carts, however, were canvas covers, which were thrown back to reveal fully clothed human forms. On all but one cart, the human forms wore the same kind of white garment, trimmed in various colors. These forms—bodies, Dan supposed—were lifted from the carts by attendants who handled them with the greatest care and respect.

On the other cart, though, the bodies wore street clothes. These bodies were grabbed under the arms, dragged to a black door like the door of a furnace, set in the wall of the building, and shoved through the door head first. As the bodies were shoved in, Dan saw the sunlight glint on what looked like tight metal cords around their necks, bearing oblong metal tags.

Several men had stopped while Dan glanced in to watch this scene. Dan now overheard their comments, which were made in tense angry tones:

"Look at that. If this referendum isn't over soon, it'll dust the lot of us over the forest."

"It's all these charges and accusations that make the trouble. Why we can't do it like civilized human beings, I don't know."

"The trouble is, there's no precedent."

The men walked away.

Dan had the out-of-focus sensation of a man who comes into a room where a joke has already been half-told.

He glanced at the low building. "Are you getting all this, Kielgaard?"

"We're getting it. But I hope it makes more sense to you than it does to us."

"Well, it doesn't."

Dan glanced around, noted the discreet word "DISPOSAL" printed on the face of the small building where the bodies were shoved through what looked like a furnace door. Dan thought he could see what was going on here, but the reasons for the things that were happening were totally obscure to him.

It was in the next block that he began to get some sort of an idea, when he saw a large poster bearing a blue triangle standing point down. Stamped over this triangle were large letters: VOTE YES!

Several blocks away was a big poster showing a green triangle, its base down, and bearing the words: VOTE NO!

***

Both posters were dented, scratched, and spattered, as if stones and rotten fruit had been thrown at them. But, though Dan watched carefully as he walked on toward the center of the city, he saw no clue as to what the voting was about. He was also puzzled to find that, though there were many stores, and a fair number of what looked like hotels, office buildings, and apartment houses, there seemed to be no factories, large or small.

The people passing here were another source of uncertainty. As Dan approached the center of the city, he began to sense the peculiar air of freedom that he had noticed in resort towns on a dozen planets. And yet this did not look to him like a resort town. Moreover, it was hard to gauge the mood of the people passing by, because nearly all seemed to react to his presence in some way. Some looked suddenly alarmed, a few looked furtive, others seemed pleased and smiled at him. A considerable number of the women had a thrilled look when they saw him.

Dan walked another block and saw part of the reason for the resort-town atmosphere. Across the street was a sweeping expanse of green. In the far end of this green was an enormous swimming pool, with floats and concrete islands dotted through it to hold diving boards that were almost constantly in use.

Dan, wanting to watch the passersby without their watching him, stepped into a quiet, old-fashioned-looking bookstore that fronted on the green. He looked out the many-paned front window and immediately noticed a change in the people. Without his inexplicably disturbing influence, nearly all of the people fell into two distinct categories. One group had a depressed and angry look. The other group looked cheerful and carefree. Aside from their mood, they didn't seem to differ noticeably in dress, age, or any other way.

Dan glanced around the bookstore and saw that it, like the other stores, could be transplanted to Earth, and—except for the unfamiliar lettering on storefront and book titles—would hardly be noticed. He nodded to an elderly woman working at a small desk to one side of the store, then walked to the rear, where the stacks of books left a far corner partially in shadow and out of sight from the front of the store. Dan stooped, glanced at the dusty row of books on the bottom shelf, and slid a mataform transceiver behind the books.

He walked back to the front of the store, stepped out on the sidewalk, and saw a cart come slowly along in the street. This was the kind of cart he had seen earlier. The outstretched figures of men lay bumping loosely on the cart, metal cords with oblong tags tight around their necks. Dan stepped over to note that the tags he could see all read:

—KILL—

UNAUTHORIZED

***

There was a buzz of indignation from the crowd on the sidewalk as the cart went by.

Then there was a sudden silence.

Dan glanced around.

Walking along the sidewalk toward him was a man about his own height and build, who moved with controlled catlike steps.

The man looked directly at Dan and called out: "Hello, Death!"

The people on the sidewalk rushed to get out of the way. Abruptly the man's arm swung back and forward.

"Catch."

Something flashed in the air.

Dan's impulse was to jump aside, then tackle the man. Instead, his body turned slightly. His right hand, already partly raised, whipped in a short arc, caught something, flicked it to his left, and blurred straight out again.

The man opposite Dan blinked and jumped aside.

At the same instant, Dan's left hand shot out.

There was a gasp from the crowd. The man collapsed with the butt of a knife jutting from his chest.

A voice behind Dan said warmly, "Superb! A return attack complete in one stroke!"

Dan turned to see three alert, strong-looking men.

One counted bills from a thick roll. The second opened up a square case with carrying handle. The third was unwinding an armband with a badge on it.

The man with the case held it out. "If you'll just put your fingertips on these plates, so we'll be sure to get your mating credits—"

Dan sensed from the waiting attitude of the people watching that this was some kind of test. Unhesitatingly, he held out his fingertips. There were also two bright flashes as a small tube was held to Dan's eyes.

Once Dan could see again, everyone seemed relaxed and friendly. The crowd was excitedly arguing the details of what had happened. The man with the roll of bills handed over a small fistful, saying, "Double, for the return at one stroke."

The man with the armband put it on Dan's arm as he rapidly recited the words of some rote formula, of which all Dan caught was a frequent reference to "the Code," and the words "peril and deadly danger," and the last words, "now say, 'I do.'"

"I do," said Dan, fervently wishing he were somewhere else.

The man with the case was beaming as he snapped the little rod inside. He said genially, "I always know an honest fight when I see it. And these days it's a real pleasure to—"

Just then, he clapped the case shut.

The case gave out a clang like the general alarm on a space cruiser under surprise attack.

The crowd gave a shout. "Unauthorized kill!"

The three men beside Dan jumped forward.

Dan's left hand lashed out to smash the nearest of the three men in the midsection. The flat edge of his right hand struck the second man just below the nose; then Dan had thrown the first man back against the third, had whirled around and seen the crowd start to surge across the sidewalk to block his escape. He sprinted directly past this crowd, so that when it completely blocked the sidewalk an instant later, he was cut off from the view of the three men he had just knocked down.

Dan did not doubt that these three men were officials of the planet, and he strongly suspected that they were armed and knew how to use their weapons.

＊＊＊

Across the street, at the edge of one corner of the green, was a tall hedge of flowering shrubs, back of which was a grove of young trees. Dan dodged past carts and small, square, silent automobiles, and ran through this hedge. Behind him there was a shout of anger.

To Dan's left were two young trees, growing close together. Dan still had with him two of his little mataform units, and he quickly thrust one of them between the two dark, slender tree trunks.

An instant later, he was in the dark corner of the bookstore, hearing the angry shouts dwindle into the distance outside. The door of the store closed as the elderly woman who ran the store stepped outside, apparently to see what had happened.

A moment later, Dan was in the shelter under the river. He worked quickly with a small brush and some dye, then got out another set of clothes. He checked his appearance swiftly and thoroughly.

Then, with more of a tanned look than he had had before, with much darker hair, and wearing entirely different clothes, Dan mataformed back to the bookstore. The elderly woman was standing by the front window as he came forward, to pick up a thin scientific volume and say, "I believe you were outside when I came in."

"Oh," she said, "the most frightful thing just happened." She then gave a highly inaccurate account of Dan's fight with the knife man, and described how the crowd was hunting him down right now at the far end of the park.

Dan took his change and said, "I'll have to go look."

He stepped outside and could see the path of the crowd with no difficulty. The flowering shrubs were flattened, and the ground under the trees showed the marks of many feet. Dan recovered his mataform unit and walked a short distance to look down toward the far end of the green, where the swimmers were all out of the pool—probably so that it could be searched for Dan.

He turned around and noticed near the bookstore a large restaurant, built in a style that made him think of an old English tavern. Several men looking well contented came out. Dan realized he was hungry.

He went in, and from a weird merry-go-round serving apparatus got a steak indistinguishable from those at home, and a selection of unfamiliar side dishes that looked good to him, but made other diners nearby wince. Dan paid for his selection and sat down.

During the meal, someone at a nearby table began to talk loudly, and someone else shouted, "Spacerot!" There was a momentary hush in the restaurant, and two burly men in white jackets quickly crossed to the table and spoke firmly to the diners. Peace was restored, and the two burly men wove back through several parties just leaving the restaurant, and separated to stand quietly but alertly near the far wall.

As Dan ate, he thought, "Kielgaard!"

"Right here."

"Do you make any sense out of what we've seen so far?"

"I get the impression something's about to snap, but I don't know what. Or as my experts here tell me, 'It's too early to venture an opinion.'"

"That," thought Dan, "is likely to be the trouble with this place. By the time we find out what's going on, it will be too late to do anything about it. We're going to have to play hunches to crack this one in time."

Kielgaard said fervently, "*How* we crack it makes no difference to me, so long as we *do* crack it."

***

While Dan ate, a considerable crowd of people went out the front door, and two couples came in. The restaurant, however, remained nearly full.

"Something tells me," Dan thought, "that there must be a lot more to this planet than meets the eye."

He got up and walked toward the back of the restaurant. What he had taken for the rear wall turned out to be merely a wall that divided one section of the restaurant from another equally large, where waitresses served individual tables.

A flight of carpeted steps led down to men's and women's rest rooms and a gently sloping, softly lighted hallway. People were coming up the hall in considerably greater numbers than they went down, and Dan was startled to see that they reacted to him exactly as the crowd outside had, before he had gone into the bookstore to watch them unnoticed.

Dan went to the men's rest room, washed, and inconspicuously studied himself in the mirror. He looked very much different than he had before. Why, then, did the people react in the same way?

Dan concealed a mataform unit in the dimly lit lounge outside the washroom, then went out and down the hall. He had gone perhaps thirty steps when a lithe man coming the other way saw him, whipped out a gun, and shouted, "*Death!*"

One instant Dan was walking down the right side of the hall. A split fraction of an instant later, he had thrown himself to the other side of the hall.

There was a swift, bright flash.

Someone screamed.

The gun went spinning and Dan had the man on the floor, both hands locked at his throat. It was a severe struggle for Dan to loosen his hands.

A crowd gathered so quickly that there was scarcely room to stand. A man carrying a small box with a handle forced his way through. Dan had his captive, half-unconscious, on his feet. Improvising rapidly, Dan said, "I think that was unauthorized."

The man with the carrying case said grimly, "We'll soon find out." He held the man's fingertips to plates in the case, flashed a small tube in his eyes, and shut the case. There was a loud clang.

Two powerfully built men wearing armbands with

shields stepped up. One glanced at Dan and said, "Want to finish him? He's yours, by rights."

Someone in the crowd said, "*Question* him! Find out which side is behind this!"

The man with the carrying case said sternly, "That's neither here nor there. The only question is, which side is *right?*"

There was a tense silence. It occurred to Dan that this planet might not be called Truth for nothing. He was still gripping his captive by the arms and wanted in the worst way to question him. But how, in this crowd? And then he remembered that he still had one mataform unit with him.

The man with the case was saying to the sullen crowd, "Maybe you think something's wrong. Maybe it is. All right, you know what to do—*go to the War Ruler—*"

Dan mentally pronounced a key word, then opened his hands as he pronounced another.

A momentary flash of dense jungle, and then he was in the corridor again, his prisoner gone.

***

It all seemed to take a moment to register. As soon as it did, someone shouted, "Spacerot!" This word acted on the crowd like a blazing torch thrown into an explosives shack. They began smashing each other violently around in the crowded corridor. Dan barely recovered his mataform unit, which had fallen to the floor when he transferred his prisoner, and had a rough time merely staying on his feet. The savage pressing and crowding in the jammed corridor seemed to drive the crowd to hysteria.

Dan realized there was no way to tell when he might get loose. For the second time, he used the mataform unit to get out of the corridor. This time he went to the shelter under the river. He got some strong cord, went to the place in the jungle where his prisoner was, and tied him up. Then he returned to the shelter, fitted a set of small filters in his nostrils, and went back to the lounge outside the washroom near the corridor, carrying a small egg-shaped object. Someone happened to be looking at the spot where he appeared. Dan ignored the staring onlooker, went out to the corridor, and found that things were even worse than when he had left.

He threw the egg-shaped object at the wall of the corridor and ducked back into the lounge.

There was a loud *bang*, followed by a number of smaller explosions. Abruptly the lounge was filled with bright points of light and little popping noises. The air was permeated with a gray vapor. The people in the room sagged in their seats or collapsed on the floor, and Dan was very careful to breathe only through the filters in his nostrils. He mentally said a key word and he was in the corridor, standing on a mound of unconscious people. He worked till he found the transceiver, went by mataform back to the lounge, took the transceiver there in case the lounge should be searched, and walked back through the corridor over heaps of people, picked up the other mataform unit, and went on down the corridor.

He wasn't happy about the people behind him. When the concentration of the drug in the air reached a low enough point, those on top of the heap were going to come to, then those under them, till there was one writhing hysterical mass that would be even worse than it had been before he threw the bomb. The only good feature—if it could be called that—was that they would all very soon be violently nauseated, with an urgent need for fresh air, and yet would be too sickened and weak to head for the outside in a rush.

Thinking this, Dan rounded a corner and came to a dead stop.

***

Directly before him was a short, wide, high-ceilinged cross-corridor with half a dozen doors swinging open as people hurried in, walked a few paces, and collapsed. Either side of this short hall was made of shiny metal containing numerous slots. As Dan watched, a man came through a door, and in one automatic motion jammed a coin in a slot, ripped off a ticket that popped out another slot, then suddenly blinked and jerked around to stare at the pile of people on the floor of the corridor. Then he collapsed.

Dan glanced from this man to the wall above the doors, which was brilliant with lights and moving letters, forming a maze that made him dizzy to look at:

SKL MACH OPS—80L6h4 s WANTED ON LEVEL 10
MNL LBRS-647L25h2°MN°MEN WITH FAST
REFLE PENSES PAID HOUSING

Dan strode forward and through a door with the numeral "1" over it.

Directly before him was a short dead-end hallway that abruptly vanished, and he was walking toward a crowd of hurrying people in an immense room.

***

Glancing around, Dan again felt at home. The immense room reminded him of Grand Central Mataform Terminal back on Earth. One wall even had the same kind of huge map of the tunnels and cross-tunnels that gave underground access to stores in the area. But the map here was even larger and more complex. Near its face were spidery walks and moving stairways, so that people could examine individual parts from close at hand if they wanted.

Dan looked over the terminal carefully, then walked slowly along looking for a place to hide one of his mataform units. He spotted, near a door in a corner, a poster on a stand showing a strong young man in uniform with a series of numbers, apparently dates, stretching out like a road before him. The stand held a poster on either side, and there was a place between them where Dan could slip one of the mataform units. An instant after he did this, he was in the shelter under the river.

Quickly, he got out a very light, strong two-man tent, an air mattress, a hypodermic, and a shiny half-globe with web straps at the back. He immediately went to the spot in the jungle where he had left his prisoner and found him thrashing furiously in an attempt to get loose. Dan injected a small quantity of a fast-acting hypnotic drug, and the man lay still. Then Dan set up the small tent and got the man inside on the mattress.

It was now getting dark outside, and, with the darkness, there was a rumble of thunder in the distance. Dan went back to the shelter, returned with a light, and adjusted the half-globe over the man's face and head, then fastened the straps behind his head. He inserted in the man's ears two little thimblelike devices, then said mentally, "Kielgaard?"

Kielgaard's voice answered, "We'll know in a minute." After a considerable pause, he said, "Yes, he's responding. Watch."

Very slowly, the man's right arm lifted from the mattress, then dropped limply.

Dan said, "You can handle it all from that end?"

"Easily. We've got a team here that will do nothing else but question him."

Dan nodded, aware that the voices of specially trained psychologists were now speaking in the man's ears, so that he heard nothing else, while he saw only what the screen in the half-globe projected directly into his eyes. Soon he would begin to talk, and what he said would be transmitted through subspace to Kielgaard's team of questioners. Then it might be possible to learn something of what was going on on this planet. But there was another way that might also help.

Dan glanced at his wristwatch and saw that it was late enough so that if this were Earth most stores would probably be closed by now. Dan didn't know how it was on this planet, but he pronounced a key word and was in the bookstore that faced the green. The bookstore was closed.

Dan quickly selected an armload of books, brought them back to the shelter under the river, went back and got another stack of them. He set up a spidery device of light metal and piled the books near enough so the feed arms could reach them. A set of rubber-tipped rods like long skeletal fingers turned the pages, while the scanner on an overhead arm oscillated from a position over one page to a position over the other page.

Dan said, "How's it coming in, Kielgaard?"

"Speed it up a little."

Dan moved a small lever. The pages turned more quickly.

***

Dan said, "We'll see how the feeder works before I leave it." Then he got out a mirror and went to work to change his appearance again.

The second book fed in with no difficulty, so Dan took four of his little mataform units, which was all he had room for, and went back to the terminal.

The crowd seemed to have thinned out somewhat, so he supposed the evening rush was about over. As in terminals nearly everywhere Dan had been, most of the people moved briskly, intent on their own affairs. No one paid much attention to Dan while he glanced around, noting the wall of flashing lights and moving letters, similar to but far larger than the one he had seen before, and a series of sizable blocky structures with large numerals suspended above them, and the stylized outlines of doorways on their four walls. People appeared in front of these doorways, or strolled directly toward them and vanished, hesitating only when a red glow outlined the door to show that someone was coming through from the other side.

In the center of the room toward either end were large silvery structures with the word "Information" hanging above them. Dan went to one and found that vertical blue lines divided it into twenty-four sections, with room left over for more that weren't there as yet, plus a section headed "General Information."

Dan studied the numerous slots, went to the General Information section and spent most of his change. He sat down with a small package of maps and folders and soon had before him a cross-sectional drawing showing a series of spherical layers one inside the others, labeled, "Level 1—Retail," "Level 2—Retail," "Level 3—Wholesale," "Level 4—Manufacturing," and so on, numbered from the outside in toward the center of the sphere, from one to twenty-five.

Dan sat perfectly still for a moment, looking at this. He leafed carefully through the folders, and was soon convinced that this wasn't a map of underground layers under just one city, but of an interconnected system that appeared to stretch over most of the planet. The surface was labeled, "Recreation—Ordeals—General."

The complex of underground layers seemed to be much thicker than separate floors of a building would be; the map showed cross-sections of buildings of many stories in the individual layers.

Dan studied the map further and found that Level 10 was marked, "Coordination—Government." Dan walked to the information machine and came back with a general map of Level 10, which was divided into sixteen sections. Sections 4 and 5 were headed "Government Sections," and Dan got large-scale maps of each of them.

What he was looking at was being reproduced far away on big screens, and instantly recorded, to be examined in detail by staffs of trained men. He was thankful this was so. The map was a maze of colored lines, blocks, and curves, with numbered lists up and down both sides and across the bottom.

Abruptly, Kielgaard's voice said, "Dan, see that dark purple oval a little to the left of the center of the page?"

"I see it." Dan glanced from the number to the list at the side of the page and read, "War Ruler's Control Center."

***

Kielgaard said, "The staff going over those books thinks there is some sort of an arrangement by which a 'war ruler' takes over absolute power in an emergency. What would be a better way to take over the planet than to get control of this War Ruler and then provoke an emergency?"

Dan studied the purple oval on the map. "Yes. But what do we do about it?"

"The first of your reinforcements will be coming down tonight. If you can get near that control center and plant a few transceivers, we might be able to make a good deal of trouble for anyone who may have seized it."

"I'll do my best," said Dan. He got up, put most of the maps and folders into a locker, and bought a ticket for Level 10, Section 4. As he turned, he noticed two men standing about twenty feet away, talking. On impulse, Dan went, not to the block that would take him to Level 10, but instead toward the station that his pamphlet had told him would take him to Section 6 of the same level he was on. As he rounded a corner and strode up a deserted corridor, he stooped and slid a mataform unit into the space between a waste container and the wall.

An instant later, he was back beside the posters where he had hidden a transceiver earlier.

Two men were walking in the same direction he had gone.

Dan followed them till they vanished, walking very rapidly now, around another corner.

He picked up the mataform transceiver and looked around for the blocky structure with the big number "10" over it. He saw it, after a moment, near the wall with the lights and moving letters on it.

"Kielgaard," he thought, "what do you suppose that wall is?"

"We think it's a sort of abbreviated classified ad arrangement."

"Sounds reasonable," Dan thought.

Dan was by now near the blocky structure with the big numeral "10" above it. Each of the four faces of the structure had four large doors outlined on it—one door for each of the sixteen sections of the level. Dan stepped up to the door marked "4" and it was immediately outlined in red. A voice said, "Travelers are reminded of the special restrictions now enforced at the governmental sections. To enter, you must present valid authorization papers, or state an acceptable reason for entering."

Dan stood perfectly still. He was fairly sure now that he must get into this section. But how?

At that moment, the lights of the huge wall of moving letters caught his attention, and Kielgaard's voice said, "Dan, look to the left, about halfway up."

Dan looked and saw moving letters spell out:

S WANTED ON LEVEL 10 ALL CREDITS PAID
SHORT TERM EMPLOYMENT °MEN WITH

FAST REFLEXES WANTED ON LEVEL 10

***

Dan realized he had seen parts of this ad spelled out twice at the terminal entrance. He didn't know if it was a trap or something he could use. He said, "I'm interested in a job on Level 10."

"You have examined the record?"

Dan had no idea what this meant. He said, "I understand men with fast reflexes are wanted on Level 10."

"One moment."

There was a short pause, then a new voice. "What we offer you is a special credit allotment sufficient for all normal mating and purchase needs. On account of these latest restrictions, I can't tell you exactly what the job is, but I can say this: The rewards are great. But you also might end up getting sprinkled over the forest. We've got a situation down here that has to be cleaned up fast. With the special referendum tomorrow, it might boil over and make an interstellar mess. We want you for a night's work. At the end you're either rich or dead. How about it?"

Dan thought of the two words "interstellar mess," used in connection with a "special referendum." He had the sensation that he was getting close.

"All right," he said.

***

There was a blur as mataform stations shuttled him from one place to the next. Then he was walking into a large room holding about thirty men, all of whom had something of the look of big cats alert for prey.

Dan had hardly come in when a lithe man walked out on a raised platform, looked over the waiting men, and said, "I'd like to wait till there are more of us, but there isn't time. I'll come to the point without delay. I'll only explain it once, so listen carefully.

"On this level, we have the War Ruler's control center. Two levels up, there is the planetary zoo. Among the animals in the zoo is an ape about our size and general shape, with a thick layer of fur, strong muscles, and a sense of humor like a white-hot rivet dropped down your collar. By some process I don't understand, about fifty of these apes have gotten into a storeroom in an arms depot attached to the control center.

"With this referendum coming up to decide whether we should join the Stellar Union, every time there is a disturbance the election committee blames it on one faction or another. Using their emergency powers, they then clap on some new restriction to keep order till the referendum is over. If there is now a disturbance near the control center itself, tempers are going to shorten further. If the blame should be stuck on one side or the other, true or untrue, it could swing the vote either way.

"We have got to get those apes out of the arms depot right away. The trouble is, there's an alarm in the arms depot that can't be shut off except from the control center. Fire any kind of impact or vibration weapon in there, or change the composition of the atmosphere by pouring in gas, and the alarm automatically goes off in guard stations all over this level. If we had more time, we could starve them out. We don't have the time.

"The result is that we have to go after them with knives and clubs. Now, the apes are fast, they gang up, they throw things, and if they can, they'll grab you from opposite sides and pull your arms and legs off. That's very funny—for them. So we'll have to work together as a team and fight as hard as we know how."

* * *

After the speaker finished, there was a silence in the room. Dan was thinking over the idea and he liked nothing about it. He had little enough time to do his job, and he did not want to spend it being pulled to pieces by apes. He called out, "Mind if I make a suggestion?"

"I'm willing to try anything. Let's hear it."

Dan said, "I don't know about anybody else here, but I am no team player myself. Let me go in alone first. You wait half an hour and then come in and see if there are fifty apes left."

Everyone craned to see who was offering to fight fifty wild apes singlehanded.

The man on the platform turned pale, but said, "Agreed. And if you win, you receive the combined credits of all."

Dan found himself walking down a corridor, surrounded by well-wishers, to a room where several tables were loaded with hand-weapons. He picked up a short weighted club, and a short double-edge, razor-sharp sword. A few minutes later, he arrived at a heavy metal door studded with rivets and painted green.

Dan had intended to hide a transceiver nearby on the outside and spend as little time in the storeroom as possible. But everything had happened so fast, and there were so many eyes watching him, that he had no chance to hide a mataform unit anywhere.

There was a loud clang as the heavy door swung shut

behind him. Then he was in a big dimly lighted room with a twelve-foot aisle running down the center, a narrower aisle along each wall, and high piles of wooden crates and wirebound heavy cardboard cartons spaced five feet apart to either side of the central aisle. There was a strong smell of damp dirty fur. On the floor partway up the aisle lay what looked like a clothed human arm.

From the far end of the building came a series of low gruff barks. A humping motion ran along like a wave up the aisle and over the piles of crates toward Dan.

He glanced briefly to either side at the solid concrete walls of the building, felt behind him. The door was locked.

It flashed through his mind that up till now he had had good luck on this planet.

Dan saw, in the nearest corner of the room, several pipes that ran up from the floor and were bent to travel along near the ceiling. He quickly slipped a mataform unit behind these pipes on the floor, then cut into a cardboard carton about fifteen feet away and put another unit inside. He tossed a third on top of the nearest pile of cartons, mentally said a key word, and was on the pile slashing open a carton to slide the unit inside. Then he was on the floor in the corner.

In the dim light, the shadowy figures came toward him. Their long arms swung up and a barrage of rifle parts, bayonets, scabbards, and helmets crashed into the corner. Dan was fifteen feet away when they hit. An instant later, he was back, kicking the rubble out of the corner. There was a repeated gruff cough, then the aisles were jammed, and he had a brief view of bared teeth in fur-covered faces, and hairy arms that reached out to grasp him. There was a grisly laugh that started as a low chuckle and ended on a high-pitched wavering note.

Dan mentally pronounced a key word and he was on the pile of cartons with a half a dozen apes. The short sword flicked out and back. Other apes sprang from the next pile of cartons. Dan dropped the weighted club, threw his last mataform unit toward the top of a pile across the aisle, and an instant later had recovered it, dropped to the floor, and raced up the aisle.

***

There was noise like teeth clicking together and then the wavering laugh burst out again as the apes turned to chase him up the aisle. Dan slid the transceiver into a slit-open carton and whirled as the leaders rushed toward him. The short sword flashed out and back in rapid thrusts, and abruptly Dan was on top of the first pile of cartons. He recovered the weighted club, glanced down at the apes turning to rush up the aisles, and then suddenly he was with them, slamming the last few of them over the heads with the weighted club.

He thrust, stabbed, and smashed, now in one place, now another, always striking the gibbering horde where they were fewest and most off-balance.

After a long, hideous interval, there came a silence. Dan could see that there were four heaps of dead or unconscious apes, the only live ones were a few clinging to overhead beams with their eyes shut.

Dan recovered his transceivers and made his way to one of the few windows in the room. This was about seven feet from the floor, heavily barred, with its glass panes broken out. Dan pulled himself up and looked out at a walk and a high wall a few feet away. He cut the sleeve of his shirt into strips and knotted the strips together with a transceiver tied onto either end, so that one transceiver hung on the outside and the other on the inside.

Then Dan was outside, in an underground part of the planet where no one was supposed to be without an official permit.

The air seemed as fresh as outdoors, while overhead there was the appearance of the sky on a heavily overcast day. There was light enough to see by, but it was apparently dimmed to provide an artificial night.

Dan saw no one, and said mentally, "Kielgaard?"

Kielgaard's voice had a hoarse sound. "Are you out of that place?"

"I'm out of it—thank heaven."

"Amen. But listen, things have taken a nasty turn."

"What's happened?"

"We've questioned that prisoner. The outfit behind this trouble is Trans-Space. But they don't have the control center. Instead, they've got the headquarters of the election committee that controls the referendum. Trans-Space is representing itself as the government of an interstellar league of planets. They have everything set up to falsify the vote tomorrow."

Dan frowned. "What of it? I can still plant the mataform transceivers and we can bring men down from above."

"Yes, but Trans-Space has a mataform terminal set up in the terminal election headquarters. It hooks into the local system and connects with an outpost in the jungle on the surface. Trans-Space has been building up to this day for over three years. The election headquarters is manned like a fortress. It's in immediate touch with the outpost on the surface where they've got an army of reinforcements."

Dan stood still, thinking. He remembered the official with the carrying case in the corridor overhead, who had said to the angry crowd, "Go to the War Ruler." Dan mentioned the incident and said, "What about this War Ruler and his emergency powers?"

***

Kielgaard said, "It looked promising to us at first, but actually that's as if someone should say, 'England is in peril. Go to King Arthur.'"

"What?" said Dan, puzzled.

"The War Ruler is a myth. A thousand years or more ago, after a terrific internal war, they had a famine. They also had a huge army to disband, headed by a very popular leader. The army apparently threatened to take over the planet, but by a clever gimmick, the government put off the crisis. They announced that their scientists had discovered a way to halt the flow of time after the famine— and the War Ruler marched the whole army loyally into a kind of big mausoleum where they presumably killed the lot of them with a quick-acting gas. That is the War Ruler's Control Center.

"Ever since then, they've been making ritual gestures. They stock new arms of standard design nearby, and recruit a number of fresh soldiers to join the old—as a population control measure. To make the illusion complete, they say that any man or woman who sincerely believes the state to be in peril can enter the control center, by passing through a lethal field that kills the insincere and lets the sincere through alive. A number of people have tried it and got killed, so now they don't try any more."

"Where is this place?" asked Dan.

"If we read your map rightly, that wall in front of you marks the edge of the field surrounding it."

Dan set down one of the mataform units and mentally pronounced a key word.

He was in the shelter under the river.

An instant later he was back by the wall, a glider and the control helmet in his hands. He clipped a transceiver to the glider and guided it toward a huge, dark-stained building with the look of a fortress. He sent the glider around to the front of the building and saw two huge bronze doors, one of which stood open. There was a totally still, motionless look about the place that Dan did not care for. But the glider had come to a closed inner door and that was as far as it could go. Dan took off the control helmet, drew a deep breath and said a key word.

He was standing in the huge hall, before the closed door. He opened the door.

Before him was a room with tall slit windows, and as Dan went in, he could see dimly, but, like a man in a hall of mirrors, what he saw did not make sense.

Distorted shapes and forms, with bright points and blots of light, shifted as he moved, and shifted again as he moved closer, to see one leg of what looked like a very old, faded table. A heavy cable ran up the leg to the top, where there was a switch, and a bronze plate with the words, "Open Switch."

Dan reached for the switch, and hesitated. If Kielgaard's theory was right, he would now be electrocuted, or otherwise disposed of.

He swallowed hard, reached the rest of the way, and opened the switch.

A pall of choking dust spread over the room, with the sound of coughing all around him and the rustle of clothing and stamping of feet.

Dan wiped his streaming eyes, and saw a man in uniform behind the desk, all but one corner of which looked new.

The man stared at Dan and said, "So soon? What's happened?"

***

Dan glanced around. The huge room was filled with tough, weary-looking men in combat uniform, all fully armed and equipped. He thought fast, turned back to the man behind the desk and said earnestly, "Peace is restored to the planet. It's been rebuilt and the damage is all repaired. But now, fantastic as it may seem, an enemy has come down to this world from outer space—"

The man at the desk angrily brought down his fist. "No one lives in outer space! That's foolishness!"

Dan said, his mind racing, "Whoever they are, they've seized a vital communications center! They've got men on guard, armed to the teeth. They've issued orders through captive government officials to seal off this part of the level from the public. They're trying to take over the whole government!"

There was a stir in the room and a low ugly rumble.

"I knew it," said the man behind the desk, jumping to

his feet. "I knew they'd lie low and then creep back again when things are quiet. If we'd been demobilized, it would all have been for nothing. But we *aren't* demobilized!"

Abruptly there were shouted orders, and someone was gripping Dan by the arm. "Just lead the way. Show us where they are and we'll take care of the rest."

Dan said mentally, "Kielgaard?"

Kielgaard said, "Good Lord! Go straight outside and turn right."

Someone threw a switch beside the door. Outside, they followed Dan to the right. Behind him, Dan heard the mutter and cough of engines starting up. They were in a well-lighted street like that of a large city, but there was no traffic, either because it was late or because of the travel restrictions.

Kielgaard said, "Next left and it's in front of you."

Dan turned the corner. Directly before him was a large white marble building with a lawn on either side of a broad flight of steps, and guards on the sidewalk, the steps, and in emplacements in the shrubbery on either side of the steps.

One of them saw Dan and casually snapped a shot at him. Dan got back around the corner fast and looked around. On both sides of the street, men were lying flat at the bases of the buildings, or crouching in doorways. Down the street, they were running up a block to the left. Up the middle of the street came a tank. It paused just out of sight from the building around the corner, and an amplified voice boomed out, "This is the War Ruler. Get out of that building before the count of thirty, or we clean you out."

A voice began to count. There was a sound of fast footsteps on the sidewalk around the corner, and half a dozen men carrying guns came into view. Dan recognized some of the men who had searched the place where he'd landed his boat. One of them, not yet quite in a position to see the tank, called out irritably, "All right, you. Get out here!"

Then he caught sight of the men lying at the base of the buildings, and crouched in the doorways. He fired.

Flashes of light came from the men by the buildings. There was a roar and a grind and the tank rolled forward. A whistle blew. Dan heaved a mataform transceiver toward the emplacement at the base of the stairs, and an instant before it landed, he mentally pronounced a key word.

In the emplacement, he jerked the men away from their gun before they could fire a shot. He knocked them senseless, grabbed a rifle, and sprang up onto the staircase, with the intent of sprinting to the other side and diving into the emplacement there. Halfway across the steps, there was a sensation as if someone had smacked him between the shoulder blades with a rifle butt. He saw the stairs coming up to meet him, and then he saw nothing.

***

He came to with a pretty face smiling at him through a sort of fog. The fog cleared away, and a highly attractive nurse was looking at him very admiringly. She said, "Sir, you have a visitor."

Dan glanced around and saw Kielgaard, a sorrowful look on his face.

Dan said as the nurse went out, "She spoke Truthian, didn't she?"

"She did. You're still on the planet."

"What's this 'sir' business and the pleasant smile for?"

Kielgaard said, "You're a hero. It shows, incidentally, how the best experts can make awe-inspiring mistakes. We gave you fast reflexes, thinking that would make you safer. But it turns out that the planet has a class of authorized assassins who hunt down criminals for a livelihood, and never get too numerous because they fight each other for extra credits and prestige. With your fast reflexes and built-in wariness, the populace immediately spotted you for one of these lawful assassins, so you couldn't have been more conspicuous."

Kielgaard shook his head. "Meanwhile, Trans-Space was bringing in hired killers to knock off the planet's lawful assassins at a huge bonus per head, in order to create an uproar so that the election committee, which they had already captured and conditioned, would clap on more restrictions, thus creating more tension, so that Trans-Space could swing the referendum at the last minute. You see, the most dangerous thing we could have done to you was to give you these extra-fast reflexes. But now, because of it, you're a hero." Kielgaard looked sad.

"Luckily," said Dan, "I'm still alive. And so were all those soldiers."

"Another mistake of the experts," said Kielgaard. "The highest authorities on Truth strongly suspected something was wrong with the protective field around the control center. This made them fearful that the scientific device to halt the flow of time hadn't worked either. This would have been a terrible catastrophe, so by a set of rationalizations that would do credit to a bunch of habitual liars, they evaded the whole issue. The experts and I made the mistake of drawing the logical conclusion. I'm glad it wasn't so."

"What happened to Trans-Space?"

Kielgaard stopped looking sad and smiled a smile of deep satisfaction. "Galactic has its contract with this planet. Trans-Space is in a very anemic condition. The Truthians don't like people who lie, and they always settle their accounts very strictly."

Kielgaard's face subsided into its gloomy look.

Dan said, "What's wrong?"

"Well," said Kielgaard, "you see, you're a planetary hero for settling that business with Trans-Space. Also, you have—let's see"—he took out a slip of paper—"the equivalent of around six hundred thousand dollars spending money for cleaning out those apes, plus—I don't know how to translate this—six thousand mating credits. They have a weird system for romance, and these credits—"

Dan grinned. "Envious?"

"It isn't that," said Kielgaard. "I'm thinking how I'd feel in your place. These Truthians don't have any give in their system. Right's right, and wrong's wrong, and they hand out rewards and punishments irrespective of persons."

There was a sharp rap at the door.

Dan tried to sit up, but he was still too weak.

Kielgaard said sadly, "I tried to reason with them, but I might as well have talked to a wall."

"Listen," said Dan, becoming alarmed. "What's wrong?"

"I don't have the heart to tell you," said Kielgaard.

***

Picking up a large briefcase, he said, "Do what you think best. I might mention that we're giving you a bonus, though I suppose that's no consolation."

The rap at the door was repeated and there were sounds of arguments outside.

"What's in that briefcase?" said Dan.

"A big version of the kind of mataform transceiver you used. There's a dreadnaught of ours orbiting the planet with another transceiver like this on board. The key word, in case you should have use for it, is 'Krakior.'"

The door burst open and three men came in, arguing with a man in a white jacket.

"That doesn't matter," said the first man, a familiar-looking individual who was opening a square case with carrying handle. "The only question is, was it or was it not an unauthorized kill, and is this the man? We have our checker set up to answer this question and that's all there is to it." He glanced at Dan. "Hold out your fingertips, please, and touch these plates. Purely a routine check."

Behind the man with the case were two men with armbands and shields. One glanced disinterestedly at Dan and cocked his gun.

Dan looked at the head of A Section and said fervently, "Thank you, Kielgaard."

The doctor in the white jacket was arguing to no visible effect as the tube was held to Dan's eyes, snapped back into the case, and the case clapped shut, to give its loud alarm clang.

The assassin with gun calmly leveled it at Dan and fired.

All he hit was a suddenly empty bed.

Dan had said the key word.

The Knife and
the Sheath

Able and Ted Andrews stood with the afternoon sunlight on their backs, the tips of their longbows resting on the stony soil of the ridge. In the distance, the yearly supply ship rose, glimmering with reflected light, above the dense forest.

Ted Andrews glanced up at his brother.

"Dad told us we might miss the supply ship if we went hunting now."

Able calculatingly eyed the tall gray trunk of a dead staplenut tree down the slope toward the forest. There was the stub of a limb halfway up the tree, and the stub was hollow. Down the side below the stub were many small scratch marks where the splintered wood showed light brown.

"I'd rather hunt than watch the ship," said Able. He selected several rocks the size of hens' eggs.

Ted said disgustedly, "We haven't seen anything *to* hunt."

431

"We've seen sign."

Able studied the tree carefully, then hurled three rocks one after another.

"Can't eat sign," Ted was saying. As Able threw the rocks, he blinked and stared.

The first rock hit the tree squarely, above the stub, to make a hollow *bonk* sound. The second hit on a level with the stub, and the third arced in just below it. Able bent to get his bow.

"*Bonk!*" came the sound of the second rock as Ted watched blankly.

"*Bonk!*" came the sound of the third rock.

Able straightened with his bow.

There was a muffled squawk. A sinuous brown-gray creature the length of a man's forearm shot out the hollow stub and turned in the air. It stretched out all four limbs and the furry membrane that ran between them, and planed to the ground, to streak downhill in darting zigzags.

Able waited exasperatedly for it to pause, but instead it took a sharp swerve past a clump of thick brush. The brush shook. Something blue-gray and big burst out with a flash of teeth and glowing eyes.

Ted Andrews caught his breath.

"Woods cat!"

Able sucked in a deep breath, and strained to judge angle and distance. The two were running straight, and he risked the shot of an arrow.

The wind gusted, to rustle the long dangling leaves of a waterfall tree by the edge of the woods. The leaves briefly showed white undersides, their edges brushing to make the low roar that gave the tree its name.

The gust moved the arrow aside, and, this done, died as quickly as it had sprung up.

Suddenly the big gray cat caught up with its prey.

Able aimed carefully, shot an arrow, shot another—

The cat sprang almost straight up, twisted, and fell full length. Able swallowed, lowered his bow, and glanced around.

"See anything?"

"No."

Able started downhill.

Ted cried, "We aren't going down *there!*"

Able looked back.

"We can't give up all *that* meat and hide."

"Dad said, 'Stay out of the woods!'"

"Are you *scared?*"

"No, but—"

"Then watch in back. I'll watch in front."

Ted glanced nervously around, and followed.

The big trees loomed taller and taller overhead.

The dead woods cat lay outstretched, one arrow through its back, the other through its neck. The wind ruffled its short blue-gray fur.

Able said uneasily, "This is the female."

Ted gripped Able's arm.

Able glanced uphill.

From under the long leaves of the waterfall tree moved an even larger blue-gray cat, with a mane that stood up from head to shoulders. Its black-tipped tail idly flicked leaves aside as it came out into the open.

Able's chest grew tight, and his hands felt stiff, as if from cold.

The cat's yellow eyes were like two mirrors that reflect light.

The yellow eyes glowed as the cat came downhill, its movements flowing and graceful, its gaze steady, unwavering.

Able faintly heard his brother's voice:

"*Able!*"

He tried to raise the bow, and couldn't move.

The remembered voice of his father spoke, as if he were there beside them:

"Never look in a woods cat's eyes. *Think where to sink the arrows in.*"

Able blinked, looked at the blue-gray mane, then at the place where neck joined shoulders.

The cat disappeared behind a tree.

Able raised the bow.

The cat sprang to a closer tree.

Before Able could move, the cat stepped out, looked at him, and then stepped back out of sight.

Able nearly let the arrow fly. He recovered his grip. The cat made two swift bounds to a tree still closer.

Ted's voice shook.

"*Shoot* him!"

"*I can't aim!*"

"He's halfway to us!"

"*You* shoot, too!"

Ted raised his bow.

The cat stepped out, then back.

There was a *twang* as Ted shot and missed.

The cat streaked behind a fallen tree resting low to the ground on stubs of limbs, its bark hanging in strips.

Able strained to find his target, but could see nothing behind the dangling bark.

From there, the cat could come out from so many different places that Able didn't know where to watch.

He glanced at his brother.

Ted, his bow raised, stared helplessly at the fallen tree.

Suddenly the rest of what his father had said came back to Able:

"A cat will stalk you from tree to tree, and never give one clear shot till you run. *Then* he'll land on your back."

Able drew in a deep breath, watched the tree, and drew his bow taut.

"Ted—"

Ted glanced around.

Able said, *"Run for it!"*

Ted blinked, then whirled and ran.

There was an explosion of bark strips.

Ted was running headlong, the cat a gray blur behind him.

Able shot an arrow, strung another—

The cat swiftly shortened the gap.

Ted suddenly caught a sapling, clung, whirled himself around, and bolted in a fresh direction.

The cat slammed to a stop, one forepaw against the bole of a tree.

Able shot an arrow, and another arrow—

The cat bounded high, whirled in the air—

Able aimed, shot again—

Ted ran up, his legs unsteady, and snatched up his bow.

Able's target had vanished. He stepped sidewise.

The big cat lay motionless.

Ted sucked in his breath.

"You *got* him!"

Able, trembling, gave mental thanks, then looked around.

Their arrows were strewn all over, and the shadow of the ridge was beginning to reach into the forest. From somewhere came a startled scream, then the eerie descending note of a wirebird.

Able took pains to keep his voice steady.

"Better stick together while we collect our arrows. We'll drag these cats up by the hunt shack and bleed them—skin them if there's time. If there's a drag frame there, *maybe* we can get them home tomorrow."

***

The hunt shack, on the far end of the ridge, was a small cabin of massive logs, with a shingled roof over heavy planks.

Able and Ted, worn out from skinning and butchering the woods cats, woke in the darkness of the cabin, listening to a distant barking and yipping.

Ted groaned. "Traprunners."

"It's about time for them to swarm."

"How do we get the meat home? They'll smell it."

"Dad would say, stay here until they hunt out the brush and go north."

"How long will *that* take?"

"It could be tomorrow," said Able frowning.

"Or next week," said Ted uneasily.

"The meat has to be cured soon, and we need a lot more salt than there is in the bin. We *can't* stay here."

The room seemed to go around and around as Able lay back.

"Are we," he murmured, "going to just let it *spoil?*"

In the distance the traprunners yipped, and something screamed.

But Able didn't hear it.

***

Midmorning of the next day found them crossing the first of three large streams on the way home. They were close to the edge of the forest, the big trees looming up to their right, while to their left the brushland sloped ever more gently off toward the swamp in the distance.

The morning, so far, had been unnaturally still, with the traprunners apparently asleep after the night's hunt, and everything else in hiding. The worst of this quiet was that they had no idea where the creatures might be.

They paused to drink from the stream, then lay down beside a tall bush for a few minutes' rest.

Atop the far bank, downstream, something moved.

A long-muzzled brown head bearing upright pointed ears appeared.

With a quick careless glance around, the creature ran down the slope, a brown animal about the height, at its shoulder, of a man's knee. The head, on a thick neck, looked oversize for the body until it turned, to briefly show its massive chest.

At the edge of the stream it crouched, braced its paws on the bank, and leaned far down to drink.

Able strung his bow.

The bank crumbled under the creature's paws, and it backed to keep from falling.

Able let fly an arrow.

The arrow struck the chest near the front legs. The traprunner fell over the bank into the water. Barely afloat, it slid down the stream.

Able looked all around and glanced at Ted.

Without a word, they went up the slope on all fours, crawled over the top, and looked back through the brush.

On the opposite side of the stream, far down the gentle slope, dozens of traprunners, of all shades of brown and gray, came leaping and bounding silently through the brush, appearing first here, then there, so that the eye seemed never to see the same one twice, while a broad stretch of brushland seemed alive with them.

In the distance, a long-legged creature with slender horns, off to the side of the pack, suddenly sprang up and bolted. The main pack paid no attention, but two more of the predators appeared as if from nowhere and bore it to the ground.

Ted said, his voice scarcely audible, "Will they cross the stream?"

"If they see us, some will split off and come after us."

In the distance, there was a single short bark.

The pack vanished.

Able whispered, "Don't move."

There was a short sharp bark.

The pack sprang up, bounding high into the air and looking all around.

Ted caught his breath.

Able looked carefully around.

From the distance came a rapidly repeated bark, high and piercing.

The whole pack turned away from the stream, as half a dozen spotted white-and-tan creatures sprang up and raced away. The pack raced after them in a V, two wings reaching to the sides to keep the small herd together. A constant yipping, high-pitched and short in duration, like the squeaking of innumerable ungreased hinges, jarred on Able's ears.

Ted whispered, "Let's go."

Able looked carefully around.

"I'll sneak away. You stay here a minute, and see if anything is watching."

Able eased through brush and small saplings.

The roar of the stream dropped behind. The high-pitched yapping faded in the distance.

Able saw nothing but brush, scattered clumps of saplings, and, ahead, a tall tree, its leaves turning freely in the light breeze to create a soothing, almost hypnotic pattern of light and shade on the ground beneath, where the grass and moss grew sparsely.

Able, soothed, walked toward the cool sheltered shade.

Abruptly he stopped, the sweat starting out on his forehead.

Ted came hurrying up, to whisper, "I only saw two. They were watching the pack chase the brush deer."

Able nodded and murmured, "Good. Watch it, there's a wire tree in front of us."

Ted started.

"Can't we go farther from the forest, now they're headed the other way?"

"We don't dare. There could be some on this side."

From behind came a chorus of cries, distant and triumphant.

Ted swallowed. "They've caught the brush deer already."

"Now, they'll turn. They'll go north, or they'll come this way. I think I heard them to the north last night."

"Then they've hunted that stretch already."

"Yes."

The wind rose, and there was a roar as of a stream, from in front.

Ted said, "Waterfall tree."

"We'll have to get farther out from the forest, after all."

Able turned to swing out toward the north, and in front of him there was a slender sapling whose leaves turned in the breeze to cast an inviting shade where light and shadow flickered in a soothing hypnotic pattern.

Ted gripped Able's arm.

Able stood still, reminding himself of the things to remember.

The forest, he was thinking, is to the south. The traprunners are behind us, to the west. We have to keep near the forest, because the traprunners live in the brushland, and usually avoid the forest. We want the forest to our right, and not far away. But we have to watch out for the wire trees. They're in the forest, and along the edge. We've got to remember the wire trees. But, now, there was the sound of a waterfall tree up ahead. We don't want to get near *that*. We had enough of that yesterday. We have to keep away from places woods cats like. So we'd better swing a little farther north here, while there's time—

As Able moved forward warily, there came a rapidly repeated piercing bark from the direction of the stream behind them.

The bark was repeated; then, after a pause, repeated again.

Ted said, "They've found our trail!"

"He's calling the pack. He won't follow until some of them are following him."

Suddenly the barking grew fainter.

Ted whispered, "It's going away!"

"Or starting down into the stream to follow us."

Able intently studied the trees at the edge of the forest. There was one, to the right of the wire tree, that was huge, with widespread level limbs.

Suddenly the barking grew louder.

"Stay behind me," said Able.

He walked straight toward the wire tree, passed outside the reach of its limbs, turned behind it, and walked toward the forest.

The barking was growing close, and now a high-pitched yipping joined in.

Suddenly this yipping seemed to burst out at them, to leap at them, from ahead, from behind, from all sides, its direction so confusing that Able could feel the urge to run, to rush this way and that, to panic.

Able glanced back.

Ted was turned with his bow raised, looking here, there—

Able took him by the shoulder, forced his own voice to stay level.

"Climb up into that tree ahead. I'll follow."

Ted ran to the tree, caught a thick low limb, and pulled himself up.

The tree's big limbs, almost like a staircase, for a moment roused some faint memory in Able's mind; but then, paralleling the edge of the brush and a few dozen yards inside the forest, a traprunner bounded into view, its muzzle up, yapping.

Able froze.

The traprunner, bounding along carelessly, shot past through the trees.

Able climbed.

He went up the smooth worn lower limbs, around the tree, sought a fresh grip, pulled himself higher, then stopped.

Through the forest below bounded another and another of the predators, muzzles thrown up, yipping.

Out in the brush, another came into view, head down, snuffling along their track. It put its head back and barked.

It seemed impossible that the yipping noise could grow louder, but it seemed now to be not only on all sides, and overhead and underfoot; it also seemed to be inside their heads, a sound that stopped thought, made time stand still, and held the attention like the points of a thousand daggers, touching first here, then there, so that the mind was constantly distracted, could not think, could not plan—

Suddenly a roar echoed through the forest.

Down below, the onrushing traprunners slowed, jumped aside.

Eyes glowing, gray fur on end, claws extended, tail

lashing, lips drawn back from sharp teeth, a big woods cat paced half sidewise, its whining growl a background to a look of sledgehammer hate like the glare from white-hot iron.

The traprunners backed away.

Out in the brush, the main pack bounded up, stopped, watched curiously, and sat down.

The woods cat herded the nearby traprunners to the edge of the forest, and there he paused. The threatening whine dropped to a low growl, rose again to a whine as a traprunner blundered forward, and dropped to a growl as the predator jerked back; then the cat settled down beneath the outspread limbs of the tree, near the edge of the forest.

Able clung to the smooth worn limbs, groping for some explanation.

Down below, the cat held the horde overawed.

From somewhere overhead came a faint mewing.

Able looked again at the tree's smooth worn limbs. He glanced up.

High overhead in the tree was a dark bulk against the sky, a place where the limbs seemed woven together.

From somewhere overhead came a gruff questioning bark.

Able forced himself to breathe slowly and steadily.

From above came a slipping, clutching noise.

A small feline form arced through the air, to seize a limb, swing, cling with a scratching, clutching sound, climb up on the limb, and then bound to the main trunk of the tree. A second small form arced down.

Able watched numbly.

The gruff bark sounded from overhead, louder.

Ted glanced urgently at Able.

Able looked around, moving only his eyes.

The radiating limbs of the big tree reached out past other trees. But any movement along them would be in view of the male cat down below, and of all the traprunners waiting at the forest edge.

Now from up above came a menacing growl. It rose to a threatening whine.

Below, the big cat gave a reassuring gruff bark.

Out in the brush, a large traprunner sat on its haunches, tongue lolling out between long sharp teeth, and looked from Able to Ted.

Able fitted an arrow to his bow.

Through the woods, panting and bounding, came a traprunner that had fallen behind the rest.

The woods cat growled a warning.

Overhead, there was a rustle and a sway of branches as a large gray shape moved out the mouth of the den and peered down at Able and Ted.

Out of the corner of his eye, Able could watch the approaching traprunner. Seeing all his fellows, this predator was not awed by the woods cat, but gave a hunting yip, and bounded straight for the cat.

The cat's left paw lashed out, ripped flesh and fur from the traprunner's side, struck again, and threw the carcass into the brush.

The nearby traprunners stood up and began to growl, whine, and yip.

From up in the tree, the female woods cat came dropping swiftly down from limb to limb, her gaze fixed on Ted. Her lips drew back from her teeth.

Able aimed, his position awkward and strained, and let the arrow fly.

The arrow struck the cat's head just above the eyes, cut fur and flesh, and glanced off the bone beneath.

The cat missed its footing, dropped, twisted, and hit Ted a glancing blow on the way past.

Ted caught another limb, his face strained.

Able quickly strung another arrow. The female cat circled below the tree, looked up, and crouched. Able shot. The arrow struck the woods cat at the base of the neck. The cat gave an abortive spring, and dropped.

The traprunners rushed the male woods cat.

The cat battered them right and left, drove them back—

One of the traprunners circled behind him, rushed up.

The cat whirled with a flash of teeth.

The yipping seemed to come from everywhere.

The traprunners from out in the brush spread out as they rushed. A knot of them passed directly under the wire tree through the flickering light and shade.

The ground exploded. Pebbles danced in the air as the dirt boiled. Dust drifted up in a cloud. The air looked filled with whips, the predators whirled in the dirt and pebbles, vanished into the soil, and from overhead there sounded the eerie descending notes of a wirebird.

Able reached out to steady Ted, and pointed to a thick limb that led straight back into the forest.

Ted nodded.

Able started out along the limb.

Around him, under him, above him, from all sides,

inside his head, exploded the high-pitched endless yipping. Twice he almost lost his footing.

A roar of murderous rage blotted out the forest.

Able clung to the limb.

Behind him, the monotonous yips were suddenly disjointed, startled.

There was a clutching, a snap and scream, another clutching sound, a strange singing tone, a yip, another sound of clutching, a startled bark, and as Able eased farther along the limb a picture formed in his mind.

The cat was using the trees.

The traprunners, accustomed to open ground, unable to climb, unused to the forest, were fighting a thing that could escape at will, return from whatever direction it chose, and, when they followed it, could lead them straight to one of the wire trees around its den.

And now the cat must have found its dead mate.

There was another roar that seemed to blot out earth and sky, and the fight moved away, a sound of slaughter off toward the brushlands.

Carefully, Able lowered himself from limb to limb, and dropped to the ground.

Ted followed, and Able led the way, walking and running, scanning the trees and the ground ahead for a particular deadly pattern of shadow and light.

Behind them, there came a bark.

Through the woods trotted a big traprunner, nose to the ground.

Able fitted an arrow to the bow, aimed carefully—

Ted yelled, "Look out! There are others!"

Able let fly the arrow.

Something hit him in the side like a thrown billet of wood. A tan shape hurtled by to lock its teeth on Ted's shoulder.

Able dropped the bow, whipped out his knife, and stabbed up, through the front of the abdomen. The traprunner dropped to the ground.

Ted fell across it, rolled free, and looked up.

"Able! Look up!"

Able glanced up.

Smeared with blood, gray fur matted, eyes blazing, the woods cat came low and fast along the thick level limbs of a nearby tree.

Able stooped for his bow.

The cat sprang.

Something hit Able like a tree trunk swung by a giant. The world spun. He saw gray fur, and stabbed the knife into it. There was a raking pain across his back. He clung to the fur with his left hand, and stabbed the knife into it again and again. Gray and brown intermingled before his eyes, flowing together and separating. Something jerked his left arm so hard it seemed all but torn out by the roots. Ted screamed. Able clung grimly, stabbed the knife home, and ripped back with the blade.

The world seemed to explode.

After a long time, Able opened his eyes.

The cat was gone.

Ted lay flat on the ground, his shoulder smeared with blood.

Able bent beside Ted, saw faint signs of breathing, picked up his bow, recovered his arrow from a dead traprunner. He made sure he had his knife, and knelt beside Ted. Beside the mauled shoulder, Ted seemed to have several injured ribs. Able straightened.

Where the traprunner pack might be now was anyone's guess.

Ahead of them stretched miles of wire trees, waiting for one misstep.

Overhead, the sun was passing its highest point and they weren't halfway home.

Too late, Able could hear his father's advice, and *understand* it.

Gently, he shook Ted by the unhurt shoulder.

***

It was after dark when Able, carrying his brother, was challenged by the guard atop the wall of the settlement.

The moon was halfway across the sky by the time his mother finished dressing the bruises, cuts, and long deep scratches he hadn't known he had. By now, Ted was asleep in his cot, wrapped in bandages.

Able's father cleared his throat.

"We didn't settle this planet to raise children to feed woods cats and traprunners. You're supposed to use your *head*."

Able nodded unhappily.

His mother said disappointedly, "You should have known better, Able."

His father murmured, "However, he *did* get two woods cats. And there *should* have been enough salt in the hunt shack."

His mother spoke indignantly to Able's father.

"Is that all you're going to say?"

"What more?"

"There's such a thing as caution. You can't say anything to Ted tonight, but you have got to make Able understand!"

His father suddenly laughed.

"Let me ask you exactly what *I* can do that will compare with being worked over by three woods cats and a pack of traprunners. They've either learned caution, or they'll never learn it. *Able!*"

Able looked up dazedly.

"Tomorrow I'll teach you a path through the forest to the ridge. Boys can't be trusted with it, but as far as hunting is concerned, *I* say you're grown up. Besides, we have to take care of that meat, and that's the quickest way with traprunners around."

Before Able could speak, his mother started to object, but his father spoke first.

"Courage is like a knife, and caution is the sheath." He smiled at Able. "You understand, you can get quite a few nicks in the blade if you've always got it out."

"I understand."

The strain released, Able became aware that he ached all over. Tomorrow they would head through the forest where the wire trees grew thickest, where thorn bushes and assassin vines hungered for the kill while awed predators edged around in search of some easier place.

Worn out and aching, Able crept into his bunk, and was asleep in a flash.

His mother glanced at him wonderingly before she put out the lamp and shook her head.

Able was smiling.

The Anomaly

Since just about everyone else who was there has written an unbiased true inside story of what really happened at the latest Human vs. Computer *Ygor* competition, and since we've even got to the point where outsiders who weren't within a thousand miles are explaining the "significance" of what took place, it seems a good idea to put my own oar in so at least a few generally undigested facts will come to be known.

And who am I? Well, someone has to snap the pictures of the grandmasters and the computer programmers. When you hunt around in some knowledgeable article, and find in tiny print the words, "Photos by Sam Bean," you may not be especially impressed, but you know the photographer was there.

After all, to get pictures, you have to keep an eye on what's happening. And there was a special reason to care how these pictures turned out. I was using one of the first of the new "invisible flash" cameras, the camera company was providing generous expenses, and emotions at the competition were running so high it was a foregone conclusion there were sure to be chances for first-rate shots. All that was necessary was to just keep thinking about pictures, and not get caught up in the terrific emotional atmosphere of the place.

Anyone who wants to understand what happened needs to realize what this atmosphere was like. The only words that really fit are "impending hysteria." For one thing, the seer who had predicted the recent San Francisco and Tokyo earthquakes came out with the announcement that the influence of the planets had "guided human history into a line of alternative possibilities," and a "decisive *Ygor* competition" was to be one of the "key determining events" down this alternate route.

Now, any reasonable person would naturally say, "So what?" but the entertainment was flowing freely, the place was full of rumors, and everyone was rattled by what had happened already.

Part of the problem, of course, was the nature of the game itself. Ygor wasn't even heard of a few years ago. As the "natural successor to chess," Ygor is supposed to reach complexities at least an order of magnitude greater, and has been called "the last refuge of the human intellect from the calculating machine." Though the computer managed to beat the world chess champion years ago, the tricky nature of Ygor had reduced a generation of programmers to nail-biting frustration. But now, the word was, even this last citadel of the human intellect, defended by its masters and grandmasters, its supreme fighters and unconquerable champions, was to fall to the mindless calculating ability of the computer.

So emotions were running high, and what had happened so far did not help.

First, of course, had been the loss of the World Champion to a rank outsider, Manuel Cerverias. Cerverias' supporters could praise him lavishly, call him "the Capablanca of Ygor," and so on, but the fact was, his reputation was as a volatile and uneven player, and no-one could say what shape he might be in when he came up against the computer.

Then there was the other half of the competition—the computer. After all, the leading computer program was more or less familiar, and so were the people in charge of it. When they accepted the challenge of "Pirates IV"—by their own claim an outfit of elderly ex-phone-phreaks and virus-breeders—everyone thought it was a joke. But the next thing anyone knew, the Pirates IV program, The Red Death, had whipped the computer champ.

So now, instead of the well liked and respected World Champion, we had a little-known newcomer, and instead of the familiar computer opponent, there was The Red Death. Just in case the name didn't give you chills, there was the team itself. Every one was thin to the point of cadaverousness, they all dressed completely in black, and the one in charge wore a set of narrow oblong glasses that looked more like prisms than lenses. If you tried to look him in the eye, you'd get a jolt of disorientation. When this Red Death crew walked past in a group, shadows and foreboding darkness seemed to glide along with them. All this compounded the atmosphere.

It would also be possible to blame quite a lot on the site, the weather (that is, drizzle, gloom, and fog), and the proprietor of the hotel where the competition was being held, who claimed that his total pay had been misrepresented, he was being cheated, and unless this was straightened out, he would throw us all into the street. Of course, somebody had to deal with this.

The previous Champion, at least, could not have been accused of political naiveté or financial unawareness. But the new champ, Cerverias, could be heard shouting, "Don't come to me with this birdseed! I am an Ygor master, not a moneybag!" The result was that a committee of backers and hangers-on was scraped together to disentangle the financial mess, and someone, doubtless sometime pretty late at night, had a stroke of genius and realized that, when you have a boxing championship, the opponents do not have a series of fights; they have only one, and that decides who is champ. If the opponents in this collision could somehow be gotten to agree to that, then one full-length game could decide the championship, the competition would be over with no delay, and then there would be no need whatever to dig up more money for the hotel. Of course, a certain amount of juggling of rules might be necessary, but enough deprivation of sleep can make almost anything look reasonable.

Cerverias, by this time, was so sick of the problem that he said, "Yes. All right! And to hell with it!" The spokesmen for The Red Death said it could make no possible difference anyway, since their program was sure to win regardless. Everyone else attending the competition was naturally outraged. But the proprietor, noticing how much this shortened the competition and so increased his profit, at once credited a generous rebate to everyone, with the result that all, in effect, were briefly and unexpectedly rich, and in a position to afford some fairly exuberant entertainment. This was a situation hardly anyone lost time taking advantage of.

All of this has to be taken into account to get a picture what things were like next morning when the human champ, Cerverias, hove into view looking hung over, pale, and sleepless, with a bad cough and his left eye twitching, to face the stick figure, like a vacuum cleaner handle with a little portable 3V mounted on top, that The Red Death used to fill the chair opposite the human champ, and to move the pieces.

In due course, silence was established, the game started, and the opposing positions were reproduced on a big angled screen above the players. Cerverias had got the black pieces, The Red Death moved first, and a groan went up as the human champ adopted a defense in general disfavor. While all this was going on, of course, there were opportunities for the camera. The "invisible flash" has been explained in different ways, the general idea being "stored photons guiding computer enhancement." Whatever the explanation, in practice the camera was delightful. Since there was no actual flash, there was no blinding, no angry fists shaken in the photographer's face, and, in fact, by moving slowly and evenly, there was almost an illusion of being invisible.

This made it possible not only to get photos of Cerverias, and of the weird mechanism in front of him with its faintly nodding 3V, but also of the programmers, and of such luminaries as the former Champion, several of his predecessors, and the formidable American bad boy,

Arnold Winner, who had threatened to boycott the event, claiming that what was being played there was not Ygor.

Winner disliked time limits, despite the fact that he was one of the fastest players around, and periodically, into the teeth of world opinion, demanded that the clock be done away with.

Rumor had it that Winner's doctors were worried about his health, that he had been warned against stress, and that he had ignored the warning, to play a tough match secretly against one of the leading players. But if he was in bad health, he didn't look it. He sat back like a well contented big cat, watching the play with a faint smile.

The picture-taking fell into a routine, so that it was a surprise, on taking a fresh picture of Cerverias, to see that the human champ, playing Black, was leaning forward with a glint in his eye. A quick glance at the big screen showed what certainly looked like White in difficulties. The room was utterly silent. The weird entity opposite the champion unfolded its thin jointed metal arm, and responded to the obvious pressure. Any mere wood-pusher could see the computer had done nothing but stay alive for another move. There was a faint murmur and movement in the room, as it occurred to the spectators that Cerverias had not picked this generally shunned defense at random. There was every sign he was thoroughly prepared. One false move on his opponent's part was all it would take.

Another memory packet went in the camera. "Ultra-hi-res" photos, which accumulated in a compartment on the bottom, came out. Time passed. The tension in the room gradually subsided. The next glance at the big screen showed Cerverias still seeming to generally dominate the play, but now his expression was of exasperated bafflement. One slip could have given him the game. But the methodical computer evidently had not made the slip. Cerverias still had an edge, but it was not what it had been. With monotonous calculation, his opponent shaved off a trifling advantage here, a niggling ghost of an improvement there, move after move. It was beginning to appear that the computer would make no oversight. In that case, its opponent dare be no less methodical; but humans have been known to get impatient.

The champion's expression was not so much glum as fed up. The various faces around the room showed different degrees of frustration, save for the programmers, who were now smiling modestly.

Here and there, low voices could be heard to mutter, "It's a draw."

Then there was a murmur. A glance at the big screen showed that White had moved a man forward. This, at first glance, seemed to do nothing. But a low groan could be heard in the room as it became evident that it was preparation for freeing White's position. Black had made an oversight. That move by White should have been foreseen and blocked.

Now the consequences of the oversight followed in monotonous succession. White gradually came to dominate Black's position. Black's grudging defense finally became tortured, painful to look upon. One by one, the advantages changed sides.

The expression of the viewers showed sadness, disappointment, and in the case of some of the leading players, a sort of doomed paralyzed awareness of what was coming.

Only the former champion and Arnold Winner looked unintimidated by what was happening, their expressions unreadable.

Cerverias, the champ, his voice ringing in disgust, said, "I concede." He came to his feet, started to turn away from the board, then he turned back. He looked briefly humble, then defiant. "I should not have played this game. I am not in truth really the human champion. I call upon—"

There was chaos in the room.

A group of players around the former Champion, apparently feeling he was about to be called on to play, came to their feet. He, however, shook his head. His voice was clear as he spoke to Cerverias: "You won the championship fairly."

There was a murmur of approval, the sound of people wearily getting to their feet, apparently to leave the room. Then the computer's chief programmer spoke, his voice ironical, but very clear:

"Our program will take on anyone here. The Red Death makes no errors. There is no-one who can out-calculate our algorithm. All you have to do is make one slip. —And being human, you will make it. All talk about the art or the science of Ygor, or of the game's 'immutable principles,' is humbug. All that is just an attempted human substitute for the range and precision of digital calculation human minds do not possess. No offense, but as of this moment, all human players of whatever rank are nothing but has-beens. So, if you've got any other so-called 'champion' out there you want to call on, never mind the formalities. Just bring him on. We'll take him right now."

Several high-ranked women players stood up, one with tears running down her cheeks. The former Champion, seeing this, abruptly came to his feet.

Cerverias, still standing by the board, cleared his throat. His voice was thick but understandable:

"I call on the true human champion, Arnold Winner."

This had the effect of a bomb. People starting to leave turned back from the door. Some looked thunderstruck. A few looked hopeful. Many looked outraged. Winner, a player in the style of chess champion Bobby Fischer, aroused strong emotions, though few players sneered at his skill.

His mere reputation was said to paralyze many opponents. Fiercely offensive players tended to waver uncertainly with Winner on the other side of the board. Unbeatable defensive players had been known to be ripped wide open and lose every game in a match.

And if Winner had any false modesty, no-one had ever mentioned seeing it. Here he came now, tall, powerfully built, smiling, his gait springy, confident, the harsh planes of his face like the slanted surfaces of a gun turret. Let Winner once get his grip into the psychological guts of his opponents, and their offense evaporated, their defense fell apart. General opinion was that only his refusal to accept the rules had kept him from being World Champion.

But he wasn't popular.

There was a shout of "No! No!" and a moment later, the shout would probably have gone up for the former

Champion. Because Winner did not accept the rules, he
was not Champion, was the thought. If everyone else has
to obey the rules, let him, too. Possibly he was the best
player here, but he hadn't proved it under the rules. He
was not the Champion.

But Cerverias' voice momentarily dominated the
gathering:

"Arnold Winner and I played a match last fall, in secret.
He won. He is the World Champion."

The chaos this produced was quieted by the computer's
chief programmer: "You settle the technicalities later.
We'll take him on and whip him now."

There was a brief silence, then a roar like the surf
crashing in, inchoate but powerful. Suddenly everyone
was back in his seat. Everyone wanted to see this fight.
Winner, grinning, shook hands with Cerverias, leaned
across the table, and studied the thing on the other side.
He looked ready to shake hands with it, then gave a kind
of noncommittal grunt, and sat down. He set up the white
pieces on his side of the board, and the slender jointed rod
came forward and set up the black.

Some official, doubtless no admirer of Winner, began
to speak.

The programmer, apparently to forestall any objection,
interrupted. "We couldn't care less who gets to move first.
It's a question of calculation without oversights. That's all
it is. He can't win. No human can."

Winner reached out, and spun the board around. He
was now playing Black. He was challenging the computer
to take advantage of the first move.

Somehow, imperceptibly, this Ygor competition

seemed to have mutated into something else, possibly a medieval tournament, with Arnold Winner as human Champion.

At his gesture of defiance, a roar went up. The crowd was on their feet. Some were chanting Winner's name. Now it was not only the women players who had tears rolling down their cheeks. Even the European players, most of whom had reservations about Arnold Winner, were shouting their approval.

The expression on the faces of the programmers was worth capturing. The blank look around the eyes told of their surprise. The little wry smile suggested the thought—"What's this? Are all these people insane?"

This seemed a perfectly valid point. Though anyone might argue that Arnold Winner could bring a power of combination to the game that the computer might not be able to match, still, suppose that were true? Then, in this one game, the computer might go down in defeat. The silicon challenge would be turned back by the human Champion. For now.

But then what?

Then the team of programmers would go off somewhere to work on their program, and the chip designers would proceed at their own work, and, in due course, The Red Death II, probably running on an upgraded computer, would be back to play whoever might then be the human Champion.

Suppose the human did win tonight?

What would it prove? And for how long?

Some of the onlookers' faces showed a realization of tragedy that argued for their recognizing this very point.

But not Winner. His face shone with a sublime confidence. His assurance was almost frightening. Before it was possible to get a second view of this expression he glanced up, and pointed his finger at the camera.

"That's a distraction. No pictures during the play." He looked around for an official. "Are we going to sit here waiting all night?"

One of the officials, his voice almost squeaking in indignation, said, "Do you accept the rules? This game has a time limit. Will you play with a time limit?"

Winner said easily, "For tonight, I'll take this hunk of metal any way it wants to come."

That produced another frenzy of approval.

Play started.

The computer, as if in challenge, chose the same opening it had used against Cerverias.

Winner, as if tossing the challenge back in the computer's teeth, played the same defense Cerverias had used.

Nearly everyone was seated now, watching tensely. Play moved rapidly. No-one could have said who had the edge. But now Winner abruptly sat up and pointed at the TV pick-up.

"This thing flashes when it reaches the end of its scan. I want it covered."

No game with Winner would have been complete without something like this, but it seemed to catch the programmers off-guard. A pair of officials came over and looked at the offending piece of apparatus.

The chief programmer was on his feet, scowling.

"We can't cover that. That takes the data input for the program."

Winner said imperially, "Fix it so something blocks the flash. I won't put up with this."

The expressions on Winner's face, and on the programmers' faces, would have been wonderful to record. But somehow, though he had no formal authority, Winner's order to stop taking pictures barred use of the camera.

A little later, there was a cut-out arch of corrugated cardboard, held upright by small stacks of books, that blocked the reflection. The moves were proceeding with startling speed. On the big display, the position began to resemble the chaotic defense Black had used the last game. That looked promising, but that defense had led to the computer's victory.

Winner straightened lazily, looked at the board from a slightly different angle, chuckled, and said, "Oh, no, you don't."

After apparently playing Black's previous game move-for-move, now he introduced a variation.

There was a lengthy delay before the computer finally moved, then the jointed arm moved out hesitantly; it made a faltering move, and—

Crack!

There was a collective gasp as Winner, moving like a cat springing on its prey, slammed a piece in place on the board.

The programmers, perspiring, glanced at each other.

Winner glanced up. "Concede?"

The chief programmer, plainly showing strain, snapped, "That's absurd! This isn't a human opponent. You can't rattle a computer. That's a low stunt, and it won't work!"

"Why are you sweating if you're so sure?"

"Hell, man, when you slapped that piece down, I all but jumped out of my skin! I'm rattled. But you're not playing me. Go ahead and try to win it. It makes no mistakes. You can get a positional advantage, but you can't win. Sometime, you'll make a slip. The best you might get is a draw."

"It's made two mistakes already. The game's lost, with best play on its part. Watch."

Winner uncrossed his legs, and reached forward to move a Black piece. There was a long delay before the computer responded. Winner promptly moved again. On the big display, White's clear disadvantage in position was compounded by an increasing loss of space. As if there were a fantastic difference in ability, a grandmaster toying with a beginner, the White pieces were forced back across the board, to end up packed together, as one then another retreated from the Black advance. Winner glanced up, and grinned.

"This piece of tin is winning?"

The chief programmer, sweating heavily, studied the board. "You don't dare to take any of those pieces. Every piece is covered by the same number of pieces as there are attacking it."

"That's routine. But how's it going to maintain it?"

The game proceeded.

Somehow, White survived the endless threats, maintaining its tortured position as the Black pieces visibly built up a greater and greater threat aimed at the White king.

Smiling, Winner settled to his task as the computer, with agonizing skill, rewove its defense, and then tried to move its King away from the danger.

In the breathless silence, certain moves seemed to

stand out. A Black Lion slid across the board and took a White Knight. A second White Knight captured the Black Lion.

A Black Dragon checked the White King.

Casually, Winner brought his pieces forward, snapping up this and that white piece, repeatedly checking the computer's King, forcing it here and there at will.

With dogged persistence, the computer calculated and replied; calculated and replied; sheltering its King here, then there, always somehow patching together a temporary defense despite an appearance of easy total domination by its opponent.

Then the last of the series of exchanges was made.

The chief programmer exhaled in a hiss, and mopped his neck and forehead. He had a wondering look, as if he were surprised to still be alive. Now he leaned forward, plainly willing himself to face whatever might be there on the board, and thereby showing how completely he had lost track of the game.

But he wasn't alone. All around the room, people were staring at the board or the display.

The computer had a King and a Soldier.

Winner had a King and two Soldiers.

A huge sigh circled the room.

The programmers glanced at each other warily, then shrugged in disgust. Plainly, they knew their program somehow was beat; but also plainly, they were not crushed. They knew this loss was temporary.

Winner, smiling, began the routine that, in this position, would win the game for any capable player.

A peculiar beeping noise sounded.

The chief programmer said, "That's how it concedes. You've won. For now."

The former champion, who had lost to Cerverias, came to his feet. "Three cheers for our World Champion, Arnold Winner!"

Winner, beaming, came to his feet.

No-one was playing now, so it seemed fair enough to take pictures. One of them was a little puzzling, showing the chief programmer with two other experts at his elbow, discussing something intently, their expressions very odd. Then Winner was talking to one of the women grandmasters. He smiled, and the last thing he said was clearly audible:

"I am completely content."

An instant later he was on the floor, the smile still plain on his face as chaos broke loose around him.

They had doctors on the spot in a moment, but they couldn't revive him. He was rushed to a hospital, where they had no better luck. The cadaverous chief programmer broke down and cried, as did one of Winner's doctors, who damned himself for allowing the game. Then the spectators crowded around, masters, grandmasters, and ordinary players, earnestly giving comfort to the doctor and the programmer:

"Look, he wanted to play. It was his life. You didn't hurt him any."

"Did you see that expression on his face? How many people die with a smile?"

"He's in Chess/Ygor heaven now. Humboldt is shaking his hand. Lasker is gripping him by the arm."

A woman grandmaster, so beautiful there were those

who credited her victories over men to her opponents' distraction, took the doctor gently by the arm.

"He was in no trouble during the game. Did you see any sign of strain? If you'd ever played him, you'd understand. When you played him, you weren't up against his calculating ability alone. His concentration was total. His attention never wavered. His will would take you like a giant hand and crush the life out of you. No medical condition killed him. He was just through here, that's all. His will let go of his body. He moved on."

She briefly drew the doctor's head comfortingly against her shoulder. He sighed, then looked up with a wondering expression. He was medically responsible for a patient's death; he could see it no other way. Yet he was surrounded by the friends and admirers of his patient, and no-one looked at him in anger. Everyone was smiling.

"He argued me around," said the doctor. "With the best good nature, somehow he convinced me he'd be all right."

"That's how he was. You couldn't stand against his will. We'll miss him. But, oh, what a triumph! What a time to go!"

Her shining face made a beautiful picture, setting off the wondering misery of the doctor's facial expression.

A glance around showed the chief programmer for The Red Death, with a look none too easy to interpret. He was holding what looked like computer printouts, happened to see me aiming the camera at him, and gestured to come over. His expression was no easier to interpret at short range.

I said, "You don't look happy."

"We've got what you might call a problem."

"A temporary problem? Back to the drawing board?"

He shook his head. "I would have said so yesterday. If this is truly what it looks like, it's worse than that."

"How could it be? A little tightening of the code, an improvement in the algorithm, maybe a faster processor— How can you lose? It's like every year or so, the strongest man in the world has to go out and wrestle the latest model Caterpillar tractor. How long is that going to be in doubt?"

"That's what I thought before I saw these."

"How—?"

"Take a look."

What he handed over was two listings of the game's moves, showing the last two games played by the computer. One list was headed "Cerverias," and the other "Winner." Comparing the lists, it seemed obvious that, at the beginning, all of Winner's moves were identical to those of Cerverias. But two of the computer's moves were outlined in yellow, and these moves differed from one game to the next. I looked up.

"There's a random aspect to the computer's moves?"

"Only when the alternative moves have exactly the same value."

"So these two moves in the first part of the game had the same values? That is, the moves the computer played against Cerverias, and the two different moves it played against Winner?"

"No."

"No?"

"No."

"Then the play against Winner represents superior moves? There is an accumulation of computer skill from game to game?"

"The moves it made against Winner were mistakes."

I looked at him, then back at the lists. Winner's comment came back to me: "It has made two mistakes already."

"But, I thought that couldn't happen?"

"It can't. But it did. That's our problem."

"Some hardware failure? Maybe some fluctuation in line voltage?"

He shook his head. "We're ready for anything like that."

There was a lengthy silence, then he said, "What that woman grandmaster said, that his will just let go of his body. You believe that?"

I said carefully, "I don't know if she meant that literally."

"But do you believe it?"

"I don't know. If 'life is but a dream,' he'd certainly reached an ideal spot to end a dream. I heard him say he was perfectly content."

"I don't want to believe it. But I don't know."

"What does it matter, anyway? All you have to do is keep making incremental improvements."

He shook his head. "That's assuming it's a question of pure calculation. We can handle that. But what's 'will'? We're always hearing about somebody 'whose iron will overcame all obstacles.' It sounds like baloney to me. Especially applied to Ygor. But here we've got it. How do we fit a thing like that into the program? The first question is, what's will?"

"I don't see where you get the idea that 'here we've got it.'"

"First, we see the computer ignore normal calculation when it's playing Winner, and decide on some other basis. Second, the woman grandmaster, a great player and well acquainted with Winner, credits his dominance to his 'will.' Third, no-one disagrees; everyone nods and smiles. Fourth, what other explanation do we have? Remember, Winner threw the computer around the board as if it were a kindergarten pupil. He was a great player, but he could only do that because of his opponent's errors. How can anyone distract or overawe a computer so it makes errors? What's Will?"

"I read a definition once—"

"What was it?"

"As I remember, will is what enables you to hold your attention focused. I think it was compared to a polished reflector, and attention was conscious awareness—Like light focused in a searchlight."

He considered it and nodded soberly. "How about what she said that when you played him you weren't just playing his calculating ability; he got you in his will—that is, in his focused attention—and crushed the life out of you? Was that true?"

I said carefully, "I only ever played him once."

He studied my expression. "And how did that work out?"

"Just about as she described."

"How, specifically."

"I forgot moves I knew. My thoughts congealed. I recorded the moves, and afterward I couldn't understand why I'd made some of them."

"His reputation paralyzed you?"

"It would have, if I'd known who I was playing. It was a wet night out, and I'd just come in, and there were two players I didn't recognize sitting beside the fireplace, on opposite sides of a game board, and one was just getting up. The other glanced at me. I wanted to be near the fire, to get warmed up, so when he said, 'Game?' I said 'Sure,' and we started to play. I blamed the results on the cold and wet, followed by the warm fire. But I wasn't falling asleep. I just couldn't think properly."

The chief programmer said dryly, "How many players like that are there?"

"I don't know. Maybe one in a generation. I don't think you can predict."

"One is too many."

"Maybe it's just that your processor has gone bad."

Briefly, his face cleared. "We can hope. We're checking that."

There was a tearing sound, and one of the other programmers came over with a sheaf of papers. The chief programmer leafed through the sheets, and gave a low grunt, as if he had been hit. The other programmer pointed to different lines marked in yellow, and shook his head.

"Twelve different times through, and we can't duplicate any of this. But that's what it did, playing him."

"We'll just have to crank everything tighter."

"Sure, sharpen our knife. Look, he used nerve gas and smart bombs."

"What else are we going to do? Besides, maybe he was the only one. After all, this whole damn thing is impossible."

The other programmer nodded ironically, then in a perfectly level toneless voice delivered a mind-stunning profanity. The chief programmer shrugged, then he looked around as if wondering what to do with the sheaf of papers. He noticed me, and held them out.

They were listings of moves, the first marked, "Winner," and the rest marked, "Trial," and successively numbered "1" through "12." The overall effect was stunning.

"The computer did one thing when it was playing Winner, and it did another thing when you gave it the same positions afterward?"

"It made two crucial errors in the beginning—as Winner pointed out. Later on, it made what look to us like no less than half-a-dozen inferior moves. Most of these weren't by themselves disastrous. Just a shaving off the position here, a little something grated off there. But it's all going to the credit of Grandmaster Arnold Winner, who smilingly cashes it all in at the end. It's as if somehow he paralyzed the computer's ability to calculate."

Finally I could understand the chief programmer's facial expression. Just what was he supposed to do now? How could you program a computer to not be influenced by something that couldn't possibly have affected it in the first place? On the other hand, for someone not faced with the problem, there was a certain hilarious aspect to this.

I said, "Look, what Winner did to you was only what you were trying to do to him, wasn't it? I mean, through endlessly refining the computer and the program, so you couldn't possibly lose? All that happened was, you got back what you dished out to Cerverias."

"Well, yes. But *we* did it by strictly rational calculation."

"Yeah, but why should that be the only method permitted? Your assumption was that there was nothing involved except calculation. And in that case, sooner or later you were sure to win. But how could you know in advance that was right? You did dismiss all talk about the art of Ygor, the science of the game, the immutable principles—All just humbug."

"Well, what the hell, we weren't planning to come up against The Psychic Powers of the GrandChampion! We didn't figure the guy could mesmerize the computer! How did he do it? Did he temporarily alter the conducting properties of the chip? Did he impose an electromagnetic field that changed the flow of the electrons? How could he do anything at all *except* calculate? I thought for the purposes of this game, Mind was just Calculation. But now, how do we know that's true? And damn it, now he's gone, so we can never be sure!"

The expression on his face was pure indignation, and it took just a second to record it. He waved his hand in disgust.

"All you care about is pictures. Look, how do we digitize Will? How come we never ran into this before? Was there something special about Winner? You realize, he passed away; the guy is dead, and somehow we're all seeing it the way he would want us to see it. Now, just think this over. If he could use will to affect the computer, how do we know there won't be some effect that works the other way, the computer affecting will? Then what?"

He glared at me. "You see how many cans of worms this opens up? I'm only getting started. And you know how many people are going to give this five seconds' thought? You can count them on one hand. What the hell, most of them probably will never hear about it! But any Pollyanna that wants to write an article on how this proves Mankind will never be outthought by a computer will probably get it in print and even be paid for it."

"Well—Just keep improving your program."

"Naturally, we'll keep improving it! And everyone else will improve theirs. And maybe we'll clobber the next human champ, and the next fifteen after that. That's not what we're talking about here. The point is, what we've got here does not fit the way we know things have got to be. It's an anomaly. It throws our main assumptions completely into question. If what those printouts suggest is true, the whole mechanism of cause and effect may work differently than we believe."

For a moment, he hesitated. "It's like when Fleming saw the wood mold had killed the bacteria. The conventional answer to Fleming is, 'That doesn't make sense; it couldn't happen. So, just clean your glassware, man. Keep at it, and you'll get the result we all know in advance you ought to get.' Fortunately for us, Fleming nailed down what actually had happened, and we got penicillin. In Science, big gains can come from noticing little anomalies, and this is an anomaly that stands out like a lighthouse! But it happened in an Ygor game. And everyone will just think it's a mistake on our part. No-one who needs to know about it is likely to see this, much less realize what it means!"

"Wait a minute. You see it."

"Pirates IV is going to win the competitions if we can, but somehow I don't see us following Fleming to the bat."

***

So, since we've had one article after another to show "What Arnold Winner's Last Victory Really Proves," it seemed a good idea to just mention those points that generally don't make it into print.

In nearly every article, any anomaly is totally overlooked. If mentioned, the suggestion is that it somehow is unexplainable, and it therefore follows that it must be an error. That leaves the problem, but disposes of the awareness of it.

Since, as they say, there isn't any point in examining errors, the focus is on what is explainable. So the facts are being gradually normalized out of existence, and Winner's unexplainable victory is credited to such things as his "sheer Ygor wizardry."

And of course, since Winner isn't here, nothing can be proved. But there's still a lesson here.

The main thing seems to be, if somebody does something impossible according to accepted assumptions, don't just say it can only be voltage spikes on the line.

Take a hard look at what happened, and the assumptions.

Remember Fleming, and:

Examine the anomaly.

In the Light
of Further Data

GATESBURG, ILL., FEBRUARY 22nd. Dr. Richard Roswell, director of the Gatesburg Medical Research Center, announced today the realization of an age-old scientific dream, the regeneration of limbs and bodily organs, using implanted "tissue-seeds." Much interest has already been aroused by published reports of research in this field by Dr. Roswell and his associates. Beginning with studies upon tadpoles, and extensive experimentation on mice and hamsters, the method was last year proven eminently practical in the successful regeneration of the injured lower trunk of the elephant "Millie." Since then, it has been used successfully on chimpanzees. In answer to questions, Dr. Roswell expressed his belief that his tissue implants will in time come to be very widely used, particularly in the regeneration of teeth.

HARBRIDGE, MAY 2nd. Dr. G. Puthrie Banks, dynamic, hard-driving president of fast-growing Oxnam Technological Institute, today addressed an audience of several thousand gathered to dedicate the new OTI Advanced Nuclear Research Laboratories. Calling upon the under-graduates present to "pursue the creative quest for excellence," President Banks pointed out that "nothing is more important than that the new generation of our nation's leaders prepare fully for the trials that lie ahead." President Banks added that "to so prepare, the most requisite need is the acquisition of true, accurate, and detailed factual knowledge. The sole source of such knowledge is Science. Thus, in a very broad and meaningful sense, we may say, 'The Source of Truth is Science.'"

HARBRIDGE, JULY 2nd. OTI President G. Puthrie Banks today publicly denied that he had said "Science is God." President Banks stated that the charge, made by a group of prominent clergymen, "evidently grew out of a misconstruction of a speech in which I merely pointed out what is perfectly obvious, namely, 'The *source of truth* is Science'."

CLINTON, W. VA., OCTOBER 4th. Doctors report that Lyell Smith, a forty-two-year old coal miner seriously injured in a mine cave-in, has recovered partial use of his left foot. The foot was regenerated by the Roswell implant method, and hopes are high that the operation will prove a complete success.

FORD HILL, VA., FEBRUARY 2nd. Dr. Raymond Schmeissner, of the Ford Hill Professional Dental Clinic, reports forty-six successful dental implants since the Roswell implant program was started last fall.

CAMP BEDFORD, PA., MARCH 18th. Representatives of several interdenominational church groups today released the final draft of the "Bedford Declaration" which reads in part, "the Source of truth, today as in all ages, is not to be confused with any single channel by which a particular truth reaches man." This was believed to be a slap at OTI President Banks, who has proclaimed Science the "Source of Truth."

GATESBURG, ILL., AUGUST 12th. More than five hundred persons in the U. S. have undergone Roswell implant treatment, according to data forwarded to the Gatesburg Medical Research Center. Dr. Roswell's most famous patient, the elephant Millie, is reported in excellent condition.

ST. LOUIS, OCTOBER 23rd. Dentists meeting here report using the Roswell implant method with "speedy and invariable" success to grow new teeth after extractions. The process is reported "more complicated but still very satisfactory" if some time has already elapsed, allowing the gum to heal where the tooth is to be implanted.

HARBRIDGE, FEBRUARY 28th. OTI President G. Puthrie Banks, angrily replying to continued clerical criticism, today charged that "certain religious so-called 'leaders' must be strangers to the modern world. The distinctive flavor of modern living is clearly due to the unlimited application of the advances of Science. Why should we not pay due homage to the source of these great advances?"

GATESBURG, ILL., MARCH 12th. More than five thousand persons in the U. S. have undergone Roswell Implant therapy, according to data forwarded to the Gatesburg Medical Research Center. No failures or complications have been reported.

MARION SPRINGS, ILL., APRIL 16th. Philosopher Michael James Henning, asked about the current religio-scientific controversy, stated that "truth, like the universe, has a number of different regions and aspects. The most expert familiarity with one region or aspect does not mean that an otherwise mortal man is omniscient." Philosopher Henning charged both sides with "airs of omniscience," but said that "Dr. Banks' extreme and widely-publicized position, in presenting science as the sole source of worthwhile knowledge, could have peculiarly unpleasant repercussions in the event of some large-scale scientific debacle." Because of the growing predominance of "scientific and pseudo-scientific methods," Mr. Henning pointed out, "the probability of such a failure increases yearly."

GATESBURG, ILL., MAY 2nd. The Gatesburg Medical Research Center revealed today that over twenty thousand persons have benefited from Roswell implant therapy. Most of this work has been dental. All of it has shown "a degree of success close to one hundred per cent."

HARBRIDGE, MAY 16th. Embattled OTI President G. Puthrie Banks, after a meeting with the trustees, stated today that he is "not opposed to religion as such," and that his statement that "Science is the source of truth," was not intended to mean that "Science is God." "Metaphysics and religion," Dr. Banks added, "have brought considerable solace to many persons in the past, and will doubtless continue to do so in the future."

GATESBURG, ILL., DECEMBER 15th. The Gatesburg Medical Research Center revealed today that nearly two hundred thousand persons have profited from Nobel-prize winner Dr. Richard Roswell's tissue-implant therapy. Headquarters of the Gatesburg National Dental Crusade predict that in the coming year "nearly fifty per cent of those suffering the effects of serious dental deterioration will be restored to a normal condition" thanks to the Roswell treatment. The Crusade announced plans for the mass-treatment of school children, and reported "substantial success" in the initial phases of the national fund-raising drive.

HARBRIDGE, JANUARY 19th. OTI President G. Puthrie Banks spoke this evening at the Northeast Regional Kickoff Dinner of the Gatesburg National Dental Crusade. President Banks pictures Science as "the source of that truth and power of action that has lifted man up out of the ruck of Medieval ignorance, poverty, illness, and despair. Once universally misunderstood, today Science goes forth like an army in magnificence and grandeur, led by such generals as Dr. Roswell, to conquer the ancient enemies of mankind."

CAMP BEDFORD, PA., MARCH 4th. Angry spokesmen

for the Bedford interdenominational conference accused OTI president Banks of "deifying science" and "mistaking a technique for a kind of beneficent supernatural entity." Dr. Banks, the group charged, is "crystallizing the attitude, already painfully in evidence, that 'science can do no wrong.'" Such an attitude, the Bedford group charged, is "emotional, partisan, and totally devoid of so-called 'scientific objectivity.'"

HARBRIDGE, JUNE 20th. First patient at the Gatesburg Crusade Clinic here was Dr. G. Puthrie Banks, dynamic president of OTI. President Banks declared that he has "one hundred per cent faith in the scientific method," and expects to throw away his dental plates in the near future.

PHILADELPHIA, AUGUST 15th. The Gatesburg clinics in this city reported treating their fifty thousandth patient this morning. Implant therapy, the clinics report, is "fast and reliable."

GATESBURG, ILL., SEPT. 30th. National Headquarters of the Gatesburg National Dental Crusade announced today that with incomplete reports on hand, the Crusade "has given over five million persons a new lease on dental health." Crusade spokesmen criticized "superstitionists" who "refuse to give their children permission to receive the benefits of this modern blessing."

HARBRIDGE, OCTOBER 6th. OTI's dynamic president G. Puthrie Banks today smilingly displayed a mouthful of new teeth, grown from transplants by the

Roswell method. He cited the success as a measure of "the growing omnipotence of an expanding Science, which has enabled man to become master of the forces of nature in the modern world."

NEW YORK, DECEMBER 10th. Sociologists report that according to recent surveys, research scientists have climbed to the number one spot in terms of public respect and admiration. Second are dentists, and third, physicians.

GATESBURG, ILL., MARCH 26th. Crusade Headquarters announced today that through their intensive efforts, over fifteen million persons have "received the blessings of truly modern medical science." Charges of graft in the program have been strenuously denied.

HARBRIDGE, MAY 16th. Dynamic, youthful OTI president G. Puthrie Banks, replying angrily to continued criticism from many clerical sources, today declared in his speech dedicating the university's new Roswell Medical Research Center, that "religion, metaphysics, and philosophy are outflanked, outmoded forces in the world of today. Today Science is the principal, if not sole, source and repository of useful knowledge and fruitful techniques."

GATESBURG, ILL., AUGUST 19th. Crusade headquarters announced today that over twenty million persons have attended the Crusade's clinics. Continuing rumors of graft were branded "scurrilous and anti-humanitarian."

GRAND FERRY, IOWA, SEPTEMBER 16th. "Millie" the circus elephant, for years the favorite of children all over the country, provides a new and unusual attraction these days. Millie's trunk, the lower portion of which was regenerated several years ago by the Roswell implant method, for some weeks this summer was swollen and looked "peculiar." Millie's keepers were later dumbfounded to discover that the Roswell-treated portion of the trunk was turning into twins, the two portions being joined at the base to the uninjured part of the trunk. Asked if they would seek veterinary care for the elephant, circus spokesmen said they see no need. "This way, she's a bigger attraction. The trunk don't seem to bother her, and she really draws people in." Both portions of the trunk move together, in exactly the same way, as if they were one.

GATESBURG, ILL., SEPTEMBER 17th. Dr. Richard Roswell, when reached early this morning with news of the elephant Millie's twin trunk, stated that he was "appalled." Assured that the report was not a joke, Dr. Roswell stated that he will go to Grand Ferry at once to examine the elephant.

GRAND FERRY, IOWA, SEPTEMBER 18th. Dr. Richard Roswell, world-renowned medical-research scientist, today examined the circus elephant "Millie," one of the first large mammals to receive the Roswell tissue-implant treatment. Following the examination, Dr. Roswell, haggard and uncommunicative, left town immediately.

GATESBURG, ILL., SEPTEMBER 19th. The offices of the Gatesburg National Dental Crusade are deserted today. It has proved impossible to contact anyone connected with the movement.

CLINTON, W. VA., SEPTEMBER 24th. Lyell Smith, 45-year-old coal miner whose left foot was regenerated four years ago by the Roswell tissue-implant method, today told reporters that in recent weeks the foot has become red and swollen, "looks funny," and seems to "itch inside."

GATESBURG, ILL., OCTOBER 6th. Dr. Richard Roswell today announced successful surgical removal, in a careful four-hour operation, of the extra foot of a West Virginia coal miner who four years ago received the Roswell implant treatment to regenerate this same left foot. Doctors who have studied the case say the extra foot was "functional, but suffered from a lack of circulation." Dr. Roswell explained that the nerves and blood vessels branched at the site of the original tissue implant, thus dividing the blood supply. Asked how the foot could have appeared normal for several years, and then in the space of a few weeks could have begun to duplicate itself, Dr. Roswell pointed out that "far more striking changes take place in the developing embryo," and the tissue-implant method "relies on related phenomena." There is, he said, apparently a build-up over the four-year period of "some chemical substance which triggers this second regeneration of the part or organ concerned." Asked if there would be yet a third such regeneration, Dr. Roswell stated that there was "as yet insufficient data to answer the question." Asked whether persons who have had their teeth regenerated would find themselves growing duplicate sets of teeth after the original regeneration, Dr. Roswell answered the he "would presume so. All the data point to it." Asked further how the condition could be corrected, Dr. Roswell replied that "surgical removal of at least one, and probably both, sets of teeth would be indicated."

GATESBURG, ILL., OCTOBER 8th. A mob smashed and burned the deserted headquarters of the Gatesburg National Dental Crusade here last night. Today, National Guard troops with bayonets fixed surround the Gatesburg Medical Research Center to protect it against threatened violence. An estimated twenty-five million persons have received Roswell tissue therapy in the intensive drive following its first public use four years ago.

WASHINGTON, D. C., DECEMBER 14th. A meeting of prominent physicians and dental surgeons broke up today without issuing any report. The meeting was originally called to make recommendations on "improving the medical image."

GATESBURG, ILL., APRIL 14th. Dr. Richard Roswell today stated that "many reports now available prove conclusively that duplication of teeth follows the same pattern as twinning of other organs or parts." Dr. Roswell noted that at present the only satisfactory treatment is "extraction of the tooth prior to twinning, as the human jaw is peculiarly unsuited to the retention of two sets of teeth at the same time." Dr. Roswell admitted that extraction of the tooth "involves unusual difficulties," because the tooth, being still "perfectly healthy from the physiological viewpoint, resists extraction." That is, the tooth won't let go. Dr. Roswell expressed confidence in the new compound-leverage devices developed to deal with the problem. Dr. Roswell advised general anesthesia in all cases.

CAMP BEDFORD, MAY 6th. The Bedford Interdenominational Leadership Conference today lambasted OTI president G. Puthrie Banks for his "airs of omniscience that have led millions into a kind of dental purgatory that is just a foretaste of what lies ahead for those who rely exclusively on science to solve their problems."

MARION SPRINGS, ILL., MAY 14th. Philosopher Michael James Henning today charged the controversial president of the Oxnam Technological Institute, G. Puthrie Banks, with a "disastrous misinterpretation of the function and position of science in the modern world." Science, said philosopher Henning, is "said to be based strictly on observable facts. As facts are infinite, however, and the human mind, as we know it, is finite, we are immediately brought face-to-face with a dilemma. Even with the most advanced present or foreseeable devices and procedures, it remains impossible to take account of all facts, known or as yet unknown, which may be relevant to a given question. Thus a process of selection becomes absolutely unavoidable. Now, selection is a function of judgment, and judgment is not, and cannot be, strictly scientific. There is, then, *a* *nonscientific element in all scientific findings.* This nonscientific element is inescapable, at the same time that it is nonfactual and necessarily fallible.

"There are," philosopher Henning concludes, "two lessons to be learned from this. The first is that as careful attention must be given to the use of good judgment as to the gathering of factual knowledge. The second is that Science, however useful, remains fallible. He who seeks an infallible and divine guidance must seek it elsewhere."

WASHINGTON, D. C., AUGUST 26th. Legislators here are disturbed by the rising tide of corrective operations, amputations, and extractions, needed to overcome the side effects of the Roswell implant therapy. These operations are already putting a visible strain on the medical and dental manpower of the nation, and it is bound to get worse instead of better as every living individual who has received the Roswell therapy returns for corrective treatment. Particularly troublesome is the enormous number of people who must, in the coming years, submit to multiple dental extractions. The present devices for carrying out these extractions on firmly-rooted healthy teeth resemble Medieval torture instruments, and dentists who have carried out extractions with them state that "an incredible amount of physical labor is involved. When a Roswell multiple-extraction is over, we are exhausted, and the patient is a hospital case." Teeth grown by the implant method are reported exceptionally healthy and firmly-rooted, and one dentist has complained that it is "damned unnerving to find yourself trying to drag a chunk of the patient's jaw out with the tooth."

GATESBURG, ILL., SEPTEMBER 30th. Troops at the Gatesburg Medical Research Center here have been strengthened by another National Guard battalion, Brigadier general James C. Burns reported today. General Burns said that Dr. Roswell and his family are now living full-time inside the Research Center Inner Compound. Now that the Guard has sufficient strength to strongly occupy all the hills overlooking the Center, General Burns feels that incidents such as last Sunday's combination rifle and mortar attack, and the attempt on Tuesday to ram a homemade tank through the roadblock, will be much easier to handle.

NEW YORK, OCTOBER 6th. Sociologists report that recent studies indicate a dramatic collapse in the public view of science and scientists. Research scientists, while not as far into the cellar as dentists, are now well below physicians at the bottom of the list.

CHUGABOG, MINN., OCTOBER 12th. Little Chugabog Junior College, enrollment 126, announced today the appointment of Dr. G. Puthrie Banks, formerly of Oxnam Technological Institute, as dean of students. College spokesmen admitted that they had had "some reservations" about the controversial Dr. Banks, but that after a personal interview they believe he will "do well in Chugabog. After all, we are a forward-looking community, and as long as he doesn't go off on that science kick again, we feel he will be O.K."

NEW YORK, N. Y., DECEMBER 10th. A team of

physicians, bacteriologists, and dental surgeons, backed massively with private funds, are reported to have cracked the Roswell tooth-extraction problem. According to information released here today, a process of "intensive suppuration" creates "artificial abscesses" which ease the problem of later withdrawing the teeth from their sockets. "Of course," spokesmen admit, "this means that before the extraction, the patient will have multiple abscessed teeth in his mouth."

WASHINGTON, D. C., DECEMBER 31st. Armed with "tooth-abscess generators" and motorized hydraulic compound-leverage extractors, the nation's capital tonight looks forward into the new year with as much hope and confidence as it can muster. An estimated ten million multiple extractions will have to be performed in the coming year.

HARBRIDGE, JANUARY 4th. Dr. D. Bonham Moore, hard-driving president recently appointed to overhaul tottering Oxnam Technological Institute, today addressed an audience of some fifty persons gathered to dedicate the new Oxnam Dental-Extraction Clinic on the OTI East Hill Campus. Dr. Moore called upon "any undergraduates who may be present" to "base their lives on the double foundation of experience and high principles and not chase off after easy generalisms." President Moore added that "obviously the acquisition of a new and useful method does not mean that everything else our forefathers built up in the preceding five or six thousand years is to be thrown on the scrap heap."

CHUGABOG, MINN., FEBRUARY 18th. Dr. G. Puthrie Banks, interviewed as he was carried out of the Chugabog Dental Clinic, admitted today that he intends to undergo training for the ministry.

Wan and pale, and speaking with some difficulty, the former advocate of unlimited Science explained:

"I feel that I may have misunderstood my calling."

Apron Chains

Fernando Columbus, Jr. peered into the viewplate at P. Hernandez, one of his best mariners. Hernandez's voice came out the horn of the all-hail to one side:

"Mr. Director, I have the seventeen bottles of seawater, from the specified depths."

"Good, Hernandez."

"And I have charted the wind-speed at all the different prescribed altitudes, using the gas sack as directed."

"Excellent."

"Also, I have conducted the current-mapping tests as prescribed."

"Very good, Hernandez."

"My equipment state is A-1."

"Fine."

"My personnel state is A-2. There has been a little grumbling."

"That is to be expected, at this stage. It will pick up to A-1 again as soon as you start back."

"Ah . . . I would like to make a request, Mr. Director."

"Yes?"

"I . . . ah . . . Mr. Director, I do not wish to return to port just yet."

Project Director Columbus winced, as with a headache.

"*Why?*"

"Well, sir. I—That is, I think—Mr. Director, I *know* I can make it *all the way.*"

The director gripped the table edge. *This* again.

"Look, Hernandez, every second mariner we send out *knows* he can make it all the way. There's even a name for it: 'Far-end syndrome.' Back when Indies Project started, my own great-uncle, one Christopher Columbus, knew *he* could make it 'all the way.'"

Hernandez looked baffled. "He was a mariner?"

"One of the first. They didn't have much education in those days, believe me. And that was using the old K-1 rig, pure sail power, and if you got becalmed, you just sat there. Well, he got this same crazy idea, he was going to go on, and on, and on, *all the way across.* Velasquez was director back then, and they had a terrific argument. Uncle Chris tried to throw the all-hail overboard, but the crew stopped him. Velasquez appointed the first mate to take over—that's what they called the alternate mariner in those days—and that was that. If he *had* gone on, he'd have had to go *four times as far as he had gone already*, in order to reach the Indies. He wouldn't have made it. His stores were inadequate. Equipment state was bad. Personnel state was terrible. All the same, he 'knew he could make it.' If Marquesas had been a few years later inventing the all-hail, or if the Venetian School had been a little slower getting a geographical analysis of the problem done, it would have been 'Good-bye, Uncle Chris.' Luckily for him, Velasquez was on hand to straighten the situation out before it was too late. Since then, we have had others. Ordaz for instance. Apparently he *did* go on. Lost without a trace. That's why we have alternates, to prevent such foolishness."

Hernandez said weakly, "I saw a seagull."

"You've been in a storm. It could have been blown from an island somewhere."

"Uh . . . I can sort of . . . 'feel' land—lots of land, up ahead. It's sort of *looming* there, almost. I . . . I *know* I can make it."

The director drew a deep breath. His voice came out low, patient, and determinedly sympathetic.

"Hernandez, our advances are made by the patient labor of many people, not by any one man. I realize how you feel. It does credit to you. But your achievement on this is already a significant contribution. There is no possible purpose in your attempting to complete the voyage to the Indies. Geographical analysis demonstrates that the direct sea route is *longer*, not shorter, than the route around Africa. In place of the curving route around the African continent, you have instead the whole bulge of the Earth to travel across. Consequently, there is *no conceivable economic advantage* in this route. That is why Indies Project is a scientific fact-gathering operation, under strict budgetary control, and on a minimal-risk basis. The gains have been, and will be, made in improved ship-design, better charts, and refined meteorological and oceanographic analysis. These gains can be realized in a deliberate and systematic way. What we need is the *methodical performance of assigned tasks.* Heroics, such as those of the unfortunate Ordaz, are unnecessary. It would be pointless—wouldn't it?—to try to start now a voyage that is still longer, from where you are at present, than it would have been if, when you started out, you *had* gone around Africa?"

"I . . . I guess so." Hernandez glanced away at the horizon, then shrugged. "I guess you're right."

"All right. The objectives of your mission are completed, Hernandez. I suggest you start back."

Hernandez scratched his head, then nodded, and said, "All right, Mr. Director." He dropped the cover over his viewplate. The *snap* from the all-hail told the director the connection was broken. The director shoved back his seat, to see Diaz, the medical man, leave his big viewplate.

***

Diaz said cheerfully, "Typical far-end syndrome. But Hernandez is in good shape, physically and mentally. His color is good. Eyes are clear. Disposition is basically lousy, of course, but whose isn't?"

The director smiled and sat back.

"No harm then, in letting him complete the mission?"

"No. None. Do him good."

"What do you suppose causes this 'far-end syndrome?'"

Diaz pulled up a chair. "It's beyond me. As long as we can get them out of it, I guess it doesn't matter. Oh . . . I suppose it's actually a form of psychic inertia. After you go on and on, and on, *toward* the Indies, I suppose there's a natural hesitation to turn back, away *from* the Indies. If it weren't for Marquesas' all-hail, there's no telling how many we'd lose."

The director nodded. "When you stop to think of it, it's amazing how much we owe to Marquesas—and to the Venetian School, of course. But then, without Marquesas, I doubt that the Venetian School would have hung together."

"Probably never have been founded in the first place." Diaz sat back, hands clasped behind his head. "It's a funny thing, when you think of it, how much the world has changed in roughly the past hundred years. And when you trace it back, sooner or later, you usually arrive at one man—Marquesas."

The director nodded.

"I read an interesting piece on that very topic. It was called 'The Unvenetian World,' or something like that. The basic assumption was that Marquesas had died in that shipwreck, instead of barely getting ashore near Venice. It then followed, and it was logical, that the Turks would have taken Constantinople, and Europe would still be split up in odd bits and pieces, all fighting each other. The steam carriage, the all-hail, the viewplate, the snafaraz, the flashscraper—all of that would have gone down with Marquesas. If Science *had* started up, *without* Marquesas, it would still have run smack into the Church. The likelihood of another person with both scientific and diplomatic genius was nil. Without Marquesas' particular viewpoint, many of those devices *never* would have come about. *Other* things would have been devised, filled the need, and eliminated the search that led to their discovery. The whole world would have been different. It's an incredible thought."

"No more incredible than the facts. Did you know, when he made it ashore, Marquesas was too weak to drag himself out of the water? A peasant girl, waiting for her lover, saw him and pulled him out. Now, if he had come in at a slightly different place, if the girl had been looking the other way, or if her boyfriend hadn't been late because of taking a wrong turn on the path—good-bye, Marquesas. Everything *would* have been different."

The director nodded.

"My great-uncle Chris would have gone 'on to the Indies,' for one thing. But then, you wonder, could things actually have turned out differently. *Could* Marquesas have drowned? Could the peasant girl's boyfriend have taken the right turn on the path? *Could an individual create such a change in history?*"

Diaz nodded. "I would say, *that* was such a slender, delicately-balanced thing, that . . . yes, *that* could have turned out differently. But *now*, could a similar individual decision, or even accidental action, at the *present* day, have an equal effect on the course of history?" He shook his head. "No. Quite impossible. We have, after all, reached a time when the course of history is already determined. The mass-effect of innumerable tendencies quite outweighs any possible individual action. It's too bad for romance, I suppose, but this *is* the Day of the Organization. Individuals don't matter much, one way or the—"

***

The all-hail gave its whistling note, signifying contact, and the director sat up.

"I wonder who *that* is."

"Not Hernandez again, let's hope."

"Surely not . . . *Contact!* India Project, Director Columbus speaking."

"*Contact!* Tenochtitlan. Mariner Ordaz speaking."

"Who? *Ordaz?* But you didn't—we haven't heard from—"

"That's right. I *didn't* obey your damned silly schedule. *I went on.*"

"Wait a minute, now. Hold it. By now you must be almost to Cathay? What's your equipment state? Personnel state?" He turned aside. "Quickly, Diaz! Get him on the big viewplate! He sounds in bad shape. Probably cracking up . . . Contact! *Contact!* Are you still there, Ordaz?"

"Yes, I'm here. I *told* you, I could sense land ahead!"

"Yes, yes. Certainly. Of *course*, you could, Ordaz. Now, calm down. Where is the viewplate? The *viewplate*, Ordaz. Do you have it? If you are too weak to find your position, just lay the plate in its gimbaled on-deck mount, so the leads don't get crushed. Leave it face up, and we'll roughly calculate your position for you, and let you know when we have it. Now, don't worry about our punishing you for disobeying orders. We view your action purely in a clinical sense. You were temporarily insane, that's all. So just relieve your mind about *that*. We want to *help* you, Ordaz."

Ordaz's voice came across somewhat faint, as if he had turned his head to speak to someone else.

"*Listen* to that. What did I tell you? Did you hear it?"

"Uncover the viewplate. Let's see what happens then."

"Just a minute . . . *Contact!* Are you there, Mr. Director?"

"I am here, Ordaz. But the question is, where are *you*? Now, we are prepared to do all we can. But you must get a grip on yourself. You must overcome this hysteria. Do not fear because of the immense spaces surrounding you. *We are with you!* Take hold of your courage with both hands! Get a grip on yourself! We will face this *together*!"

A bad word came out the horn of the all-hail.

The viewplate flared with color.

The director found himself looking down from a height at a city of low blocky buildings topped with parapets, with towering pyramids rising on every hand. The streets were filled with bustling people, hurrying to and from a great square where a busy trade was being carried on, while swift canoes bearing garden produce flashed up the canals that interlaced the city. The canals led in from a big lake where flowery islands floated, rising and falling with a rippling motion on the gentle swells. Snow-capped volcanoes rose in the background, and the turning of the viewplate brought new scenes to view, to leave the director dizzy.

***

"Mr. Director," came Ordaz's voice, "how many times have you told us the purpose of the project was to accumulate data in order to improve our ships and our knowledge of the ocean. But *what for*, except to get some use out of the knowledge? I could never get a clear answer to that. Finally, I saw the reason. The human race, Mr. Director, has a short memory, and is ruled by fashion. The Greeks, for instance, tried to reason all things out in their heads. Experiment was *not in style* with them. We, having discovered the value of experiment, are busily accumulating mountains of data. With us, you see, *reason*, as such, *has gone out of style*.

"Now, once I saw that, I realized that your arguments about Science, and collecting data, were merely a *statement of what was in fashion at present*. Like the ladies' latest mode of piling up their hair. It had nothing to do with sense, utility, or anything else. It was just *the style*. It would be sacrosanct until it got so overblown it was ridiculous to everyone, and then it would be discarded— the good part along with the bad—and some *new* style would come in.

"Well, I hope you will excuse me, Mr. Director, for not waiting for all that to take place. I just decided to use a little reason, and a little trial-and-error, that were in style back before reason, and a little intuition, that was in style back there somewhere, and a few scientific data that looked useful—there's nothing wrong with Science, as such—and just try it and *see what happened*. Now, what do you suppose? The things that were out of fashion worked just as well as those *in* fashion. Even prayer works, Mr. Director. Fashions don't sway God any more than they do facts."

"Yes, yes. I'm sure—"

"And so, we just continued west. It was just a short distance, compared to what we had already covered, and here we were."

"Here you *what*?"

"Here we were. You see the scene. *We found a new continent*, or perhaps an old one. Perhaps this, indeed, is fabled Atlantis."

The director craned around to look at Diaz, staring wide-eyed at his own big viewplate.

"*Hsst*! Diaz! What do you make of this?"

"I don't know. It sounds like delirium. But—"

The director said to Diaz, "Do you suppose a return to routine might straighten him out?"

"Ah . . . I don't . . . I don't know."

"Worth a try." The director straightened up.

"*Ordaz!*"

"Yes, Mr. Director?"

"Enough of this nonsense. All this chatter is to no purpose. Now, do you have your samples in the water bottles? Have you taken your current readings faithfully? Is your gasmaker still in condition to send up the gas sacks? All of this is very important, you know. Science advances insensibly by many little steps with the accumulation of data. Your small bit is part of the very—"

"Mr. Director, *we have discovered a continent!* Surely that is more important—"

"If true, it would admittedly be one more datum. However, Cathay is *not* a new continent."

"This is *not* Cathay."

"Not the *known* part of Cathay."

"Not Cathay *at all!*"

"The projected course, allowing for time-lapse, places you near *Cathay*."

***

There was a brief silence. Then Ordaz said, "Did I mention that when we arrived here, we were greeted as gods? For a practical man, this puts quite a useful handle on the situation."

The director craned around at Diaz.

"Off his head?"

"Sounds like it. Poor devil. After a voyage like that, who can wonder?"

Ordaz said, "Did I also mention that this place groans under the weight of gold in it? That my friend, Emperor Cacama II, has a tremendous army, and powerful fortifications, and that his ancestors in Taxcuco gave great emphasis to the arts and sciences—emphasis which is starting to bear fruit. You regard all this as of no more significance than so many water bottles?"

"No, now of course, Ordaz, your little bit, added to the rest, *is* significant."

" '*Little bit*' ?"

"The *important* thing, however, is to complete your voyage as planned. Do not be concerned that you will suffer any punishment, or reduction in grade . . ."

"*Punishment!*"

". . . As we will simply regard this, as I say, in a clinical light. Temporary insanity. That is, as long as you straighten up *now*. But our concern for your welfare, while very great, is nevertheless limited by—"

"So you expect us to just drop everything and fill water bottles, eh? What can I say to get it across? Did I mention that we are not only regarded in the light of gods or demigods, but that some really beautiful maidens—"

Diaz said pityingly, "Completely off his nut. Typical. The whole crew is probably the same."

"I suppose," came Ordaz's voice sarcastically, "that our discovery will not change your schedule at all?"

"Certainly not. The direct voyage, even to Cathay, is too long to be practical—as witness your own experience."

"And the fact that Cacama, purely in self-defense, is building a big navy—"

"Very interesting. But more interesting yet, your location, off Cathay, would fill a gap in our charts, and—"

"*Why waste breath?*"

The viewplate went blank, and the *snap* from the all-hail told of the breaking of the connection.

"Poor fellow," said the director. "There goes his last link with sanity."

"Too bad," said Diaz, "that his account was untrue. For a moment there, he had me wondering."

The director shook his head.

"No, I didn't believe him for a moment. It was easy to tell that what he said was false. It *had* to be false. It would have been *too big a discovery*. Advances now are made only by small steps, owing to the enormous extent of our knowledge, which dwarfs any conceivable new discovery. After all, when one is whirled across the continent at the speed of steam, it is obvious, isn't it, that nothing could go much faster? Where are the new discoveries to come *from?* And there is a further proof."

"What is that, sir?"

"Never have we had so many devoted highly-trained workers laboring in so many fields, and guided by men of such impressive qualifications. If any startling new revolutionary discoveries were to be made, *they* would make them."

Diaz nodded, and selected a chair.

"It must," he said, "have been wonderful to live, like Marquesas, in a great age of discovery."

The director nodded and sat back with a sigh.

"We were born," he said, "in the wrong era. This is just not the right century for it. Marquesas had all the fun."

The Power of Illusion

Colonel Valentine Sanders of the Interstellar Patrol passed a hand over his close-cropped iron-grey hair, leaned forward at his desk, and did his best to speak politely and persuasively:

"Sir, I just don't think I should put this off onto someone else. I wouldn't feel right about it."

He heard his voice come out with a quality suggestive of a crooked dealer in used spaceships. To expect anyone to miss that would be asking too much.

Just across Sanders' desk, where the bulkhead normally presented its neutral grey surface, was the convincing electronic image of a lean broad-shouldered man wearing the same style of uniform as Sanders, but with two stars at the lapel in place of Sanders' silver eagle. He, too, spoke politely, but with a frown that was becoming more pronounced as the conversation wore on.

"Val, you do understand, regardless who does it, it's against regulations to intervene on a planet classified as, in effect, alien?"

Sanders gave up on persuasion and tried stubbornness. Now, at least, he sounded natural. "Whose regulations, sir?"

"And this planet is so designated."

"By whom, sir?"

"By PDA, of course."

"Then, sir, Planetary Development Authority is insane. And I don't remember any regulation of *ours* that forbids intervention, provided we use some sense when we do it."

"PDA makes the rules for new planets. As for their being insane, that may well be—but why do you say it?"

"There are two intelligent races on this planet. One is so much like us that we can forget trying to find a difference that means anything. Their hearing and vision are unusually sharp, but that's it. The other race has a shorter average build and a kind of close dark hair or fur; people who have never been off their own home world might think the furred race is alien. Yet, when they're not killing each other, the two races trade, and interbreeding produces fertile offspring. The planet is earth-type. They even have rugged quadrupeds that look like and serve the function of horses. How does PDA see this place as an 'alien planet'?"

"No doubt they've got some esoteric reason."

"But does that make it so?"

"No. It also doesn't change regulations."

Sanders, feeling as if he were making his way across thin ice over deep water, again tried hard to sound reasonable:

"Sir, Planetary Development is bound by regulations. So is the Space Force. This tends to make their actions predictable. Yet they both can go on operating by the book, because every large-scale thug, racketeer, and confidence artist, human or alien, also has us to contend with. The rules of the Interstellar Patrol aren't known, and can't be worked into their calculations. Sir, if we adopt PDA's regulations, how do we do our own job?"

Sanders thought this was reasonable. He didn't see how anyone could object to it. But the expression on the General's face told him he had miscalculated somewhere.

"Now you're explaining my job to me, Colonel?"

"No, sir."

"That's what it sounds like to me."

"Well, sir—if we're bound by PDA's regulations—"

"There is such a thing as judgment."

"But—if we follow the same rules—"

"PDA obeys them slavishly. We use them voluntarily."

"If we use them 'voluntarily,' then we can suspend them at will. Sir, I think we need to suspend this rule that any planet they think is alien is automatically off-limits."

"So I gather. Look, Val, I have here your requisition for all this theatrical equipment, and an H-class ship and crew. This came in along with a mess of routine house-keeping stuff—glance at it, initial it, and forget it—but this requisition adds up to a traveling magic extravaganza, to be used on a planet listed by PDA as 'alien-inhabited.'"

"Sir, they aren't aliens. But if we follow PDA's rules, the planet could end up alien."

"What do you mean?"

Sanders decided to try taking the offensive. "Sir, are you aware that this planet is part of a star system so close to the border between Stath territory and ours that the

Stath can use it to test us? That collection of murderous overgrown weasels can run rings around PDA. PDA thinks aliens are there? They are. But they aren't either of the races that inhabit that planet. The aliens there are the Stath!"

Sanders had expected the General to at least be startled. Instead, he looked faintly bored, and irritated.

"Spare me the red flags, capes, and picadors, damn it, and *get to the facts*. Naturally I know where the planet is, and of course the Stath can use it to test us, if they don't mind getting another bloody nose or broken jaw out of it. How does this answer the question?"

"Sir, that's the point."

"Look, Val, the point is that on the basis of some need I don't understand, *and which has yet to be explained*, I am to provide equipment, plus scarce personnel, for a peculiar junket that will take my Chief of Operations completely off the scene for who knows how long! Meanwhile, PDA is getting into what looks like the mess of the century, and I expect the yell for help any time. When it comes, I'll need everyone I can lay my hands on."

"Yes, sir. But—"

"But when I try to find out what this is all about, what happens? It turns into a philosophical discussion on accepting the rules of other organizations, followed by a shocker revelation that the Stath would like to eat us alive. Is that supposed to be news? This isn't an answer. It's a smoke screen."

"Sir, the main problem is that the Stath are working a stunt that PDA is too blockheaded to understand."

"That's the main problem, eh? All right. Specifically?"

"This planet has two races. The clearly human race has a feudal society. The other is a collection of warlike tribes. There's a wide river that separates them, and though they raid some, they usually respect each other's territory."

"I get the picture. What of it?"

"For several years, the Stath have been visiting the less obviously human part of the planet, disguising the visits as emergency landings, treaty-approved mapping missions, navigation errors, and so on. This spring, the furred race crossed the river, and, using weapons they never had before, started slaughtering the humans."

For the first time, Sanders could see his superior's interest. "And you think the Stath are behind it?"

"Yes, sir. While PDA piously bars us from the planet, the Stath are already there. That pack of bloodthirsty weasels backs a local race, and in return gets a useful ally in disputed territory. And having got away with this stunt, they will have a lower opinion of us in the future. Who knows what they'll try next? Sir, to obey PDA's regulations could be an expensive proposition. This is exactly the kind of thing we're meant to take care of."

Abruptly, it dawned on Sanders that, with the argument all but won, he had just said a few words too many.

The General nodded slowly, and looked up.

"Then why is this the first I've heard of it?"

"Sir, I just found it out myself—and only because of unusual circumstances. PDA didn't mention it, because they haven't caught on."

"Look, Val—Why didn't you make a little more noise? Why just send me this requisition?"

There was the catch. As Sanders had just said, this was

the exact kind of thing the Interstellar Patrol was meant to take care of. Why, then, hadn't he handled it as usual? Of course, *he* knew why, but he desperately did not want to mention that. Sanders, who rarely acted impulsively, was even worse at explaining an impulsive action than the average person, who at least had a little more practice at it.

But the General was still waiting, with rapidly evaporating patience, for an explanation.

Inspiration failing to provide a way out, Sanders still had to say something. And improvising plausible-sounding excuses was another skill Sanders lacked. In horror, he heard himself say:

"Well,—I—ah—Sir, I just didn't want to bother you—with—ah—"

Across the desk, the strongly built uniformed figure leaned forward. The silver stars glinted. Sanders felt like an onion whose outer layers were rapidly being stripped away.

"Val—"

"Sir?"

"Why are you approaching this backward?"

"I—Ah—"

"We have here a legitimate request which you present to me hind-end first. There has to be some reason. The most obvious is to conceal something. Say, you want to go yourself, but don't want to explain why. A routine requisition might just slip through unquestioned. Val, do you have some *personal* interest in this mess?"

"Sir, I—"

"Well?"

Sanders could feel the perspiration trickle down.

"I—Ah—"

"It must be even worse than it looks. All right, let's have the whole thing. Have you been on this planet? What are the 'unusual circumstances' that told you what's going on there? Is there an extra booby trap somewhere in this sinkhole? Let's have it, and from the beginning, for a change."

Sanders, pinned in his superior's searchlight gaze, with an effort began to talk.

"A long time ago, sir, a ship crashed on this planet. There was apparently just one survivor—" He hesitated.

"Just keep going, Val. A ship crashed. There was one survivor. I follow that. Go on."

Sanders took a deep breath. "The survivor was a baby in a safety cradle. The ship was on fire when it crashed, and there was the danger that it might explode. A second ship followed it down, but couldn't get there before the first ship blew up."

"Were you there?"

"Yes, sir. In the second ship."

"All right. I follow it, so far. Keep going."

"The father of the baby and the crew of the second ship rushed to the wreck, searched the remains, and found no survivors. After they had given up hope, there walked through the smouldering debris a local chief or king, carrying the cradle. He had risked his life, and gotten the baby out just before the explosion."

The General opened his mouth, then closed it without speaking. He nodded slowly.

Sanders said, "The crew of the second ship took the

safety cradle. The father was overcome with emotion. He took the guard ring from his hand, and put it on the hand of the local chief."

"A *guard ring?*"

"Yes, sir."

There was a lengthy silence. It was this detail, which Sanders could not even explain to himself, that he had wanted to avoid mentioning.

The General stared at Sanders. "The father, of course, was a member of the Interstellar Patrol?"

"Yes, sir."

"He was a member of the Patrol when this happened?"

"Yes, sir."

"Was he aware of the PDA rule that no technological device is to be introduced onto an unclassified planet?"

"Yes, sir."

"This ring was not dropped, or lost inadvertently, in which case—"

"No, sir. It was placed intentionally on the chief's hand."

"In full awareness of the technological nature of the guard ring, and of the rule barring exactly such actions?"

"Yes, sir, and in full awareness that the rule was a rule of PDA, and not a rule of the Interstellar Patrol."

"This ring was, of course, a technological device *of the Interstellar Patrol*? Granted that there are other outfits—including the Stellar Scouts—that have devices disguised as jewelry—rings, pins, belt buckles, bracelets, watches, and so on. This was one of ours?"

"Yes, sir. It was one of ours."

"What justification for this could there be, bearing in mind that the guard ring was equipment of the Patrol, not the property of the person giving it away? Incidentally, where did this guard ring come from?"

"From an agent of the Patrol who had passed away—a retired member on a partly settled planet."

"Passed away how?"

"By natural causes, sir."

"This ring had not been issued to the member who gave it to the local chief?"

"No, sir."

"Had the ring been collected on orders to turn it in?"

"No, sir. It was being brought back voluntarily."

"I see. Was the transaction reported?"

"No, sir, it was not."

"Why not?"

"It might have been disapproved."

"I see . . . How long ago did this happen?"

"About twenty-three years ago, sir."

After a silence, the General cleared his throat. "You'll have to report it, Val. Never mind the details. Just state to me verbally that you do now report it."

Sanders, caught off-balance, hesitated, then said, "Yes, sir. I do now report it."

"Disposition of the guard ring is approved. This local king is obviously a capable individual, well suited to be an involuntary agent of the Patrol on the said planet, allowing for the possibility of subterfuge by the neighboring Stath. Now, what happened? Did the baby survive?"

"Yes, sir."

"And is now where—and what?"

"He's grown up, sir. A second lieutenant."

"In what organization?"

"The Interstellar Patrol, sir."

There was a brief pleasant interval as the General smiled. Sanders understood the reaction. In the Patrol, perpetually shorthanded, each recruit was precious.

"Well, now I can understand, at least. But Val, if there's anything more technological than a guard ring—"

"Sir, PDA wouldn't know one if they saw it."

"Granted. But *we* know what it is. All right, now, let's see. We not only have the Stath, and the local invasion, but this guard ring, introduced into this tinderbox years ago. Is there anything more?"

"That's most of it, sir. When the patrol ship took off, an outphased watch satellite was left in orbit, just in case. It would note landings on the planet, and could, to some extent, at our signal plant spy devices, so we could learn more if we needed to."

"This satellite transmitted reports at intervals?"

"No, sir. There was no interest in the place then. The satellite was set to send any accumulated information on our transmit signal. Since there was no suspicion of what the Stath were doing, no transmit signal was sent—until the guard ring alerted the communications net about three weeks ago."

"Three weeks?"

"Yes, sir."

"That's the unusual way you became aware something was going on?"

"Yes, sir."

"Okay. Now, let's be sure there's no misunderstanding.

This guard ring was keyed to the person whose finger it was put on?"

"Sir, there wouldn't be much point giving a guard ring inactive. It was keyed."

"You know guard rings have been taken out of general use?"

"I didn't think they ever were actually in general use. I know they're dispensed with great caution."

"But this local king on this barbarian planet has been walking around all this time with this ring on his finger?"

"Sir, I don't know. The signal we got recently shows no change in identity, so he was wearing it then."

"In the meantime, it could have been traded back and forth for cattle, or nubile girls, for all we know?"

"Yes, sir. But I think he would have kept it, and worn it. We know he has it now."

"What style is this ring? Is it a plain regulation type, or an ornamental ring?"

"Ornamental, sir. The control crystal appears to be a large gem—like a star sapphire—until it's activated. There's a lion to either side of the gem. The setting looks like gold."

"Then he probably has worn it. Well, I don't know what the damned Stath gave their fur-bearing allies, but I can scarcely wait to find out what happens when they run into this ring."

Sanders kept his mouth shut. Right there was the reason he was anxious to get to the planet.

The General cleared his throat.

"Has the invasion got to this local king yet?"

"Not yet, sir. When we got the alert on the communications net, we sent the transmit signal to the satellite, and that's when we found out the Stath had been visiting the planet. Then we had to learn all we could in a hurry."

"I can imagine. We didn't know any of this before?"

"No, sir. Supposedly, PDA was taking care of it."

"PDA doesn't understand how the Stath think. So, this requisition you've sent in—All this theatrical equipment, an H-Class ship and crew—this was to try to recover this guard ring?"

"No, sir, it was to stop the Stath from taking over, through their local allies. Of course, in the process, that would hopefully keep the device from becoming fully activated."

There was a little silence, during which Colonel Sanders had time to consider how many different organizations would have had him drawn and quartered by now. Yet the General, who had had him in just the right position for a verbal beheading, or worse, instead had buried the really deadly question with a harmless one, then legitimized the impulse Sanders still couldn't explain to himself: Why *had* he put the guard ring on the local chief's hand? He could remember no calculation, no reasoning, no thought; he had just acted, and become aware of it afterward, as if he were a spectator in his own life. How did anyone explain an impulse? Then a clearing of the throat warned him the questioning wasn't over yet.

"How close is this invasion to our—ah—involuntary agent on this planet?"

"I think we might just have time to get there before he's hit. We've flooded the place with subminiaturized spy devices, and been pretty well swamped with information we haven't had time to digest. There's even a local prophecy of what sounds like our intervention on the planet."

"You've located the opposing forces?"

"Yes, sir, that's clear enough. Though there aren't two equal forces. The invaders heavily outnumber the defenders."

"Okay. I'm approving your requisition. I don't think we should fool around with this, whatever PDA might think. The planet may be near the boundary, but it's in our territory, and the mental processes of the Stath are as you describe them. We can't let them get away with this. However, these local inhabitants on both sides are also people, and the less gratuitous slaughter we inflict, the better."

"We aren't planning to use force alone, sir. With luck, we may be able to get by with something else, that PDA should incidentally find it harder to detect, or to understand if they do detect it."

His superior smiled. "All this theatrical equipment?"

The colonel nodded. "Yes, sir. Illusion. Of course, to use that effectively, we have to know how the people on this planet think, so we have to watch them closely."

***

The Chief stood by the stone parapet atop one of the high central towers of the fortress dominating the river valley. He stood a little apart from his remaining advisors, looking down over the lower walls and towers as, across the valley, the morning sun flashed on the shields and breastplates of the heavily armed troops, once his own, but now under the command of traitors, who were emerging in large numbers from the forest that rimmed the valley.

The same sun made visible the thinness of the numbers of defenders on the massive walls of the fortress. And, beyond the stone fortress itself, he could see the emptiness in his outermost works of earth and timber, where behind the pointed upright logs of the palisade built out on the rightmost side of the fortress, to menace the flank of any hostile approach, no-one waited to break the enemy's first attack.

Arion, the Chief's long-time friend and advisor, spoke quietly. "There is Summa's standard. Among the first."

The Chief's eyes, no longer young and sharp, sought out across the valley the red and orange banner, and spotted it coming in where an intervening slope still held off the sun. Briefly, his gaze blurred with emotion.

Marron, the state councillor, spoke in a wondering voice. "Who would have thought he could be bought?"

There was a murmur from the troops on the walls below, as the numbers of traitors and hirelings was made clear in the glitter and flash of the armor emerging from the forest.

Then, carrying clearly in the early morning stillness, came the low good-natured voice of Tarvon, the War Leader, second in command only to the Chief:

"The more traitors for us to kill, men. And if they should win, we are no deader if ten times as many come to do the deed."

Tarvon's voice soothed the Chief, inside, where the blows of life had left their unseen wounds. Most of the nobles were gone, turned traitor, and with them the clever luminaries of the court. But Tarvon, greatest of the great, was loyal. True, the hosts needed to properly embody his skill were turned traitor, bought, or fled, but his presence alone must weigh on those who approached. The Chief could almost hear the warnings of the approaching sergeants and captains:

"Tarvon is there, still with the King. Look right and left, men. Steady. We are fighting Tarvon, remember. Keep closed up, there!"

Arion spoke sharply.

"Hold that bolt! Wait till they're closer!"

The Chief glanced to his left, saw the flatbolt catapult on the open top of a tower, and the shame-faced crew that manned it.

Tarvon spoke again, his voice low and good-humored:

"Wait till they're closer, men. For now, just watch the show. They're trying to come forward, but their feet want to go to some other place."

The Chief noted the hesitation in the advancing host, and smiled despite himself. Though more were emerging from the forest, those in front had slowed. Seen from this viewpoint, the left of their line had actually halted, and a few there visibly drew back. It would pass, but for now it was pleasant to look upon.

For an instant, the Chief could see the scene from the enemy side. The sun, flashing impressively on their shields, was also glaring directly in their eyes, blinding them. The stone fortress on its rocky height before the river dominated them below in the valley, its massive walls rising menacingly high above them. And there before them waited their own King, justly angered by their treason, along with his shrewd councillor, Arion, and mighty Tarvon, whose mere presence on a battlefield was said to change a mob into an army, and an army into a conquering host.

What greeted the traitors was silence and menace, with God alone knew how many of the loyal, lances and swords ground sharp, with uncountable stocks of arrows and heavy bolts. Hidden high on and within the walls, unseeable in the glare of the sun, were the huge kettles of smoking oil that could blister and cook an attacker inside his armor. Behind the wooden outerworks of the palisade, there could be massed horsemen jostling in impatience to throw open the gates and kill the turncoats.

Out in the open, conscious of their treasonous cause, burdened down by their heavy armor, and weary already from the march here, the approaching troops were showing no enthusiasm for the fight, however it might profit their leaders. And, of course, they had worse if more vague worries.

The Chief absently fingered the intricately formed ring on the third finger of his right hand. His thumb slid over the cool smooth surface of the blue star jewel, then across the golden lions recumbent beside the blue star to the left, and to the right. The contact took his mind back to a night long before, when he had seen the flash streak down across the sky, wavering flames at its head, and realized that a star traveler was here and in trouble.

He had overruled the cautious Arion, ridden out in the night, and crossed the river, to find on a wooded hill a burning shell of metal—What metal could burn?—and his retainers had fallen back in fear.

With Arion trembling beside him, he had dared the dying flames and briefly entered the wreck, to see a charred corpse amidst the twisted shapes, and there, in clouds of white smoke, cold where he touched it, the Chief found a kind of closed cradle, with a baby moving fretfully under the cradle's transparent cover.

The Chief had put his cloak between his hands and the frosted surface, and carried the cradle out, and down the far slope of the hill. He had set it down, and Arion was bent at the closed cover when there had come from the wreck on the far side of the hill a dazzling burst of bluish whiteness, and the trees atop the hill were thrown flat with a rending crash, their budding leaves and outer twigs aflame.

Inside the cradle, the baby apparently saw Arion's face in the brief glare, smiled, and swung its hands to thump the inner surface of the cover.

Already, a second brightness was descending rapidly from the sky, there were the sounds of approaching voices, and then an anguished cry from the hill.

Arion had said, "These come to save the first, but are too late."

"Then we have good news for them." The Chief bent to pick up the cradle.

Arion said, "Their affairs are dangerous. Best we keep the child and raise him as our own. You have saved him, at least."

"He isn't ours. Call to them!"

"My voice will not function."

"Nor mine. But my legs will." The Chief picked up the cradle, and went back up the hill. Arion and the rest of the reluctantly following courtiers saw him outlined in the fading bluish glare, saw two figures in strange armor take the cradle, saw another figure in armor come and clasp him, heard a low voice rough with emotion, the words unrecognizable, then the armored figure had stepped back, and raised its hand in salute, and the Chief had come back down the hill like a man in a dream, and spoke to Arion.

"The baby was theirs. But for some reason, I miss him."

"Let us hope you get no hurt from this. My skin burns from those flames."

"And mine, too. The river is still cold. Let's see if it will draw the heat."

Arion and the Chief had bathed in the river until their teeth chattered, and to the touch their flesh felt like the flesh of a corpse in wintertime. But the next day, their burns were mild, and now the word of what the Chief had done had begun to work its magic, as his awed followers told of the flaming metal of the wreck, the magical cradle, the child, and the Star Man's clasp of affection and brotherhood. Now, too, the startled Chief made a discovery. On his right hand was a golden blue-star ring, and the wise men outdid themselves in interpreting this visible evidence of the Star Men's favor.

The Chief said privately to Arion, "The talk of these wise men can be as hard to follow as the gabble of drunkards. Does it make any sense to you?"

"No. To believe the half of it would be more dangerous than it was to go into that wreck. I trust none of it—and least of all that the ring is a 'crystallized omen of good fortune and invincibility.'"

"Let's hope our enemies believe that."

"That would be useful. But the ring is very beautiful, that is certainly true."

"There is a strange thing. Any other ring I have had is either too tight, or else at times it is loose. The fit of this is perfect. I can hardly tell it is there."

Arion examined it carefully. "It was formed by craft far beyond ours. Would that I had had the courage to go back up that hill with you. Perhaps I would have one like it."

"Here. Wear it if you like."

"No, it is yours. Anyway, I am not jealous. I have baubles as pretty as that. I only regret that I lacked the courage."

But all that time had passed, and now they stood together by the parapet, and the Chief thought to say to Arion that he had lacked no courage to stay beside him in this disaster. But at that moment, the wavering ranks of shields and armor across the valley were roughly broken from behind by a rush of unarmored alien horsemen.

Even at this distance, the Chief could recognize them by the thick short dark hair or fur that covered brow and cheek and throat. Seeing that, he could imagine that he saw their eyes, with a glint of craft and cleverness. On the walls, his men straightened.

Down below, the enemy rode in, spreading across the valley, undeterred by the menace of the fortress, no doubt content that they had conquered others like it, and could conquer it, too.

Tarvon's voice, reinforced by the low tone of his trumpeter's signal horn, warned the defenders, "Hold your bolts—Wait for the command—Let them get closer."

Behind the aliens, the armor again began to move, perhaps unaware that they had hung back. Pressing forward at the head was the red and orange banner.

The voice of Tarvon, the War Leader, was quiet but clear: "Catapult crews, see the traitor lead the way? He is the one in front, with fresh painted royal bearings on his shield. He is to be tyrant once we are dead—That's how they bought him. Hold your bolts till he is near. Wait till you hear the King's warhorn. Let Evertrue speak for us, who are loyal. Then, when Evertrue does speak, put the wax plugs in your ears so you can have your minds on the job. Then aim careful, and work fast."

The Chief gauged the height of the sun, looked down at the alien horsemen, coming straight for the wooden outerworks. He watched these horsemen, their drawn knives glittering as they rode to the base of the palisade, vanish from sight, then their flexible lines and hooks briefly appeared atop the palings, caught, then the lithe hairy forms were up on the wall, glancing over, and as suddenly they dropped onto the high footwalk, inside. The gates were opened, and the others rode in.

Down in the valley, Summa's men were rushing closer, losing their order in their haste. The other armored troops were coming on much less quickly; but Summa, who should be most loyal, must now prove his new loyalty to the invader.

The horsemen, meanwhile, having taken the wooden outerworks, were making no further attempt. Some sat grinning atop the palisade, speculatively eyeing the walls. Others, out in the valley, seeing no effective resistance, were coming forward now at a casual walk. From the direction of Summa's men, the Chief could actually hear a small excited voice:

"They've run away. There's no-one there!"

The Chief smiled, noted the angle of the sun, the men waiting at the catapults, and, behind him, the bare pole atop the massive tower. Everything must be done now, in order. He kept his voice low and even, the first time today his men would have heard him:

"Raise the war flag."

He turned, waited a few moments:

"Ready at the catapults."

He heard Tarvon's murmured repetition, then the trumpeter raised his signal horn, and he saw the men at the catapults stand ready to loose their first bolts.

With the sun behind it, its long ends like claws, the climbing flag would be a cheerless message to all but the grinning hairy aliens below. To them, all this was nothing but foreign play-acting. But the Chief could see the flashing line of armor in the valley waver, as at a blow, and he turned to two pages wearing dark green and leather, and spoke quietly. "Lift up the voice-thrower."

They lifted a long wide-flaring instrument, and held it on their shoulders.

Down there, Summa and his men were approaching the already captured palisade, perhaps to man it, releasing the aliens for other jobs, perhaps to try to take the fortress by entering the hidden tunnel that opened behind the outerworks.

The Chief drew a deep breath and spoke carefully and forcefully into the mouthpiece:

"Hear me, men of Summa! I, your King, before

Almighty God sworn to defend this land and people, now strip from your traitor baron all right and power to command! The penalty for his treason is death!"

The Chief turned from the voice-thrower, keeping one hand on the shoulder of the nearest page, to warn him not to move, looked back at the main central tower, looming behind them, and spoke clearly:

"Let Evertrue speak!"

At once, a tone like a sound made of silver hung in the air, subtly turning, riveting the attention. Down below, the traitors' armored foot troops came to a halt, banging into one another. The mounted aliens, coming on at a walk, looked up in surprise. The aliens atop the palisade stared in wonderment.

Beneath the tone, as if somehow acting on a different level than those hearing the tone and held by it, there was a low creak of cord drawn tight, a metallic scrape, a sudden jarring snap and hiss as a metal-tipped bolt streaked out flat through the air, a thump as the parts that launched it struck the pads from whence they were hauled back with a clink of gears and iron dogs that drew the mechanism tight again as the next bolt was put into place—then a cry from below.

Atop the open towers, the men at the catapults, their ears blocked with wax, straightened and bent. The sounds of the catapults were repeated again, and again, dominated by the clear tones of the warhorn, whose silver note seemed to hang in the air, than vanish, still holding the minds of the hearers, involuntarily seeking to find it.

Abruptly a shout rose up from below:

"The Baron's down! Baron Summa's down!"

There was another shout:

"Evertrue has killed him!"

The Chief had time for a brief ironical thought that it was not Evertrue, but a bolt from a catapult that had done the job. Then he had drawn another breath, and spoke intently into the voice-thrower. The voice-thrower magnified his words in the sudden stillness:

"True men, will you fight for Right?"

From some one of the towers came the carrying voice of the chaplain, praying for the penance of those who had fallen into evil ways, calling upon them to repent while time still remained.

Through the minds of those below—except the aliens—there would now be moving a grim familiar prophetic chant:

> "Above them rear the walls of stone.
> The war flag climbs upon the wind.
> The warhorn speaks in silver tone.
> The traitor to the earth is pinned . . ."

Arion said, "They've passed the word up. Summa is dead and his men are milling around."

The Chief drew a deep breath, and spoke into the voice-thrower. He kept his voice even, but it came out like thunder:

"Men of Summa! Your place is at the palisade! You are stronger than the enemy there!

"Now is your chance! *ATTACK!*"

There was a shout from below. The armored men, already near, rushed the palisade with its wide-open gates.

Tarvon's voice rang out. The aliens atop the palisade, some still watching bemused as if they were spectators, were struck by a hail of arrows from the walls and towers. Out in the valley, the long glittering line of those who had other treasonous leaders stood as if paralyzed. The mounted aliens for a long confused moment looked on as if baffled to understand what was happening.

The Chief noted the distance of the long line of armored troops still far from the fortress, remembered their weary and hesitant approach, noted now the movement among them of their traitorous leaders, doubtless steadying them with threats and offered rewards. He wanted those men back in the fortress, manning the walls and watchtowers, and he wanted them as a starving man wants food. He could sway them, could challenge the hold of the aliens and their own treasonous leaders—but he could only do it effectively once.

Down below, there was the sharp blast of a whistle. The Chief saw an alien horseman race forward, carrying a pole with one red and one yellow pennant whipping in the wind. The alien horsemen came awake, raced toward the palisade. The entire floor of the valley seemed suddenly in motion.

Tarvon's voice carried, his tone pleasant.

"Catapults, set your aim by the west marker! Line your shots up abreast, straight to the front. Let's get a few horses down. Archers, cover the palisade. Aim careful— those are our men coming in now! Men of Summa, welcome! Man the palisade! We'll cover you!"

The sound of the catapults was almost continuous. The dark heavy bolts blurred out, the horses reared and fell, the air filled with arrows, and beneath the fusillade the armored men of Summa crossed the front of the fortress, and fought their way into the palisade. They were scarcely inside when the palisade wall was freshly topped with loops and hooks, and the invaders pulled themselves up, but now Summa's armored men were atop the footwalk, and more than a match in close fighting on the wall.

The Chief looked around. The fortress, barely manned, lacked lookouts, and nothing would be more natural than a party of furry invaders with ropes and grappling hooks coming down the river in boats, and up the rocky slope on which the fortress stood, to attack it from behind. But from here, at least, there was nothing in sight yet.

Arion, apparently with the same thought, was looking around, away from the battle, while Marron now pointed excitedly toward the valley.

Out there, more and still more horsemen were coming, but the host of armored men under traitor command stood stock still. Arion turned, and saw them. His voice was surprised. "They're uncertain."

Once again, the Chief saw it as it would seem to those below—except the aliens. He saw the high walls, and above them the war flag; he heard still in memory the silver tone; he saw the archtraitor struck down, heard the chaplain's call for repentance, heard the King's command, and saw before his eyes the troops of Summa change sides. He saw the invaders knocked from their horses, saw them picked off from the palisade, and in the distance heard the voice of Tarvon direct the battle. Those armored hosts might well be feeling desperately which side they should be on.

Marron pointed. "Could we not sway them, too?"

Arion glanced at the Chief, who shook his head.

Marron said, "The warhorn—"

The Chief said quietly, "Summa's men were close. These are still far away. Their armor is heavy, and they are already worn from the march here. Summa had just been struck dead. Their leaders are still with them. The men might try to obey, but they could not. Moreover, the aliens must not become accustomed to the warhorn. And Evertrue must speak only when the time is right, when its orders are possible to obey, and when hopefully the enemy is confused and uncertain."

"But the men hang back. Their leaders are traitors, but the men are loyal. If we could call them in—"

"At any moment the enemy main force may come onto the field. From the accounts, what we see here is only the beginning of them. Then our men out there would be slaughtered. Evertrue must give the order only when the men can obey it. They cannot obey now. We will wait."

Arion said, "Look, the palisade is ours!"

Down below, the armored troops of Summa had finished the enemy resistance inside the palisade, manned the wall and shut the gates. The mounted aliens swirled outside like waves against a rock. Here and there, ropes or hooks topped the sharp-pointed logs, and hairy warriors climbed up, to be enthusiastically struck down by the heavily armed defenders.

The Chief watched thoughtfully. So far, these aliens were not unbeatable fighters. Save for bribery and treason, the fortress would still be secure.

Just then, there rode rapidly over a rise before the

forest, a squat horseman surrounded by pennant-bearers. This new arrival turned his horse, and in a flash he and the pennant-bearers crossed the front of the armored troops, followed by uncountable numbers of unarmored horsemen.

The Chief glanced briefly at Marron. Above the thunder of all those hooves, his voice could not be heard, and even Evertrue would be made faint, while the size of the alien force would intimidate or crush opposition. If he had managed to bring those armored troops actively into the fight, they would now be destroyed. A single glance at Marron's look of horror showed that Marron realized it.

Below, the valley filled with onrushing horsemen, some of whom spread out to go up and downstream, no doubt to work their way through the rocks toward the sides of the fortress. A fresh cloud of dust now betrayed the arrival of something new—riders leading separate short teams that pulled carts.

Tarvon called out, "Catapults! Let's fool these newcomers! Drop bolts at three quarters pull, aimed at those carts."

Below, the carts were coming to a stop, were disconnected from their teams, and rushed forward by small groups of men pulling at the tongues and sides of the carts.

The Chief, watching, considered the disconnected rumors that had preceded the arrival of these conquerors. In these rumors, thunder, earthquakes, and lightning bolts shared the credit for the speed of the conquests with dragons that belched fire, and iron falcons that plunged from the sky. If anything as commonplace as carts had been mentioned, he could not recall it.

Below, the carts were stopped and swung around. From some were removed, with heavy effort, curious objects like very deep black iron cooking pots. From others came odd-shaped lengths of wood or metal. But then, from the fortress, the bolts reached out, and fell short. The bearers, setting up their curious objects, glanced up, watched, took fresh holds on their heavy burdens, and moved them in closer.

Tarvon called, "Catapults! Elevate! At three-quarters pull! Try again!"

Again, the bolts failed to make the distance. The aliens showed brief grins as they set up their odd-looking devices. They worked fast and smoothly. Already, there were puffs of smoke.

Tarvon said, "Catapults, from left to right, divide the target! Full strength! Strike at will!"

From the aliens' curious devices down below, things like black large-size children's balls were blurring up into the air.

Now the catapults, too, were in action. The iron-shod bolts flashed out.

The Chief, frowning, looked up, and it went through his mind that no fortifications, of whatever strength, had stopped these outlanders yet. For generations, they had been held beyond the line of the North River, and, save for raids, they could not come south, though in return few who raided their territory had come back to tell of their deeds. But now that had changed.

Now, they came south, through counties, duchies, and kingdoms, and nothing stopped them. With the plunder from one conquest, they bribed the faithless of the next conquest, slew the loyal, took their goods, and bribed the faithless of the next, creating a huge empire subject to them alone.

This went through the Chief's mind, along with the knowledge that, great though their numbers were, even such numbers could have had the work of half-a-year at the least to subject Great Keep, just below the North River, while Pinnacle Rock, inaccessible, with walls that were said to be a hundred feet high, could have held out as long as the food in its storehouse and the water in its cisterns. Both were lost before swift-riding messengers could bring help from the south.

Looking up as the black balls dropped, it once again came to the Chief that there was something else, and these black balls could be part of that something else. He seized Arion roughly.

"Below! Get to shelter, quick!" He turned to the pages. "Set down the voice-thrower! Follow Lord Arion!"

He saw that Tarvon must already have gone below, glanced around for Marron—balanced whether he should follow—

There was the beginning of a great wind, the start of a loud noise. A redness briefly surrounded the Chief. There was the start of another wind, the beginning of a heavy thunder. The redness faded. Again, the wind began, and the thunder. Dazed, he could not count the beginnings of the roar and the times the redness rose to shut it out. Then again the redness faded, and this time there was no wind, and no roar.

Beside him, Marron lay on the floor, half-turned, a black dart sunk in his head, the blood oozing out around it. Other black darts were in his body, or on the stone floor, and embedded in the mortar between the stones.

Half the crew of the catapult on the open top of the tower were stretched out, bleeding, while the others held their hands to their ears, stunned.

He looked far out, to see the crew that had worked the weapons that had dealt this slaughter. The bolts from the catapults had reached them. From behind, others were coming forward.

There was a cry from down below. "Tarvon! They've killed Tarvon!"

The Chief, stunned at Marron's death and the sudden loss of Tarvon, kept his countenance unchanged, straightened, saw the voice-thrower with two holes knocked in its sides; but it should still work. Resting the end on the parapet, he spoke into the mouthpiece, toward the men at an exposed catapult:

"All right, men, This is the King. Let's take a few more of them with us, for Tarvon. Crank up that catapult, and see who you can hit, around those black pots."

The remaining men looked around at him, their eyes wide, then raised their hands in acknowledgement, and bent to the work.

He turned the horn, calculated its aim.

"Archers, this is the King. Pass the word. When those black pots spit out those black balls, take cover behind stone, with stone overhead. Those balls burst apart into iron darts. But the stone will stop the iron. Pass the word."

There was a shout as the archers, dazed from the shock, noise, and sudden losses, recognized his voice, and went back into action. As he repeated the warning to other of the defenders, the fortress, temporarily silenced, again began to work ruin on the exposed hosts below. At the voice-thrower, the Chief straightened, drew a deep breath, and then saw the squat alien seated down below on horseback.

For an instant, they were looking directly at each other. The Chief was not certain how, with that fur on his face, it was possible for the alien leader to have any visible expression at all. But a look of intent wonder was clear on the alien face right now.

The Chief turned the voice-thrower toward another flat-topped tower. "Catapults, Tarvon's trick worked, but they're trying to get new men to those heavy pots. Let's pick off the men, and see if we can wreck the pots."

The heavy bolts flashed out again, and there came a cheer. Looking down, he could see one of the pots, burst into pieces where a bolt had hit it head-on. As he watched, another bolt slammed over the top of another one of the pots, missing it by less than an arm's reach.

If that aim could be maintained, it might conceivably be possible to wreck every one of them. If not, the aliens were certain to sneak in after dark to drag them off, and next time use them from out of range of the catapults. But, if they could all be destroyed now—

Obviously thinking the same thing, the enemy chief below gave a command. Messengers left his side to race through swarms of horsemen, who rushed toward the spot. Then another of the pots burst into fragments. The angle of the bolt indicated the crew of the main central tower, and the Chief turned toward them.

"Good work! Let's make them pay!"

There was a visible increase in the bombardment. The alien horsemen converging on the spot made a momentary confusion in which everyone there was in somebody else's way. In such a crowd, a bolt that missed one target might strike another. Men were thrown to the ground. The horses screamed and plunged. The thrown men were trampled under the horses' hooves. Fresh bolts slammed into the panicked mob.

The enemy leader sent new messengers to the spot.

The Chief, looking down on this chaos, balanced the odds if he were now to give the word for a sortie, but he shook his head. Even with Summa's men massed behind the palisade, he lacked the numbers.

Down below, the ruinous shambles was sorted out. At heavy cost, the remaining pots were dragged back out of range, the struggling panicked horses were killed, and the dead and wounded carried off.

The Chief used the voice-thrower. "Good work, men! They don't have quite as many of those things as before!"

The men were grinning. From below, fresh bolts were carried up. The captains were studying how best to take cover when the next bombardment of black balls should drop out of the sky. On the walls and towers, the dead and wounded were being carried below.

Down below, some of the hairy horsemen were shaking their knives at the walls—a change from their easy manner at the beginning.

Arion spoke close by.

"They're closing in—coming up the rocks from behind with sacks the size of grain bags. I've got archers picking them off, but the angle is steep, and we can't hope to hit them all."

"Sacks?"

"Leather sacks."

"At the north and south walls, or along the river?"

"All three. Naturally, they're having more trouble on the river side."

"What have they got beside the sacks?"

"Hammers, picks, bars—We don't know what there is inside the sacks, but the whole thing looks like some kind of working party. The ones that are armed seem to be just in case we should go out and attack the working parties. We don't have the men. But we're a lot better off than we were."

"Best we bring most of Summa's men inside, to help man the walls if need be. But for now keep a strong force near the main gate. We may want to hit the enemy once they're back inside the palisade."

"It's being done. Tarvon gave the orders just before he was hit."

"When these alien working parties get close enough, let them have a little oil."

Almost as he spoke, there was a terrible scream from somewhere behind and below.

Arion said drily, "I've already given the word."

"I wonder—what can they do with sacks?"

"What could they do with pots?"

"Yes . . . Look at them down there. They're *waiting*."

Below, the alien horsemen, from a safe distance, were looking up. Amongst them, some archers vainly tried to send their shafts up to the walls, then occasionally darted into motion as answering shafts came close. But there was no rush to get near the walls. Long ladders had been brought up, but no-one was using them. At a respectful distance, the peculiar deep pots were again being set up, so there would be that to live through before long. The Chief considered the situation.

"Where could we put our catapults, except at the tops of the flat-roofed towers?"

Arion frowned. "There's no other place right for them. We can't very well shoot them out an arrow slit. Maybe on the walls, here and there. But that's no better."

"What hit Tarvon?"

"He'd gone below, and crossed the covered bridge to West Two tower, to look out. One of those balls burst overhead, and the pieces smashed through the roof of the tower."

The Chief glanced at the conical roof of the tower called West Two, directly in front and on a lower level than where he stood. The tower was low enough not to block the view of the battlefield from here, but Tarvon, having gone below, would have found it in the way, and crossed the covered bridge to it, to get a better view.

"We'll have to reinforce the roofs." The Chief could see the holes plainly, along with a number of darts stuck in the cone-shaped roof. "The darts broke through the weathered shingles. Where they hit the timbers, they didn't go through."

He glanced up, to see the sun still well up in the sky.

"I don't see how they're going to take us before dark. By dawn, we can have some of these roofs reinforced."

From down below, toward the upstream side of the castle, there was a piercing scream, then another.

More hot oil, no doubt.

But if enough of the enemy were that close—

The stones jumped underfoot. There was a roar, and the sound of a crash, of an avalanche, and another heavy crash shook the fortress.

From the distance, a black ball blurred up into the air, followed by another, and another.

The Chief noted that the bulk of the enemy remained unmoving. He called to the exposed catapult crews. "Get below! Quick!"

The crews dove for the trapdoors.

He looked around.

A huge cloud of dust was rolling skyward from the wall along the river. At a second glance—

Arion said, "The wall's gone!"

"It can't be!"

"Look at the end tower. See those few rocks sticking out? That's all that's left! Look further. There's the wall again. In between, a big length has gone down!"

"You're right!" The Chief glanced up, and grabbed Arion. "Quick! Get below!" He thrust him toward the steps, saw out of the corner of his eye the concerted movement on the field, toward the fortress. He looked up, wincing as he glimpsed the black balls dropping. He lifted the end of the voice-thrower, calculated where below, under cover, his men should be.

"Archers! Put some arrows in that crowd! In that pack, anywhere you hit will do good! When they're close, tip some oil on them!"

He glanced around, to see that Arion had gotten below. There was the first rush of wind, the start of a roar, then a redness that cut out wind and sound, a flash as if he saw the scene around him briefly through a closing door, another roar, cut off by the redness, and another—

He was standing, one hand on the parapet. Below, the whole valley was alive with rushing horsemen. Behind him, there was a roar, a crash, an uprush of dust. He turned to the voice-thrower, saw it was holed from end to end, useless. He looked down, saw the enemy chief sending off a messenger, who rode hard toward the face of the fortress that looked upriver. Closer at hand, he saw the hook of a ladder over the outer wall, saw a hairy face rise up—

From the slit of a nearby tower, an arrow flashed. The climber, struck in the throat, toppled from the wall. The ladder was still there.

A warrior in armor stepped out of a tower in the wall, briefly studied the ladder, and swung an axe. The ladder dropped from sight. The warrior stepped back into the tower.

The Chief looked up, saw the sun still well overhead. Out of the corner of his eye, he could see a blurred motion. The black balls were dropping in again, one after another.

It came to him then, looking at the black balls coming, and down at the voice-thrower, shot full of holes, that he must be dead, his body lying somewhere on the stone floor, or perhaps fallen over the parapet to down below, but he did not yet know it.

His consciousness, seated in his soul, looked out the eyes of his soul, and for now he could see, but surely not act in the world, because his worldly body could not be alive after this. And the teaching of those who had studied the matter was that the real man was in the soul, which, like the rider of a horse, at least in theory mastered and controlled the body, with its wild impulses and sudden unruly nature.

Uneasily, he rubbed his left hand across the Star Men's ring, felt the hard facets, glanced at it in surprise, saw the two lions risen up, their forepaws outstretched, their claws out, the ruby gemstone glowing as if lit from within.

There was the beginning of a wind and a roar, cut off by redness, and this time he was thinking: Did rings have souls? Did, then, a blue star gem have the soul of a ruby? Was a gold standing beast the soul of one lying down? No. It made no sense.

Then it followed that he was still alive, and since he could not possibly live through what had cut through the voice-thrower, killed half the catapult crew, and smashed through the roof of West Two to kill Tarvon—since he could not possibly have lived through that, it followed that he had not lived through it—something had kept it from him.

And since no known thing had powers that could have kept it from him, something of unknown powers had kept it from him. It could only be the ring, given him by the star traveler, in gratitude for a baby's life.

Just as an arrow could strike down the fiercest predator from a distance, the Chief thought, just as the enemy's sack of unknown substance could bring down the fortress walls, and just as these clearly impossible things were done by routine once understood, though they seemed like magic until understood, so the ring, like a beautifully decorated bow, was much more than an ornament.

Then once again the world was there, and the redness gone. The remains of the voice-thrower were scraps of metal against the parapet. The floor was covered with chips of stone and bits of mortar mingled with the black darts. There were black darts stuck upright in the mortar, and lying on the stone floor like hail after a storm.

From below, faintly to his deadened ears, came a muffled sound of hooves, then a ringing silence.

Looking down, the Chief saw the horsemen drawn back, like a tide that has pulled back from a shore in a huge wave, in order that it may smash more heavily against the rocks in its next blow.

The Chief, frowning, saw the enemy messengers, with their pennants, grouped around the squat alien leader, who was looking directly at him.

From behind, there was a rush of feet on the steps. Arion's voice was breathless.

"The river wall is breached at ground level! There's nothing but a pile of rocks they can climb over!"

The Chief looked around, but could not see through the dust.

Arion said, "The wall is all down between the middle tower and the northeast tower. But we've got archers to pick them off as they climb in over the rubble. Thank God we've got plenty of arrows!"

Looking back toward the river, it dawned on the Chief that this latest catastrophe was partly concealed by the massive bulk of the main central tower. But that tower must be as vulnerable as anything else. He looked back at Arion.

"They're not in anywhere yet?"

"No."

"Is the main gate still unhurt?"

"Yes, but the outer entrance, through the palisade, is partly blocked with fallen rocks. The tunnel entrance is clear, but the tunnel is too narrow to put men through in a hurry."

"Good. Now tell me, what's this?"

Arion stood beside him, looking down where the aliens had withdrawn.

Arion's voice was wondering. "Why should they—"

"Look at their faces."

The aliens' hairy faces as they watched the fortress were marked by three openings—two where their eyes looked out, and one where their mouths split into what appeared to be grins of anticipation.

Of all the aliens, only a few, here and there, appeared somber. Amongst them, squat and stolid, the Chief saw the alien leader, watching him with a look that was alert, and almost fearful.

In a brief flash of comprehension, it came to the Chief that just as he had unleashed carefully timed strokes against the waverers under Summa's banner, so the alien chieftain worked to a similar pattern in guiding his attack. And where his own alien men saw no reason to fear the outcome, the alien chief was conscious of a break in the accustomed pattern.

In this brief flash of insight, the Chief seemed to look up at the fortress, to see through a hell of fire and iron a single motionless figure which stood upright, unaffected, to counter blow with blow, waiting, knowing in advance the sequence of strokes that must follow, biding his time to let loose the final blow.

The stone floor of the tower jumped underfoot. There was a roar from all around them. Clouds of dust, on all four sides, rolled skyward.

Unbidden, the prophetic chant came to him:

> "The alien host that bought our spears
> With magic dust brings down our walls.
> Still know, the trumpet has no fears.
> Through smoke and flame, our duty calls."

The Chief looked back at the massive bulk of the central tower, looming through the rolling clouds of dust. He raised his voice, but kept it even as he called out:

"Let Evertrue speak!"

Back there, somewhere, was the trumpeter. Let him quaver just the slightest, and there would be a false note. The pattern that so far gripped the loyal might break. The prediction of the chant would be shown false. The alien pattern would prevail.

The silver tone spoke, over the noise and the dust.

The tone turned in the air, flawless, riveting the attention, holding the listeners motionless.

Then it was gone. The ear still sought for it, but found it only in memory.

The dust, slowly, blew away.

The Chief caught his breath.

The outer walls were down.

It was not just one part of a wall now. Looking around, it was clear why the enemy had pulled back. No-one would want to be close when those heavy rocks came down. The towers of the walls, here and there, still stood. Behind the rubble—and the Chief could see now that that rubble in places rested on structures that had not wholly collapsed—the towers *behind* the collapsed walls still stood. But the effect on the mind of the crash of those walls should have been crushing—except for the tone of the warhorn, and the remembered words of the prophetic chant.

Looking down across the wisps of dust still trailing from the collapsed heaps of masonry, the Chief could see the unmoving aliens in their hosts, and their squat leader somberly studying the fortress. From somewhere to the rear came a roar, a faint jar, and a heavy crash of falling rock, as some blast, that should have taken place earlier, joined in belatedly.

Illogically, the Chief felt cheerful. This time, there would be no holding the aliens at the wall. The wall was no longer there. They would get over the rubble, into the courtyard, would succeed in using their magic on the inner walls and towers—if they lived. But many of them would never make it through the hail of arrows that would greet them. And many who got in would never emerge from this place on their own feet. The Chief, foreseeing the attack, drew his sword.

There was a motion amongst the mounted enemy hosts, as if they sensed the order to attack just as the Chief had sensed it, before it came. But faintly across the gap between the enemy and the fortress, strewn with dead horses and the bodies of the enemy, there came a snarling repetition of sharp commands.

The enemy line of soldiers on foot, backed by a heavy mass of horsemen, had begun to move forward, but now stopped, and even, with much jostling, drew back.

The Chief, prepared for an attack, sensed what had happened. In the fortress, even in the rubble of the fortress, a determined defence might inflict untold casualties. The enemy chief had no desire to expend his strength in a killing match in a rock heap where his horses were worthless, and his tough but lightly armored troops were at a disadvantage.

The command to close for the kill, once given, could not easily be withdrawn. His war machine could be wrecked here against an unshaken enemy whose leader watched smiling from above, plainly looking forward to the finish fight at close quarters. And how did that leader still live after the bombardment that had burst around him? The alien chieftain sensed a trap, and suddenly turned on his horse to shout a fresh command.

Watching intently, the Chief realized with a shock that the pattern still held. That, in fact, so far from the aliens breaking it, it was coming to dominate them, through the mind of their leader. He turned to Arion.

"We have another voice-thrower, don't we?"

"Yes, in the armory downstairs."

"We may need it."

"I'll get it."

A moment later he saw the armored figure being brought forward, and realized that the alien leader was already working to free himself from the dilemma. As the Chief watched, an alien on horseback was leading one single man in armor slowly and reluctantly toward the fallen outer walls. A brief clatter beside him told the Chief that Arion had brought the voice-thrower. Down below, somewhat more than halfway to the fortress, the armored figure stopped, and called out. His voice seemed small, but clearly audible:

"Will you parley?"

The Chief sheathed his sword, and the click carried. He raised the voice-thrower, and his voice seemed unnaturally loud:

"What do they say?"

"They offer terms."

"So do we."

"Give your word of loyalty to their chief—their king— and pay the equal of one tenth of the yearly crop's worth to his collector. If you give your word, he will leave at once, and you may settle matters here as you choose."

The Chief spoke as much for his men, who would be intently listening, as to the enemy leader. He spoke also for those to hear whose leaders had been bought by the enemy, and who would just have heard their new hairy ruler offer their lives freely as part of the barter.

The Chief spoke carefully. "Tell him we thank him for his offer, but our word is pledged in an ancient oath that must be upheld by all those who are true. And we do not need to yield. We are at the center of our strength, and his force, though great, is not sufficient to break it.

"But he is far from home, and behind him for many days' march, there is no-one he can trust if he should have ill-fortune. There is no-one back there bound to him by blood, love, or loyalty. Save his own men here, there is no-one at his command but those who are cowards, who are unwilling, or whose loyalty could be bought. Here, if he attacks further, we will break his strength, and he will see what, in the final clash, false hirelings and those betrayed into his service by their own false leaders are worth. But we will make an offer of our own. Will he hear it?"

There was a silence, then, with an effort, the armored figure spoke: "He will hear it."

"Tell him that he has won so far by new and subtle means of unleashing force. Tell him that there are still subtler means that can lift men to the stars, set metal aflame, blot out the lightning and silence the thunder. His coming has been foretold by prophecy, and he who would defeat the prophets in their power must take care, lest unwittingly he fulfill the prophecy instead. We offer that he may withdraw now, and we will let him go with no further hurt. Neither will we, if he leaves at once, summon those whose loyalty will cast aside bribery and betrayal to join the true cause at our first call. We know their real feelings.

"We decline his offer, and remind him that he knows the subtle might of the stars. We call upon him to soberly weigh our offer, while there is still time."

The armored figure raised its gauntleted hand in salute, and the Chief returned the salute, knowing now which side this warrior wished to be on. He watched the armored figure return to the alien chieftain, saw the hairy interpreters confer with both, to clear up points that might be uncertain. There followed a silence, in which the predicament of the alien leader was clear enough to the Chief.

Obviously enough, to the alien ruler and perhaps a few of his leaders, some new power was in evidence here. Otherwise, the King who had just spoken from the fortress would have been killed in the first bombardment. Worse, this King was said to have friends amongst the star men, so the possibilities for unpleasant surprises were practically unlimited. On the other hand, the outer walls were down, and to turn back now, with his army convinced that one last assault would take the place—that would breed doubts as to his judgment and his courage, and be possibly even worse than a defeat.

The Chief, looking down, saw the enemy chief look up. Even at this distance, he could read a message of angry irresolution in the alien's gaze.

Briefly, despite himself, the Chief smiled. Suddenly, another part of the chant came to him:

> "Look, a streak is drawn across the sky,
> In answer to our King-Chief's cry.
> Now see the enemy stand silent by,
> As a mightier host comes marching nigh."

Down below, they were all looking up.

The Chief glanced up as a peculiar traveling thunder crashed and rumbled overhead.

There in the sky hung a long narrow cloud, at the head of which, like an armored forefinger, was a glittering something—a star ship!

The Chief felt his breath stop, but with an effort kept a grip on his sense of reality.

What was happening, so far, fit the chant with

unvarying trueness. But prophecies had been known to fail before.

Arion spoke at his shoulder, his voice awed.

"They've come!"

The Chief spoke in a low voice. "They can see us from down there, and you aren't the only one with eyes as sharp as a bird of prey. Keep your own features impassive, and let me know how their ruler looks to you. He's the squat one, in the center of that group of messengers with pennants."

Arion said more soberly, "With all that fur on his face— H'm—To me, he looks stubborn, but none too easy in his mind."

"That's what I thought. Now, how do we take advantage of this?"

"But do we need to? Certainly it's the star men come to help us?"

"How do we know that? Is that the first star ship we've ever seen pass overhead?" The Chief kept his voice low. "Even if it should be the star men, how do we know they *can* help?"

"It fits the chant—the prophecy."

"It fits part of it, but let's not take leave of our senses just yet. How about that line that goes, 'The fallen walls with iron ghosts are manned'?"

"True . . . Unless it means, which is true, when those walls fell that we lost heavily . . . But, at least, we'd gotten the best part of Summa's men safe before the collapse, and they didn't get hurt. They're all loyal. The rot only touched the Baron."

"Now look, down there."

Down below, the armored figure came forward again. This time, with the visible streak across the sky overhead, he saluted before speaking.

"Chief and King, the alien knows of the prophecy, but he wants proof it is true."

The Chief glanced at the collapsed outer walls, considered the men lost in that collapse, and considered also the form of address, 'Chief and King.' That meant acceptance as both head of the clan and ruler. The armored figure below was now leaving no doubt as to which side he was on. To his natural loyalty was added, no doubt, an earnest desire to be on the right side when the forces of Justice proved mightier than the aliens. This same emotion might very naturally be shared by the bulk of the armored troops betrayed into the alien service by their self-seeking or overawed leaders.

The chief raised the voice-thrower.

"Tell him," he said carefully, "to open his ranks between the fortress and the landing place of the star men, and he will have proof. Tell him that, if he had attacked earlier, the star men, in their might, would have come onto the battlefield while his men were enmeshed in the ruins of the fortress."

The armored go-between glanced around, obviously uncertain just where the star men had landed. Overhead, the streak was still plainly in evidence, but, as usually happened, the star ship itself had disappeared. Certain wise men, the Chief remembered, surmised that the star ship, as one means of travel, used a mysterious fire which left its smoke behind it, but also, they thought, the star ship could glide, like a hawk, so that the fire was only lit at intervals, and hence the track of smoke appeared only now and then.

Down below, the armored figure looked up hesitantly and then asked, "The landing place?"

The Chief carefully raised his arm to point. The direction in which he pointed was not seriously inconsistent with the path of the streak overhead, and it incidentally would open up a route for the body of armored troops outside, whose leaders the aliens had bought, who were much closer now, and who by now might earnestly want to be on the right side when the rest of the prophecy came true. Those armored troops could make a big difference in the price the enemy had to pay to win—if those troops could be brought to change sides.

Arion cleared his throat.

"I think they have something to try to hear our words with."

The Chief noted a thing like a voice-thrower, the wide end now aimed roughly at him, the narrow end just being taken from the ear of someone near the alien chieftain.

The Chief nodded. "Look."

The enormous horde of mounted aliens was now separating, as half-a-dozen messengers on horseback moved through the ranks. But, the Chief noted, the path they made was curved to miss the armored troops. And yet, if those armored troops should move forward—

"Shrewd," said Arion. "I wonder—"

A small voice, oddly accented but understandable, reached them from below:

"Prove your prophecy."

Down there, one of the hairy translators lowered a voice-thrower.

The Chief considered the situation. In the little group around the alien leader, his couriers waited for orders. In the sky, the streak was still plainly visible, but spreading, and before long would begin to fade away. There was an intense and waiting silence in the motionless host below. This tension couldn't last forever. It would break, in one way or another.

The Chief turned to look back at the central tower, and was jarred as if by a physical blow. Back beyond the tower was the reflected glint of light on the river. Though he knew that the outer wall of the fortress was down, he hadn't expected to see the river. But the dust was settled, and there was nothing there now to cut off the view. He drew a deep slow breath, then faced the tower, and spoke slowly and clearly.

"Let Evertrue sound the Assembly."

When he turned back to face the aliens, he could feel the loss of the fortress wall behind him. It was as if his back were naked, exposed to whatever blow might be aimed at it.

Then the silver tone hung in the air, turned, fell and rose, its message more complex than before.

Across the field, the armored troops began to move. Down below, a single armored figure separated itself from the enemy messengers and interpreters, to walk with steady pace toward the fortress. Across the field, the entire mass of armor was thrusting its way into the wide cleared aisle, turning, the low-voiced commands clearly to be heard, even the rattle and clink of metal, with the sun glittering on the armor and the unsheathed weapons.

At once, two alien couriers raced up the cleared aisle. But the mass of the aliens, still held in the trancelike grip induced by Evertrue's clear silver tone, did not move as the tone rose, fell, and then faded insensibly away.

The armored troops were coming now, massed and purposeful, straight down the aisle toward the fortress. As they came, they threw up the visors of their helmets to stare, desperately earnest, toward the fortress and the two unmoving figures who looked down upon them from its high tower.

The Chief drew his breath carefully, looking from the approaching troops to the plainly baffled alien leader. However the alien might have been affected by Evertrue's tone, he could hardly guess the effect of that particular call to assemble by the colors. Neither could he tell by the purposeful advance whether conceivably an attack on the fortress was in progress, or an open changing of sides in the teeth of his own superiority.

The Chief let the uncertainty stretch out till he saw the alien leader turn to a messenger. Then he turned back toward the central tower and spoke very clearly.

"Let Evertrue sound the Welcome."

A cheerful call climbed into the air.

A shout of mingled relief and exultation burst from the armored troops as they realized they were welcomed back into the fold. They could have been treated as traitors, and once close enough, greeted with bolts, arrows, and taunts of contempt.

The Chief, feeling the sudden increase in strength like

a man waking from a nightmare, reminded himself the
odds were still none too good, and he had now the
problem of getting these reinforcements into the fortress.
The outer walls were mostly down. The mounted men
among them could never get across that shambles of
tumbled blocks. The palisade still stood, but from here he
could see that its normal entrance, ordinarily dominated
by the outer wall, was buried under a wreck of fallen
masonry. But to judge by the clear ground that he could
see, the main gate of the fortress still stood, and almost
certainly the tunnel was undamaged.

Once inside the palisade, the way into the fortress,
through the main gate or the tunnel, should be clear.
But exactly how could he get these troops inside the
palisade?

The leaders of the approaching armor were evidently
contending with the same problem, and the called orders
and direction of march showed that they intended to try
to get in as close to the normal entrance as possible, over
the fallen blocks, or through a gap in the palisade where
the blocks had thrown down the upright logs.

The Chief glanced at Arion.

"We have to hold the palisade. Otherwise, the aliens
will be over the outerworks and hit our men as they come
in."

"Summa's men are still handy. I'll send the main body
through the gate. The tunnel's too slow. Then I'll be back."

Down below, as if caught in a dream, the invaders
stood unmoving. Then the alien leader, possibly uncertain
at first what the shout of the armored troops had meant,
turned sharply to the men around him. The messengers

raced out with signal flags. The massed enemy horsemen gave a sudden roar, and surged forward.

Down below, the armored men, caught between the collapsed wall and a host of attackers, turned to fight. Behind them, on the palisade, armored men appeared. The mounted aliens were greeted from the fortress with flights of arrows and heavy bolts. But before the fight could be truly joined, from the far distance came a remote but clear golden tone.

This tone climbed, turned in the air, climbed again. It wasn't Evertrue, but it had Evertrue's ability to pin the mind, to stop the thoughts.

The clash below died away, everyone staring into the distance, no-one certain what this meant.

The Chief turned back toward the main central tower.

"Let Evertrue sound the Welcome!"

The passage of the chant rang in his head:

"Shall Evertrue call for help in vain?
No! Where was one, there shall be twain!"

The silver tone rose behind him.

From the distance, the golden tone responded, note for note.

Out there now, he could see dust drifting up, in the distance.

A quick glance showed him the alien chief, rapping out orders. Messengers raced over the field. The enormous host of horsemen moved like a single living thing, and now the enemy had changed position, and was drawn up with his main body facing to the west.

And there, passing across the flank of the enormous host of aliens, came a glitter and flash, and now the Chief could make out a small band—At once, even at this distance, he recognized the strange armor—that marched with solid unvarying tread straight for the fortress. The armor told him it was the star men. But now, for the first time, he felt a touch of fear.

They were few.

They had come. Years, decades, in the past, he had helped them. Across what unknown spaces the call had reached them—it must have gone out in some way from the ring—he could not know. But they had not hesitated. They were here.

But they were few.

Here seemed the first break in the accuracy of the prophetic chant, and the Chief damned himself for having felt relief. There was a tradition that the star men might, occasionally, mingle in human affairs—but that when they did, they would not openly use the tools and weapons of their full power. How had he imagined that the trouble was over because the star men had come? They had come to share the danger with him, that was all.

With equal illogic, he at once felt cheerful.

Let the aliens consider the meaning of such courage.

Arion, beside him again, and watching intently, gave a low exclamation.

"What?" said the Chief.

"I was," said Arion, "frightened at first by the smallness of their numbers. Now—"

"The aliens are not hastening to the attack."

"No," said Arion drily.

The Chief's vision, less sharp than Arion's, now revealed to him a curious fact. Where the little group of star men in armor walked, dust rose from the contact of their feet with the ground. That, at first, seemed natural. What was curious was that the dust *continued to rise* after the armored men had passed.

Looking from that compact little group, back across the field to the distant point where they had emerged from the forest, an unvarying drift of dust was rising still, fresh and none too thin.

Leaning forward at the parapet as the Star Men approached, the Chief caught his breath. He had begun to notice the details.

Before the staring motionless aliens, the armored men moved with a briskness unusual for men in armor. To move with such ease suggested that they bore a light weight. Yet, behind each of them in the packed dry earth, there stretched a line of footprints, and these footprints, looked at even from this distance, appeared to be two or three inches deep.

The only conclusion the Chief could reach was that the few men approaching in glittering armor were no ordinary warriors. Each individual must be bearing a weight of metal far beyond that of any normal armor. That they bore it so lightly could only suggest the strength of giants.

There was a movement in the close-packed ranks of the watching aliens, as if those in front, closest to the star men, and best aware of their nature, sought to draw away, while those behind, and hence less afraid and more curious, tried to get a better look. Only the alien leader and those close around him stayed truly unmoving.

Now the star men were passing the alien chief, and as if in greeting, salute, or possibly just out of exuberance, they did something that caused those around the alien leader to suddenly draw back, openly staring. For an instant, the Chief could not grasp it.

The star men were marching in unison, the left foot of each striking the ground at the same time. At this distance it was possible to hear the good-natured rhythmic chant with which they kept the beat of their pace. Their shields as they marched, hung on their left arms, while their right arms bore short thick spears slanted back across their right shoulders—save for their leader, who carried a naked broadsword in his right hand.

Except for the thickness of the spears and the size of the sword, there was nothing unusual in any of that. But as they passed the alien chief, the leader of the star men gave what appeared to be a greeting or salute with his sword—there was no menace in the gesture itself—and his men behind him at once changed their hold on shields and spears to the sound of a clashing of arms so harsh, loud, and ringing that it briefly left the Chief, looking down, feeling faint and dizzy.

There below, the Star Men marched, and as the right foot of each struck the ground, the shields were abruptly on their right arms, and the spears slanted back across their left shoulders, and the marchers enthusiastically banged the butts of their spears—the long sharp points thrust straight up in the air—twice against the shields.

Then, as their left feet struck the ground, the shields were again on their left arms and the spears on their right shoulders, and again there was a mighty ringing clash as the butts of the spears were banged twice on the shields. It happened so fast there was no way to see how it was done, yet it was done good-naturedly, exuberantly, as a boy tosses a ball and catches it in his hand.

And now something that had no doubt already dawned on the massed aliens dawned on the Chief. That deafening volume of sound could never have come from so few men. He took another look.

Down there, the dust was still rising where the Star Men marched, and now they were close enough so the Chief could get a better look behind them. Coming along in back of them were another set of fresh footprints, and another, and another—until it dawned on him that while he could *see* only a few men, the sounds, the visible dust, the trampling of the dirt—all the indications were of an uncountable host of fighting men in massive armor, and of such might as to bear such armor lightly. And most of these men *could not be seen*.

They were still passing the near end of the aliens, who were drawing back, and now they tossed their spears in the air and caught them. Now they clashed their spears on their upraised shields, making a clanging noise that hurt the ears at this distance. Then the head of the column was approaching the fallen walls, and there appeared ladders, and the ladders were swung up, so that the upper ends leaned forward as if against walls still there to receive them.

The sun was now low enough so that, even holding up his hand to protect his eyes, the glare was dazzling. Leaning forward, the Chief peered again at the ladders. They were up above the collapsed masonry, to where the walls had been before they had been brought down, *and the ladders remained solidly upright, but now bent slightly as if unseen weight bore down upon them.*

Now, passing the alien host as the sun descended, came different prints in the soil, and the Chief recognized the dust and the hoofmarks suggesting a formidable host of armored knights, invisible like the rest, that drew up outside the walls and faced the enemy.

At the fallen walls of the fortress, fresh lines of footprints reached the ladders, and there was the clang of metal, the scuff of feet, the clink and rattle of an uncountable host coming up the ladders and along the walls, spreading out on the vanished battlements ready for the fight—if anyone here should care to make a fight—and there was nothing wrong with it anywhere save that there were no walls, no battlements, no outer towers there to defend, but that did not trouble the Star Men. From them, now, there came a clash of spears on shields that traveled from the walls back up the dusty trail to echo from hill to hill from the fortress down the valley up into the forest and out of sight in the distance.

The sun was now low in the west, and the Chief peered down at the enormous and motionless host of silent alien horsemen. Amongst these horsemen, he located the enemy chief, looked at him steadily, and the enemy chief slowly turned his head and looked back. Written in the slowness with which he turned his head, and in the wideness of his eyes, was an acknowledgement of defeat. Solemnly, the Chief looked back, feeling no triumph but only a great relief as the prophecy completed itself.

Before the motionless and wide-eyed aliens, the dust

was still rising. The earth where the Star Men passed was churned and pitted to such a degree that the entire surface looked beaten down below the general level of the fields to either side. From time to time, a good-natured clashing of weapons on shields broke out somewhere among the invisible marching host, to travel in both directions, and roll and echo like iron thunder, back and forth, from the walls to the valley, to the forest and back again.

Each time, this clashing was louder, and the sound now from atop the walls, as the walls would have been before they fell, was such as could have been equaled only by a solid mass of troops, shoulder to shoulder drawn up on the battlements three or four deep. And now a none too subtle change was there to be heard in the clash and shout and the gathering steady throb of drums—The sound was no longer so good natured. It began to carry a threat. It began to suggest the gnashing of the teeth of innumerable large and hungry beasts of prey.

The Chief looked down at the leader of the aliens.

The alien chief looked back. Then he glanced around.

The dust no longer rose from the beaten ground before him.

Abruptly the mounted messengers with their pennants raced in either direction along the front of the silent mass of horsemen. How it was done, the Chief couldn't grasp, but abruptly the huge mass moved, almost as one man, and with a pound that seemed to shake the earth, they went across the fields, over the hill, up the far side of the valley into the forest, and away.

They were gone.

The Chief exhaled slowly, and thanked God.

Arion gripped his arm.

The Chief turned.

There before him in the fading light was the armor he knew from long ago. The voice, too, was familiar, and this time the words were in his own tongue:

"We star men, as you call us, differ among ourselves, as you differ among yourselves—But there are those among us who believe in paying our debts. Your ring is like a knot in a net made of strands of force, and this force can defend you, while waves moving along the strands can travel at speeds well above that of light. So we learned of this trouble and came to try to repay you."

The Chief said carefully, "I have no way to thank you. Any debt is more than repaid." He twisted off the ring, and held it out.

The voice from the armored suit was warm, but no hand reached out to take the ring.

"Perhaps we have repaid our debt, but such things are hard to measure. And there is more to it."

A second figure in armor stepped forward to clasp the Chief's arm. The voice was like the first, but less deep:

"I was in the cradle that you saved from the wreck. This is my first chance to thank you."

"When," said the first voice, "we find those who do what is right, we remember them. We cannot be truly friends, because of such things as disease, and differences in customs and skills. But it is a pleasure to help, albeit that our help is at times mostly illusion. But there is a part that is real, as our gratitude is real. You risked your life for us, and we have not forgotten."

When they were gone—and their departure was a simple thing compared to their coming—the Chief saw that his friend, Arion, was standing apart, tears rolling silently down his cheeks. It struck the Chief with a pang, and he felt, found the ring again where it had been, on his finger, and was about to twist it off to try to comfort his friend; but Arion held out his own hand, where on his finger a wide silver band showed a lion seated, with two tiny bright white stones for eyes.

"The young Star Man," said Arion. "When he passed, he clasped my hand. He said, 'For courage,' and afterwards this ring was there. It soothes my soul, but it isn't right." He began to twist at the ring. "I showed no courage. I was afraid to go back to that burning ship."

"You were with me when we saved the boy. It is that that counts."

"When you saved him, not I. And I would not have given him back. I was afraid. I do not deserve this ring."

"H'm," said the Chief. "It is a ring from the Star Men, Arion. Who knows what power it may possess. It should not be lost."

"Then you take it," said Arion. "I am ashamed to cry, but I cry only that I do not deserve it."

The Chief turned the new ring in his hand, but did not put it on. Neither did he put it in the small leather pouch at his belt. He examined it, and then looked up.

"It is very pretty."

Arion did not reply, but nodded miserably.

"Arion," said the Chief, "I am not only your friend since childhood. I am also your Chief and your King. As you know, I have the power to reward those who deserve it. Now that you have given this ring into my care, I have, I think, the right to reward someone who has been true to his duty, who has courageously stood with me against hosts of alien horsemen so thick they covered the ground. So courageous as not even to think of this as courage. I am speaking of you."

"But that was my duty."

"It was also courage, beyond any doubt. Cup your hand so we do not lose this over the edge. If you had wavered, who knows who else would have gone over to the other side? The younger star man said, 'For courage.' He spoke truly."

Arion, eyes wondering, took the ring in his cupped hand, hesitated, then put it on. He smiled, looking at it, then looked up. "It eases a hurt, from long ago."

"Perhaps he sensed it." The Chief looked around at the wreckage in the moonlight. "Would that we had the skills of the Star Men. To rebuild this—" He paused.

Arion shook his head.

"We can never rebuild this, except as a monument."

"True. It would be useless against such weapons. In the future, our fortresses must be different."

They went down the steps to where the newly lighted torches smoked and flared in their brackets against the blackened stone of the tower. Tomorrow, they would start to think about correcting such of this terrible wreck as could be made right.

But, he thought with relief, at least, now, there could *be* a tomorrow, and at that thought, he felt also a flood of gratitude to the Star Men. Where, he wondered, were they now? What inconceivable deeds did they perform, up among the stars?

***

Colonel Valentine Sanders, speechless, watched his son, Lieutenant Colin Sanders, say earnestly to the General, "Sir, for weeks we've been immersed in the records from the spy devices. These are real people! It's impossible not to act toward them as we would toward our own people."

"Listen," said the General, "you were sent down there to straighten out that mess, not to compound it. To have *one* guard ring down there is bad enough. Why did you have to deliver another one?"

"Sir, we've seen the records of what happened down there. For more than twenty years Arion has been blaming himself that he didn't show courage when, in fact, he did. Besides, he helped rescue me. And, whatever the psychologists say as to how soon a person can remember things, I can remember Arion's face—I must have seen him when the ship blew up. When I met him, I was over-come with emotion."

The General said, very carefully, "I wonder if this is one of those sins of the fathers that is passed on unto the seventh generation? Just where did *this* guard ring come from?"

"Sir, from my uncle. He said that in thirty years, he'd really never felt the need to use it. Now that I was in the Patrol, Uncle Basil thought maybe I could use it."

Colonel Sanders looked blankly at his son.

The General looked equally blank. "Val, do you have a brother in the Patrol?"

The Colonel shook his head. "No, sir. I'm afraid not."

There was a considerable silence, as the General stared at the Colonel, while the younger Sanders looked on in puzzlement. Finally, the General said, his voice sounding a little hoarse, "You don't mean—"

Colonel Sanders said hesitantly, "Basil is a Stellar Scout, sir."

The General gave a grunt, as if he had come down a staircase in the dark, and stepped off with one more step still at the bottom.

Colin said, "But what's wrong with that, sir? They scout the planets ahead of the classification teams, ahead of the colonists—They're even ahead of the trapminers and freebooters. The Stellar Scouts are the most advanced outfit there is!"

The General managed a sketchy smile.

Colonel Valentine Sanders growled, "They're advanced in a different way than we are. They use *the newest equipment available*."

Colin began to ask what was wrong with that, then noted the expressions of his two superiors, and kept quiet.

The Colonel went on. "Ask Basil about his friend, Barnes, some time. Barnes spent a chunk of his life imprisoned on a planet in the Forbidden Zone, back before it was the Forbidden Zone. He wound up there courtesy of several pieces of exceptionally new equipment."

The General said carefully, "Very few people in their right senses use experimental equipment on a day-to-day operational basis. We ourselves use new equipment, *when we think it's proven*, and now and then we get a black eye or a broken arm out of it. But the Stellar Scouts, if they see something that looks interesting, will raid the research lab for it. I have it on good authority that Stellar Scout ships have gone through the middle of territory controlled by commerce raiders, and the raiders have come boiling out to surrender to the Space Force. Anything to keep away from the Scouts. Years ago, the Scouts had a thing that fired 'holes'—If they aimed it at you and pulled the trigger, chunks of your ship would vanish and reappear unpredictably all through adjacent volumes of space. They still use it—though with a little more discretion."

Colin Sanders blinked. "The chunks reappear *unpredictably* all through the adjacent space?"

"Right. Including, now and then, the space occupied by the ship using this weapon."

Colin grappled with this revelation.

The General added, "A little imperfection in their equipment won't stop the Scouts. They're used to it."

"I—I see, sir. But the guard ring—"

Colonel Valentine Sanders said thoughtfully, "What was it Basil said? That in thirty years he hadn't really found the need for it? *He'd had it thirty years and hadn't tried it out yet?*"

"Yes, and now I was in the Patrol, I could have it."

The General growled, "Generous of him."

Colonel Sanders nodded. "Aren't they always generous?"

The General said, "And if he had it for thirty years—"

"Then it's almost certainly one of their early models." The Colonel looked back at his son. "You see, Basil had it for thirty years. *And he never used it.* As you've pointed out, the Scouts get in dangerous spots. Why hadn't he used it?"

"I don't know. Unless—" Colin hesitated.

"Unless what?"

Colin said indignantly, "Unless he was nervous with it and wanted *someone else to try it out first*?"

The Colonel nodded. "The first time they go out, when they're still new to the Scouts, little more than recruits, they tend to use all this wonderful stuff. Once it blows up in their faces, provided they survive, they get wary. When two Stellar Scouts get together, what do you suppose they spend the first few hours doing?"

Colin said angrily, "Comparing notes on the equipment?"

"Exactly. And there may be items they both left strictly alone. It looks as if you've passed along one of those."

"But, if that's so—*What about Arion?*"

The General said, without enthusiasm, "What about him?"

"Sir—We can't leave him with this—this experimental guard ring—"

"Now you've given it to him, how do you take it back?"

Colin looked blank.

Colonel Sanders said, "It is keyed to him, isn't it?"

"Yes, sir. Otherwise, what would be the point?"

"All right. Considering what a guard ring *is*, how do you or anyone else now take it away from him? If you try to do that, you'll activate it. Then what?"

"That's true . . . Still, he'd give it back if I asked, wouldn't he? And I could replace it with a more reliable—"

The General shook his head. "One involuntary agent on that planet is plenty."

Colin said bleakly, "Poor Arion." He hesitated, then said miserably, "I *meant* well."

Colonel Sanders said, "Arion seems level-headed. He shouldn't wind up imagining he's a god because of the power of the device. And until it's activated, there should be no great risk. Then, who knows? It might even work as it should. Seeing who made it, *probably* the greatest risk is to these hairy invaders. And it could be quite a risk. The Stellar Scouts don't pull their punches."

"What if, some day, the wrong person should get it?"

The General said, "Why do you suppose we try to keep track of these things? Why does PDA have the rule against technological devices? Sure, it could make trouble. Lots of it."

Colonel Sanders said, "If Basil offers you anything else, think twice. He means well, too. But, just incidentally, you end up testing the thing for him."

"At least, there was no warning against it in that prophetic chant—and I don't understand that chant, either. How *could* anyone predict what would happen?"

"Well—When a given culture finds a method that seems to work—that they have the right talent to use— they tend to standardize it, and skip the rest. There may be another method that works, but they pass it by. We used to have prophets. But science seemed more useful and reliable, so we've put more effort into it, and developed it. You have to be prepared for these differences. We even have them from one generation to another."

The General nodded. "There used to be a good deal of wisdom in proverbs. Our ancestors relied on them as guides."

Colin said unhappily, "I could have used one for this situation."

"No problem," said the General, "I'll adapt one for you. A little late; but it might still be useful."

Colin blanked his face and stood straighter, in preparation for what he sensed was about to hit him.

The General thought a moment, then smiled benevolently, though he spoke with real feeling:

"Beware of nearly anyone who comes bearing free gifts. *Yourself included.*"

Afterword

With the publication of this volume, the eighth in Baen's reissue of the writings of Christopher Anvil, Baen Books has now put back in print everything Anvil wrote in the way of science fiction. Anvil died recently, on November 30, 2009. The last science fiction story he ever wrote, "The Anomaly," was written for this volume and is now seeing its first publication.

What follows is a complete bibliography of Christopher Anvil's science fiction works. The bibliography is arranged in chronological order, by publication date.

TITLE	DATE	FIRST PUB	VOLUME
"Cinderella, Inc."	Dec-52	Imagination	7
Roll Out the Rolov!	Nov-53	Imagination	7
The Prisoner	Feb-56	Astounding	4
Pandora's Planet	Sep-56	Astounding	1
Advance Agent	Feb-57	Galaxy	4
Compensation	Oct-57	Astounding	5
Sinful City	1957	Future SF #32	5
Torch	Apr-57	Astounding	6

TITLE	DATE	FIRST PUB	VOLUME
The Gentle Earth	Nov-57	Astounding	5
Truce by Boomerang	Dec-57	Astounding	6
Achilles' Heel	Feb-58	Astounding	4
Revolt!	Apr-58	Astounding	2
Top Rung	Jul-58	Astounding	4
Cargo for Colony 6	Aug-58	Astounding	4
Foghead	Sep-58	Astounding	4
Goliath and the Beanstalk	Nov-58	Astounding	3
Nerves	Nov-58	Fantastic Universe	5
Seller's Market	Dec-58	Astounding	4
The Sieve	Apr-59	Astounding	3
Leverage	Jul-59	Astounding	3
Captive Leaven	Sep-59	Astounding	5
The Law Breakers	Oct-59	Astounding	5
Mating Problems	Dec-59	Astounding	3
A Rose By Any Other Name	Jan-60	Astounding	6
Shotgun Wedding	Mar-60	Astounding	5
A Tourist Named Death	May-60	IF	8
Star Tiger	Jun-60	Astounding	2
The Troublemaker	Jul-60	Astounding	3
A Taste of Poison	Aug-60	Astounding	8
Mind Partner	Aug-60	Galaxy	4
The Ghost Fleet	Feb-61	Analog	4
Pandora's Envoy	Apr-61	Analog	1
Identification	May-61	Analog	7
The Hunch	Jul-61	Analog	2
No Small Enemy	Nov-61	Analog	7

TITLE	DATE	FIRST PUB	VOLUME
Uncalculated Risk	Mar-62	Analog	6
The Toughest Opponent	Aug-62	Analog	1
Sorcerer's Apprentice	Sep-62	Analog	6
Gadget vs. Trend	Oct-62	Analog	6
Philosopher's Stone	Jan-63	Analog	6
Not in the Literature	Mar-63	Analog	7
War Games	Oct-63	Analog	6
Problem of Command	Nov-63	Analog	6
Speed-up!	Jan-64	Amazing	7
Rx for Chaos	Feb-64	Analog	7
Hunger	May-64	Analog	3
We From Arcturus	Aug-64	Worlds of Tomorrow	5
Bill for Delivery	Nov-64	Analog	3
Contrast	Dec-64	Analog	3
Merry Christmas From Outer Space	Dec-64	Fantastic	5
The Day the Machines Stopped	1964	Monarch	8
The New Boccaccio	Jan-65	Analog	7
The Plateau	Mar-65	Amazing	5
The Captive Djinn	May-65	Analog	4
Duel to the Death	Jun-65	Analog	5
High G	Jun-65	IF	7
In the Light of Further Data	Jul-65	Analog	8
Positive Feedback	Aug-65	Analog	7
The Problem Solver and the Spy	Dec-65	Ellery Queen's Mystery Magazine	6
Untropy	Jan-66	Analog	3

TITLE	DATE	FIRST PUB	VOLUME
The Problem Solver & the Hostage	Feb-66	Ellery Queen's Magazine	8
The Kindly Invasion	Mar-66	Worlds of Tomorrow	4
The Coward	Mar-66	Adam	8
Devise and Conquer	Apr-66	Galaxy	6
Two-Way Communication	May-66	Analog	7
Stranglehold	Jun-66	Analog	2
Sweet Reason	Jun-66	IF	12
The Missile Smasher	Jul-66	Analog	8
The Problem Solver and the Killer	Aug-66	Ellery Queen's Magazine	8
Symbols	Sep-66	Analog	4
Strangers to Paradise	Oct-66	Analog	2
Facts to Fit the Theory	Nov-66	Analog	3
The Problem Solver & the Defector	Dec-66	Ellery Queen's Magazine	8
Sabotage	Dec-66	Magazine of Fantasy & Science Fiction	4
The Murder Trap	Jan-67	Man From UNCLE Magazine	6
The Trojan Bombardment	Feb-67	Galaxy	6
The Uninvited Guest	Mar-67	Analog	4
The New Member	Apr-67	Galaxy	6
The Problem Solver	Apr-67	Ellery Queen's Mystery Magazine	8
Experts in the Field	May-67	Analog	2
The Dukes of Desire	Jun-67	Analog	2
Compound Interest	Jul-67	Analog	2
Babel II	Aug-67	Analog	6

TITLE	DATE	FIRST PUB	VOLUME
The King's Legions	Sep-67	Analog	2
The New Way	11/12/67	Beyond Infinity	7
A Question of Attitude	Dec-67	Analog	2
Uplift the Savage	Mar-68	Analog	3
Is Everybody Happy?	Apr-68	Analog	7
High Road to the East	May-68	Fantastic	8
The Royal Road	Jun-68	Analog	2
Behind the Sandrat Hoax	Oct-68	Galaxy	5
Mission of Ignorance	Oct-68	Analog	4
Trap	Mar-69	Analog	1
The Nitrocellulose Doormat	Jun-69	Analog	2
The Great Intellect Boom	Jul-69	Analog	7
Test Ultimate	Oct-69	Analog	2
Basic	Nov-69	Venture Science Fiction	2
Strangers in Paradise	1969	Tower	2
Trial by Silk	Mar-70	Amazing	3
The Low Road	Sep-70	Amazing	3
The Throne and the Usurper	Nov-70	Magazine of Fantasy & Science Fiction	3
Apron Chains	Dec-70	Analog	8
The Claw and the Clock	Feb-71	Analog	3
The Operator	Mar-71	Analog	3
Riddle Me This...	Jan-72	Analog	3
The Hand From the Past	May-72	Alfred Hitchcock's Mystery Magazine	8
The Unknown	Jul-72	Amazing	3
Ideological Defeat	Sep-72	Analog	6
Pandora's Planet	1972	Doubleday	1

TITLE	DATE	FIRST PUB	VOLUME
Cantor's War	5/6/74	IF	3
The Knife and the Sheath	1974	Future Kin	8
Warlord's World	1975	DAW	3
Brains Isn't Everything	Jun-76	Analog	4
The Golden Years	Mar-77	Analog	7
Odds	Jul-77	Amazing	3
A Household Primer	Jan-78	Amazing	7
While the Northwind Blows	Nov-78	Amazing	3
A Sense of Disaster?	Jan-79	Fantastic	8
The Gold of Galileo	Oct-80	Analog	8
"The Steel, the Mist and the Blazing Sun "	1980	ACE	6
Top Line	Jan-82	Analog	6
Superbiometalemon	Jul-82	Magazine of Fantasy & Science Fiction	7
Bugs	Jun-86	Analog	7
Rags From Riches	Nov-87	Amazing	7
Interesting Times	Dec-87	Analog	7
Doc's Legacy	Feb-88	Analog	7
The Trojan Hostage	Jul-90	Analog	3
The Underhandler	Nov-90	Analog	5
Negative Feedback	Mar-94	Analog	7
A Question of Identity	Jul-95	Analog	4
Of Enemies and Allies	8-Aug	No first publication	4
The Power of Illusion	6-Oct	Jim Baen's Universe	8
The Anomaly	First published in this volume		8

EDITOR'S NOTES TO BIBLIOGRAPHY:

Note 1. The column titled "Volume" refers to the volume in the Baen edition of Anvil's writings. Those volumes are:

Pandora's Legions, Baen Books (February 2002)
Interstellar Patrol I, Baen Books (April 2003)
Interstellar Patrol II, Baen Books (March 2005)
The Trouble With Aliens, Baen Books (August 2006)
The Trouble With Humans, Baen Books (August 2007)
War Games, Baen Books (December 2008)
Rx For Chaos, Baen Books (December 2008)
The Power of Illusion, Baen Books (this edition)

Note 2. Most of the stories which were included in *Pandora's Legions,* including the original novel *Pandora's Planet,* were reworked by Anvil into a unitary novel for this volume. The only exception is "Sweet Reason," which was reissued in the same form in which it was originally published.

Note 3. The first three stories in the Interstellar Patrol setting—"Strangers to Paradise," "The Dukes of Desire" and "The King's Legions"—were reissued by Tower Books in 1969 as a novel under the title *Strangers in Paradise.* The editors of that volume ignored Anvil's advice, and he always disliked the end result. So, when I began putting together the first of the *Interstellar Patrol* volumes for this edition, I followed Anvil's desires and we reissued the three stories as they were originally published in *Astounding Science Fiction*.

Eric Flint

IF YOU LIKE...
YOU SHOULD TRY...

DAVID DRAKE
David Weber

DAVID WEBER
John Ringo

JOHN RINGO
Michael Z. Williamson
Tom Kratman

ANNE MCCAFFREY
Mercedes Lackey
Liaden Universe® by Sharon Lee & Steve Miller

MERCEDES LACKEY
Wen Spencer, Andre Norton
Andre Norton
James H. Schmitz

LARRY NIVEN
Tony Daniel
James P. Hogan
Travis S. Taylor

ROBERT A. HEINLEIN
Jerry Pournelle
Lois McMaster Bujold
Michael Z. Williamson

HEINLEIN'S "JUVENILES"
Rats, Bats & Vats series by Eric Flint & Dave Freer

HORATIO HORNBLOWER OR PATRICK O'BRIAN
David Weber's Honor Harrington series
David Drake's RCN series

HARRY POTTER
Mercedes Lackey's Urban Fantasy series

THE LORD OF THE RINGS
Elizabeth Moon's *The Deed of Paksenarrion*

H.P. LOVECRAFT
Larry Correia's Monster Hunter series
P.C. Hodgell's Kencyrath series
Princess of Wands by John Ringo

GEORGETTE HEYER
Lois McMaster Bujold
Catherine Asaro
Liaden Universe® by Sharon Lee & Steve Miller

GREEK MYTHOLOGY
Pyramid Scheme by Eric Flint & Dave Freer
Forge of the Titans by Steve White
Blood of the Heroes by Steve White

NORSE MYTHOLOGY
Northworld Trilogy by David Drake

URBAN FANTASY
Darkship Thieves by Sarah A. Hoyt
Gentleman Takes a Chance by Sarah A. Hoyt
Carousel Tides by Sharon Lee
The Wild Side ed. by Mark L. Van Name

SCA/HISTORICAL REENACTMENT
John Ringo's "After the Fall" series

FILM NOIR
Larry Correia's The Grimnoir Chronicles

CATS
Sarah A. Hoyt's *Darkship Thieves*
Larry Niven's Man-Kzin Wars series

PUNS
Rick Cook
Spider Robinson
Wm. Mark Simmons

VAMPIRES & WEREWOLVES
Larry Correia
Wm. Mark Simmons

NONFICTION
Hank Reinhardt
Tax Payer's Tea Party
by Sharon Cooper & Chuck Asay
The Science Behind The Secret by Travis Taylor
Alien Invasion by Travis Taylor & Bob Boan